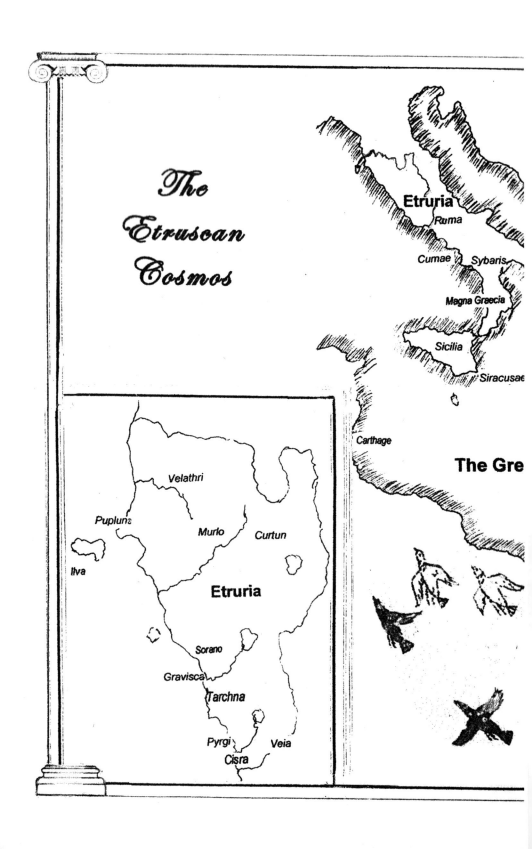

The
Etruscan
Cosmos

Etruria
Ruma
Cumae Sybaris
Magna Graecia
Sicilia
Siracusae
Carthage
The Gre

Velathri
Pupluna
Murlo   Curtun
Ilva
Etruria
Sorano
Gravisca
Tarchna
Pyrgi   Veia
Cisra

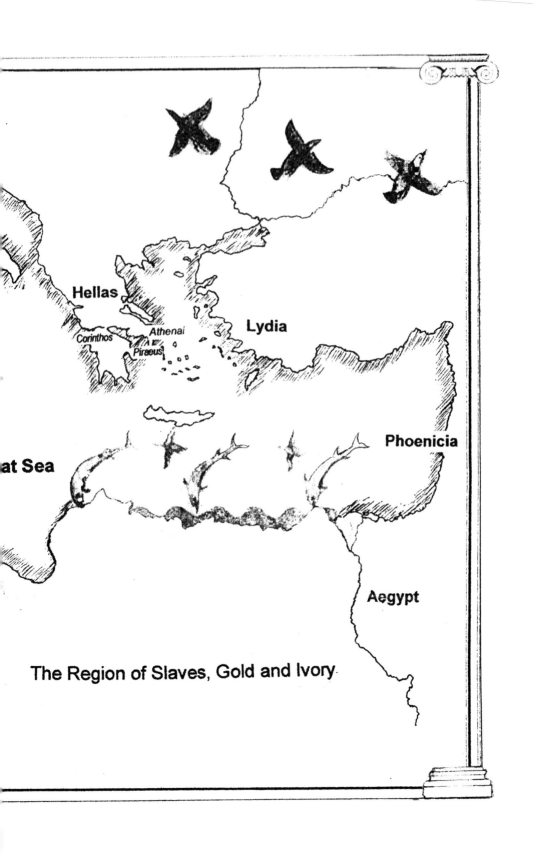

The Region of Slaves, Gold and Ivory

ALSO BY ROSALIND BURGUNDY:

Odyssey of an Etruscan Noblewoman

Tuscan Intrigue

Song of the Flutist

Epic of the Ancient Etruscans

Rosalind Burgundy

iUniverse, Inc.
New York Bloomington

Song of the Flutist
Epic of the Ancient Etruscans

Cover design: Rosalind Burgundy and iUniverse

Editor: Richard Ekker, Professor Emeritus of English and Film

iUniverse books may be ordered through booksellers or by contacting:

iUniverse
1663 Liberty Drive
Bloomington, IN 47403
www.iuniverse.com
1-800-Authors (1-800-288-4677)

Because of the dynamic nature of the Internet, any Web addresses or links contained in this book may have changed since publication and may no longer be valid. The views expressed in this work are solely those of the author and do not necessarily reflect the views of the publisher, and the publisher hereby disclaims any responsibility for them.

ISBN: 978-1-4502-5660-5 (sc)
ISBN: 978-1-4502-5662-9 (dj)
ISBN: 978-1-4502-5661-2 (ebook)

Library of Congress Control Number: 2010913320

Printed in the United States of America

iUniverse rev. date: 11/01/2010

28 January 2011

Dedicated to Readers:

May the Etruscan spirit smile on you because you are special yolks

love, rosalind

Song of the Flutist

Hierarchy of Etruscan Society

(from highest to lowest social order)

Etruscan gods:	male mythological rulers of the cosmos
Etruscan goddesses:	female mythological rulers of the cosmos
Prince-priest:	The supreme leader in each village or city, each named *Zilath* or *Maru*
Augur-priest:	philosophical and religious codifier of law
Fulguriator-priest:	observer of bird flights for omens and portents
Haruspex-priest:	reader of animal entrails for omens and portents
Magistrate:	lower than the prince-priest, manages a segment of industry or economics
Court official:	An advisor or henchman to the prince-priest
Citizens of Etruria:	Elder Noble Skilled Professional Trade Worker Grower (farmer) or Fisher
Servant:	Descendant of captured enemy, freed of obligation
Slave:	Recently captured enemy, never freed, descendants may become free

Succession of the Laris Family

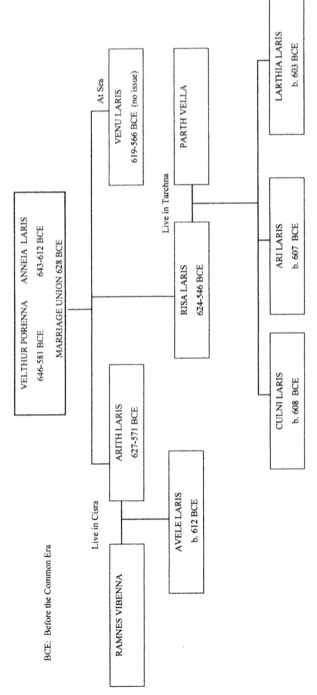

BCE: Before the Common Era

VELTHUR PORENNA 646-581 BCE — **ANNEIA LARIS** 643-612 BCE
MARRIAGE UNION 628 BCE

Live in Cisra

RAMNES VIBENNA

ARITH LARIS 627-571 BCE

AVELE LARIS b. 612 BCE

At Sea

VENU LARIS 619-566 BCE (no issue)

Live in Tarchna

RISA LARIS 624-546 BCE

PARTH VELLA

CULNI LARIS b. 608 BCE

ARI LARIS b. 607 BCE

LARTHIA LARIS b. 603 BCE

Reckoning of Etruscan Time

Traditional dates weren't accurate until about 644 BCE, after the Chalcidian (Ionic, from Hellas) alphabet came into use. The calendar was measured in *saeculae* and Etruscan civilization was granted ten, varying with "the length of the longest life of all those born in the year in which the preceding oldest inhabitant died." (Censorinus, *De die natali,* 17.5;cf Zosimus ii.i.). Time-division was the day, beginning at the sun's zenith.

Prologue:

"Open the gates of the past
And let me enter.
Sweep aside the mists
That hover on your roads
So that I may clearly see
and understand
who you were and what you did.
Who you are and what you do."

The Flutist spoke, guiding the people long before the rise of archaic Greece and ancient Rome.

Like a soup of blended flavors, the Indigenous Tuscans, Hellenics and Lydians of Asia Minor melted into the bucolic land, understanding the workings of the cosmos.

Clever! Cunning! Courageous! How active they were when stars aligned in the heavens! Goddess Uni's moon lit the way, shining through the landscape, turning forests to fields. God Tinia shaped settlements into villages and flourishing cities. How mighty the Etruscans of the Italic Peninsula became!

The Flutist steered them on, nurturing their spirits, ripening the soil to tell their tales to you, dear Reader.

A chain of events started the Porenna-Laris-Vella-Vibenna Clans. Their stories are within…

Wealth and Wisdom
The Porenna-Laris Generation

1

"We require more copper. Only you can find those veins." Prince-priest Zilath raised his voice, tightening his grip on the ivory throne.

"One moon's time is all I ask," Vel Porenna confidently protested. He lowered his eyes respectfully to the man of higher rank, although they were of equal age, height and girth.

"You're needed to thwart Cisra," Zilath sulked, swinging the jewel-encrusted medallion around his neck. "Take a quarter moon."

"Cisra can't match us. Our resources flow," Vel replied evenly, stroking the point of his razored beard. "Besides, what is wealth with no family to share it? My mother and father would be proud of my nobility. This visit is to honor parents and ancestors. My sojourn will be short, and I again shall serve you well."

"Go if you must. Make sure you're back in a half moon. Don't fail me." Zilath stomped out, his threat hanging in the air.

After having his curled hair shorn to shoulder and his cheeks shaved, Vel packed his leather pouches. Wearing earth-color wool tunic under ankle-length cloak, he tramped towards his birthplace, home of his forebears. He carried five days of victuals for his journey on paths up hills, through lush valleys, skirting lakes and land unmarked by habitation, ripe for human sustenance.

Walking was a part of his life, dictated by the gods. Near Sorano village on a crown of rock overlooking mountainous beech and fir trees, he admired the pristine landscape. Craggy hills of contorted formations rimmed steep canyons, sloping to woodland and forest where wildlife prowled until hunted by the growers.

Hunting wasn't Vel's specialty. Rocks intrigued his waking days. Nothing was more satisfying than to fracture a boulder where he might find rainbow-colored chunks, silver-white crystals or reddish-brown stone, the source of bronze.

If it hadn't been for Tarchna's Magistrate of Mines, Vel would have been a grower like his father and grandfather. The memory came as clear as yesterday.

"I've searched these hills for metals and minerals and heard you have the gift of discovery. You don't want to stay here, child, where ancestors were hunters and shepherds. They were like those barbarians over the mountains. Come to the best city in all Etruria, Tarchna, more powerful than the eleven others, and we'll make you rich," the Magistrate enticed young Vel. "Once we were a primitive settlement, then a village that grew into a town. Three generations built trade and culture to make it a great society. Indeed, the cosmos blessed us Etruscans with earthly abundance, and peopled the region with brilliant minds like yours. In Tarchna, you'll have the life of a city man and noble."

So he had. Showing off would be pleasing reward for his hard toil. He did what other men could not, scaling shear cliffs to find deposits of metal. Zilath was pleased enough to give him an opulent dwelling of ten rooms around a courtyard that held a cistern to collect rainwater for the cooking room.

Over the next hill were the weathered thatch and mud hovels of the poor. Sorano was still an outlying village of soil tillers who often slept in pastures with sheep. From what he knew of his parents, they stayed growers. Their hair must have whitened since he saw them. Anticipating reunion made his steps jaunty on the downward path to their farm on the edge of a terraced hill.

Perhaps he was on the wrong path. There was no laughter of sisters and brothers. No noises of food preparation. No laundry flapped in the breeze. No goats butted heads, no grape harvesters sang.

With the wind at his back, sinister silence greeted. He rounded the final curve and stopped breathing. Outlined against the bleak sky, charred skeletal remains of his childhood home were exposed to a raw rain. He reeled among the ashes in horror, stunned with revulsion.

"Vetisl, god of Darkness and Night came and left his mark. A roving band of Italic tribesmen beset them," the distressed voice of a village elder wheezed.

"Were they Cisra?"

"Cisra, no. Cisra is Etruscan. Our brethren wouldn't war with us. These were Umbrian murderers." The Elder dug his staff into the ground. "You walk too fast for me. You were 'the brilliant youth of Sorano,' weren't you?"

"This was my home."

"I've followed you, loath to tell of your family."

"What are you saying, Elder?"

"Dead. Your father, mother, older sister and husband..."

"Surely, not everyone," Vel trembled.

The venerable elder clamped the younger man's hands. "And two brothers and youngest sister. Had you been here, you would have been slain. But you were sensible to leave this crumbling village."

In shock, Vel could only nod.

"Those Umbrians defined the land as theirs and destroyed those who opposed them. Your family was massacred, flesh hacked to bone. Now, you are alone."

"Alone." The elder's voice echoed within Vel. He collapsed on the scorched bench he sat on as a child, head in hands, and wept. "Charitable gods once rained magic on me. What have I done to deserve this?"

Dazed, through pouring rain that turned the path to sliding mud, Vel slogged toward Tarchna, missing trailheads, stumbling on pebbles and scrub brush. Exhausted, he tripped on a root and fell head-long into a ravine. Thorns pierced his flesh. He lay throbbing in pain.

When day cleared, two men emerged from a mountain glen and hiked along the escarpment with pheasants slung over their shoulders, the sun glinting on their bows.

One stout, one lean, Vel thought. They don't have helmets, spears or shields. They may be hunters, not enemy warriors out to kill me.

Weakly, he shined his gold belt clasp. Then he fainted.

Sent to scavenge for poultry and bird, both hunters were of the lowest category, rejected for lack of courage.

"What's that light? It moved."

"Aargh, no one but us in these hills. An underbrush animal."

"No animal. A man!"

They craned their necks into the ravine.

"Not dead."

"Almost. Let's go. We're late and these birds stink."

"He could be the stag hunter who went missing after the frost."

"So what? He's too far gone."

"Known or unknown, we go against the ancient laws if we don't help one in need. If he's mortally wounded, we end his life. That's what the elders train."

"We could fall and die."

"We would do no less for a wounded animal."

"I'll starve," the stout man said.

"A meal less won't hurt you," the leaner one answered.

They planted the pheasants to ward off vultures, unraveled sling bags and dexterously knotted a rope of weeds.

"You've the strength of an ox. Hold the rope," the lean hunter said.

The stout hunter complied, slipping in mud as he lowered his partner to strap the rope around the unresponsive man.

"Haul me up," the lean one called, yanking on the rope.

Slowly but roughly, they lifted Vel's bloodied body, scraped more from their efforts. On top of the escarpment again, the hunters laid him on wet ground and examined the leather pouch of serrated and hooked tools tied on a belt with a gold clasp.

"Odd trappings. Not like ours," they agreed and tore off Vel's rain-soaked cape. Underneath, the bloodstained tunic was of rich quality. From within the cloth, a chain of ingots fell out.

Lean inspected the links. "Whoever he is, he's from Tarchna. The stamp of nobles is on this prize."

"Give it here." Stout grabbed and bit an ingot. "Gold. It's true fine gold."

"We'd better see his wounds." Lean ripped the tunic with his knife. "The man doesn't have flesh worms."

"He's stuck with thorns. His head bleeds."

"If we don't keep him alive, someone might think we threw him off the cliff."

"We'd be caged until death. I told you we should leave."

"If he is to live, the skin needs lacing," Lean protested charitably. "Let's take him to Anneia."

"The Healer?"

"If anyone can bring him to life, it's her. She cures the ill with herbs."

"Drag him," Stout said woefully.

From wet branches, they deftly constructed a bier like for a common corpse.

Close to a sacred dell where prince-priests of Etruria met, they concealed the unknown man with thickly piled leaves, leaving a hole for air.

Under the night sky and bright full moon, Vel's eyes fluttered open. His body couldn't move if the finest banquet were offered. "My promise to Zilath is broken. His wrath will be upon me."

2

With haste, the scruffy game hunters entered Tarchna's center. Men and women folk were dressed in flax tunics and mantles from knees to ankles. They walked, noses covered with cloth against the smell of human waste. Inquiring where the Healer might be, Lean and Stout were directed to the prince-priest's court. Closer to the walls, the highborn rode in carts driven by ponies or donkeys. The bearded, curly-haired men wore cleaner tunics. The women's tunics were embroidered at neckline to show plaited or piled hair under tight-fitted caps.

Their search brought them to Zilath's palace guards.

"She's masterful curer to warrior, merchant, gymnast and the prince-priest's wife. What do you want with her?" asked a guard charily.

Another guard put out his palm. "She knows me. I could take you to her if you have the means. She lives in the sacred temple of priests, augurs and fulguriators."

They gave him a hunting arrow. With this improbable gift to offer, the guard led them to Anneia's quarters.

Two women, taller than male guards, each stood with a spear. "No one enters without just cause."

The drape parted. The Healer came fearlessly towards the hunters.

Agog at her long flowing chestnut hair streaked with Aplu's sun and her serene goddess face, Lean sputtered, "True citizens we are, not miscreants of society. We beg your tolerance for secrecy. A rich man is dying in the woods."

"Not right," Stout said and drew out the ingots. "We don't know which to save, him or the gold."

"Bring him in," Anneia said. "My service is open to everyone in need."

The hunters went no farther than her first room, lined with clusters of herbs, jars, bowls, razors and tools for cleaning human orifices.

She appraised one of the stamped metal balls. "A predicament you have. These gold ingots are from the magistrates. Who's the fallen man?"

"We can only show him to you."

"There's talk of a missing noble named 'Soil Sampler.' He's a mysterious one, not to be seen at the temple. I've heard him called *'Nenfro.'*

"Nenfro, the gray stone for a sarcophagus? Pity us the toil to retrieve a nenfro," the hunters complained. "We could have stolen the ingots and melted its gold for our own."

"A stroke of fortune you didn't. If he is the Soil Sampler, he's far more valuable than his gold," Anneia replied, inspired to take on this new task.

Inner strength showed on her determined face as she strapped a belt of herbal pouches and poultices around her tunic. She covered her head with a hooded cloak to leave the palace without being noticed. Not wanting her attendants to blab about this unusual mission, Anneia walked alone with the hunters on the same paths they had trod. The two day journey brought them to the remote hinterland.

On her direction, the hunters brushed leaves from Vel's inert body. Anneia knelt beside the body. "He breathes faintly. Blessings of the Letham gods! What good god of fate made him live?" She examined his life signs. "From his injuries, he's not been attacked." She sewed up the worst wounds, bandaged cuts and oiled weather-exposed flesh.

She was drawn to the man with the rugged face and a sorrow-burdened look.

The hunters and Anneia brought him to a shepherd's rarely used hut at the edge of the forest.

Days and nights went by. Vel's body was still numbed by pain. Anneia sent the hunters for discreet priests to chant divine laws of the cosmos to boost his life.

"No movement." They shook their heads. "He dies soon."

"He won't," Anneia said, boiling juniper berries and yarrow to soak on his swollen skin, but the treatment didn't cure.

At highest moon, she went to Tarchna's river to pick an herb that might reduce inflammation. Though scraped by brush, she scrambled over boulders to the water. Hoping the river gods would steer her path, her own life tethered to the mission of bringing life to the Soil Sampler, she leapt over rushing foam and gathered the rare wild weed.

Successful, she returned to the hut. With mortar and pestle, she worked the weed to a paste, adding freshest oil of olive and aromatic flowers. Applying it to Vel's brow quickened him into restlessness.

"Have mercy, ogres of death!" Vel slashed at the air. "Demons, don't devour my family."

"Speak louder," Anneia's voice floated at him, compressing the moonflowers to his mutilated body.

"The light of day confuses. What vision do I see?" Vel asked in his fog. "Old woman or young?"

"Old as night, young as dawn," she said, her face near his.

Vel fondled the rippled surface of her tunic. "This velvety softness embodies your spirit. Lovely vision, you make my lips quiver."

"Kiss the cloth if it pleases. It will bring you closer to me."

Vel brought the cloth to his lips as she invited. Awakened by her lavender fragrance, his blood surged. Warmth repossessed his cold body from slumber. Lacking strength, he whispered, "Are you real, Vision? No, not so. I must be on my afterlife journey."

She smiled. "You barely live. Pain fragments the body. Touch restores."

"Who are you that I escape the netherworld at your hands?"

"Anneia, the Healer."

Her melodious voice, like a harp's full rich tones, dared Vel to say, "Touch my cheek so I may feel your caress."

Her fingertips traced the lines of his wounded face and stroked his forehead.

Vel rose onto stiff elbows. His bones and muscles moved like they were pinned under a load of *tufa* bricks. "Am I the same man who left Tarchna? How well do you know me?"

"Your wounds improve. They respond to my hands. God Tinia requests the pleasure of your life."

Desperately, Vel wanted to live to see her again. Her smiles lit his being. Her touch melted his self-importance. Never before had he such comfort with a woman.

3

"Velthur Porenna is your responsibility," Zilath told the Magistrate of Mines. "Find him."

"He hasn't returned from Sorano. There's talk he's dead."

"He can't be. He's indispensable."

"More than me?" the burly magistrate asked sullenly.

"If he's dead, wealth stops for Tarchna. Dishonor will be yours."

The magistrate's inquiries brought slow results. Blending into the late cooling season shrubbery, the hut was difficult to find. When located, the Magistrate rode his horse to get Vel. Brashly, he kicked the door open.

"Where is he? Do you hold him prisoner?"

"Who?" Anneia drew the curtain to shield her sleeping patient from the Magistrate's sight.

"I call him 'Nenfro.'"

"A jesting name. Why do you think I have him?"

"My men saw him with you, carried on a bier by two hunters over a hill path."

"Why do you detest him?"

"Because Zilath favors this tufa lover, Velthur Porenna, and made him his Soil Sampler, who I discovered, me, Magistrate of Mines."

12

"Obligation brings you here," Anneia deduced, confirming her patient's identity.

"Only that."

"If he dies, you will lose status."

"You can't let him die! Other than Zilath, he's the most important leader of our saecula."

"Not true. I lead. I'm Zilath's most important healer, the one who keeps our people in health. I must know more about this Soil Sampler to keep him alive."

"I believe you," the Magistrate said, awestruck by her demeanor. "Porenna is arrogant, but he knows how to pull rich deposits from bedrock with pick and hammer. Zilath gives him hundreds of Tarchna slaves to cleave the earth for every trace of valuable resource. What wealth Zilath begets."

Anneia offered the Magistrate a bench and goblet of wine. "Getting more bronze would make Tarchna greater than Cisra."

"Of course. I try to do the same with my deposits of iron minerals." He swigged the wine. "The malleable iron smelted in furnaces, form durable axe blades and hand instruments, bits for harnesses, cooking cauldrons and numerous items. I supply Tarchna with export trade and wealth, but Vel Porenna finds more new metals." He wiped his lips on his sleeve. "That son of a mangy dog is given newest inventions—sledges, chisel blades, drills, rakes, trowels, shovels, axes, and slaves to carry the loads. The more ore he detects, the more approval he receives."

"He surpassed your expectations?" Anneia poured another goblet for the talkative man.

"So much that Zilath gave Vel Porenna the house that should have been mine, not far from the court and temple. Columns and walkways around rooms with windows. A roof of tiles, not thatch. Constructed for a magistrate, not a youth. He even has cooking servants and slaves to tend chickens, milking goats and white oxen."

"Oxen for luck," Anneia commiserated, realizing how the magistrate wallowed in jealousy.

"I should have gotten that house," he repeated. "I have a family."

"Doesn't he?"

"He isn't married. He's only interested in his rocks."

"Why didn't you get rid of him?"

"I couldn't. He worked hard. I worked him harder. He found more streaks of metals." The Magistrate slouched on the bench. "Zilath sent him to the Tolfa Mountains, into valleys and broad plains for the most mundane materials. Porenna found marl, mixed it with paint and had craftsmen use it for sculpture. The same with tufa. He took deposits of common tufa and made bricks for construction."

"You and Zilath used Porenna's talents."

"Zilath called him 'Brother' and added him to his family. Porenna was no fool. Pressing his forehead against the back of Zilath's hand, he displayed service to seal the contract," the Magistrate bridled.

"Vel Porenna ousted you from Zilath's affection."

"That he did," the Magistrate said, "but I learned his weak spot. Porenna hated the results of gouging the land—smoke, fumes, lacerated mountains, rubble and debris. He missed the pure landscape. He was a villager at heart, a dolt from the hinterland."

Anneia was delighted. Vel had a secret soul after all. His rocks were like her herbs. New industry demolished beauty of trees and coastline.

"My healing herbs die when forests are cut. What did you do about his weak spot?"

"I interfered with Zilath's decisions and made Porenna stay in Tarchna to sort and inspect rocks brought from fields. That way, he wasn't able to make other discoveries."

"You made him do trifling work. That wouldn't have made him happy."

"He wasn't. He spited me and gave our workshops a secret formula of powdered dirt to mix with water. The potters turned the metallic clay into black earthenware. Widely admired, they were sent to markets in distant lands."

"I suspected he was the one who invented *bucchero*."

"You guessed, Healer. He watered excess clay and let it run off on a slab of wood. A potter baked it in the firing oven to become a flat surface. Porenna framed the edges in wood so it wouldn't shatter and applied pig fat. With a metal stylus used for picking stones, he incised numbers. He didn't know how to write words, just the alphabet, so he gifted it to Zilath and magistrates to keep accounts."

"So he's the one who popularized the writing slate."

"Zilath ordered thousands. Porenna's final glory. Zilath honored him with a banquet fit for gods, and bestowed the title: 'Devoted Soil Sampler of the Tarchna Realm, Revered Noble to the Prince-Priest.' Now he's considered god-like, for he rules Tarchna's fate with discoveries."

"Vel Porenna searches for worth to bring Tarchna. You get glory for being his sponsor. Is that so bad?"

"Not bad," the Magistrate admitted.

"Who gains more from this joint venture, the prince-priest, Soil Sampler, or you, Magistrate of Mines?" Anneia pondered. "Our joyous city pulsates with opportunity. The three of you have made us mighty and respected for your knowledge and sound advice. Shouldn't you work together?"

"You shame me into agreement."

Anneia pulled aside the curtain and dabbed cloth in chamomile water to cleanse Vel's matted hair. "You've given me answers. I can make him whole. See him now, Magistrate."

The Magistrate admired Anneia's ministrations and sent a covered cart to transport Vel to Tarchna. The Healer accompanied the Soil Sampler to his dwelling within Tarchna's walls, as lavish as the Magistrate described.

4

Anneia made Vel live. His girth reduced from the Sorano journey, she fed him remedies in boiled eggs, puls, meat and dark wine to restore his blood. At dawn, they drank her herbals and spoke thoughts not shared with others.

As she attended his wounds, he sought her fingers to bear the soreness until they clinched hands. Vel's grief spilled out over the brutal loss of his family.

"You were given life, here and now. Don't be ashamed you didn't die with them. They left you as a link to history," she comforted as she shaved his stubble. "Delight in what you have."

Comely as she was, Anneia hadn't slept in the prince-priest's bed. She had declined Zilath after he accoladed her as his personal healer. Rumor spread she didn't know how to love a man. She wondered if it was true, that she favored work over magistrates and nobles.

But she saw the good in Vel and gave her secret heart to him. He received it by seeing her pure and lovely soul.

Struck by Turan's arrow like the Hellenic legend of Paris and Aphrodite, Vel was rapturously in love, a miracle that advanced infirmity to wellness. When he thought of life without her, his cosmos paled. He reentered life as a changed man.

Word of Anneia living in Vel Porenna's home reached her parents, vineyard landowners from Blera, a well-to-do village outside Tarchna's gates. Infuriated, they rushed into Tarchna.

Complacently, Anneia met them at Vel's door.

"You bed a man of mountain village origins? How could you stoop so low? You were raised properly," her mother reprimanded as if to a four year old. "You've disgraced us."

"You believe all you hear," Anneia answered, her face buoyant, not refuting the accusation. "There's a honeyed aspect to his being. I felt sorry for his plight, but now I'm filled with joy at seeing his eyes. I belong here."

As they spoke, Vel watched her and thought, infatuation for me shows in her face. Adoration. Love must show in mine, too.

"You've lost practicality," her father chastised, "Come home, misguided daughter, before you're spurned."

The hunters arrived to show their new status, each wearing a gold ingot draped on his neck.

Lean said, "We aren't mere hunters, but heroes glorified in the community, given extra foodstuff and bounty due to our courageous rescue of the Soil Sampler. We come to pay homage to the man and wish for his survival. How is the honored noble?"

"And who might that be?" Anneia's mother asked disdainfully.

Stout grinned. "Vel Porenna's the most respected of the new kind of noble, for he earned his title with knowledge and good judgment."

"Titled? Then chitchat about our daughter sleeping with him is just that," her father said. "She is his Healer."

From the recesses of the court, an exquisite whistling blew towards Zilath, a melody that recalled joy of the cosmos, the dances of sun and moon, the poetry of the gods. Distracted from his duties, the prince-priest moved toward the sound. "What hails?"

Hunched at a pillar base, a servant held double reed pipes.

"Why aren't you doing chores?" Zilath asked.

The youth sprung to his feet and bowed. "Dearest Prince-priest, God of our Realm, I'm not needed until next meal, so I make these hollow sticks play."

"Those hollow sticks are 'flutes,'" Zilath corrected, overcome by the music's passion. "The best flutists call stags and foxes from the hills, but novices play at banquet. Mediocre ones barter for puls and onions in the market place. We categorize musicians by age and talent. Which destiny is yours?"

"I play what comes from the soul."

"Aah, the soul! The spirit that comes from within," Zilath said. "You are better than those of cresting years."

"Song is the essence of life, enhancing our beings, eliminating desperation. Song releases sorrow and tears, bringing joy and smiles," the youth clarified with the simplest words.

"Your melody was of the ancestors, stories of the ages." As sunlight filtered the sky, Zilath lit with discovery. He, not the gods, knew that his people needed one flutist per generation to mark life's passages—birth, marriage, and death—one stupendous flutist to shape the sound and mood of Tarchna. "Why are you here today?"

"I'm waiting for the augurs' orders."

"It is I who give orders. You'll be my personal *subulo*, my flutist, who will play announcements throughout Tarchna."

Growing taller in stature, the youth solemnly pledged, "Prince-priest, I'll repay you with honor. My descendents will be flutists."

"Come with me. Don't dally." Less moody with every step, Zilath pulled the youth to his next audience, nobles Vel and Anneia.

"Humbled by Anneia's love, I've become a man of dimension," Vel began. "Grateful for my revived life, I'm here to vow for marriage."

"My Soil Sampler? My Healer? You want to marry?" Zilath berated as he strode through the court hall, The Flutist's tune in his head. "You tricked me by secretly meeting."

"Nothing of the kind, Zilath." Anneia's serene voice broke his stride. "We are two of your most credible subjects for we are unwavering in our service."

"I continue to bring wealth to Tarchna. Our union won't interfere," Vel reasoned.

Zilath couldn't deny that. Vel filled his coffers. "You spited me with this man, Healer."

"Zilath, when I refused you, you restricted me to marry only with your consent."

"Did I?" Zilath said, mollified that she would bring up her lack of interest in him.

"We ask for agreement, not strife," Vel said calmly. "Sanctify our lives with matrimony, Zilath, and we'll begin a noble family."

Pacified by the echo of The Flutist's pipes, Zilath chuckled, forgetting his exasperation with the couple. "Know that your allegiance comes first to me before you make issue. Nonetheless, if you must wed, the new moon brings the warming season. Marry then."

"O glorious day! Praise the gods! Praise you, Zilath!" Vel and Anneia wished. "We're beholden to you."

At the sacred altar, Anneia and Vel coupled in traditional pose, forehead to forehead to solemnize marriage, forever binding the Laris and Porenna families into grander Etruscan blood.

The Flutist trilled happily on his pipes, his notes rising as doves flew to the trees around the new couple, their wings applauding the union.

5

"Each Etruscan couple must procreate six to eight times to populate and expand society. There must be many descendants to farm and look after parents and grandparents," the *Book of Tages* declared.

Shame to the Porenna-Laris family came from not having enough offspring. There were only three.

The gods granted two females and a male. Arith was an incomparable girl with a good mind, fluent in language and movement as a babe. The second, Risa, suckled little milk from her mother's breast. She was a disappointment, short of bone, long of black curls, but smiled sweetly from her first feeding, a smile that began at the center of her lips and widened radiantly. Astounded, Anneia and Vel forgot to use her birth name and called her, "Risa, child of the beautiful smile." Then the gods rewarded the couple with a male to carry the lineage. Venu was a dreamer, smitten by water play and his mother's healing powers, blathering about places he had never seen.

"Will our few children be able to carry our bloodline?" Vel asked the augur-priest.

"They're able-bodied. Your children will be perpetuators of life, a fruition of the gods."

Between births of the Porenna-Laris children, Zilath demanded Anneia's skills when the contaminated Maremma air struck, and she had to prevent illness from spreading to Tarchna. Anneia went farther afield than Vel, leaving him to spend more days with Arith, Risa and Venu.

Vel and his children watched for Anneia's homecoming at Tarchna's outer wall overlooking the coastal forest and vast sea.

"How can the cart bring her home if we can't see the road?" Venu asked.

"We can't see the road because there are too many trees," Risa said patiently.

"She's gone more than she should," Arith impatiently said.

"Stop wagging your tongues." Vel separated his daughters. "Zilath commands and we must wait."

"Tell us again about your strange family ancestors," Arith said.

"They weren't strange. My grandparents rowed the waters from Anatolia and settled in Sorano, a place no one wanted. They had hardships that we don't, taming the stock and working to clear the Tyrrhenian soil. Their children, my parents, prospered from growing beans."

"And Mother's family?" Risa asked.

"They came to Etruria from Hellas when priestesses ruled, long before my ancestors. They raised goats and harvested grains. We don't live like our parents, for the gods gave your mother and me knowledge to advance Tarchna's wisdom and wealth."

"Your family must be happy in Sorano because they don't come to see us," Venu said.

"They don't invite us to visit them either," Arith added.

"Our grandparents must be tired from all that work," Risa said with the caring of an old woman. "Maybe they don't like to journey."

"What smart judges you are," Vel said, hiding the truth and pain of his family's massacre.

Putting his children to bed at night was a chore for Vel. They jumped around, spatting over where to lay, tweaking each other's toes, restless without their mother.

"Tell us about her," Arith coerced with phony tears as Risa and Venu threw cushions at each other.

Vel grabbed a cushion mid-air, laid it against the wall of their bed and struck flint to an oil lamp. He sat and pulled Arith and Risa to his sides. Venu camped at his feet.

"When Anneia was your ages, she lived with her parents in Blera, a village higher than Tarchna's hills, where the sun rises sooner. As a child, she roamed the forest to smell fresh plants and trees. One day, she brought a branch home to tickle her kid-goat. This goat, no higher than a man's knee, was a mangy runt. Anneia minced the branch leaves with mash and gave it to him. He ate like a greedy pig. What do you know? The goat began to grow!" Vel rhymed, getting in his children's mood.

"Kiddy-goat, kiddy-goat. Greedy pig, greedy pig," the children sang.

Vel laughed at how silly the words sounded. Maybe his children weren't so unruly after all. He began to enjoy his own story. "The next day, she gave the goat more. A hare, fattened for the seasonal feast, had the same illness, and she made it well."

The children fluffed their cushions, ready for his tale's length.

"Her parents marveled at the hardy animals and bragged to the village elders that Anneia wasn't a goddess, but imbued with spirit to heal." Vel sipped wine and warmed to his tale, forgetting his annoyance that his wife wasn't there to put the children to bed. "The elders understood and encouraged Anneia to seek other plants. When the warming season rains scented the hillside and opened her senses, Anneia went into fern forests to pick herbals that smelled right. Some she ate, mixed with water, oil or honey."

"What were they?" Venu eagerly wanted to know.

"Your mother's secrets," Vel said. "At meals, Anneia put her weeds and roots into bland stew meat and beans. What flavors the family tasted on their tongues. They felt clear-headed or strangely calm. After that, the herbs were used often."

He had held their interest. The children could almost taste the stew, a regular addition to cold season meals to keep a layer of fat on their bodies.

"The villagers saw Anneia's healed animals and the good health of her family. They wanted her to make the emaciated or diseased stock well, too."

"News of her abilities was on everyone's lips as she grew up. Our prince-priest summoned her to Tarchna for treatments so often that he invited her to live on the palace grounds." Vel paused, conceit swelling. "But it was me, the man who fell into the nasty gully thickets she was called upon to heal. I am the man who changed her life."

"You're a good yarn-teller, Father," Risa said sleepily.

Vel laughed and tousled her hair. "More another time. Now rest."

From the doorway, he overheard their talk as they took out blankets.

"Father's stories aren't like Mother's," Arith said. "They each tell the same story but only one is the truth."

"They're both true. Mother and Father love differently." Risa snuggled into her feathers. "What we have to decide is who loves who more, a Healer or a Soil Sampler?"

"Father loved Mother first," Arith avowed. "The priest at the temple says that men love women."

"Mother tells me how much she loves Father," Venu said.

"Doesn't matter. This is an honest love, an example for us to follow when it's our turn," Risa said. "Ideal love is to meet a life partner."

Venu piped up. "Will we have a chance at love as our parents did?"

They giggled at the thought.

6

Anneia came home to celebrate the coming of age of her firstborn, the beautiful daughter whose loveliness was formed in childhood.

Supple curves rose from Arith's skinny torso. Melon round breasts grew high above her waist and hips. She sauntered as if she owned the cosmos. With flawless eyes, nose and kissable mouth, her face was framed by tresses of black hair.

"She has the grace of Goddess Turan," young and old men said and eyed her voluptuousness. By their glances, Arith knew they wanted to touch her. Nais, the neighbor who lived on the next path was first.

At a morning market for ship goods from far off Aegypt, Arith saw Nais trading for a glass vial to gift his family. From that barter, she learned his family was wealthier than hers. Interested in his rich accounts, she bumped into him in the crowd. Her body heated and radiated warmth as he apologized and offered to carry her parcels.

Arith and Nais walked in narrow streets where Tarchna's well-to-do citizens lived. When a carriage servant pushing grains yelled for access, they flattened their bodies against a wall. To avoid the cart grazing her, Nais put his arm across Arith's chest. The cart rattled on. They were the only two on the street.

"You stir me up with your stares." Nais pinned her to the wall.

She licked her lips, then his. He kissed her hard.

Giddy, she thrust her enlarged breasts. "Pleasure me. Touch me where no man ever has."

Her primordial instincts, as inborn as the rutting of a stag in heat, unleashed the right words, the right undulations. She unwrapped her tunic. He undid his skirt and thrust his erection upon her. Like an animal in heat she panted. Ecstasy shot through her being. His hand covered her mouth when she screamed.

"Hush!" Nais warned. His manhood softened. "Someone's coming. Arrange yourself."

To Arith's advantage, he was dimwitted.

"I won't tell of your wickedness," she threatened, poking him with her brooch's needle before weaving it into her tunic's seam, "unless there's cause."

"See me again," he pleaded. "I'll gift you with treats from the East."

Moments later they appeared wholesome, two citizens taking a stroll homeward, the first of many strolls to fields behind the animal yard, lying in the spelt wheat. When they met at the river, they lodged between boulders, not speaking but gratifying their bodies with goatish climax.

"Arith, your mother and I are looking for your marriage mate," Vel said one day as she matured, not knowing it was from this randy coupling. "Nais, of the Coesidia Clan would be a good complement, but…"

"No," Arith protested. "Please, not him."

Doubt formed in Vel's mind. "He's betrothed already."

"Repetition spoils after awhile," Arith frigidly told Nais when they next copulated. "Your tricks don't entertain."

"But they satisfy, don't they?" he said, and brought Arith a sacred cup etched with two men facing each other, holding a hetaera with her legs apart. One man was ramming his shaft into the hetaera's mound, the other into her buttocks. Their eyes were in a trance of fornication.

"Let's try this." He turned the cup to show its second scene. "My friend will join us."

"Did you steal it?"

"Yes. From Zilath's augur-priest."

Arith recoiled, smart to know he wasn't a safe lover. "Don't nag me again."

She sought other men to instigate intense cravings, needing to bite skin and muscle of her lovers, wanting to be scratched until her skin was raw, desiring whatever act brought release. A series of men ensued, a traveling jewelry merchant, the young temple priest who wasn't as holy as he should be, and the overseer of official building construction.

"I've heard snickering as I've walked to town to give my latest find to the elders," Vel raged at Arith. "They say, 'there's the father of the wanton beauty, the seductress.' I assure you that our family will not be scandalized should their words be true."

"Father," Arith whimpered, clinging to his arm. "I'm pure. Your reputation will be blameless. I honor you."

"To make sure there's no babble, we'll hold a seasonal hunt for eligible men to meet you, if we have to find one from Norchia or Veii," Vel said, his testiness lessening. "We'll hold a day's entertainment to chase hare and woodland creatures."

By luck or work of the gods, the merchant Ramnes of the Vibenna Clan of Cisra, came to Tarchna to buy new stock from a sheepherder. Vel invited the impeccable man to the hunt feast. With his quick smile, Ramnes pleased Anneia and Vel by telling of his heredity, that he was son of an ancient family. Although not a noble, he proved to be the best choice.

"He's not Tarchna. You want me to condone Arith Laris Porenna to marry a Cisra man?" Zilath stormed. "We'll lose a citizen to them."

"Not lose," Vel said. "Blood ties will keep Tarchna and Cisra from ever warring."

"This intermingling has possibility. Your daughter could keep us informed of Cisra's workings," Zilath said.

"She'd be a spy?"

"She could tell us how Cisra keeps wealthy, and we won't let Cisra rise higher than Tarchna."

"This union is our answer from the gods," Vel told Anneia. "Zilath gives Arith her cresting banquet accolade."

"Her marriage brings us tranquility," Anneia said.

Zilath said to his sacred priests, "We'll show our success to Cisra. That worthless city will cower at the brilliance of my eminent Soil Sampler. Tarchna will continue to rule supreme."

"We unite Tarchna and Cisra," Zilath introduced Arith to Cisra's young, audacious Prince-priest Maru at the first meeting of the clans, having to look up at the taller, broad-boned man.

Maru beamed. This union was a plum from the cosmos. Stealing a noble's daughter from Tarchna could strengthen his city.

Vel loved the pomp. He was treated like a celebrated magistrate. Arith's cresting banquet was added to the wedding with rarest delicacies and golden gifts from the East. Days of feasting became a quarter moon.

Vel forgot that his daughter wasn't pure.

Arith and Ramnes married in the year of the terrible thunders when leviathan downpours soaked the ground and many sickened of dampness and infections. On their marriage night, Arith inserted red berries up her mound. She pretended chaste coupling, acting as if she had never seen flesh of a man. Timidly, with one finger she stroked his body to prove purity. Then the berry juices gushed forth.

"I've heard false rumors about you," Ramnes said, entering her again.

"Free your mind. My untouched blood guarantees you." Letting him play the hunter and she the hunted, her wildness in bed pleased him. She kept more of her sexual techniques unknown to him.

7

Tarchna had been given the sacred books by the pansophic gods. Within were the mysteries of the cosmos, its structure and division of responsibility for upkeep. These complexities were told to the highest sacred priest of each generation, all named Zilath. Enlightened, the highest priest would instruct each sacred augur-priest, fulguriator and haruspex of duties to construe relationships between gods and humans.

"Fulguriator, study the heavenly stars and auspicious bird flights to predict our fates. Interpret the meaning and effects of thunder claps and lightning with omens indicating each day of any-named year, divining to explain the gods' wishes."

"Haruspex, read entrails of hens, roosters, sheep or hare for portents and omens. Slit the throat of your kill and gut them with blessing."

Down the hierarchal ladder, from nobles and regular citizens, to crafters, servants and slaves, all had prescribed duties. None protested, not wanting to be strangled, smothered, submerged, stoned, or exposed to beasts in the forests.

"This system makes Tarchna great," the most recent Zilath said, patting his belly as if he had the most satisfying banquet. "We have advantages. Wisdom of the cosmos."

The augur picked up his stylus and wrote on sheepskin: Greater than Cisra and the rest of Etruria.

Every bit of the superstitious cosmos was sacred, recorded in the holy books:

Objects are dormant until seen or touched by humans.

A vase shows movements in its contour and charms the eye. Dedicate vases to the gods.

Smells from perfume vials hold significance. Aromatics have life.

Animate and inanimate forms are bound harmoniously in the cosmos.

Everything that can be pushed or pulled, placed or thrown, holds life. The cosmos is alive with wonder!

Food for our bellies comes from animals that provide skins for our shoes. Cushioning feet with shoes give comfort and warmth.

The Porenna-Laris family strictly obeyed Zilath and Tarchna's logical philosophical laws, the Etruscan order and procedures of hierarchy, but they kidded over a life riddle that Zilath brought up at market: "Which came first, the chicken or the egg?"

"The chicken had to lay the egg," Vel said. "It feeds on soil."

"No, the egg birthed the chicken," Anneia said. "The chicken has wings. It's a bird. A bird is from the sky. The sky gods began the cosmos."

"Neither," Zilath laughed when he told the crowd, "Tages was first."

After the fanfare of Arith's wedding, the family adjusted to life without her. She moved across the mountain to Ramnes' home in Cisra. Vel was relieved that Arith's sexual exploits hadn't brought revengeful talk. In the early days of her marriage, Arith sent Zilath messages through Vel on how Cisra's society was becoming rich.

A respite from healing obligation, Anneia stayed in Tarchna and tended Venu. Of her children, Anneia was fondest of her son, and they went into fields and hills to gather wild yarrow, thyme, basil, or chamomile. She taught Venu wisdom of the herbals, claiming sun and healing god Aplu gave her knowledge.

At riverbanks, she found the herb with silvered green leaves that bloomed in the heat season. "Goddess of the moon, Uni, shines on this one. The bitter taste makes sore bodies mend by soothing the skin."

Venu scrunched his nose. "It smells like wet, burnt grass."

"When I was birthing you and your sisters, it worked well. I wasn't dull. It's special for mothers, but you don't need to know that." Anneia put a handful in her apron pocket. "There's more to being a healer than herbs. A healer cures out of love for the wounded or diseased. Even as you learn my remedies, you're not meant to cure like superstitious shepherds who use lupine to ward off wolves. Healing will not be your life's pursuit."

Vel and Anneia didn't worry about their middle child. Because Risa smiled, they didn't think she required tending. Her face glowed like Aplu's dawn as she did assigned tasks while growing up. At dusk, she picked dandelions, set fragrant oils in bowls or plumped cushions. Vel and Anneia's own importance made them thoughtless, not acknowledging their daughter's efforts, nor seeing her subtle aura emanating through the secret smile the gods gave her at birth.

"Sweep and mop, bring in the crop, a servant's life for me. Gods give wealth, priests give health, some day I'll be free." Risa sang the servants' tunes as she braided thread bits into a waist belt for her handed down tunics. She let her long thick hair curl around her face to hide the envy that Arith and Venu had more worth.

Vel went about his business of rock discoveries and soil analysis during the day. Nights were for official banquets where Zilath, magistrates and nobles rambled on about Tarchna's brilliance.

"We have ascended and have stabilized our supremacy," Zilath said after the fifth course of meats.

"Still, Phoenicians speak unfavorably of us. They say Etruscans are eccentric, but how would they know?" Magistrate of Commerce said. "They live in an arid wasteland, not idyllic like ours."

"What about those Egyptians? They condemn Phoenicians for stealing our ideas and and then do the same," Magistrate of Construction added.

"Our ship masters report that Hellenics, Phoenicians and Egyptians speculate about our origins. They say Etruscans come from nowhere because we speak a tongue they don't understand. Keep them confused. What does it matter how we talk or where we're from?" Magistrate of Import-Export guffawed.

"Cisra wants to know our Etruscan origins, too. They think they can claim our heritage if they find out how we Tarchna live," Vel told them.

"What have you been telling them about us, Soil Sampler?"

"Only what is generally known, Zilath. I don't speak our secrets, although Cisra pries. My informant tells of Cisra's theories and shrewdness."

"So if I alter the myths, Cisra will have notorious traditions," the prince-priest rationalized to the magistrates. "Tell Cisra we came from Lydia in Anatolia. Or tell that we're a lost Semitic tribe. Or that we intermingled with the native population on the Italic peninsula. Tell them the Hellenics mottled our bloodlines. A joke on them!"

"Those are stories of Prince Tyrrhenos, son of King Attis of Lydia sailing west," Vel said over his goblet of wine.

"Right. Our true secret that we Tarchna are pure Etruscans, originators of the cosmos, born of our sacred ancestor, Tages, who bored a hole up from the center of the earth, set the perimeters of the land and wrote holy codes and laws to live by, our *Book of Tages*. This we will keep to ourselves."

Stuffed from banquet, the magistrates and Soil Sampler bowed at the prince-priest's words. "O Zilath, by falsifying these origin myths, it will show Cisra we are supreme. You are greatest of great leaders of Tarchna."

8

"The scourge erupts in the swampy lowlands of Gravisca near the Great Sea," two of Zilath's servants yelled from a regal cart that scattered the chickens. "Prince-priest Zilath commands The Healer to tend the sick."

"I've been expecting you. These should be taken first." Anneia pointed to the cooling season herbals stacked in the yard. "They'll bring down fever."

"You can't go. People die when they go within a quarter day's journey of Gravisca. We hear of people going to the port and never coming back." Struck with terror, Vel clutched Anneia's hand.

"Who can refuse the Zilath?"

"I won't let you go."

"Vel, I'm a healer. People are ill and need me. You find wealth in rocks for our city. The city needs you. Can I tell you to give up your rocks? You wouldn't permit it. I can't give up my cures. Please understand."

"It's dangerous work."

"So is scrambling up cliffs. How often you tell me about someone falling."

"That's different."

"Load these other plants," Anneia told the servants and yanked her hand from Vel. "No, it's the same. If I don't go, the gods will be angry."

Appalled by the onerous task of driving her to Gravisca, they lifted baggage and assorted herb pouches into the wagon, procrastinating to know their own fate.

"And us?" Vel's brow shot up. "You justify Zilath. What about us? Shouldn't we be angry?"

"Shush, my darling." Anneia went to Vel with her warmest smile, kissing away his frown. "Remember that my loyalty is repayment to Zilath giving us permission to wed."

"That was years ago," Vel griped.

"The prince-priest is very powerful, isn't he?" Risa asked, fear for her mother growing. "He'll keep you safe."

"That he will. He needs me for a short while and will send Lethi to care for you."

"I don't need anyone to care for me. I'm going to the training hunt." Venu mimicked a hunter with bow and arrow.

"My son, she'll keep you disciplined when you get home."

"Lethi? Isn't she a servant in Zilath's house?" Vel asked.

"Not a servant. A wise woman who cares for the prince-priest's family. Her long straight hair hangs to her knees in a single braid and she wears boots. She'll fascinate the children."

"Zilath thinks highly of your healing to send her."

"Lethi will make sure you're not bothered."

Vel kissed Anneia and held her tightly. "Your lips taste like ambrosia."

"You approve then?"

"No, but have your way. I'm proud your special powers keep Tarchna healthy."

With a basket of herbs on her lap, Anneia left Tarchna, full of life. The family watched her go until she was a dot on the landscape.

"She's convinced that her mission is right," Vel said. "But can she keep more from death?"

9

The citizenry adored Anneia, often wistfully reminiscing about her goodness after she courageously left for Gravisca.

Vel went into the hills. Without ambitious plans made for her upbringing, daughter Risa spun flax for cloth and helped do Lethi's chores. Housebound with servants and yard animals, her tunics weren't prettied with finery.

Son Venu went on a training hunt. He loved the hilly woodlands spotted with oak and chestnut trees, where pheasant, hare and partridge frolicked, where he targeted prey with bow and arrow, and retrieved dead animals.

After trotting on a horse and sighting wildlife, Tarchna lacked adventure for Venu. Risa played knucklebones with him, bouncing the grape-sized ball and swooping bronze metal bits with her practiced hand. She, too, was unhappy their mother was still at the port. "I'm done with this. Do your chores, Venu."

He did what he was told and went to the courtyard with the family dog.

"How rumpled you are. You stink of dog dung," Vel reprimanded. "If your mother saw you, she wouldn't let you in the house. Change your filthy clothes."

Rainfall was a time to stay indoors. Vel set a wood panel on his lap. "Boredom is the culprit of inactivity. Risa, you need skills to stretch your mind."

"I like the markers. They look like little people," Venu said. "Can I play, Father?"

"You're not old enough for games of strategy." Sarcastically, Vel plunked his marker on the wood. "Take your place, Risa."

Obediently Risa sat, stone-faced from Vel's affront to her brother.

Hotheaded, Venu rolled with the dog on the floor mat. The game roughened when Venu rapidly shook the mat by its tasseled edge. The dog nipped and missed, tearing Venu's sleeve.

Vel threw off the markers with the back of his hand. "Get away with your noise. You're nothing but a child."

"I hate you! Mother doesn't talk to me like that." Venu stalked out of the room, wanting to be on the other side of the cosmos from Vel.

Venu rushed to the back of the house. Anneia's workshop was sealed with a plank of wood. He pried it off and kicked open the door. Shut since Anneia left, a musty smell permeated the pitch-black room of cures.

With light from the hall, Venu could see the center table covered with roots, stems, leaves, flowers and fruit. He recognized a few by names Anneia had taught. Mustard seed, rosehips and chamomile were wrapped in flax-clothed pillows. Drying herbs of calendula and mugwort hung from walls upside down. Holly suspended from the rafters. Clusters of lupine, lavender and hyacinth had fallen, reminding Venu that he picked them with his mother.

The air freshened. Breathing in the fragrances, Venu flopped onto straw. Idly, he stripped leaves from a yarrow twig used to staunch open wounds. His mother hadn't packed this cure, nor the plants that were good for the soul. She would need those. He got up and tied them with deer sinew.

"Come to me," a tiny voice called from the shadows.

"Mother, are you here?" Venu asked. "You can't be. It's your herbs I see."

Moonbeams streamed from the thatch roof, lighting a carnelian stone on the table.

Anneia's voice spoke again. "Take the amulet. It drives off disease and brings luck."

It had to be the peculiar amulet that Vel gave Anneia, the stone of the gods. Venu stuffed it into the folds of his clothes.

He had to help his mother. She'd be proud if he brought the herbs to her and would let him stay. "Should I take these dried pods and seeds? They're right for grinding into paste."

The wind replied, rustling the bundled plants into his hands.

Venu pushed the workshop door in place and tiptoed past the room where Vel slept. The house was quiet, except for servants at chores. Creeping through the dim hall, he stole his father's wool cloak. He went to his room for his hunting pouch. From there, he searched the food storage shelves for barley cake, but found only mash that he scooped into a sack. What he'd have to do was forage like the older youths at training.

Stealthily, he ran from the house through the animal yard without disturbing the geese. Crouching low on the hill path leading seaward, he avoided the main road and the guards who watched for possible enemies. They would catch a boy running in the night, and tie him with hemp.

A blowing wind prodded him towards the cliff's edge. Down the embankment he went. Mud oozed into his boots. Dark shadows blasted heat as he squished around gnarled trees bent by the sickened flora. A skull appeared on one tree trunk. Another looked like a gorgon. Gorgons were supposed to ward off evil spirits of the dead. Maybe dead beings were in the swamp? Outgrowths and stumps of vegetation that couldn't survive the climate were on the uneven ground. Erratically he walked, hearing sissing and croaking noises from things he couldn't see. Dank smells of stagnant ponds pricked his nostrils where herons and bitterns rotted from last season. The odors made him queasy.

Frightened by these grotesque surroundings, he sloshed through spongy moss and rancid water. The gods must hate this fenland too, for they hurled a thunderbolt that stung marsh trees with fire.

Those fire gods, demons of the netherworld, increased his dread. The elders had warned not to turn against them. Disaster would be one's fate.

Hammering rain poured over Venu. Covering himself with the wool cloak for comfort, he kept the herbs dry in the pouch. Tired and shivering, he squatted under a thick tree branch. Frugally he nibbled a few grains of mash. They were almost gone.

The dawn's pale light showed his way again. Nothing edible was in these uninhabited marshes. Not that it mattered. His hunger had soured by the abominable odors. Crawling over decaying logs, fumbling through confusing mazes of bramble, he walked towards the hazy sun.

Venu had done the unthinkable, disobeying laws of the cosmos. He shook off slime of the swamps and hurdled onto the main road.

Had goddess Menvra—the only name he could recall—taken his hand to guide him out of the putrid bogs?

10

The stench of Gravisca came on a foul wind recalling ancient animals and fetid crevices, the smell of marsh fever, the sickness that had wiped out half the port's population.

Looping his pouch over his shoulder and holding the cloak to his nose, Venu wondered where he would find his mother. No one paid attention to the small boy with a sack. Dirty, untidy folk were on the road between Tarchna and the port town. Wrapped in their own wretchedness, the haggard ones scuffed along in muddy ruts. Apprehension showed in the eyes of those standing, wincing with fear of contracting The Disease.

"What cures are you trading, lad?" An old woman, brittle and bent in her afflicted pose, hobbled to Venu and leaned on her stick. She grinned with crooked teeth.

He smelled disease on her. She lacked pride, yet there was kindness to her being. He had never seen a person like her.

"Are you Tarchna?" he asked.

"No, boy. I'm from here. Give me your cures."

"They're my mother's. She knows well-making remedies. She's Anneia, the Healer, as wise as Goddess Menvra. This one might do for strength." Venu drew out a few chopped twigs of wort plant. "Have you seen my mother?"

"Never heard of her. Perhaps she's at the ships. Those sea merchants are

smart. They're quickening to get out before the sickness reaches. Go there."
She shook with fragility.

Where she wagged her bony finger, Venu saw a shimmering mass of sky-blue and tree-green water that changed hues at each step he took. The western wind lifted his tiredness from the marsh. Soon he was racing, cleansed of the noxious odors that had filled his body.

Eyes on the enchanting view, he passed through the village, a blur of people, carts and animals. What was this sight, lit by golden speckles shot from the sun? Ship after ship was at the dock, structures as big as Tarchna's temple, rocking on water. Waves slapped at these wooden hulls, saying, "Come with us."

He had never been close to a boat but had seen a tiny one painted on a vase. In awe, Venu went among them, not knowing what they were for. Upturned prows of the grand ones looked like snakes about to strike. Were they sea demons? The creatures stared out with open jaws, tongues about to lick the water. These had to be the monster seafaring ships the Tarchna spoke of when they told of sea bandits.

Long sleek ones could be pirate warships built for speed against enemies.

Boats that could hold six men, decorated with symbols of favorite gods, had to be for fishers who sometimes arrived in Tarchna bartering catch.

All were of woodland pines, oak and spruce, nailed with bronze pegs with a cabin centered on the deck next to a tall pole sheathed in woven canvas. On some, the prow was a pointed rod. The other end was squared and broad, weighed with amphorae.

No matter what they were, he loved them already.

Mariners and sea warriors milled around the imposing vessels, not admiring their merit but asking for work. Venu mingled among them, and went to a second dock where ships and people waited for olive oil, sea fish and grain. They were ordinary townsfolk of spotless or squalid variety, not of Tarchna's quality but suited to port life. Acting like a merchant's helper, he inspected goods in the market place so that people would think he belonged.

"Take me, Alfnis!" pleaded one of the men to a shaggy-faced man leaning on the railing of a ship. "I've been with you before."

"Come aboard," the man named Alfnis shouted back amidst the talk, calling men for his crew.

Continuing to the end of Gravisca, Venu carried his bundle of herbs, cloak thrown over his shoulder with the day's heat. Tall grasses and coarse sand ended at a path through the dunes. Another amazing sight met his eyes. Round pebbles dusted with glittering blackish sand led to frothy waves.

He wrenched off his mud-clad boots and put his toes into cold brine. It bit him, sinking his feet.

An unknown force made Venu forget his mother. The undertow sucked him into the foaming sea.

11

Gigantic to most Tarchna, unswerving in stance, Zilath's flutist with his mantle caught by a draft, his skirt whipping his knees, skimmed through Tarchna's streets with double flute pipes held high. Blowing hollow wails, he heralded Anneia the Healer's death.

Tearfully, the Tarchna spoke of Anneia as if she had been a goddess infallible to strange cosmic forces, the absolute Etruscan, joyful and gracious. Yet in the gloomy region of the death-ridden port, Vel's wife perished, the moment and place unknown. Not a goddess, but mortal, she met her fate like other humans.

When the family learned of her death in the season of bare trees and frost, Anneia had been away from Tarchna for three moons.

Living in the near empty home, housekeeper Lethi attended only Vel and his younger daughter, Risa. Soon after Anneia's departure, Venu, the last child of the Laris clan, was nowhere to be found.

"Gone. Where is anyone's guess," Lethi said ruefully.

"Did father's rage make Venu run away the night he was spoiling the dog?" Risa asked this woman who would substitute for her mother. "Was father angry because Zilath demanded Anneia's aid, or was father impatient because he was left to care for us?"

Zilath's flutist made his rounds again with a distressing message from Gravisca. Six-year old Venu drowned in the wake of an Etruscan ship leaving the harbor. There was no funeral. His body wasn't found.

Vel took to his rooms. Risa stayed in hers when not needed. Her aura had burned low when her mother died and went lower from Venu's demise. Without family, the animal yard was the liveliest place. The sky above was full of chirruping swallows. Each day Risa threw grains to quell their hunger, and soon she could differentiate one from the other.

"You uplift my spirits," she told them. "You're my only friends to help tolerate this dreary existence."

"Enough misfortune you've had, Soil Sampler," a well-dressed messenger confronted Vel.

"Who are you to know?" Vel asked.

"I'm a magistrate to Cisra's Maru, sent by our all-mighty prince-priest. Our metal-bearing hills are unexplored. You are the man who finds copper and tin. We know of your life and talents." He narrated Vel's attainments. "We'll pay for your genius."

"Why does Cisra need metals?"

"The same as Tarchna. Utensils. Tools. Bronze figurines of the gods, those offerings to make the gods laugh with delight. Candelabras and metal incense holders."

"We already make them for Etruria," Vel contended. "You'll cut our trade."

"Masking death's smell is part of our commerce. We must appease the gods' nostrils. Incense distracts the gods from imposing ominous judgments on the dead. We need to make our own statuary and ornaments."

"Is Cisra going to war against Tarchna?"

"No. Our enemies are as yours. There must be enough metals to make Etruria the strongest power of the Great Sea. But you have a greater enemy."

"Who might that be?"

"You don't know? Zilath of Tarchna sent your wife to an early afterlife."

Vel gagged. That was the truth he repudiated. Swallowing hard he said, "What do you need?"

"Bronze helmets and breastplates outlining the male chest, nipples and rib cage for warrior chiefs. Spears for sea warriors to stab life from a victim."

"Weapons. What's in it for me?"

"Zilath keeps you leashed. We offer leeway."

"How?"

"Greater remuneration. Maru elevates you second to him. More wealth shall be yours than what your prince-priest gives. We'll send our best stallions and chariot for your journey," the magistrate wheedled.

"Your offer isn't frivolous."

"Do not ponder long, Soil Sampler. Like Tarchna, we have a right to lead."

12

Forlorn without laughter, the grand Porenna-Laris home was as neglected as a straw hut gone to seed. Vel didn't mention his bereavement but invited no one in, not relatives, acquaintances or traveling harpists and lyrists who had once brought gaiety. The silent dining place had tattered cushions and few candles.

"See what I've picked, Father. Aplu's sun shines in these flowers. The black eyes wink." Risa centered the stems in a bucchero bowl on the low table. "I painted those borders on the walls. Do you like them?"

"Too bright. We'll have none of these decorations," Vel scoffed, repressing any attempt to enliven the house.

With Anneia's death, Risa blossomed, not because of her mother, but from womanhood. Vel saw his daughter's growth but denied it. No bronze mirrors were kept in the house. Risa's chiseled cheekbones, creamy skin and masses of locks, went unseen. She heightened and slimmed, but she was small-breasted, dissimilar to voluptuous Etruscan women.

Risa wasn't a healer like Anneia, but every once in awhile, her intangible goodness reminded Vel of his dead wife's beauty. Never praising Risa's graces, talents or intelligence, he made sure she stayed home, not visiting neighbors or meeting new friends, nor going to the prince-priest's circus, the entertainment of the mid-heat season where acrobats, dancers, citharists and animal acts competed.

Anneia's distraught parents argued that their son-in-law, whom they once acclaimed for his astuteness, had led their daughter into danger and death by consenting to her mission. In warped hysterics, they disowned him and his offspring. Cut off from Anneia's family, Risa couldn't see grandparents, aunts, uncles, and cousins.

"Don't mind, Father," Risa tried to cheer Vel. "The cousins are rough with games and grandmother's food tastes revolting. You have me. I'll take care of you."

"Lethi's competent. She takes care of me," Vel replied grumpily.

Lethi hadn't moved back to Zilath's house. In a show of mourning and appreciation for The Healer, she was given to Vel. The arrangement worked. Lethi enjoyed the accolade, staying in the small household as favored head housekeeper.

When Vel worked, Risa sneaked from one unoccupied room to another, each full of abandoned memories.

Arith's room was immaculate, kept with blanketed bed and trunk as homage to the firstborn. Risa peeked into the trunk, full of night linens and pre-wedding banquet tunics. She slammed the lid, glad that her sister married and left Tarchna. Arith's sinful lusts were against Tarchna's code. Once Risa had come upon her in an act with an unknown man, and Arith tweaked her lips until they hurt. "Keep your mouth shut or all your hair will fall out. First, the hair on your head, then your eyebrows and eyelashes and the hair up your nose. Then your nose, eyes and ears will shrivel and decay!"

Venu's undusted room was the same as the night he disappeared. His clothes were in a box, the learning slates, bow and arrow on the wall.

Risa went to the most honored room of the house, Anneia's, still piled with healing herbs from hills, forests and beyond the river. Stale blood smelled from the far corner, bundled with yarrow and rosemary. Maybe a yard animal was burrowing in the herbs. Feet pattered across the floor.

"Who's there?" Risa called out. "If you're a servant, you shouldn't be in this room."

Woosh! A bundle was flung at her, the stalks shooting out like knives thrown, settling at her feet. Unnatural noises came from the walls. Risa shuddered, feeling eyes at her back. The workshop was embodied with Anneia's spirit. She darted to her own room and dived under a blanket.

Her heart beat like a parade drum. Her mother might be alive in the workshop, hidden from Zilath's command. No, that couldn't be. The Flutist had announced Anneia's death, yet the circumstance of how she died was inexplicable. Double-talking Zilath gave no answers. The healing sun god Aplu might have turned against Anneia and sent sudden death with his arrows. Aplu might have killed Anneia because she left her family to care for non-family.

Risa could remember her mother's face and gentle manner. What she couldn't remember was being held at her mother's bosom. Arith was hugged, Venu kissed on the forehead. They had received devotion given to prince-priests and gods.

The house was unnaturally quiet. Risa uncovered herself and ran to daylight, bemoaning, "There must be something wrong with me that I wasn't cuddled or touched. I cared for others. Couldn't they see my love? Perhaps they saw only my outer form, the shell of my being. Am I who I am, just to me?"

A crested-plumed hoopoe bird fell from the sky, its wing askew. Risa calmed it with spelt kernels while she straightened the wing on a cloth. She patted the bird until it flapped and perched on her arm, tweeting before flight. A simple cure that lifted her heavy heart and reduced the hurt of Anneia's demise.

An ache penetrated within Risa, spiraling as if she was falling into an abyss. That grief subsided with time but not the sadness that she hadn't said farewell to her mother.

She wondered how the gods would punish her.

Deceit and Honor

Noblewoman Risa Laris

13

"Our dining place can hold twelve without crowding. Twelve is a magical number. My age. The number of Etruscan cities. The number of magistrates," Risa fidgeted, mashing boiled spelt in her bowl during an evening meal.

"Your mind is elsewhere. Did you hear me say I've been to a fulguriator?" Vel asked. "He's read the gods' portents for me."

"Why, Father? Lethi says a haruspex is as good. He takes a forked bone out of a chicken without breaking it and makes wishes."

"The wishbone doesn't bring luck. The hands of a haruspex are covered with blood, always messing with skin, fur and intestines of whatever neck he can wring. A fulguriator is talented. He knows fate."

Alarmed by his foreboding tone, she mixed a dried millet cake into the slop served as food to make it palatable. Anneia's death had made her father an ascetic. He punished the household with simple food of the ill or poor to honor what his wife must have suffered.

Apprehensively, she asked, "What did the fulguriator say?"

"Mostly not for your ears, but he told me Zilath prepares a quest for more iron and tin. I knew that already."

"Can I go with you, Father? I'll walk all day and sleep under the stars. I'm not afraid of night, howling wolves or screeching owls."

"Traipsing the hills? Not what females of marriageable age do." He cleared his throat. "Arith had union at your age."

Risa knew that he had made a decision that would destroy her known cosmos. To her mind, he didn't want or love her. Neither had her mother.

"If you won't let me go, I can stay with Lethi and tend house. The servants and slaves do my bidding," she tried.

"No man will be here to protect you. You need a husband, Risa."

"A husband? I'm not ready to wed."

"You don't need to be ready. There's a man who will do you well."

"I want a love story. You and Mother had one," Risa objected. "Give me a chance at great love. Let Turan make it possible."

"Cease pestering, daughter." Vel lorded over her like an adversary in battle. "The heavenly priest has spoken to the gods. Balance will bring harmony to our house. You'll marry who I say."

Her being quaked as if the roof caved in. She threw over her bowl and left the room. With nowhere to go, Risa clomped through the mud yard to the dove coop that a servant had hastily made from old timber. The coop shook as she raked the doves' detritus with furious strokes.

"You are like me, my lovelies. Caged, unable to fly at will. Now, my master traps me." She undid the catch and shooed them out. "I snared you. Forgive me. Fly! Seek your way!"

They squawked, flapping wings at cross-purpose, whether to stay or go free. Their indecision frustrated her further. Fervidly, Risa chased them across the land and into the hills.

Weeping, she cradled herself in the arm of a tree and slept.

At dawn, a white dove roused her. She lamented, "The gods give me a lesson by your coming, to undergo whatever happens next."

14

The man who came to dine with the noble Soil Sampler on Porenna Street in Tarchna's finest part of the city wasn't put off by the stark table setting. Local word was that Lethi's meals were atrocious, gruel and water at morn, vapid stew for the main new day repast, cheese and barley cake at sunset. Unperturbed, he reclined.

Cooking servants grumbled about what they had to serve. "We can't cook decent food without Anneia's herbs. The master won't let Risa get fresh ones. Gods help us!"

Risa heard the stranger's voice before she saw him. Without being told, she knew he was part of her punishment for not wanting to marry.

"Serve our guest, Risa."

Speechless, mindful that her tunic smelled of the day's chores, unclean like a disheveled servant of the animal yard, Risa spooned stew into the man's bowl. Her father hadn't told her that he would be here.

Vel and the man ate the tasteless meal, talking about an arched bridge that the city of Vulci built over its river. Neither spoke to Risa, snubbing her as if she didn't exist. She seethed, cheated to have no say.

The next night the stranger came again.

"Parth has walked a long way today. Bathe his feet," Vel bullied.

His feet? Risa's jaw dropped. Father is like a demon god, a monster. He feels nothing for my needs. I must submit to him and to the ancestor priests who scribed in Tages' sacred books, *Children must heed parents.* Loath to comply, she rose from her couch and filled a water pail.

Vel lay back on his cushion, having chosen the right man. He would tell the cooks to make the food tastier.

When Parth was invited to a third supper, he avoided Risa's face, scrutinizing her tunic. Rebelliously, Risa had opened the forbidden trunk and wore one of Arith's best tunics.

He's a heathen, probably imagining what is underneath. Never would a man want a woman with small breasts and slim hips, Risa thought.

The cooks obeyed the master's scheme and chopped onions, garlic and parsley into the stew. The savory food confirmed her doom. Words died on Risa's lips.

Parth spoke only to Vel.

On the night when a shrill chirring of cicadas came through the courtyard, Vel said to Parth, "Sup without me. Those insects scare the animals. I'll send a servant to herd the sheep from the yard. Risa will serve."

Comfortably, Parth ate as he would in his own home.

Risa scraped plates and bowls, banging them like pans to call slaves to a meal. Wanting to be away from this beastly man, wanting him to fall into a water hole, she stood and wobbled the low table in front of the reclining couch, sending the wine jug at him.

He grabbed the jug after wine dribbled on his white tunic. He stood and reached for her hand. "Who are you?"

Heat spread up her arm from his harmless touch. Feeling graceless for such a crude trick, Risa's eyes followed the stain to his hem. Reluctantly she broke her silence. "What do you mean?"

"You're not the Soil Sampler's servant. You're his daughter." Parth released her hand, watching her move as light as a dancer. "Why haven't you spoken?"

She dipped a serving cloth into the water pitcher and handed it to him to lessen the stain. Then she saw his face. Stars of the cosmos! He was the same man from her dream who walked towards her on a pebbled forest road, draped with a stag fur skin, swinging a tear-shaped weight from a coil of rope on one shoulder. His shaggy-bearded face had greeted her with an Etruscan upturned smile and kissable lips.

Kissable lips? Her dream questioned. She had never kissed a man's lips, but this man's whole face was endearing. Golden from Aplu's sun, he had high cheekbones, dark eyes with amber flecks and the longest eyelashes she had ever seen.

"I haven't wanted to," Risa said to the man who wasn't a dream. He was younger, livelier and beardless.

Grinning at her, Parth said, "I've caught you out. You can talk."

"Of course I can."

"I know. I heard you chatting with the servants." He sat back and rubbed his beard stubble. "And you can laugh, too."

"Are you from a forest village?" She looked at his perfectly formed lips and dimpled chin.

"I'm Tarchna born but test roadways through the mountains. That's where your father and I met. He came to the wilderness when he could have sent his helper. To my surprise, he asked me to eat with him on our return."

"You must have expected better fare. Our foodstuffs are awful."

"Sometimes," Parth admitted, shamefaced. "He invited me again."

"You kept coming."

"If a nobleman invites a lesser one, it's not to be denied. Your father is a great man."

"You could have said you eat with your family."

"The food got better. Ewe cheese and garum sauce. The stew was laced with spring berries."

"My mother's dish."

"When you brought wine, I couldn't help seeing you."

"You've seen me before."

"Vel let me assume you were a servant. Guests don't look at a servant. But I felt you weren't. I glanced once, then twice and saw the family resemblance," Parth said.

"You didn't know who I was?"

"I figured it out. Vel knew I wouldn't gawk at a noble's daughter."

"My father played you with a game." Risa folded her arms across her chest.

"You're not the only one annoyed. Vel is persuasive. He has wily ways and played us both."

"I'm mortified by his lies. We've been set upon."

"Perhaps his game was a different way of introducing us so I would find interest in you," Parth drawled demurely. "Under your insolence, your face pleases. You listen well and your comeliness shines."

His approval was subtle. In unspoken words, he had given the compliment that she had attained an Etruscan life goal, inner beauty.

"Forgive me. I've been rude," Risa said and sat on a cushion opposite him, hoping tears wouldn't fall.

"Yes, you have. You acted as if I wasn't good enough for you. Just then,

51

lightening crossed Tinia's sky and I understood Vel's purpose. He wanted me for marriage union with you."

"He deceived you."

"Maybe Tinia's lightning was a sign. Maybe it's not bad to be deceived."

Ensnared by his eyes, she was melting, responding to him against hate for her father's authority.

"Your honesty amazes," Parth said. "Our moments together have been foolish, haven't they?"

"The gods cheer honesty." Risa reached for the wine jug.

Parth's hand blocked hers. "Don't throw it again."

"Why would I throw it now? You're already drenched." Good-naturedly she poured the liquid into his goblet. "This wine has a clear ruby color. It's of last harvest, blessed by the elders."

"Drink with me, Risa. I like your name, uncommon to the Etruscan tongue. Does it mean 'beauty of the sunrise'?"

His warmth made her cheeks shine like copper. For a moment, a smile dawned on her face, the gods awakening her aura. "It means 'the one who smiles.'"

He gazed at her intently, startled by her godly lips. "You have possibilities of being one of the most fascinating people in the cosmos. Tell me what you smile about."

"I haven't truly smiled since Mother's death. I give false smiles to not upset."

"Upset? So you always cause trouble."

"When I'm angry I get stubborn. An old village granny once told my parents: 'Don't cut her hair until she has three years. It will give her character.' They didn't. You see the results."

"She was right. You have character."

A rush of playfulness filled Risa. "There's humor in these maddening nightly episodes. Since the truth is out, you don't have to attend me. You can leave."

"I'm not here by force. You may be stubborn or angry, but you obey." He sliced a wedge of barley cake, gave it to her and took a piece for himself. "I'm staying to see a real smile that won't stop. Another goblet to thank the gods for good fortune?"

She felt an impulse to sing. Her instinct told her Parth was nobler than her father.

They sipped wine, savoring the sweet rich drink. A sensual giddiness passed between them in that toast, as if Turan had impassioned the moment.

Heady from Fluflun's wine, Risa blurted out, "You're old for marriage."

"I am." A shadow crossed his cheeks.

"I didn't mean to say that." Her cheeks flamed.

"You have a right. My parents found a young girl for me to wed. On eve of betrothal, she sickened of poison berries and convulsed to death."

Unrestrained tears welled in Risa's eyes. "You've felt the pain of loss as I have."

He drew her close and wiped her tears with his fingertips. "Have we other common bonds?"

"Perhaps a dislike of bland food. This barley cake needs fennel."

"We're Tarchna born," he said. "You're hot-tempered."

"You're not."

"You're witty."

"You're bold…"

"…swift-minded…"

"…alert…"

"…pleasant under your pretense."

They compared what came to mind, from interests and upbringings to similarities and differences. In accord, a promise of compatibility grew, one of caring and joyous intimacy. Neither wanted the night to end.

Dawn came on the horizon. Parth touched Risa's wrist. "I didn't love her. I met her twice but never knew her."

From deep within Risa, a glowing light surfaced into a joyful, loving smile.

"You're beautiful," he stammered, caught in the glare of her aura.

Shyly, she turned her cheek. "No one has ever said that to me."

"That's because I was meant to be first."

Risa smiled again, washed in the enchantment of happiness that could shape her destiny. She was so happy that if stars could jump out of the sky, she would catch them.

15

Hot with desire, the first kiss between Parth and Risa didn't come soon enough. As the late cold season began to warm, they dined with or without Vel, at odds in front of him to keep his game.

"I know your pretense." Vel came in, hearing more than social conversation. "Parth, I've spoken with your parents, but they haven't answered. Will you have my daughter in union?"

"How could you be so blunt?" Risa cried out, inclined to run to the courtyard. "You bruise me with talk that should be made by parents behind doors."

Parth caught her shoulders and swiveled her to face him. "A direct question takes a direct answer. Yes."

From the amused look on Vel's face, Parth knew he acquiesced too quickly. "Have you seen Zilath about it?"

"I see him every day."

"Is her portion substantial?"

"One that will pleasure you both. I'm tired. I'll leave you alone and go to my pallet."

Loosening his grip on her, Parth drew her face to his. "So, that's that."

"How could you accept me without knowing the portion?" Risa drummed with rage even as his proximity thrilled her.

"I want you, not your portion." His feather kisses lengthened, covering her

54

mouth until her lips parted and her hand touched his cheek. "I've wanted to stroke your hair and tawny skin. What is underneath your tunic arouses me. I want your body with mine."

Her resistance melted. "Great Tinia! You do care for me."

Risa's lessons in lovemaking weren't from her mother or Lethi's tutoring, but from sacred bowls at the augur-priests' temple where she offered wild rosemary sprigs to win favors from the love goddess.

"Turan," Risa stooped in front of the revered statue, "has the unbelievable happened? Will I have an honorable love union?"

"Ah, you're early, but it will do." The augur-priest came from behind a column and said irritably, "I'll leave you with the bowls and will be back at high sun."

Grousing about this ritual, he snagged his cloak on the door and left.

He's a novice like I am, but he's scared of having to perform initiations of life passages, Risa thought.

If there was one lesson Risa inherited from her mother, it was not to fear. She walked to the center of the sanctuary. Perforated holes under the roof eaves cast rays of light on three vases, each on separate tufa stone pedestals.

At eye level, the first appeared to be an ordinary water pitcher with flaking bands of paint around incised outlined figures. Startled, Risa moved nearer. This wasn't a usual Etruscan story on ceramics. Faces in profile, a naked smiling woman sat on a stool, her arms around the man who was kissing her open thighs.

On the band below, a second portrait of the couple showed her legs raised to his shoulders as he stood with his erection pricking her mound.

This is the mating that the initiated giggle about. Could I do these positions? She wondered, looking at the middle vase, an amphora with reddened nudes cavorting in un-human contortions.

It took her breath away. A full-bodied woman sucked the tip of her lover's manhood while a second male lover entered her from the rear, holding her, stroking her hair. Next to them, a woman stood in front of her lover as he pushed up her garments, looking at her mound.

The other side of the vase depicted two lovers jumping in the air, their faces in dreamy preoccupation. They're not kissing. Gods and goddesses they must be! The gods' myths are more complicated than the innocent version we're told as children, she mused.

The two-handled grand cup to the right was Turan's love story. Both lovers knelt towards each other, head to head in an intimate moment. They were enjoying the sexual act, preparing for intercourse. Delight grew in Risa, imagining herself the smiling woman giving sweet looks, exposed breasts caressed by a brawny lover, his countenance like Parth's.

The augur-priest returned. Without pausing, he recited the vase lessons. "The pitcher is Lust, desire for carnal fulfillment. The amphora is Lasciviousness, supreme joy of gods-like-beasts debased into vice. The cup is conjugal Love, Eros and Beauty of Affection. Hellenic gods sanctified Eros and we Etruscans do the same. The ancient elders call love 'perfection of the cosmos.' The divine phallus is reward in your wedding bed. Fascinos, god who gifts you with offspring, grants his power."

Contemptibly, he looked at Risa. The assignment of teaching virgins was not his calling. "This is your marriage training. Your mother will tell you of union night duties."

"My mother is deceased."

"That can't be. I spoke to her at the market place. Aren't you Ramtha, about to wed?"

"Risa Laris is my name."

"Risa, the Soil Sampler's daughter? Your initiation is for next season. You sneaked in. Leave! Leave before the gods curse me, before the dead curse me."

"Turan..." Risa protested, trying to tell why she was there, but the priest shoved her through the sanctuary door to the sacred temple steps. Shamed, she huddled in the temple's shadows.

A girl tapped her arm. "Hisst, I heard the old snake. He waited for me. I couldn't get away from the market. New metals came from the hills and some nobles were tussling over them. A crowd gathered and wouldn't let me pass."

"Metals coming from the hills made you late?" Insight made Risa smile. "You must be Ramtha. Your height and skin are like mine. The bowls were for you."

"I wed come the new moon. Tell me about them. Are they what you expected?"

"The bowls are of great happiness," Risa answered, absurdly tickled. "The gods trick us with this vex!"

Vel suppressed a grin at the blundering augur-priest and said to his daughter, "You've had instruction before your time."

From her father's expression, Risa understood. "You conspired with the augur and then detained Ramtha at market place so that she missed her instruction."

"How could I conspire with an augur? I was exhibiting our newest finds at market. Now you've seen the bowls. You must wed quickly."

"But what about my cresting banquet? Surely, the prince-priest will give the accolade. Parth and I can marry next year."

"A speedy marriage union or Turan will be angry."

Risa didn't mind. Her banquet would come later.

The marriage portion was given: Anneia's vanity table, one white ox for luck, and mattress and linens sewn throughout Risa's youth.

"I'm disappointed for you, Parth. A meager portion. Arith had gifts of tunics, robes and shoes, gold earrings and bracelets, gold chain necklaces, ivory combs, matrimonial linens, marriage bed, reclining couches and tables, pans and cauldrons, platters and bowls of quality."

"Quite a list. Did she get the other white ox?" Parth ribbed.

"It's required. There must be a pair. You can decline to wed me."

"Decline you? Never. Arith moved to her husband's city. She needed a houseful. Besides, Zilath gifts us with a mating ox. I'll work for you all my life, and we'll live on my accolades."

16

"Now that you'll marry a good man, I don't have to worry about you." Vel dumped his tunics and cloaks into a chest. "I'm moving to Cisra."

"Cisra? Does Zilath send you there?"

"He doesn't know I'm going."

"Zilath would protest. He depends on you." Desperate to delay him, Risa said, "You've made your life in Tarchna."

"He meddles in my life, directing what I do. Not anymore! Prince-priest Maru of Cisra makes me a unique offer," Vel said. "The Cisra will accommodate my every request. They've given me a profitable mission and promise that the gods will let me control my own destiny."

"That's bribery."

"My obligation to Zilath is fulfilled," Vel snapped back acrimoniously. "Cisra entices with wealth and power, the gods' bonus for my life of sincere labor."

"Don't go, Father," she begged. "You have me here. You have this magnificent home."

"Your portion was sparing." He put his hand on her shoulder. "Take the house."

"But this is your home, given to you before you met Mother."

"Parth and you will stay here. The Porenna-Laris dwelling passes to you both and shall be re-named 'Laris-Vella' to honor Anneia and your coupling with Parth Vella. He thinks it's sufficient. Arith and Ramnes take me in," Vel said, confirming his decision in detail.

"This has been settled already?" she asked, riled that the family knew what was to happen, but she didn't.

"Yes."

"Then I want to emulate your union by making your marriage room Parth's and mine."

"Arranged marriages don't account for a love bond but for merging clans to procreate. Your mother and I were exceptional. We adored each other and bonded in love," Vel said, the cold wound from his wife's death upon him.

"Our love union may be similar."

"Take another room," Vel said. "Fix it to your liking. Give more children to Tarchna than we did."

"None but this will do," Risa replied as pitiless as he. So much for clever Vel. She didn't want to tell him how much she loved Parth. Her father wanted to believe the arranged marriage was all his doing.

Vel didn't quibble. He was in a hurry to rush the wedding and leave. To remove the spirits of his dead wife, the room was stripped to bare plaster walls on sand brick. With a fresh feather mattress, the marriage bed frame and trunks remained on the tiled checkered floors.

"The course of my life changed when you demanded I marry, but you've been generous, Father."

Had she not said that, she might have been disowned. He hadn't mentioned her cresting banquet, the next rite of passage.

The morn before Risa's wedding, Vel bore good news. "My wishes are doubled. Venu is alive. He's been at sea!"

"You jest to make me less jittery before my union," Risa said. "It couldn't be true. My brother was a child, lost to the fishes. Venu wasn't a seafarer. What do you mean he's been at sea?"

"Truth, I swear to the gods. I've been looking for Venu since Anneia's death. The elders influenced Zilath to locate him. A messenger from the port just came. The gods keep him alive and well," Vel replied. "He arrives, but not before your marriage."

"Miracle of miracles! That my brother lives is the best wedding gift—and you'll have your son."

"Venu can't come to Tarchna until the ship he's on is unloaded. He's been with one of Zilath's seafarers, somewhere in the Great Sea. Who knows how wild he's become? He'll need re-training. You and Parth must rear him."

"Us?"

"I can't take him to Cisra. My work will keep me in the hills. He's fonder of you than Arith."

"Then, willingly. Venu must have suffered," she answered, knowing she had enough love for Parth and could give her brother the care he needed.

17

Rising like a star in Tinia's heavens, the hilltop shrine glistened on their wedding day, anointing the small gathering with approval. Dressed in white tunics, Parth and Risa walked hand in hand up the stony path, pleased they outwitted Vel.

"We're not supposed to be in love," Parth whispered in Risa's ear. "Remember it's an arranged marriage."

Turan, who could make love bloom or fade, saw their embraces and smiled on them. Not only had they agreed to marry with rushed minimal preparations, they were eager to marry as Vel wanted.

Zilath's youngest flutist, newly practiced, played ceremonial melodies on his ivory instrument to announce the wedding procession. His music sang, "The gods made this union. Consecrate this marriage with joy."

Vel strutted behind him, his wishes honored, hurrying Parth and Risa to the shrine's platform.

Parth's parents followed, gladly welcoming the union. Their son had surprised them when he declared Risa his bride. The marriage made for Parth seasons before had failed miserably. He refused a second, then a third female. What his parents hoped for, didn't happen. They left him alone about marriage, fretting that they wouldn't have grandchildren through him.

The witnesses, Parth's two brothers and their wives, paced to the music.

Risa took to them and they to her like they had always been family. They'd be new relatives to replace the one she lost.

Risa's only witness was Vel. Arith was too occupied with her newborn to travel from Cisra. Relatives sent excuses. Planting for the warming season was more important than going to a second daughter's marriage.

"I try not to care that my family didn't come."

"Never mind." Parth kissed her earlobe with the tip of his tongue. "Who else but us need bliss today? I want to satisfy our love."

Her body hummed from his last words. At midday, they neared the shrine, the three sacred bowls utmost in her mind. Parth's shaft would soon enter her mound.

What will my life with him be? Would he be as he appears? Risa thought, biting her lips.

Prince-priest Zilath stood on the shadowless platform between high columns, his costume as marriage magistrate gleaming with gold thread. He had been told Risa accidently saw the initiation bowls and needed to wed. Giving consent, Zilath blessed them, his hands on their heads. "This celebration day marks the beginning of cresting, the third phase of an Etruscan's life. Birth, youth, cresting, twilight, death, afterlife—the span of time in the cosmos. Forever you will be together. Turan binds you and rejoices in your union."

He hasn't mentioned my cresting banquet, Risa thought fleetingly as the sun's rays glowed favorably on Parth and her.

After the wedding meal, Vel hugged Risa clumsily, the first time he had embraced her since her birth. "Now that you're married, I say farewell. You're matron of the Laris-Vella house with its luxury and joy as well as burden of memories. Make your way into Tarchna society. This is where your life's opportunities begin, Risa."

"May the gods protect your journeys." Tears streamed down her face. "Cisra wins more than your talents. That city will delight in dividing our family."

"Zilath divided our family, not Cisra," Vel said as he abandoned Tarchna.

Few would start a journey through the metal bearing hills in late light, but the dark would make it easier, should Zilath try to hinder.

Dusk became night, the beginning of their cresting phase of life.

Risa and Parth entered the newly prepared marriage room. He cupped her face in his hands, caressing her cheeks softly, touching her tongue with his. Responding to his kisses, pleasure flowed between them, her body pressed against his.

His fingertips moved down her neck and shoulders to unfasten her tunic brooch. The tunic fell to her waist and he tasted her tightened nipples.

"Nectar of the gods." Parth licked and stroked her breasts.

So this is what the sacred initiation cup meant, Risa thought, heat waving to the root of her being, down to her toes.

Parth undid the clasp tying the tunic at her waist. He pulled it over her head and let it slip to the floor.

"For the first time, I stand nude before a man, you, my dear husband," she smiled ecstatically, remembering the instruction bowls as he probed his fingers in her woman's secrets, the folds of her sacred mound.

He went into her moisture and she breathed, "You make me soar like a skybird."

"And you make my manhood quicken." In one easy motion, Parth also was unclothed. He scooped her up to the mattress.

Knowledgeable of love's ways taught by elder men, Parth lowered himself on top of her, his arms supported his chest while his erect shaft made entry with a moment's violence. Vesta's fiery torch swelled fire into her, starting a fierce new rhythm as recognizable to life as Tinia's sun and rain.

"My body will puff like Tinia's cheeks and three seasons later a newborn will appear from the slit within my mound," she said, rubbing the white salve on herself.

"Then Tinia must be watching our union."

"Our children shall bear the looks of the gods' joy on their faces from our coupling."

It suddenly humored them that they were being seen. Cozily they spoke of their new intimate lives. When desire overcame them again, they explored each other's bodies until dawn.

Drained by love making, Risa dreamily laid her head on the pillow. "Are we with child yet?"

"If the gods will it."

Clouds of Disharmony

18

Someone pounded on the hollow tufa brick walls. The reverberating blows awoke Risa and Parth. In the dark, Parth groped for his tunic. "Stay abed, Risa."

"No. I thought this might happen." Distress brought a lump into her throat. "Zilath doesn't give me a cresting banquet accolade. Instead, he sends warriors."

Risa and Parth went to the front door. "What do you want at midnight?"

The head warrior stepped forward. "Prince-priest Zilath wants this house owned by Velthur Porenna, Soil Sampler."

"Zilath gave his word that this dwelling belonged to my father, and he could do with it what he wanted. The prince-priest gave his medallion." Risa held it out like a shield. "This is my house, gifted to me as my portion."

The warrior stared at the shiny metal disk, conflict in his eyes. "Porenna knows Tages' rules too well. You have rights of ownership."

"So he told me." Risa laced the medallion through the chain around her neck.

"But he's gone to Cisra. The Soil Sampler abandoned our city!"

"I am here, loyal to Tarchna and the prince-priest. My husband is your Noble Road Builder. We care for this house with honor."

"You are strong-willed as the rest of your family."

"I respect their interests."

"I'll tell Zilath."

"Forget Vel Porenna and that house," the highest augur-priest advised Zilath. "You have other involvements."

"I do." Zilath's eyes gleamed with greed as he went to meet the other prince-priests.

Etruria's highborn prince-priests from each of the Twelve Peoples convened in secret at a hidden wooded glen beside a brook. Like their tribal ancestors, at the warming season they sat on their knees in a circle, crowned with gold-dipped oak, olive, pine or plane tree leaves, native to their cities.

"We come peacefully. Among Mediterranean nations, this is a calm era, non-violent, non-warring, " Velathri's prince-priest, the presiding head of the conclave began. "For eons, we haven't been enemies with Carthage nor their relatives, the Sea People of Phoenicia, who go from the Great Western Rock to eastern coasts. Hellenics stay on the south peninsula and in Sicilia but skulk by our coast with Ionic Phoecaens in their wake. On northern shores, they've established Masalia and Nikea as strategic forts. They won't invade us because they're scared of our sea warriors."

"Sea warriors don't scare them," Veii's prince-priest sniveled. "If they fail, they would have to submit to our way of life. We treat men and women the same. They keep women home, out of sight. Our women stroll freely and walk with men in the streets. At banquet, our people dance together and compete at games together in the great yard."

"Of course that should be," Curtun's prince-priest said. "Barbarians over the mountains lack intellect."

"The gods made two genders for life's pleasures, to make splendid love. Women have like souls. Those scornful Hellenics and prudish Latin tribes think we're improper. Outsiders opposed our ancestors and us," Rusellae's prince-priest chimed in.

"They hate us. Could it be we're superior to our neighbors? Do we war with those countries for exposing their savage ignorance?" Arreti's prince-priest postulated.

"Such nuisances," Zilath inserted, ready with his plan. "If we merge with Carthage, Hellas won't be able to take possession of the Great Sea."

"We don't want to be Hellenic, but they do have marvelous vases and sculptures," Vulci's prince-priest put in his only words that day.

"Do you mean to offer trade to Carthage and Phoenicia in exchange for protection from future Hellenic threat?" Maru asked shrewdly.

"Now, this is thinking! If we form an alliance, we combine our industry," Velathri's prince-priest wisely nodded. "An efficient use of Etruscan wealth."

Zilath didn't expect such discussion. He wanted wealth just for Tarchna but he had to show brilliance. "Unify Etruria? Then all of our cities would have to work together. We could call it a new word—*unification*. And then we advance what Hellenics call an *oikonomia*."

The prince-priests were pleased with themselves as they rarely agreed.

19

Challenging Zilath for the Soil Sampler's dwelling, Risa barricaded the yard with tufa stone, placing tubs of oil to light flames in protest. She sent Lethi and the cook for provisions, thinking Zilath's warriors might come if she was gone.

"I didn't realize how willful you are. Defiant." Parth watched her tactics and tightened his arms around her. "Don't worry, love of my life. Let's keep time away under the blankets."

Vel's house became Risa's as she did chores and beautified rooms for future use, anticipating where each child would go. Devoted as she was to her husband, there was no child in her womb.

Many leather soled shoes stomped in unison after dusk. A second warrior group bordered the house with the outcry, "Come out, Noblewoman of the Laris Clan. Zilath wants proof of your medallion!"

"They taunt me." Mustering strength to face them, Risa watched from a secret slat in the wall. "I won't give it."

Suddenly the warriors became quiet.

"They've dropped on their knees," Parth said from another peephole. "Their arms are up."

"What now?"

"Augur-priests are coming."

"Twelve," Risa counted as torchbearers lit the path for the priests who didn't glance at the Laris-Vella house.

"They're chasing a wind of dry leaves," Parth said as the warriors followed the priests.

"The priests are chanting. I can't make out exact words, but I think it's a prophecy. Maybe we shouldn't go to sleep. We might not wake up."

After that night, there were more omens. The Flutist walked the city with two hunters raising a trussed mountain goat. Risa saw the goat that should have been proud of its contribution. She could smell the goat's fear.

Most unusual were changes in Risa's yard—oak leaves folded when they should have uncurled, hens molted when they should have renewed, birds flew to Aplu's sun and plummeted to death.

A mysterious power bigger than leaves, hens or birds, shook the most complacent Tarchna. There weren't clouds in the sky, but darkness appeared. Uni's moon rose and turned black. Tinia's sun vanished.

All were afraid—priests, nobles, even Zilath. "What celestial phenomena is this?" They protected their eyes as they watched the heavens. "Don't look!"

Some said it lasted four hundred twenty heartbeats.

Others claimed it was five hundred, enough to flush skin and burn eyes.

When it was over, daylight went on. All were alive.

Risa worried to Parth, "When will the warriors come back?"

Tarchna's highest sacred augur-priest ominously deplored, "Where, but in our city of sacred philosophical life, would a sign from the gods be given first?"

"The momentary death of Aplu's sun happened throughout Etruria," a lower augur spoke up. "Seen everywhere."

"We are the ones who must tell our brethren Etruscans what we know, that this solar event is a divination. There are clouds in the future," Zilath declared, reading aloud from the *Book of Tages*. "Nature leaps in cycles with variations, growing, blossoming with meaning, then withers into the earth and dies. This is the cyclic cosmos growth and decay, life and death."

"This is about our destiny," the highest augur-priest stated, "part of the Great Prediction."

"The end of the cosmos as we know it," another augur-priest said.

"Chaos will abound," the magistrates moaned. "This Great Prediction hangs over our heads, a menace to our lives. We're doomed."

"Doomed? Not us," Zilath said and relayed Tages' words to those closest to death, the most revered elders.

"Our gods behave badly," the elders moped.

In picking sticks for seating at the prince-priests' conclave, Zilath and Maru were next to each other, wearing more ornate tunics than last year, sewn with gemstones.

Revolted by Zilath's inflated piousness, Maru patted Zilath's shoulder with stinging sharpness. "Your interpretation of the Great Prediction coming soon is to frighten us from competing with you. Our economy booms with new markets throughout the Great Sea, the 'Mediterranean' as Hellas calls it. We trade with more Aegyptians and Phoenicians than ever."

"And we with Hellenics of Masalia and Carthage," Zilath replied unflinchingly. "Our bucchero moves northwest."

"That Soil Sampler Vel Porenna who worked for you has developed a finer bucchero, the most lucrative export that our shipmasters trade for gold blocks to bring home. Our craftsmen make the blocks into gold-ware for Cisra noblewomen," Maru said with rancorous pleasure.

"Humph," Zilath emitted dryly and let loose a string of curses about Vel under his breath.

"Our metals are of better quality than yours. Do you blame yourself for not keeping Vel Porenna in Tarchna?" Maru jabbed.

Zilath squirmed like a hare to be skinned.

"What conceit, Maru," prince-priests of Perugia, Vatluna and Clevsin frowned, bored by their repetitious sparing.

"You're envious of our fortune. We reap ideas from Hellenics, Carthaginians, and even barbaric Italics. Why limit one's thinking when others have proven products," Maru justified. "The Hellenic gods grant us barter of vases that bring harmony. We have united their customs and rituals with gods of our own foundation."

Veii's prince-priest exclaimed, "Goddess Voltumna guides our economy. We're satisfied."

"Don't forget that all Etruria is prosperous," Rusellae's prince-priest retorted, about to leave the conclave. "We Rusellae have grains. Flufluna has iron, Velathri timber for ship keels, Arreti bronze pikes and spears."

"The hue of your face matches your purple robe, Zilath," Maru said, enjoying the effect he had on his rival.

"You're too self-important with your claims." Zilath thrust out his fist.

"Enough animosity. Restrain!" Their princely peers held the two at bay. "You've gone too far, Maru."

"Maru of Cisra is vulgar," Zilath confided to one of his priests. "Despicable. Eliminate him."

"It goes against the *Book of Tages* to destroy your brethren. One city turning against the other could bring the Great Prediction sooner."

"He's my opponent. That makes him an enemy. Our code condones imprisoning or getting rid of adversaries."

"We should deal with this matter subtly, Zilath. Cisra can't know it's us who assault."

"Do it if it takes more seasons than my lifetime."

20

Through rainstorms and cloudbursts, the augur-priests sought a portent in Tinia's clouds. Tinia rewarded the Etruscans. With the flick of his fingertips, the god sent lightning bolts to clarify the ultimate law as starbursts crossed the sky.

The Great Prediction means death for Etruria will be ten saeculae.

Augur-priests counted to be sure they were correct. "We are in the fifth saecula. Etruscan society spans five saeculae more."

"If that's the Great Prediction, that will be when we are dust," Risa said to Parth when their first child, Culni, was born in a season that leaves budded, verdant shoots of crops flowered, and Etruria's abundance was extolled.

Risa showed off her son at the market place, hoping a noble or augur would remind Zilath that he hadn't granted her cresting banquet, usually given before a first birth.

"Etruria provides naturally," the elders at the market boasted. "At stock farms in mountain glens, our cattle, pigs and sheep breed faster than we can eat them. That confounds barbarians. Coniferous forests are alive with birds, deer, hare and boar. Great Sea yields weighty nets of fish. Fields produce more millet, barley and flax than we eat in a season. Vines are as big as trees, clustered with grapes to eat or press for wine. Olive and fruit orchards go on as far as the eye can see. Servants pick wild berries and shake down enormous quantities of nuts. Masters select the best and the rest is left for birds. Our good land enlivens everything planted, making produce succulent. Every city concocts imaginative meals from harvest and stock—beans, boar, chiana beef, cheeses. A culinary society has evolved through the gods' bounty."

The talk made Risa hungry as she bundled her newborn and went home. Zilath hadn't noticed the child.

Three conclaves later in the coolness of the Volsinii glade, Vulci's prince-priest gave assessment. "We are wise to trade with those Phoenician seafarers who come from Carthage, a most convenient North African port. In turn, our sea merchants ships sail there for goods. A bonus! The Phoenicians protect our coast to keep Hellenics out and don't come inland."

"As well they shouldn't," Curtun's prince-priest agreed. "Strange men, those sea lovers. They live in temporary quarters, shacks strung about the Great Sea's rim, but they build walled fortifications in coves and hide wares to re-barter with Assyrians, Babylonians, Aegyptians or us."

"Interesting how they barter," Populonia's prince-priest said. "They bring bunched wares, coming one moon with medicaments of balm and calamus oil, honey and cinnamon, and kohl cosmetics, the next with indigo dyes from sea-snails, Aegyptian linen and Persian carpets."

Veii's prince-priest laughed. "When they come again, they bring silver, polished ebony and ivory."

"They know what we want," Cisra's Maru said. "They bring us gold jewelry and precious stones."

"Phoenicians don't trade with Hellenics," Vulci's prince-priest replied, "because they think Hellenics are narcissistic."

"They are but we need trade with Hellas. Praise gods of good fortune that Phoenicians are allies," Veii's prince-priest concluded. "A triangular trade. A balance of power is now among nations."

"Congratulations to the Etruscans," the gods confirmed to sacred augur-priests who passed the message to prince-priests at the Alliance conclave. "Our city-states are so organized that abundance spreads throughout the central Italic peninsula. Even settlements run smoothly."

"Except Cisra and Tarchna," Prince-priest Zilath slurred, his tongue tart on harvest wine. He pointed at Maru. "Cisra covets Ruma, the territory my ancestors settled a saecula ago. You cause trouble."

Agitated, Prince-priest Maru said, "You've sent batches of Tarchna citizens and goods past our gates, south to Ruma."

"What if I have? Ruma is just an immigrant village of Etruscan and barbaric Italic tribes."

"Ruma becomes a city, a location so idyllic that sacred temples and construction rush to completion."

Veii's prince-priest intermediated. "Zilath, Maru is half your age. Appease him with a treaty."

Tarchna ambassadors went in formal dress and crowns of spiky verbena to present the treaty with a bar of eastern gold. They brought Zilath's words: "Bloodshed and battles do not delight us, and we, Nobles of Peace, repress vengeance from our Etruscan brethren."

"We accept your gift," Maru answered contemptuously, making sure shavings of the gold bar would go into his pouch. "The Tarchna may pass if we get what we want."

"We've been reasonable. What more could you ask for?"

"Our part of the gods' wisdom."

"You already have it. We gave you the ancient sacred *Books of Tages*."

"No, you didn't. You gave us a gold book with Aegyptian laws, Hellenic translations and the Etruscan alphabet."

"Tages' books stay in our possession," Zilath said. "We keep them holy."

"We'll tell no more. We were imbeciles to let those underling Etruscan cities have ancestral secrets," Zilath's priests resolutely affirmed to each other. "They've become stronger and more authoritative."

Tarchna's magistrates had their say. "Vetulonia stole our laws of gold metal craft techniques. Veii used our methods to produce malleable clay to make sculptures of our favorite gods. Cisra swiped clay formulas and diverse metals that Vel Porenna gave us and asserts the ideas were originally theirs.

At the next Alliance conclave, Zilath cursed Maru after learning that the gold shavings became a finger ring. "Scoundrel, don't spit on the graves of the ancestors lest the gods malign you!"

"I am prince-priest. I can do no wrong," Maru laughed and snubbed Zilath by turning his back.

"You envy Tarchna. You're jealous of my strength."

"You repel me with your invented piety."

To the lowest servant, both cities heard arguments. Lies escalated between the two prince-priests. Then blatantly, Tarchna and Cisra citizens debated, punched and kicked over which city was more blessed, wealthier, had more luxuries and held larger populations.

"God Tinia throws lightning rods, thunderbolts and torrents of rain at

Tarchna if you don't find means to prevent this drivel," Zilath's highest augur-priest warned. "It will be war with Maru of Cisra."

"It's not Hellenics or Phoenicians who provoke, but Zilath of Tarchna. Kill him," Maru ordered his top murderer when he got back to Cisra.

"Yes, but how?"

"He hates bees. In the sacred glen, his face swelled when touched by one. Find a way."

"Bees swarm every seventeen years. We have many to go."

"I will wait," Maru said. "Then no one will suspect us."

21

"Etruria is distinct from foreign people of the Great Sea. We're opposites. We're profound and ambitious, for our abundant land has made it possible," Cisra's Maru smugly compared at an Alliance conclave.

"Separate though our ways are, we are vibrant," Arreti's prince-priest commended.

"Our crops grow as we sing and dance," Clevsin's prince-priest said. "Those foreigners grovel in the dirt for onions and moan at night over their dismal lives."

"Our heritage is agreeable," the prince-priests coalesced. In unison they chorused, "Praise the ancestors for giving us this land. Praise Tinia for guiding us. All is well. The Great Prediction means nothing."

Risa and Parth's second son was birthed in that golden age of gilded splendors. Ari's entry to the cosmos was a good omen at that time when Etruscans were kinder to each other.

In Tarchna, Zilath knew the time was ripe. He invited citizens to a general meeting. "Life contains a series of valued sacred objects and events. Death holds value. We must honor our dead with reverence. Tages instructed the ancients to inter bones and ashes in impasto clay urns shaped like a priestess, or warriors or earthly homes, placing these urns in pits."

"How wise the ancestors were to use urns," his highest augur-priest approved.

We don't know where those pits are." Zilath waited for his audience to digest this fact. "Then the gods thundered: 'Build homes for the dead.' The ancients abided. Where there were hills, they blended in hill-shaped tombs. Where there were cliffs, they carved tombs. Where land was flat, they built cone ceiling rooms and populated them with the dead, placing corpses upright to look at sky gods Tinia, Uni and Menrva. Less important folk were put on hillsides unfit for planting."

"Holy leader, Zilath, may I continue?" the augur-priest asked.

"Unfold the story."

"Within two saeculae, Etruria's population multiplied and they found more space on village paths or outside towns. But we needed better. Our leaders dug into the soil—trench tombs. Since body spirits journey to safety in the afterlife, offerings to the gods must accompany them—razors and weapons for men, fibula and spindles for women. The trench tombs were topped with tufa slabs."

"This isn't new knowledge," a noble said crassly. "Tarchna has measly tombs. Cisra had elaborate mound tombs a saecula ago."

"The ancestors didn't mind, but we do," Zilath lashed out. "Granted, cone-shaped mounds on the hill are small, but now we're grander than Cisra. Their mound tombs are above ground and can be plundered. Our tombs will be..." he paused for effect, "underground."

"Underground," the audience gasped.

The prince-priest had their full attention. "Underground homes for our proud, religious Tarchna people, with roofed large chambers for family clans, benches for the dead to sleep and niches for worldly possessions."

"Would homes be for everyone?" A noble spoke up.

"Everyone who counts—you, other nobles and citizens of Tarchna."

"Where that upper land has a path to Tarchna?" Road Builder Parth Vella stood with the noble, beginning to understand his role in the new plan. "Where barley and wheat fields are."

"Right. Farming covers our new secret afterlife necropolis."

"Our old style tombs will still be seen," an elder discerned.

"We can't change that," Zilath said. "They're built and are closer to Tarchna."

The elders spoke among themselves and chose one elder to say, "It would be a comfort to stay near our beloved Tarchna. What's more natural then to dig into our uplands, a small stretch of the legs from Tarchna, towards the setting sun, the end of day, the end of life on this earth?"

"Our elders, who will be ancestors soon, are perceptive. We'll build our afterlife chambers for Tarchna's souls on the uplands," Zilath promised, having set the idea for that answer.

Growing interested, the eldest of elders said, "What contentment we could have on afterlife journey if we turn our chambers into homes with household goods."

His friends rallied to the idea.

"I want my tools displayed on my chamber walls."

"I'll have plates and goblets from my last banquet."

"Eternal joy," younger citizens said, taking on the elders' ideas.

"My people, we must secure our afterlife now," Zilath encouraged.

Consensus came as swift as a thunderbolt.

"Truly the gods are shining on me to reveal Tarchna's destiny," Zilath crowed his own wisdom. "And we'll have better tombs than Cisra."

22

"Our underground burial chambers will be our biggest secret," Zilath decreed to his twelve magistrates who kept Tarchna proficient in land, sea and commerce. "The Cisra are too inquisitive. They want everything we have and try to rob us of fame. We have cause to keep Tarchna's affairs confidential. One of my magistrates spies for Cisra against me."

His eyes took in every face for innocence.

"There are always secrets within cities. That's why there are spies," Magistrate of Ship Building said, "but it isn't me."

"Tarchna keeps secrets well," Magistrate of Tarchna's Economy supported Zilath. "We don't speak our confidences."

"We wouldn't want any to know about our new tomb construction," the newly appointed Magistrate of Sacred Building said, responsible for organizing this project.

"Some secrets have leaked out to neighboring Umbrians and Ligurians," Magistrate of Trade with Barbarians complained.

"We have enemies in Great Sea countries, but not among us," Magistrate of Exchange with the East said.

"Guard our secret like a mother protective of her children," the prince-priest finished.

"We will, Zilath." The magistrates maintained their positions on secrecy.

Perhaps none of them was guilty of spying. Perhaps an augur-priest, elder or noble was. Zilath had to rely on his magistrates. He had to trust them.

Magistrate of Sacred Building tested the posts. "Tarchna's earth is right for this construction. These rocks, mud, clay and soil are consistant and sturdy."

"Draw up plans for tomb locations," Zilath said satisfied.

The Magistrate put Zilath's own chamber high on the uplands, concealing its actual spot should Cisra or barbarians plunder.

"Delightful." Zilath ceremoniously relayed the scrolls to the temple gods for blessing.

Word spread fast. Crowds lined up at the temple to petition for burial chambers. The elders came for audience. "There's little time before our afterlife begins. We'll need workers to finish our tombs, Zilath."

"Get slaves then. We can take those natives from across the Great Sea. They're tough animals and toil from dawn to dusk, moving stone and uncut rock with ease. Physical power is what we need. They'll build our tombs."

"We haven't had slaves from the Hot Countries for two saeculae. How do we do that, Zilath?"

"Don't play innocent with me, Elders. As the ancestors did. Abduct them. Our sea warriors know the winds. At full sail, they can glide over Nethuns' waves and board rickety tubs."

"We're building a road to the quarry. That's where tufa stone will come from for inner walls in the elders' tomb chambers," Parth said to Risa as they drank early dawn water, waiting for Lethi to bring puls to the dining place. "I've been given twenty slaves, but not all are fit."

"Why not?" Risa asked.

"Some aren't strong. They're thin and lack muscle. The magistrates assign a number to each slave, based on strength, and distribute them to work at different locations. They didn't send the best. I need ones who will lift boulders. They sent carriers who sort rocks and haul earth for walls, bridges and fortifications."

"If you feed them puls and meat, they'll get stronger."

"Zilath won't allow that. I can only treat them as I would our servants, without meanness, but fairness. I don't beat them when they can't lift. These new slaves are glad to be captured and not killed in sea battles."

"Then life is bearable for them." Lethi entered the family's talk as she brought their bowls. "At least, Zilath rewards them with nightly rest. For their efforts, they have time for dance and song. I remember my peoples' history, how they worked naked in sun, rain and mud."

"Naked slaves were of the past. These are issued tunics for identification," Parth said.

"What if you let the weaker rake the roadbed, or level, smooth and polish road stone? The magistrates don't have to be told," Risa suggested.

Parth hugged Risa. "You know about my work."

"Of course. You and my father talk," she said. "What about exchanging slaves from road building to fertilizing fields or serving food to laborers?"

"My family descended from Carthaginians and did menial tasks. They served food," Lethi said.

"And wore clothes, more fitting to citizens than slaves. They became proper to grace beautiful Etruscan homes like ours," Risa smiled. "You're the best example, Lethi, of this generation who blended into Tarchna society without calamity."

"I'll tell your ideas to the magistrate, my dear."

"Tell him these ideas are yours, Parth," she encouraged as he left for the road.

Excited with what was being done, the elders spoke of tomb chambers but little else, judging what slaves were most skilled at construction, where tombs might be on the uplands, which talented artisans would model sculptures, who would paint scenes on walls, and when chambers would be finished. Each wanted the most popular artist, potter and crafter for every detail.

Chambers were tested for many moons to learn of endurance. Many marveled that walls didn't topple. Clouds of Tinia's rain never disturbed. Crashes of Tinia's thunder and strikes of his white light didn't harm.

"The first set of tombs are ready, but we need thousands to thwart the Great Prediction," Zilath said, anticipating what underground riches could be his. "We can't do more."

"We can. We make life better in our cosmos. The Great Prediction is the result of Etruria's overindulgence. We became too confident with abundance. The gods were angry that we didn't thank them enough," the highest augur-priest corrected. "We can build another temple."

"Their wrath set the Great Prediction upon us," another augur said. "We didn't stay humble."

"Each citizen must work on humbleness to propitiate the gods' wrath," the highest augur-priest intoned, "and contribute to a peaceful, secure afterlife."

"Humbleness means being meek and shy," Zilath said snidely. "Build another market place, more dwellings, a second and third sacred temple."

"The people will have to pray more. Even prince-priests must pray to Tinia and Uni. Think of kindness. Forgiveness!"

"I don't have to," Zilath said contentiously.

"Especially you. Forgive Vel Porenna's daughter, Zilath," the augur-priest harked. "A kind deed to appease the gods."

"Risa Laris? How dare you suggest that? Never a day goes by that I don't curse that Soil Sampler."

"That clan has been worsened. You've torn them apart with your snub. Your forgiveness will bring family to family. There will be less hostility with Cisra," the augur-priest persisted.

Zilath's blood rose. "She owns the marvelous property I gave Porenna for metals he found."

"She's a noblewoman. It was given with a scant amount of furniture, braziers, candelabra, ceramics and linens."

"A miserly act."

"It isn't the daughter's fault that Vel Porenna absconded to Cisra and brings them success. Do as I advise. Accolade Risa Laris with cresting banquet. The gods will be happy and keep us wealthy. What's a little forgiveness?"

"I'll think about it," Zilath said gracelessly. "Just don't mention that man's name again."

23

"How did Tarchna know about the Great Prediction first?" Maru croaked at his augurs.

"The Tarchna are a more spiritual people." The augurs repeated the common fact. "They were gifted with a more sacred history."

"Sacred history, bah! It's time we learn how to get wisdom before them." Maru went among his staff of magistrates and nobles, looking for the low-ranking court official who had saved him when a jumpy horse lost its footing at a seasonal hunt. His horse would have gone into the ditch had Ramnes Vibenna not galloped up to tug the rein and right the animal's course. A simple act for which Maru retained dignity as a prince-priest. In recognition, Ramnes was accoladed with title.

"You, Ramnes," Maru called out. "Come here."

When a deed or favor was requested, Ramnes sprung into action. His actual title, Politicial Advisor to the Elders, was a slight misnomer. When the acuity of an elder could no longer be certain, Ramnes would report to Maru on an upcoming funeral.

"My magistrates and nobles are tricky and wear ordinary tunics to the market to barter for exquisite wares from the East. Someone must watch them, lest they get luxuries fit for me," Maru said.

"Then you need someone who will never be suspected." Ramnes' hands itched with keenness. "Rely on me."

"You're too obvious, Ramnes. There is one close to you who will do," Maru prompted.

Ramnes looked baffled.

"Your wife."

"Arith?"

"She's the daughter of Vel Porenna, isn't she? My Soil Sampler brings such wealth to Cisra that I'll repay him and his heirs, and you too, Ramnes."

Maru's scheme was uncomplicated. He would test Arith.

Arith was thrilled to spy for the prince-priest. Impeccably dressed, she went through the market, listening to trivial banter over new wares. On pretense of bartering, Arith picked up a necklace that caught the sun like jewels. It would make a fine recompense from Maru.

"I can identify which buyers are connivers and which importers deceive," she told Maru. "One buyer is an unfaithful augur-priest."

"My augurs are faithful."

"The one I saw bartered with an import merchant. Your augur-priest saw an Aegyptian faience vase depicting a ruler with his gods on a background of palm trees, chained slaves and apes. The merchant said it was a rare vase for flowers. Your augur-priest wanted it for his tomb. When no one was close, they swapped five sacks of grain for the vase."

"Real faience should have been sent to me." Maru considered which priest could be disloyal. "The augur-priest shouldn't have it."

"The foreign merchant has more than one. I saw the same a few markets ago. The importers must copy these items to barter after originals are bought," Arith said.

"Brilliant deduction." Maru traced a line from her forehead to chin with his pointer finger, knowing she would do as an informer. "I don't mind the copyists. They bring trade."

"Do you want something more from me?" Arith asked seductively.

"Go to Tarchna. Report to me on what Tarchna does to thwart the Great Prediction. A reward is yours should you bring vital news," Maru tempted.

In the heat season, five years after her marriage, Arith went to Tarchna under the pretext that her young son, Avele, should meet and play with cousins Culni and Ari.

Her cart went through Tarchna's streets, empty of other carts, carriages, or children who usually played noisily in mud puddles. The city had grown in size and wealth. More grand dwellings, temples and a second market place spread to the hill beyond Tarchna's perimeter. Prosperous but not lively. Arith had her driver take her around the city twice.

People moved about, fraught with unknown interest. They gabbed in stilted words, unspoken words in the air. The workers she saw labored as if each task was most important, hauling stones, carrying wood and hemp, slinging odd-shaped bundles. The metal workers were at their forges, but production seemed limited. Something was happening but it wasn't talked about.

At the Laris-Vella dwelling, home, there were few celebrations with minimal meals. Risa was preoccupied with spinning thread, sewing tunics and feeding geese. Parth was hardly there. No one gave invitation to banquet.

Tarchna mystified her. Those on the streets walked like they were dead. Perhaps the gods were causing mischief, making people act dull-witted. Their attitude might be part of a new burial custom, perhaps the Spirits of Mystery.

Bored from these thoughts, Arith walked Avele and her nephews to the uplands.

"Shoo, children. Run about so you sleep well," she said to have respite from three rambunctious boys who ran into the barley field to play amidst the stalks.

She followed their direction and heard freakish rumblings, The lone guard at the top of a distant field couldn't be making that sound, more a sound of construction. Work had to be going on somewhere, although no new buildings were on the horizon.

The boys disappeared. With indignity that she had to chase, she walked fast enough to see that there were many holes in the ground. At the spot where she last saw them, a stairway led to a room below. There, Avele, Culni and Ari played with stones at the bottom. The large humid room was fitted with niches.

Arith reviewed what she had seen. She had found out Tarchna's secret. She could tell Maru what he wanted to know.

The gold necklace would be hers.

24

"Tarchna thwarts the Great Prediction by going under earth." Arith bowed to Maru and told details of her visit.

"What deceit! That Zilath misleads us." He tied the costly necklace around her throat. Her price had been high. "You've done service to Cisra. Never mention who gifted your necklace."

Tarchna thinks they have more wisdom. Why have the gods told Tarchna to fortify against the Great Prediction?" Maru asked his augur-priests.

"You need to know how the rest of Etruria views afterlife," they advised.

Sobered by Tarchna's deviousness, Maru summoned Ramnes. His faithful Political Advisor soon stood before him.

"Are you acquainted with all elders?"

Ramnes cleared his throat. "Most. Some stay confined in their twilight."

"Ancestors," Maru steamed, plagued by having them. "Ramnes, you know of ancestors. Arith visited Tarchna and learned of burial customs."

Ramnes shrugged. "Slight talk. An unimportant subject. Arith, not I, claimed the Tarchna brood over the dead. They're sent to the hills, whisked away without ceremony."

"Could you have missed a crumb or two?" Maru bent towards him and hissed, "You lack reverence for custom. You've known about Tarchna from your wife's mouth. Go to every city. Stop at towns, villages and the tiniest settlement. Find what customs and tomb building they do."

Ramnes knew his blunder would cost extra work. He took to the road, fleeing like an exile.

Gone a heat season, Ramnes journeyed to towns or cities that paid homage to the dead with memorials for afterlife. Disguised in his merchant's costume, he bought the confidence of merchants with a cartful of Cisra's tradable goods and wine. When drunk, they related gossip of magistrates and priests.

"Honor the dead with wine to show devoutness, and don't forget to pay the tomb caretakers with a flask," Arith had cautioned.

Ramnes heeded her words, although he couldn't understand why she mentioned caretakers. He gave offerings to sacred priests, ingratiating himself with gifts of bucchero goblets and Cisra's grains. The more wine he tendered, the more expert on rituals and customs of cousin Etruscan places he became. Soon he was privy to information of sacred priests.

Vigilantly, Ramnes traversed paths through uncharted hills, forged wild rivers where no bridges crossed, to dusty roads on the hazardous coast. With increasing precision, he spied on tombs built in each city's necropolis, memorizing layouts, construction techniques and landforms. Shrouded as a mourner, he followed hearse wagons and the bereaved to gravesites, watching their actions, seeing worldly goods deposited in sepulchers.

Upon return, Ramnes went to Maru's small reclining room and kneeled at the prince-priest's feet. "I went to the Gorge of Villages. How active Etruria works for afterlife! Slaves bore holes for chambers into the cliffs to make space for new population. I befriended a man who took me inside one. We entered from a crack in the cliff and went through passages that led to chambers with uneven configurations because the rocks are jagged. Not yet occupied, those chambers have carved funerary couches. I almost got lost in a passage. When we left, we were on the steep side of the mountain. There were the tomb fronts. They look like wooden dwellings of the living, with carved rock trimmed door frames and indented columns."

"'Cliff chambers'…lots of them…cliff cemeteries…" Maru mulled over Ramnes' words.

"Flufluna deals with earthly matters, smelting ore on its beach. Iron is from an offshore island. Slaves drip sweat over hot fires. One worker pointed to ancestor tombs on a hill away from the heat. Those tombs were square houses, lifeless without ornament," Ramnes related. "Velathri, the most northern city, is a hard climb from the sea. The city houses the dead in chambers built in soft limestone on the mountain's edge. What folly! They'll soon slide into the ravine."

Maru bit off a hangnail and spit it on the floor.

"An oddity from my journey." Ramnes took a chunk of rock from his bag. "It's the color of white rain and carves like tufa stone. The Velathri call it 'alabaster.' "

"Hmm." Maru picked up the white stone, turning it in his hands.

"Hold it to the light," Ramnes urged.

"Translucent. It shines like Uni's moon."

"Our Soil Sampler didn't find this rock in Cisra."

"The Aegyptians have alabaster. I didn't know we have it in Etruria."

"Velathri keeps it secret."

"Hmm," Maru grunted.

"Their tomb chambers are typical, but they house the burned dead in alabaster boxes. Craftsmen carve these arm-length boxes with war scenes and myths that their Hellenic slaves tell. The carvings are not about the deceased one's life."

Maru toyed with the golden seal ring on his mid-finger.

"What possibilities this rock brings. Velathri claims Etruria as brethren. If we bond our ties with them we can get this stone. Then we'll have Hellenic crafters carve boxes for our chambers. Ah! Hellas will envy alabaster. We can use it for exchange. Tarchna will drool. An opportunity," Ramnes tried his best to persuade.

"I don't care how weary of travel you are. Unless there is more to tell, you've failed."

Awaiting his doom, Ramnes squealed, "What cities have in common is that prince-priests and families are buried near magistrates, nobles and elders, not like us who are separate. Their graveyards are like friendly towns. All cherish and guard their dead."

Maru closed his eyes and sat as stationary as Tinia's statue, ignoring Ramnes.

The sun dipped to dusk.

"Bless the stars!" Maru sprung up. "If they have towns, so can we. Already we have stone and hewn rock mounds for Priestess Larthia and other ancestors in those fields outside Cisra. That's the area to use for our very own City of the Dead, a city so colossal that Tarchna's underground dung holes will pale in comparison. We'll build these new afterlife domes of solid rock that can be as large as stallion meadows. To get to them we'll have streets with drainage from Tinia's rains for procession carts. Our design and construction will last the ages. And for me, I'll live in a chamber tomb with grand rooms for my prizes. Incredible idea, this enormous city, the greatest necropolis throughout Etruria!"

"It's a good one," Ramnes replied, strained by his audience with Maru. "You'll have space for your descendants."

"I congratulate myself on this idea. It will bring me more glory. A miraculous journey to my afterlife!" Maru said, possessed by his own aptitude.

25

Prince-priest of Cisra got wisdom.

It came when he questioned why Tarchna was given cosmic knowledge before the rest of Etruria and how those cities and villages dealt with the Great Prediction.

Maru showed off his divine logic to augur-priests. "Why was Tarchna foremost in wisdom? Because the cosmos moves in a pattern that creates conditions of growth. Their land was ready first. It solved the *Which-came-first-the-chicken-or-the-egg?* riddle. By cosmic chance! Animal and vegetable eggs were fertilized in Tarchna's rocky soil. They made life grow with barley, spelt and fruit under Tinia's rain and Aplu's sun. Tages was a nutrient of that soil, coming up to bless the land, bringing flocks of birds and stocks of animals. People arrived to populate the landscape and use its resources the best they could. Tarchna was born, a fluke that it wasn't our land."

"A fluke, Wise Leader," the augur-priests replied.

"Happenstance!" Maru slapped his thigh in satisfaction, no longer caring why Tarchna was so sacred.

"Happenstance," the augur-priests chanted.

With wisdom came forethought. Maru was able to declare, "We'll do the same as Tarchna. We'll get slaves to build greater tombs for the citizens of today, to grace eternity of tomorrow."

The Alliance's trade treaty with Carthage and Hellas started to crumble, driven by lack of agreement over *oikonomia* and slave treatment. Zilath and Maru set argument. Not to be outdone, other leaders made disparaging remarks. Damaged, the eminent prince-priests no longer met every fourth season. They stayed in their cities.

Maru and Zilath continued nagging. Like a contagious illness, their quarrels passed onto noble clans, specifically the Vibenna Cisra clan related to the Laris-Vella Tarchna clan.

Arith and Ramnes sent hurtful messages. "You Tarchna are too pious, praying to old gods."

Risa and Parth replied, "Cisra becomes loose and disrespects the gods."

There was no love and goodness between the two families, only bickering when the subject of each city's newest achievement was lauded.

"Venu brings Tarchna fantastic cloth from the East with each journey."

"Our fabric from Lydia is better. And we're trading father's bucchero with Nikea."

Sons and daughters of the previous generations of servants and slaves became rivals, yipping their woes.

"Cisra's Maru gives us three barley cakes a day."

"Tarchna's Zilath gives us four."

"We rise before dawn."

"We rest only at late dark."

Carthage and Hellas took advantage of Etruria's internal conflict, hoping to dominate and colonize the peninsula. "Shamelessly, you Etruscans loudly proclaim your impregnable strength up and down the coast and inland to the high mountains," Hellenics said.

"We curse your sea warriors who steal our people, our sea travelers out for a bit of sun," Carthaginians said. "You've taken men and women, chaining them together like necklaces with hot forged metal."

The trade merchant Carthaginians strengthened their ties with other Hot Countries, not bringing wares to Etruria.

The Hellenic colony of Cumae attacked Etruria's southern villages.

From the northern to eastern peninsula, the perfidious Ligurian and Italic tribes laughed at the destabilized city-states.

"We'll endure," Maru ranted. "Without the Alliance, we'll go after Carthage for slaves and kidnap Hellenics for servants, fishers and crafters for bucchero and sculpture."

Cisra vanquished this weaponless enemy. At first, the captives frothed with anger and struggled, taken against their will.

"Did our warriors relent as they saw the kidnapped cry out anguished tears, dragging shackles? No. Forcefully, the warriors threatened with beatings and torture. We killed those who rebelled," Magistrate of War laughed maliciously, "Have you ever heard cries of the drowning?"

This ruthlessness intrigued Maru. He imagined the mutilated cadavers, blood dripping from orifices. When he judged the slaves at the docks, he picked one to torture personally, tying the live slave to one already dead, its body infected and poisoned by death. It amused him to see horror on the live one's face as he writhed in death's stench.

The tale of Maru's cruelty spread among the Carthaginians. They became docile, their souls humiliated.

Cisra's territory swelled with gory conquests as it gathered new population, becoming a repository of great culture and wealth because of its abundance of manual labor.

Subsequently, in skillfully manned warships, Maru's valorous warriors surprised the Hellenics when seas were in high storms.

"We succeed in our piracy," Cisra's sea warriors said, returning with little blood lost in battle. "Much is destroyed of their fleet."

The Hellenics surrendered. Taken ashore, the fishermen, like their ancestors who had established Pyrgi as Cisra's port town, stayed near the waters.

"Their worth at harvesting the sea will help our economy," Cisra magistrates convinced constituents. "They've mixed with us for more than a saecula."

"We keep welcoming their commerce," Maru told the elders and magistrates as he took captive a few exceptional men or women to breed with Cisra's pure stock. "It's to our benefit that they're here for we admire their pristine arts."

"We give hospitality to the allegiant Hellenic servants and artisans whose skills make Etruscan arts flourish and multiply under their tutelage," the elders approved.

Maru wanted those heavenly portrayals of myth and life etched on Hellenic amphorae and urns. They would be perfect for his collection.

"Our population swells with these conquests. We must instruct Cisra citizens to accept this newer element of our society," the magistrates alleged.

In trepidation, the Cisra complied. "Our style of life satisfies and we enjoy favors that, to our ears, are not like the rest of the unrefined cosmos."

"Get more slaves!" Maru stabbed his scepter on the floor.

"There are few left. Carthaginians have stopped riding the waves," the Magistrate of War said.

"Then we must get slaves from Hellas. They've been our servants. Make them our slaves," Maru hounded.

"Don't make slaves of them for we learn from their craft," the augur-priests advised.

"A grand war with Hellas or Carthage would be disastrous for trade and industry since we have prospered," all of the magistrates agreed. "We must align with those countries."

"It's time to reconcile violence with love of peace," the highest of the augur-priests reiterated, "or it will be your downfall."

Maru wasn't pleased. Violence was exhilarating.

Passion and Purpose

26

"Look to the gods," the augur-priests said to the prince-priests.

"Look to the gods!" the prince-priests said to the masses who laughed when Aplu's sun shone and prayed when Tinia's rain flooded paths.

All Etruria expected the Great Prediction and that it would bring instant ruin. Instead, a surge of trade, wealth and foreigners at their shores brought prosperity. Indoctrinated into Etruscan life, slaves from the Hot Countries became servants. Immigrant crafters from the East brought beauty. Pride of heritage showed through city construction of courts, temples, market places and dwellings. Competition between prince-priests Zilath and Maru escalated without war.

"Prayers must help," Risa said as she and Parth went about their daily lives. "There's no sign of the Great Prediction's prospect of doom."

"Fortunate for us," Parth said.

Their marriage union fit the noble Etruscan family pattern. They stayed in Vel's plush home that Tarchna's slaves had built with materials supplied by Tarchna's quarries and forests. The house of Risa's childhood was gone. Her decoration and orderliness created a sanctuary even in the fiercest weather.

Zilath hadn't harassed.

"In the excitement of the Great Prediction, Zilath must have forgotten me," Risa joked as the years rolled by without accolade to commemorate the most important day of a woman's life, the cresting banquet.

Her marriage portion was secure, but all her life she dreamed of the day when that banquet would recognize her mature place in family and society. It hadn't happened after marriage union, before the first child's conception or birth. When Parth's third child swelled her womb, there was no accolade.

In quiet embarrassment, she performed defined obligations of her noble rank within her clan, set standards to make Tarchna's achievements better with every birth. Risa's days were divided between house and family, ensuring that the family ate, slept and behaved according to law.

As Aplu's sun fell each night, she tended her children.

This generation patterned the future with rituals and traditions after the gods evoked sweetness:

Cherish the kin for they inherit the cosmos.

Most clans reproduced six to ten but not the Porenna-Laris-Vella-Vibenna Clan. As the seasons grew to years, they had a paltry number of offspring. One male for Arith and Ramnes, two males and one female for Risa and Parth, none for Venu.

To amend for this failure, Risa cuddled her children, warming them at the hearth in the cold season at dusk.

"Who did you name me after?" Risa and Parth's eldest son, Culni asked.

"Your father's father. Your brother, after my mother's father," Risa said. "You were named to bring esteem to our heritage."

"What about Larthia?" Ari, the middle child asked, a youth who could adroitly run through fields or climb rocks and trees.

"She's named after the princess-priestess."

"Zilath's princess-priest is 'Zayla,'" Culni said.

"I mean the heroic and wise 'Ancestor Larthia, most Revered Princess-priestess of Etruria.' She lived a saecula before us, a Cisra, not Tarchna born," Risa answered. "Gods of the east sent magic with her birth and made her a warrior, an artist and a defender of truth. She went everywhere, turning towns into city-states, uniting them to become Etruscans."

"We're Tarchna, not Etruscans." Culni said, his chin high.

"We're both. Tarchna-born first, Etruscan in the land of Etruria second."

"She must have been special," Ari said.

"As special as a god. They built a mound house for her pleasure. Her couch was bronze lattice and her gilded throne was ornamented with stags and leaves. Silver cauldrons and gold-jeweled vessels shaped like birds, lotus flowers, griffins and lions were beside the throne. At her death, she was robed in gold, with a sacred gold moon-shaped breastplate of plants and animals. A gold fibula engraved with lions and leaves held her garments in place. The clasp had rows of ducks studded with tiny sprinkles of gold. The house became her tomb chamber. A gilded chariot and a four-wheeled hearse decorated with palmetto leaves carried her safely to the afterlife."

"You made up this story," Culni said. "No one has such wealth."

"People speak of her. She's a legend."

"Can I see her tomb?" Ari asked.

"Everyone in Etruria would like to, but Cisra keeps it secret," Risa said. "I think our Larthia will justify her namesake."

"I haven't been away from our city, not to Cisra or beyond," Risa told her sons.

"Why not, Mother?" Ari asked. "Father goes outside Tarchna."

"The gods gave me the fate of stillness, restricting my surroundings. Once as a child, I walked the hot dusty road to visit my mother's parents in Blera. Still, my feet carry me to wash in the river and trek in the upland grasses. No horse, cart or chariot takes me about."

"Grandfather Vel went to Cisra and so did Aunt Arith. We have to go away. The elders send us males to train in the hinterlands every fourth season. You don't go anywhere because you're a coward," Culni said nastily.

"She's not. She doesn't want to leave Tarchna. Uncle Venu rides waves of the Great Sea. We don't. Does that make us cowards?" Ari put up his fists like a dancing boxer at the prince-priest's circus.

"Uncle's not a traditional noble landsman but a seafarer like Shipmaster Alfnis." Culni pushed down his brother's undeveloped arms.

"Ari's right. My life of family, home, market, river and uplands, makes me happy. I have no need to do anything else." Risa said, separating her boys from further wrangling. "It's remarkable how our family moves about like skybirds. The gods cause their movement."

She hadn't told her children she was the only Tarchna noble unappreciated, overlooked. Her wish hadn't been granted, a banquet to honor her, denied by Zilath.

27

On every eighth day Risa went to market for rations. City coffers paid for Parth's skillful road and bridge building work with extra grains from its bins, meats from its hunts and wines from the nobles' vineyards. This routine day was like others. Lulled by strumming lyre players, she strolled with her two lively sons amidst fruit displays, vegetable piles, barley bins and seasonal kill of wild fowl, tabulating Parth's bounty to keep accounts on the food storage wall.

Risa blended in with higher nobles. They were no different than she, wearing similar belted flax-colored tunics, ground length for women, knee length for men, banded with ribbons at the hem. Both genders wore cloaks on shoulders to ward off Tinia's rains. From baskets of quail, Risa chose three live squawking ones. "They're a tasty treat to be roasted over Vesta's hearth. We're fortunate to be granted Prince-priest Zilath's bounty."

"That's because we're nobles. Meat eaters," Culni said, his active feet never touching the ground. "Our servants and slaves don't eat meat."

"These provisions are distributed to your father for his service," Risa replied. "You should be grateful."

"I'll carry the quail home." Culni disregarded his mother's reproach, having stoned and netted one in the oak hills during hunt training.

"No, I will," Ari countered, his small fingers itching to root out the quails' quills.

"No, me!"

"Hush, or you'll not eat any," Risa scolded and clutched the quail. "I'm glad Larthia isn't here. Your sister would snatch them and run like Tinia's wind."

Lethi shambled over to Risa with a heavy sack of grain on her back. "Hurry! Zilath calls you."

"You mis-heard," Risa said to her lifelong servant. "Zilath drones on about sacred laws, market trade or taking over enemy ships. He doesn't call me."

"He does."

"Risa," an authoritative voice of one of Zilath's officials boomed, "Risa of the Laris Clan, step up!"

This time Risa heard. "Why does Zilath want me? I haven't done anything bad. I keep the sacred laws."

"It's the third call. You'd better step up, Risa."

Risa's hands shook as she thrust the prized fowl at Lethi and brushed feathers from her clothes. "Am I presentable?"

"You're too thin by Etruscan standards, but you meet the dress codes as a good Tarchna." Dropping the grain, Lethi struggled to hold the quail and pushed Risa forward.

"Give way," the crowd ogled in disbelief at the prince-priest's summons. "Zilath wants her."

Looking straight ahead, she hoped they saw her only as a woman of average stature, not to be jeered at. She tried to maintain her practiced grace. Inwardly, she quivered. The gods had thrown her a thunderbolt. She hadn't been near Zilath since he performed her marriage union.

Does Zilath want to banish me? She asked herself as ordinary citizens helped the nobles get her to the wooden podium.

Lower than the prince-priest, her eyes were level to his handsome jeweled boots. Etruscans wore shoes, more civilized than barefoot Italics and Hellenics. Irreverently, her own footwear came to mind. She adored shoes and had five pairs, more than anyone she knew. Open low-strapped sandals. Laced leather high boots. Leather half boots with elegant pointed toes. Slippers of sheepskin for cold seasons. Mud shoes for the yard.

Aware of his duties, Zilath grabbed her hand and pulled her up, ignoring her fingers pecked by the quail. He drew her to face him.

Risa tensed at his seriousness, aware that tendrils of wavy hair stuck out from her snugly capped hat, unfixable before him. All she could see of the prince-priest were his eyes, color of rich harvest earth. A trace of kindness, treachery and mirth were in those eyes. He was the same age as her father, but they were as different as Tinia was to a shepherd.

"How may I serve you, Zilath?" she had the wherewithal to say.

"Daughter of Anneia Laris, the Healer, and Noble Wife of my Road Builder, Parth Vella, are you?" His lips curled.

Risa flinched at the named titles. "My mother is deceased. You didn't mention my father, Vel Porenna, the Soil Sampler. Do you ridicule me?" She wished she had shut her lips. Her barbed words might give him cause to hit her.

The prince-priest held her hand tighter with controlled hostility, yet he said gently, "No, Noblewoman. I bring your destiny, ordered by gods of the cosmos, divined through wisdom of our augur-priests, relayed to me. Your life story is calculated by Aplu's sun and Uni's moon: the day chosen for your cresting banquet shall be at the heat solstice when the sun is longest in the sky. You'll have your day of honor in your twenty-fourth year. Use it well. Make it joyous, full of laughter."

"My destiny is a cresting banquet," Risa rasped out in a voice not her own, stunned by his poetic words. "Yes, Zilath, I will."

As if he couldn't allow what he had done, Zilath dropped her hand and proclaimed to the citizens below, "Remember that in our land of Etruria, food rituals must be foremost, for food means pleasure. Epicurean and carnal pleasure are life's greatest joys."

That profundity signaled one of Zilath's flutists to take up his pipes and trill a triumphant riff. Timidly, everyone applauded, uncertain if they heard Zilath's accolade correctly. Risa wondered if she had died and was in afterlife. Her dearest wish had been granted. A smile, as radiant as a rainbow, grew on her lips and reached Tinia's sky.

Through her awe, she saw Ari, Culni and Lethi clapping enthusiastically. Excitement shot through her as she backed away from Zilath, bumping into a short, charcoal-robed creature with bushy brows, nubby cheeks and ancient eyes.

"Your recognition delights," he tittered. "Your dazzling smile shows joy."

"My smile marked me at birth."

"Crafters sculpt smiles like yours on terracotta gods."

"You shouldn't say those words to one you don't know."

"The gods gifted you with smiles and laughter, but you haven't been light-hearted for many seasons."

"Who are you to taunt me?"

"Guess, Noblewoman."

"You must be a haruspex-priest."

He nodded. "And you are the 'Neglected Noblewoman' as other highborn call you."

"They talk of me like they speak of rancid venison, but they'll have new gossip to chew and spread like wild wind. A banquet will be mine, a luxurious repast served with entertainment. The Laris family is again favored and I will lead. I am neglected no longer," Risa said defiantly. "My infamous reputation will be put to rest."

"Ah, yes. Your cresting banquet. Perhaps jeweled sandals will be your gift," Haruspex egged on. "You'd keep them in good condition like your other pairs."

His words bit. "Who told you I indulge in footwear?"

He didn't answer, engulfed in the crowd as her family rushed to hug her.

Uneasily she thought, Zilath had forgiven me and I don't know why. A haruspex spoke to me familiarly, one I've never seen. Was he friend or foe? Yet, a blessing has come my way. It could be a foretoken, an augury of the gods to change my fate."

"I avoided that woman to spite him. When I summoned her, she was undaunted after I belittled her for ten years," Zilath told his highest augur-priest. "She's positively Anneia's daughter. She expressed herself truthfully, but she was something more—sweet. I liked that."

Primly, the augur-priest said, "She is very beautiful."

"Beautiful?" He recalled how she strode to his podium and looked at him with hard-to-forget eyes, chiseled nose and cheeks like a goddess statue, and a mass of thick curled hair. "Yes. *Charisma* surrounds her. When she smiled, the sun popped through clouds."

"Gladdening the recipient to disperse negative ideas…"

"A gift from the gods…"

"A beauty. If you hadn't given her this accolade, it would have been against the Laws of Tages…"

"And thwarted our work of the Great Prediction."

28

With soothing melodies, an unidentifiable flutist roamed though Tarchna's hills, playing his pipes, luring animals from their lair for sacred feasts and banquets. The Flutist's magically hypnotic tunes were known to overcome the animal's fear until snared by Zilath's hunters.

Tingling with newness of her accolade, Risa heard those pipes whistling from the outer walls. She danced from the market place, revitalized as if she was rising from a restful sleep.

"This day has changed me forever!" She twirled through the house. "Life will be easier for our family. I can claim a freshly slaughtered boar or stag for my banquet. God Tinia praises me. I was sought by Zilath at market!"

"Why did he wait so many years?" Parth asked coldly. "Zilath accolades you the day there are rumblings that tomb construction for nobles is next in line, now that his, the augur-priests' and magistrates' are complete. Zilath wants better tombs built than Maru of Cisra has for his citizens. What do you know, Risa?"

She came to a standstill. Visions of disaster raced through her mind. "One has nothing to do with the other," she said, her joy deadened.

"It's a relief your time has come." Parth lifted her up and spun them both. They tumbled into the reclining couch. "Honor is mine as your husband."

"Relief?"

"You were the only one of our class not accoladed."

"Has it harmed your love for me?"

Parth took wine from storage and poured it from jug to goblets without answer. The wine was fizzy, not aged. Swirling the goblet, Risa sipped. It smelled better. She drained the goblet's mysteries, her tongue tasting heat seasons' fresh grasses, olives, lavender and loam. The bitter aftertaste made her realize the cruel damage caused by Vel's defection to Cisra, and Zilath's omission of accolading her with cresting banquet. Those two men had devastated her marriage.

Parth doesn't care for me as he once did, she thought. In the early seasons of our marriage, we were absorbed by love.

Dribbling water into a basin, she cooled her face with a cloth and faked a smile, too proud to let him know how much he hurt her. "Tinia blesses me twice. I feared today a bad omen. Your honesty makes me think I'll enjoy banqueting."

At the sun's zenith, the family ate the new day meal together. The children chattered like hedge sparrows, telling rhymes and riddles they just heard. Risa laughed with them. Parth was vague and inattentive.

"Our territories will link if we slice through hills into valleys, forests and make roads straighter. We'll bridge streams and rivers with barreled arches," Parth said.

Risa passed a bowl of plums to Parth. "Think of our meal and family, not your work when we're together. The augur-priest says we must make the traditional gods' myths and legends important."

"Then teach the children."

"You're more devoted to your title and position than to your children," Risa flared, thinking of how exhausted he was at night, talking about ways to cut channels for pond and wet meadow drainage, then flinging himself on the marriage bed, asleep before she blew out the candle.

He isn't the same man. I'm not the same woman, she thought. I'm to blame. I haven't objected to treatment given me. I dissatisfied Parth with little status. Not anymore. My banquet will make him love me again.

Respect for Etruscan customs swept over Risa with her cresting banquet accolade. She left the confines of home more frequently, enjoying benefits of being a Tarchna born noble.

She brought the children to the highest point of the city facing the mountain, where the tufa and sandstone square temple glistened in rays of golden sun. The steps went to a porch held up by nine columns under a triangular pediment decorated with Etruscan and Hellenic gods. Terracotta antefixes in the form of Flufluns' maenads covered rainspouts. Eaves were tiled with hideous faces of Medusa or demon Charon. Three doors led to worship altars for the triad, Tinia, Uni and Menrva, sanctuaries of mysterious rites for augur-priests.

"Our laws and artistic splendor sprang from this holy spot. Life's ways were determined here when Master Tages emerged from Tarchna's earth, giving his rules to priests who told sculptors how to carve stone gods. Religious creed was proclaimed and warfare against barbarians announced here," Risa explained, showing the circle of mosaic tiles laid on the platform before the steps. "This is a place of good omens."

Ari looked at the top of the building. "Why does the roof have people on it?"

"They're not people but terracotta statues of our gods. Because they're so high above us, they have to be big and painted."

"I like their faces and all the colors," Larthia said.

"They're all moving," Culni pointed up. "There's one who might fly off."

"The sculptors make them look like they move, but they're fixed to a base with mortar."

"They're smiling at the sky, not at us," Ari observed.

"Yes, at the sun, moon and stars." Risa patted his shoulder affectionately.

Larthia tugged at her mother's tunic. "You told us about Tages, but I don't see him. Where is he?"

"Tages has no sculptures. We've got to imagine what he looks like."

"He was muddy when he came out of the earth," Culni said.

"Mud! The augur-priests say he was a child, but he might have looked like an elder with wrinkled face and white hair because of mud," Risa replied.

"That's silly. Children don't look like old men."

"We believe in him. He told secrets of the cosmos."

"He wasn't a god," Ari decided.

"No, but he knew about gods and gave us God Tinia," Culni sneered.

"Where did you learn that, my son?"

"My friends and I hear augurs and servants talk in the streets."

"Which one is Tinia?" Larthia asked.

"He's in the center since he's the sky god of deities, ruler of the cosmos. His hair has waves like our river. He puffs clouds with his cheeks. That's why his face is rounded and the ridge of his nose furls his eyebrows. His eyes twinkle and light the sun. He's handsome as a man, not grotesque like a satyr." A light steady rain began as Risa spoke. "We're talking about him and he hears."

Thunder rolled in the distance. They sheltered under the porch roof.

"He's also Lord of the Thunderbolt, charged with nine kinds of forces that strike oxen, people or trees at random. When he walks the heavens in anger, storms rage. Winds and rain flood the land."

"Will he do that now?" Ari asked.

"Not today. There's no lightning. Look up at Tinia's wife, Uni. She shares his power. When she soothes his brow, storms abate and Tinia orders Aplu to dazzle with his sun ball. Then barley and grapes grow, and wildflowers bloom."

"Uni's statue never looks the same, Mother."

"That's because she's the Moon Goddess. She sets the sun and raises the moon. Nightly, Uni romps across the sky, shaping her round moon into half, quarters or slivers, and lets you see it at dark. She polishes her silver moon to shine sleep in our eyes, bringing good dreams."

"My dreams are sometimes joyful, sometimes sad," Ari said. "I dream about ancestors and the cosmos and hunting in the hills with The Flutist."

"Then Menvra can help you," Risa said, knowing that this son would be a wise man one day.

"What's so good about Menvra?" Culni demanded. "Show me her."

Risa pointed at a statue with flowing robes and a spear. "Menvra, Goddess of Wisdom and the Arts, is courageous. She's best loved by Tarchna as they get older. She blesses people with the gift of creativity, and they're inspired to beautify Tarchna with craft and decoration."

"Why does she hold that spear?"

"For protection. She's a warrior goddess. We've borrowed her image from the Hellenics, but we're not at war so we pray to her for courage to have a peaceful, beautiful life."

"You haven't brought us here before, Mother," Culni said less sourly, taken by his mother's tales.

"You were too young to understand this sacred place. From now on, we'll come and I'll tell you about all the gods." Risa kissed her oldest son's forehead. "They're everywhere, in the clouds, the trees, among flowers and under stones. The rain's over and Aplu's sun comes."

Risa's need to bring back her husband's love started her mission. To keep her promise to her children, she went to the sacred temple alone to gain insight about celestial gods of nature, earth and river, the comforting gods of home and hearth, gods of death and the underworld, even imported legendary Hellenic gods of love, hate, war and tragedy.

Often, she stood with other worshipers in front of the three doors as they prayed:

"Tinia! Menrva! Give me advice."

"Help remove turmoil and bring order to my life."

On Risa's way home, a woman stood at an open door holding up her household gods, Lares and Penates metal stick figures. "You have the gift of cure. Banish my child's fever."

Many worshipers were only interested in solving daily setbacks. Risa pondered greater issues. Why do the gods roam the sky but not the earth? Why does Aplu bring his sun up from the east? Why does Uni's moon fluctuate?

She couldn't pose such questions to priests, lest she be considered a traitor to Tages. The myths, the sacred sculptured gods and the grand temple monument had made her mind restless. She strove for something more, something unknown.

When no one was near, she prayed to the statue of Love Goddess Turan, high on the temple roof. The statue breathed with love, showering her with its beauty, inspiring her to feel more love for herself and for the cosmos that radiated in glory. Tinia's sky was clearer, Aplu's sun was brighter, and Risa became livelier.

Her ten-year punishment was receding. Allegiance to Tarchna grew, replacing shame from Zilath's persistent wrath. She was beginning to be accepted as one of the community. Her banquet would be seasons ahead, but there was much work to do. Tarchna would have its harvest, the hunt, the cold season, and then the warming.

What else would it take to rekindle Parth's love?

29

When the heat season became the cooling season, Tarchna's yearly hunts and feasts were held in the great yard.

"Honor me with your presence. The gods reward us with a temperate climate that looks after our wilderness. Bring your spouse, for the spouse is the one who encourages you," Zilath proclaimed, soliciting his audience of thinkers, planners of city construction, designers of sepulchers, temples and homes, builders of the community who had been recruited for tomb building.

"We have a double honor now that you're accoladed. We're invited to Zilath's annual hunt and entry into Zilath's higher group." Parth brimmed with pleasure.

"He's made our lives more agreeable."

"That he has. He's named me 'Thinker' for my invention, so we can ask for venison or wild pork. We'll need more meat this cold season with Culni and Ari growing like chickweed."

"Your *groma* helps Tarchna. I'm proud for you."

Parth's device of two iron crossbars, accurately balanced with hanging plumb lines, pivoted on the tip of an arc shaped brace, fitted to a shaft in the ground, was used to lay city streets. He would survey sights across one crossbar to a pole held by another road builder. A third assistant would peg a straight line to establish where a street should be built.

"How unfortunate Father is in Cisra. When he was a favored guest at past hunts, he received much meat," Risa said.

"So shall we," Parth replied. "More for us since the potters and crafters aren't invited."

"Why aren't they? Zilath says they're exempt from animal and field labor."

"They'll tag along with import and export merchants, sea mariners and miners. Zilath holds a secondary hunt for them this season, simpler than ours. He honors us more since new tomb excavation has begun."

At half dawn light, Parth and Risa sat on the stone bench under the roofed walkway of the great yard. Parth drummed his fingers. Risa stared at scuffs on her sandals. Other nobles lounged, waiting to take places inside.

The head trumpeter blew into an elaborately curved bull's horn and announced, "Stand for Prince-priest Zilath!"

"Zilath's yard is six times bigger than ours," Risa said as they went in. "The arena is so grand!"

Ceremoniously pressed in by magistrates and elders, the Tarchna leader arrived. Prudently, all watched.

"Don't say anything," Parth said, not looking at her, hardly parting his lips, "or we'd be disciplined for offensiveness."

Zilath's servant brought a plate of last season's dried femur of a stag. Imitating a lion, Zilath attacked it, gnawing the gristle, spitting its waste, picking out meat in his gums, expecting adulation. The audience cheered. Zilath nodded to the trumpeter's musicians. Tipping trumpets skyward, they saluted the immortal gods.

Early sunrays slanted across the crowd. Barefoot flutists entered the yard, vividly dressed like painted terracotta antefixes on the sacred temple.

Sixteen hunters, the same number as celestial gods, patiently straddled Arabian horses. A horse snorted and pawed the ground. With blinding glare, the sun grew into a ball. From a distance, an acerbic flute note broke silence.

"We call sleeping prey from high mountain woods, not only for meat but as practice for war. Now start," Zilath commanded.

Avidly, the hunters sprang into startling action, each quick as an arrow released from bow, fanning out from the yard, east, north and south.

The roar of horses faded away. The spectators remained.

Zilath raised his palms to the cosmos. "May the hunters bring great bounty so we may dine in pleasure. While they struggle, we will have contests."

The assiduous thinkers sat alert for their chance.

"Who will sport in races first?" Zilath spitefully asked the Thinkers who were more cerebral than physical.

Not light of heel but like noisy children at a new game, the Thinkers got ready. Both men and women selected teams to race around the court's rim.

Parth raced. Risa declined, not wanting to have Zilath's eyes on her, afraid he would negate her banquet accolade if she displeased him.

Servants brought trays of straw balls encased in linen. The thinkers threw them nimbly without unraveling, high or low to outdo the challenger, chortling when they lacked agility.

Zilath clapped his hands once and announced, "Gymnasts are ready. Play your tunes for them, Flutist."

Three bare breasted dark-skinned slaves, one man and two women, entered the yard and hopped up to the central platform. The pliant man extended his leg and one of the women climbed it as a tree, one foot on his shin, her other leg stretched to his shoulder. The second woman did the same and they formed a balanced triad, a sign of divine godliness. Next, the first woman got on the man's shoulders, and the second climbed on top of her to form a pole, a sign of oneness and unity, and gyrated into other contortions.

Straining under this weight, the male grew an erection. His engorged shaft prompted delight in the genitals of spectators.

Parth nudged Risa. "An extra feature of this sport. Isn't an erection a sign of prowess?"

Some thinkers sniggered, postulating about the gymnasts. "Are they strong because they're black, or did the gods make them strong but inferior?"

Zilath clapped twice and the gymnasts left, smiling. They had pleased. Two servants came to the platform, struggling to lift a two-handled bronze oil bowl.

In homage, a pair of hefty nude wrestlers fell to their knees at Zilath's throne. Reverent in his ministerial robe, the prince-priest mumbled a blessing over them. They rose, bowed to the audience and went to the platform where servants rubbed them with fragrant wildflower oil from the bowl. Zilath's flutist stopped playing. The grim wrestlers locked arms around the oil bowl, butting heads, grunting like swine. Their sensual muscles tensed, concentrating to throw the other off.

"The victor will be freed from bondage. The defeated one works in the fields. Which wrestler do the gods destine for a better life?" Zilath shouted at the audience.

Poor wrestlers! The gods sent them to earth as entertainment for others, Risa thought, watching the sport. A sad purpose and destiny. What destiny will be mine?

A roar from the crowd went up as the stronger disgraced his opponent.

With a blithering cry, head hung, the loser was led away by field hands. Risa felt sorry for him. Gods of fate would not treat him sympathetically. The winner strutted around the great courtyard, raising his muscled arms to Tinia.

His victory was brief, drowned out by the hunters' galloping horses. From lightning speed they halted, sweating and grinning, towing slain boar and stags on biers.

Aplu's sun peaked. Zilath walked among the kill, counting the bounty that was more than the number of hunters. A bevy of servants from the cooking rooms unhooked the biers and carted off the lifeless animals to be skinned and roasted over preset fires.

"My friends, the afternoon is for leisure at the garden court." Zilath waved to the thinkers with a sharp twist of his wrist. "Down wine and bread while the meats roast."

Appropriately, they separated to talk of respective works and of how Tarchna was bursting with advancements. Parth rushed to his friends instantly. Risa tagged wordlessly at his side.

The wives formed another circle. They were enjoying the day, charming each other with wit. No one beckoned Risa nor did she join in.

Until her cresting banquet, she would still be an unacceptable noble, treated like a wrestler who lost.

30

Risa moved along the yard's walkway toward the prince-priest's compound, areas not for the citizenry. Parth wouldn't miss her nor would anyone else.

Smoke came from the doors of Zilath's cooking rooms. Opening the latch, she sneaked in like a thief. Uniformed servants were rhythmically stuffing a boar's head with puls, heaping glazed vegetables and poached fruits onto sink-sized platters, stirring pots of boiling soup. A mixture of sizzling boar fat, basted pheasant, peacock in broth and hare in juniper and garlic clung to the servants' thigh length tunics. Her mouth watered. Wine and bread had whetted, not curbed her appetite.

Through the smoke, a beardless shorthaired servant hunched over a table with an expression of grim concentration as he carved irregular slabs of deer loin. His light-skinned bare chest sweated to a swath of groin cloth. At her presence, he stood without stooping to her as he should.

"Entertainment is in the yard."

"It's over," Risa replied.

"Then chatter with your friends."

"As usual, they talk of Tarchna's glory."

"What would you talk about?" he asked impudently.

"You make fun of me." Risa's resentment at Parth grew to include this bad-tempered servant. She moved to the end of his table. "I'd be foolish to tell you my thoughts."

"Thoughts come from within. They are who we are," he said with eyes too intelligent for the cooking room. "What would you say?"

"I would talk about what I want to learn. Why are we here? Why does the earth let us live?"

"Women don't discuss these things with men. Men do with other men."

"Hah!" she said. "You sound like a Hellenic."

"I'm not." He dipped a slice of venison into larded gravy.

Her belly hungered for it.

"Would you like this morsel, fair wife of Parth?"

"If it tastes as good as it smells. You know who I am, yet I've never seen you with my husband."

"The invited are my concern."

"You're too bold," Risa forewarned as she ate the slice. "Servants have no right to talk of masters' ways. Keep to your place."

His rebuttal was to wield the knife at the meat. "This venison isn't fibrous, not caught in chase as in other lands, but subdued by Etruria's flutists."

She watched him until he looked up from his board and closed one eye. Angrier, she said, "You mock me with your wink."

He rubbed the back of his hand across his forehead and she knew her mistake. Sweat had shut his eye.

"Servants are accustomed to heat and smoke, but you're not."

He pursed his lips and clicked his tongue.

"Your fingers have splayed tips. Your hands are non-callused. Who are you?"

Slowly, he worded his reply. "I'm a servant to Zilath, but not as you might believe. In truth, I'm here to observe."

"You spy for him?"

"I report what I see."

He puzzled her. Flustered, she turned to leave.

"You misunderstand. I draw what I see."

"How strange," she said derisively. "Aren't words to Zilath's ear enough?"

Reflected from the cooking fire, his eyes glinted with amusement. "I am Asba."

"Your name was mentioned at a meeting about building the tombs."

"Could be."

"The elders praised your work. Are you a Thinker?"

"No."

"You said you draw. Do you paint, too? Could you be a crafter, a painter, a great painter?" she guessed, enjoying the game. "Why are you cutting meat?"

"How else can I learn what to put on chamber walls? The cooking place has much action to enlighten me. Food blends with the elders' philosophic talk. Where else could we say why the cosmos lets us live? Besides, invited guests are to be assigned tomb sites with this feast."

He came around the table and studied her face.

She blushed, nervous at his proximity.

"Would you have your likeness painted with lust for grilled meat in your eyes?"

"You joke." Up close, she had seen Asba's brown eyes that took in everything with a falcon's speed.

"Your body holds truth of unspent love. Your lips are ripe for kissing." He analyzed her rosebud mouth. "If there wasn't an obstacle in your eyes, you could hold sentiment."

"An obstacle?" she asked woozy from his appraisal.

"Have I been forward? My response comes from what I see you thinking, not from what you've said. Sometimes, working below wearies. The air isn't always clear. The candleholders keep torches high, but light flickers when they shift stances. Enjoyment for me comes when my brush flows by itself and tells truth in each scene. I hardly help. What springs from my mind and hand is the same as a mountain stream flowing purest water. The force in my body is so strong that I forget where I am."

Risa's disdain for his earlier conceit melted with his candor and she tilted her head, smiling. "You love your art, don't you? Would you know how to paint my entire cosmos, my family and me?"

Asba speared the venison onto a platter and moistened the meat with gravy and olives. "Your smile pleasures me, Noblewoman Laris, enough to want to preserve moments of your life dancing on your walls, making tender love, singing with the cosmos. My paintings will dominate your afterlife tomb with movement and keep the spirits tamed. My figures won't weep in death."

The trumpeter's horn blasted.

"Zilath calls his guests. Please don't tell anyone you saw me here or that we met," she pleaded, wanting to stay.

"Be confident that I've never seen you before," he agreed simply.

Risa's mind whirled. Impulsively, she said, "Painter Asba, if we should be granted a tomb, we would be honored to have your painting talents."

He bowed his head courteously. "You want to know why the earth lets us live. This question is mine too." Gallantly, he swirled the palm of his hand at her. "You'll have magic on your walls made by me and my paint pots. Didn't you know that's why we met here?"

31

"We Etruscans have a joyful life. You Thinkers take pride in toil. At night you play and dance, smile at friends and add kindness to your household. It shall be the same when you pass to the afterlife, facing death with courage. Now, who will choose family tomb chambers?" Zilath asked at the end of the hunt and feast.

"Magistrates, elders, high ranking nobles and at last—Thinkers!" They responded as they should, knowing the scheme since its inception.

Overfed with meat and drink, each toddled forth to receive his sepulcher and praise the prince-priest for his generosity.

Aplu's sun crossed the sky. Risa and Parth listened to the ongoing call without being summoned to Zilath's platform.

Parth was rigid, his face and eyes impassive.

Risa silently prayed to Tinia. God of gods who grants wishes, give Parth a family tomb. Don't ostracize him like I was. Please don't damage his position.

"Come. I'm assigned the task of leading you to your tomb site." An elder took Parth's elbow. "Noble Vella, haven't you heard your name?"

"Aplu's sun is hotter than yesterday, Elder." Parth said politely, glancing at Risa for the first time that day.

I embarrass Parth as spouse, Risa thought. He sees that I ruin his nobility.

Checking the waxed slate scribed with a list of Thinkers' chambers, the elder led the way. For a man of years, he walked jauntily.

Perspiring, Parth and Risa kept step with him on the trek from Tarchna. When they got to the uplands' farthest edge, the sun was low in the sky and stars were rising.

The elder pointed at the ground. "You're lucky ones. This chamber is bigger for the earth slices easily here."

They stared at the grasses and weeds, and then at each other, agreeing without a word.

"We see only a smooth rock of rain-cloud hue, Elder," Parth said apologetically.

"Good." The elder unfastened his tunic's belt and took off two metal hooks. He bent over the semi-circular rock, located an embedded bronze loop and gave a hook to Parth. "Find the other loop."

Parth dropped to his knees and ran his hands over the rock. "Not there— but here in this grassy patch that covers the rock's true large size!"

The elder gave Risa the second hook. She engaged it through the loop. Together, the couple tugged the rock off its snug base. Underneath, rectangular blocks of tufa formed steep steps.

Parth took the candle from the elder. Descending, he reached behind him for Risa's hand. At the lowest step, they stood in cool dampness.

The tufa walled chamber, wadded with hardening mud, was as grand as bed quarters for the entire family. Blocked in with wood posts, beams and arches, it seeped with condensation. The ceiling pitched upward and met at the center. Where walls were hard, niches were cut for sleeping souls.

"Two beds are already built. Which do you want?" Parth asked, talking like his old self.

His mischievousness refreshed Risa's spirit. "This one. I'll have cushions made, filled with duck feathers. Here's a good place for Culni. One for Ari. Larthia over there. And for future spouses. Their children will have to go elsewhere."

"They could have their own tombs," Parth suggested, knocking on walls to confirm their sturdiness.

She walked after him, tracing irregularities on the undecorated surfaces with her fingertips. "The workers couldn't finish these rocks with carpenter tools so they pasted cracks with watered mud."

A vision of Asba tamping mud walls and painting multihued colors with a lover's care, made Risa wistfully say, "If I could have images from my forthcoming banquet to ornament this wall with winging birds, it would be a tribute to Turan."

32

Six of the twelve holiest men and women sat on three-legged stools in the market, monitoring mounds of foodstuff for the magistrates' slaves to distribute. A spokesman for the group preached, "Gods of the heavens decreed to our ancestor augurs that sacred ritual is significant to every aspect of life and food is at the core! Why? Because beings must be sturdy. The gods bless us. We eat twice a day—not once like barbarians."

An elder woman chanted, "Our founder, Tages, insisted that celebration with food is the crux of a joyous society. To banquet is to feast in refined style. Do not refuse any occasion, a renewed time of refreshment on a god's day, a couple's union or death banquet. Banquet is highest invitation!"

"What funeral banquet could be morose for the deceased on way to afterlife? What marriage rites could be appropriate without food for family and relations? What joy would cresting days hold without banquets?" a holy elder queried.

Another elder said, "Appreciate tastes that linger in memory."

Risa kept to herself and listened, stacking fruit in her basket. Her mother hadn't had a death banquet because of The Disease. Her father hadn't given her a wedding banquet. Parth received his accolade before they met. Arith and Ramnes' union banquet had been the only celebration she attended.

The spokesman pointed at Risa. "You walk through the food stalls admiring Tarchna's bounty but take a flea's amount."

"I follow food rituals and get what my family needs."

"You could have more than for a simple repast, maybe to serve your clan or friends."

"Could I take more for my banquet?"

"Ah!" Understanding showed in his eyes. "So you're the noblewoman of Zilath's Road Builder, the one your peers talk about."

"I don't mind the gossip. My husband suffered more than me."

"Humble you are, humiliated you were."

"The moon's calendar dictates time and place to feast or banquet," the spokesman for the elders said when he saw her again. "Zilath ordered yours. Noblewoman Laris, isn't your cresting banquet in three seasons? Nobles befriend you at market and ask about your family and banquet plans, suggesting an invite. Who have you invited?"

"No one yet."

Smelling of garlic, the bandy-legged elder left the holy group and loped to her. "The nobles ostracized you for being the daughter of the defected noble."

"They're not friends. They didn't issue me invitations for their cresting banquets."

"Zilath's accolade with cresting banquet marked your ascension to upper Tarchna society. You have a new life and don't want those shallow guests, do you?" Scratching his beard, he evaluated her. "Perhaps I can be of assistance."

"Honorable Elder, your offer is valued. I don't know how to get started for a feast," she confessed.

"Invite the people you care about."

His words calmed and cleared her mind. "You mark me well."

He laughed. "Answers are within us. To start, tell what you consume now and how it's cooked."

"Fish, fowl and animal flesh—stewed, boiled, roasted or grilled. We stay limber from work and muscular from strenuous games."

"Tsk. Basic meals. For banquet, one needs to cultivate the palate with oiled olives, onions and cured meats before the main courses. Drink from premium vines to invigorate the most inert souls. Don't forget to surround your ears with gentle music."

Risa memorized his words as they went through displays of hooked carcasses and caged fowl.

"Some birds are nourished in areas of plenty to become fat for the kill," he said.

"I don't eat skybirds, Elder," she protested. "They're friends."

He bent to her height considering what she had said. "Your companions? Then stew stag meats in blood juices to enhance flavor."

She smiled at his broad-minded answer.

He spoke over the din of citizens who argued for their market ration. "The time of day must be compatible to the body so the belly won't swell."

"We eat at high sun."

"Rules accompany eating, and those who eat improperly are not invited to banquet," the elder advised. "Children are little beasts. They would spoil the festivities."

"Culni and Ari will be at training during my banquet season. My youngest, Larthia, thinks she owns the cooking room and pulls pots off shelves. She wants to cook too," Risa replied, taken aback by his distaste for the young. "Larthia will stay with a milking woman. My children aren't included."

The elder scooped up puls kernels and shook out weevils. "Come to the next market. You'll see what I can do."

The elder taught Risa to select guests. When settled, invitations were delivered two seasons in advance."

"Only forty-eight," Parth counted on his slate.

"Increments of twelve, omen of good fortune. There's no one else I wish to invite."

"There should be a hundred," he said querulously, "and in Zilath's hall."

"Maybe Zilath didn't offer because I'm older. We can give it at home," she said adamantly. "We'll put half in our dining place and line the courtyard with couches for the rest."

Risa visited potters on the far side of Tarchna, most known for banquet-ware.

"Your bucchero is expertly turned." She held up a rounded clay cup mounted on a high-stemmed base. The proportions fit her hand. Drinking wine from this goblet would be perfect.

The potter saw her critical appraisal. "The finish isn't crackled. You know more about bucchero than most. You're the daughter of the man who formulated this black clay, aren't you?"

"Does that make a difference? The bowls must be ample for serving and eating. I'll take extras, should any break at the meal."

"I'll have them ready. Platters we spin on our wheels are balanced and flawless."

She chose large, round platters on pedestal bases for fruit, cheeses and cakes of garlic and herbs; sky-bird shaped jugs for wine; two-handled rimmed bowls for gravies; small bowls for nutmeats or olives.

At the metal crafters, she found bronze platters imprinted with vines and leaves for grapes, and went to the beekeepers for hundreds of candles. Given by the elder, her list of necessities ended with wild flowers to strew on tables, woven garland rings for walls and ceilings, and incense for perfume braziers.

Magically, superlative foods became available to her in greater measure at market, freshly hunted from forests, without bugs. If it hadn't been for the feasting wisdom of my elder, Risa thought, my banquet would be bland. The small price I pay is to hear every lesson and opinion on Etruscan rules for eating.

Risa stocked the cooking room to be a floor-to-ceiling storehouse of pungent ingredients. Rich, extravagant food accumulated. Jugs of wine and olive oil. Jars of honey. Staples of barley, spelt-wheat, hazelnuts, cheeses, eggs, root and garden vegetables were hung under cured hill animal meats, forest berries and herbs.

Lethi hadn't made a meal since Risa and Parth's marriage union. Three former men servants became house cooks. For Risa's banquet, they began chopping, slicing and pounding. Tantalizing smells wafted from Vesta's unceasing fires in the raised hearth that took up the whole wall.

The Vella head cook tossed meat chunks and onions into the simmering soup pot. "This season of Shifting Winds keep our fires stoked and lift black smoke from Tarchna."

The elder had opined, "Servants and slaves become disrespectful if you eat with them."

But Risa couldn't alienate these cooks who were part of her life. They had always eaten together, in and out the cooking room. For solution, she wove a wreath of bay laurel and capped it on the head cook. "May we savor the sustenance you give. Feed us well."

Short-staffed for a banquet, without butcher boy or grain pounding slave, the three cooks applauded.

The second cook said, "You're like a regal princess-priest giving an accolade."

"My specialty, boar on spit, will be succulent." The head cook angled the wreath as the prince-priest did with his crown. "Cheeses will be from top cream. Olive oil will be the most sublime that Hellas offers. Artichokes will be most tender, quail eggs of best hens. My delicacies will be remembered on your tongue."

The third cook perceived her problem. "Noblewoman Laris, we'll eat after the banquet."

"Your loyalty pleases. Each undertaking brings us to the most perfect banquet."

The cooks would make her feast a success.

Her elder said, "Seeing food whets all sensations—taste, touch, smell."

"You're so wise, Elder. My spouse, Nobleman Parth Vella must enjoy my banquet, too. Obligations to road construction keep him away until a few days before."

"Surprise him."

"Wonder of wonders!" she said when Parth arrived. "The gods provided for my very own bounty."

Padding their feet in the darkness of night to keep the household abed, Risa interlocked fingers with Parth and lead him to the cooking room.

"Sight of this food makes me reckless." He nibbled goose on the spit, stuffed peacock, fish gravies, venison, bean and carrot soups, roasted onions and garlic.

"Taste of this food awakes passion." He slathered olive oil and ewe's cheese on her palm, licking the melding flavors.

Amorously, he took her among the sacks of grain and rounds of cheeses.

The elders knew how food and lovemaking paired. It had been long since she felt Parth's white spurt on her mound. His manliness smelled as good as the food.

33

Aplu's sun awakened Risa on Tinia's solstice. The children had left. The house was quiet. A rainless day, just as she wished. Her banquet day, a bit humid, had arrived. She faced Parth as they lay in the marriage bed, their bodies draped by a cloth, sharing a tranquil moment before getting up.

"I've planned each moment. A few bites of puls. I'll offer a spray of columbine to Goddess Turan at the temple. Praise the gods!" She smiled like she was the first to ever rejoice.

Parth rolled to her, holding thick-looped gold earrings. "For you who inspires this banquet. While it's your celebration, it's mine to give a sumptuous repast and entertainment."

That old familiar desire for him grew. She wrapped her arms around his shoulders. "Today will be unforgettable for both of us."

"Tonight I promise you hot blankets," he tempted.

"And I promise you a gift that isn't visible."

"Is it behind your back?"

"It comes in time. The crafter from the hunt will do our tomb chamber walls. The magistrates think Asba's a great painter."

"You're jesting, Risa. If Asba paints for the magistrates, how can we have his talents?"

"He'll paint us in glorious moments of our lives," Risa said, getting robe and toilet box to bathe at the river.

"How can he know of our wedding night?"

"He won't paint that," Risa laughed.

"Until dusk." Parth kissed the tip of her nose. "Prepare yourself for more than your banquet."

Lethi rubbed ointments on Risa's skin, scraping residue off with her bronze strigil, crooning songs of the ancients, ending with, "Rest until the best night of your life comes."

Bathing and exfoliation reduced her to jelly, yet she couldn't rest. Applying honey paste to her sacred opening, her cheeks glowed as she readied for Parth's entrance, bubbling like effervescence rising from beneath river rocks.

"Have the gods swindled me with a short day?" Risa asked when Lethi came for her.

"Zilath says it's half light, half dark, the most equal day of Tinia's year. Sit at your vanity table while I brush your hair," Lethi replied.

"You fuss over me like a bird flapping its wings."

"If you try to coil your hair, it would be dusk before you finish." Lethi weaved strands into braids, piling them high into a crown, draping the rest on Risa's breasts.

Delicately, Risa pulled a new tunic over her head, straightening it on her hips and smoothing wrinkles. Banquet wear wasn't coarse linen. The slender tunic was a luscious creation of sea hued sheer fabric with embroidered bands at the base. Venu had brought the cloth from his last voyage. For the tunic's closure, she pinned a gold fibula of an intricately wrought bird, threw a matching scarf over one shoulder and pleated it into the belt at her waist. She slid her feet into new leather sandals, set with glossy oval stones.

Around her neck, Lethi clipped the gold link chain link that held a new gold ingot inlaid with a red bloodstone. Her father had found the gem in the colder hills and sent it for her banquet. That made five ingots; one for her marriage, three Parth had given for the birth of the children, and this one to mark her cresting.

"Your hat maker sewed this headpiece with fine amber and glass beads." Lethi pulled the cap snug on Risa's piled up hair. "Look in your mirror."

Risa unknotted the string of a velvet cloth sack and withdrew a polished bronze mirror engraved with a picture story of Turan, her favorite goddess on the reverse side. She held it up to her head. "The headpiece is a good fit, just like what Zayla would wear."

"Now your face," Lethi said, putting out unguents, powders and brushes. "I'll hold the mirror."

She sat and concentrated, painting cheeks, forehead and chin. With a thin brush she outlined eyes, glowing more than that morning.

"See? Your smile is like Turan's. You're as elegant as a goddess," Lethi approved.

Risa gazed at her reflection. "The bronze shows me grimacing like a gargoyle on the temple frieze scaring evil spirits."

"You don't have evil spirits in you."

"The mirror plays tricks. My face shows both youth and antiquity."

"It's not a trick. The mirror casts ageless wisdom. Smile, Risa."

She forced a smile, worrying about the unfavorable number of guests. Of the forty-eight invited, there would be forty-five. So close to banquet, she couldn't ask others.

Venu was at sea on a voyage of unknown length. He had told her he would come if the ship caught the right wind. By the banquet dawn, he hadn't. The sea kept its own schedule and Venu would be missed.

A messenger had brought Vel's reply to Risa's invitation. "It's the best season to find iron boulders, before the higher land ices. I'll be in the Tolfa." With this slight, he sent the costly ingot.

Arith's husband, Ramnes wasn't here. Four days past he came but left before Risa awoke this morn at Cisra's demand. Risa distrusted him. She had seen him snooping around the market place, listening to trade.

"Arith stayed. She's the only Laris family member, still she visits her Tarchna friends on my banquet day because she doesn't want to help," Risa had grumped to Parth. "She waits for others to do the work."

"And they do," Parth chuckled.

"Arith insults. The colorful scarf she gifted me for my banquet dulled when she told me it came from Cisra's prince-priest. He gave all his council's wives the same Anatolian cloth and Arith wouldn't wear it," Risa fumed. "She passed it to me."

"That scarf on the shelf?" Parth said. "It's as gaudy as Arith."

Risa drubbed her lips to relax and smiled at the mirror. Her smile reflected back.

"Turan, whose exalted face and body symbolize love, made you beautiful tonight," Lethi admired. "She gave you joy."

Suddenly, Risa felt content. "The goddess has washed me with her love. I do feel beautiful, Lethi. I want to dance, to sing and frolic like the gods across the cosmos."

"Your needs are met, Risa. Your cresting banquet is upon you."

34

A newborn goat arrived, bleating as the late sun diffused in the dismal western sky.

"This offering to the gods in honor of Risa should be made now. Rain clouds threaten," Spurie and Tita, bearers of the goat, said.

"Please, no sacrifice," Risa entreated. "The kid will be milked."

"Tinia's storm may cross the sky tonight," Tita said.

"You're so superstitious," Spurie told his wife. "The receiver of the gift decides."

Parth led the disgruntled cousins and the goat to the animal pen, leaving Risa at Tinia's votive statue in the hallway niche."

Those superstitions of an unfavorable number of guests and goat sacrifice to make a banquet perfect were crazy! Let tonight be faultless, she prayed.

Lethi waited at the front entrance. Viewed as a nonentity, guests walked past the servant. Risa affectionately squeezed Lethi's hand.

Sophisticated in her striking attire and stately pose, Risa walked through the hall of rooms to the courtyard and received guests on the top step of the three-sided dining place. Smiling her true smile, she gave each man and woman a floral garland from her basket.

To tread from one end of Tarchna to the other took no longer than boiling water for a pot of soup, but carts carried the invited. Risa's few childhood friends, Parth's relatives, Tarchna's nobility from nearby quarters and acquaintances who would be assets to Parth's future works, gathered in the courtyard.

Under the flickering candelabra, the resplendent women swooshed in, adorned with sheer fabrics that outlined breasts and nipples. Firm or flaccid didn't matter, for the gods had created each woman for her life's calling.

"Is not the suckling of the young the source of life?" the elders would question the uninitiated. "Our ancestor gods roamed the heavens in purposeful activities. They became mischievous when they gave women's breasts a second function, to grant men pleasure. A man's touch on a woman's breast could stir them both, quickening a man. Thereafter, generations of women draped thin tunics over their breasts for men to see underneath."

Not to be outdone, the men ebulliently bared virile chests, displaying curled hairiness, compensation for not having milk for the young. Wool cloaks covered one shoulder, the other showed muscle and sun-darkened skin. Finely woven skirts, hemmed at the knees, met leather shoes strapped up their legs.

Orgasmic feelings by males and females were aroused by these semi-nude fashions. "Shriek! Shriek with glory!" was written in the clothes-for-banquet section of the morality code within the *Book of Tages*. Ancestor priests, who scribed this original phrase, reckoned it meant, "Desire is hastened by proper clothing."

"Did a sybaritic god design diaphanous women's tunics and men's scanty drapery for the banquet to fit the code?" The augur-priests deliberated as they perfected the sacred books. "The gods created two genders, bodies to complement each other. Have they also made the banquet a time to celebrate beauty of the body?"

This code lived on. Proper clothing enticed genteel nobles to prevail with animal sexuality in bed after feasting.

Most brought gifts more appropriate than animal sacrifices. Anina gave an ivory comb. Gaia presented a bolt of cloth. All were ready for leisure.

"Warm greetings. May the gods be with you." Thana, whose hair was styled high like her noble family rank, bestowed Risa with baked bread, an egg inside for luck.

"In your honor, Risa, the gods send nectar for long life and good health." Noble Sethre held a flask of wine from his yard.

"For the Master's lovely wife." Noble Marce gave packages of lavender incense.

"Remember that perfume enhances coupling." Ramtha hugged Risa to her bosom, jangling gold and silver jewelry, ornamented with brilliant stones inherited from her mother and grandmother.

Risa laughed with the matronly noblewoman who she had met after accidently seeing the augur-priest's marriage bowls before her union with Parth. "I'll use this vial of rose water tonight."

Called in for the banquet, pairs of cupbearers carried double handled bowls inscribed with euphoric antics of god Flufluns, keeper of the vineyard. They stirred water into Etruscan wine and ladled the drink. The formula had to be right: light wine before food to not spoil the belly. Sipping wine mellowed the guests. They milled about under the gleaming lights in their gossamer garments, introducing one friend to another.

They wouldn't know everyone. Who could in a city whose population doubled every generation? This time of interaction could be formal, but the Laris-Vella home was congenial with decoration, candlelight, and the musician at his cithar.

"Where's Arith?" Parth asked when all arrived and sundown had begun. "We can't start without her."

35

Glowing like hundreds of winking fireflies, beeswax candles lit the feast tables set with bowls of steaming meats, vegetables, cooked grains and delicacies of quail eggs and suckling pig. Twigs of herbs and spices interwoven with hanging berries, bedecked the walls. Lavender incense infused the air.

"Where's Arith?" Parth repeated.

"She's still primping." Lethi said.

At last, with a grandiose swish of her gold-flecked transparent tunic and a scarf of brightest rose, Arith stood at the top step. Hatless, not of Tarchna style for a formal banquet, her straight hair flowed over her shoulders. She glittered like a bejeweled goddess.

With eyes as round as Uni's full moon, the bemused guests stared at the human goddess who walked among them.

"I'm here. Your banquet can start now," she said, looking over the tables. "Where's grilled partridge and pigeon skin? Could it be you won't eat your so-called 'friends,' Risa?"

Risa didn't answer but watched Arith's immodest display with the same amazement as her guests. A twinge of panic caught in her chest. Her face flushed and a ball of fire grew in her belly. My sister begrudges me pleasure, she thought. Why am I not used to her ways after these years? Why does she have to make a grand impression? Will my guests prefer her?

To deflect their interest from her sister, Risa sprinkled wildflower petals among the guests, forcing herself to chat gaily, hoping all would see the festive scene she intended.

When she rested, doubt grew again. Would guests think this banquet shabby? An image came to mind: that of the gymnast at Zilath's hunt whose fear threw off his balance. He had lost confidence in his abilities and made one wrong move. The audience had booed. Risa shivered in the night's warmth trying to shake off these wild thoughts that had started with Arith's entrance.

A laugh from Ramtha jerked Risa out of her miserable reverie. The guests had quit their rude gaping and resumed conversation, glancing sporadically at this unknown person who had confused them with her vibrancy. Jovially, they surveyed the feast tables, salivating over assorted platters of steaming, fragrant smells. "Such hospitality! The gods' bounty! What pleasure!"

There were neither frowns nor smirks as they anticipated their most favorite pastime, the luxury of banquet.

I imagine too much, Risa admonished herself. No one seems annoyed. Arith is already forgotten. My guests are of my choosing. They've come to my banquet, not Arith's. I won't let them find her better than me.

36

"Elegance is a distinctive Etruscan trait," the elders drilled, "but comfort at a banquet adds consideration for the invited."

"Choose courtyard or dining place as you prefer," host Parth invited to abide with the elders' advice.

Each man found the couch most suitable to his clothes and heft, looking for convenience to reach for dishes, bowls and goblets. Before reclining, he placed his narrow-tipped deerskin shoes on a foot bench near his couch. Each woman displayed her best leathers from the crafters, making sure they were buffed, jeweled, strapped, gloved or sandaled, hiding the rough undersides of feet.

When they settled, a cupbearer handed Risa a goblet for the customary opening libation. She raised it high as her elder had coached. The guests took up their goblets.

"All-knowing Tinia who rules day and night with justice, who causes storms to rule the sky and trees to sway with brawn has given me this banquet, named on the lips of our majestic Zilath," Risa thanked in her rehearsed speech. If she hadn't paid homage to the most revered god of the celestial cosmos and to Tarchna's leader, more disfavors might fall on her home.

Guests cheered affably.

Heartened, she went on, "To Goddess Menvra who steers my life, and to my honored guests who give value to my years of growth and womanhood, I drink this wine."

Again, everyone raised goblets.

Breaking apart a loaf of spelt bread, she passed around chunks. "Be it grand or simple, our feast is to delight in life's enjoyment. Welcome."

All ate a mouthful of bread.

"Family and friends, there's food to gorge the soul's longing for satisfaction, wine to rejoice, music to sooth, and Risa of the Laris Clan to dignify with your presence," Parth proposed. "This occasion is willed by the gods."

"Willed by the gods," Risa reverently repeated under her breath. "Thanks to Turan for Parth's love."

Adeptly the two younger cooks rushed more platters of roasted meats, asparagus, wedges of cheeses and mounds of cherries and apricots.

With first courses done, the cooks hoisted the roasted boar.

On muscled shoulders, they displayed the animal speared on an iron prong, glazed skin smelling of lard, garlic and herbs. Head intact, an added laurel sprig in its mouth, the fatted boar was positioned as if in a race, front legs forward, hindquarters back.

Parth honed his knife on a whetstone. In one sharp stroke, he sliced off a boar's ear and paraded it high like a trophy before holding it to Risa's lips. "Only for you."

Risa tested its crustiness. "The best delicacy I've ever had. Be ready, my guests, to fill your stomachs."

The cooks set the boar on the sideboard that bowed under its weight. Carving into breast and ribs, the head cook saturated slabs in blood gravy and offered pieces on pronged skewers.

Smacking lips like wolves devouring prey, the banqueters ravished the chewy wild boar, grinding sinewy meat to pulp, saying between bites, "What flavor. What aroma."

Washing down meat with wine, they gobbled everything on the table from veal to venison to nuts, seasonal greens and ripe fruit.

"The gods send Risa the sweetest fruits," they flattered as they gorged on berries or dried pears.

"Cheeses melt in the mouth," they said, sampling fresh curdled sheep milk.

They toasted each other and the charitable gods of hearth and home, providers of the repast. "Praise Lares and Penates who give bounty so our hosts can feed us well."

Risa and Parth smiled at attaining this banquet, tasting morsels as they went from group to group, not able to relinquish hosting duties to sit with guests until everyone had fully eaten.

Food and drink turned strangers into friends as they chatted about Zilath's arena sports of horse racing, boxing or wrestling. Tongues wiggled like dogs licking water as they delved into personalities of known figures.

"A good magistrate. He supervised grain bins and fields adequately."

"No, I've heard he's put too much spelt flour in his own sacks."

Couples mingled with scathing talk about the ruling nobility's garish, wicked ways. At the end of the couch, Risa could hear their loud whispers.

"His wife has been seen with that visiting noble from Nepi." The voice dropped to name a high official. "He'll be ousted come next meeting."

"Ahal's wife eats more berries than she should. Her face has changed to earth color," Mammarce, Parth's older brother said as he ate strawberries. "They say the noble's been tending more than his orchards in Tuscania village."

"Do you think she's been rash?" his cousin Senna questioned, peeling grapes.

"Clearly. Her tunic doesn't hide a growing bulge."

Mean-spirited but interesting gossip. Risa had been subjected to it for many seasons when Zilath's wrath painfully crushed her spirit. Now she wanted no part of tittle-tattle. She went to guests who spoke of open-minded topics, of the crafters' artistic works, of Tarchna's architecture, of dance and music.

Having fasted earlier, the banqueters overindulged. Contented, they reposed on cushions for the night's entertainment. One by one, the women let their scarves slip. The men dropped cloaks in the heat of banquet, exposing naked torsos.

37

Dancers tiptoed into the courtyard, dressed as Flufluns' maenads of wine orgies. Naked under thinly veiled layers, they leapt high and bent low to the cithar's strums. The women twirled on light feet, flexibly twisting into forms only they could do. Convex out-stretched hands curled with ardor for the music. Ending in delirious drama, they raised fingers to click wooden cymbals.

The lethargic guests applauded, all but Sethiti and Velcha, oblivious to the dancers. They sipped wine and fed each other bits of boar meat and quail eggs. Turan had seen that the two were in love.

That's how love should be, Risa mused as the dancers left.

From across the dining place, a bare-chested flutist strode in like a prince-priest, commanding attention with magnetic authority.

Shocked, Risa stared at him. He was no younger than she, of gentle beardless face, hair plaited from scalp, her own image in manly features. His face broke into a smile.

Holding his sacred talisman, the double pipe instrument, he began to play, the humid air vibrating his poignant love songs. Guests reclined closer to partners, stroking exposed skin provocatively. Inquiring hands slipped under tunics to explore private flesh. Although aroused, they didn't shriek with glory, conduct only acceptable for the sleeping room.

"What music of mine would delight your ears?" With a deer's quietness, The Flutist stood at Risa's side, as intimate as a lover.

For a moment, her breathing skipped. "Do I know your music, Flutist?"

"You do." The smile on his lips matched his eyes. "Love is the instrument of life." He blew a few random notes. "If I play sweetly, it will flood your soul and bring harmony."

"Music drifts over Tarchna's hills and city, but I've never been close to a flutist before. Are you of the cosmos, a living person?"

His laugh sailed to the stars. "Many flutists play. I'm chosen for you because your life flames with love that pushes you forth along your path."

Why did he seem to know her? She wanted to touch his chest to see if he was real. His nearness enclosed her, sending waves of heat into her being. His skin absorbed her, taking her until she was one with him.

"Yes," she replied firmly. "Love exists to give life meaning."

The Flutist began a tune, a dreamlike mixture of ancient myths, enchantments and wishes.

Stars kiss and send love on a sultry wind
Destined to earth
Seeking lovers entwined, caresses
Lasting through life time...

He strolled away through the courtyard to lull others with music.

"Wait," she called to him, "Please, another verse."

No response came. An increasing breeze billowed the canopy over the courtyard.

Whoever he is, I shouldn't have spoken with him, Risa chided herself. Parth planned music and dance, not I. Music is to sooth my guests. As the honored one, I must keep attentive.

Gregariously, Parth walked among the languishing guests, occasionally checking for their needs. Gratefully, Risa watched his tactful way with friends, looking after her banquet with ease.

He's my life's love and I'm proud we're together. The divine gods have bound and blessed us, Risa told herself.

38

In the courtyard, Arith was charming men, telling about Cisra's festive life. Witty and lively, she flirted as if she knew each, making them forget wives.

Asba, the painter of tomb walls was the only man not attentive to her. He had come in through the cooking place after the boar's presentation, wearing a nobleman's tunic, observing like a spy with pent-up secrets. Sucking pomegranate seeds, spitting the waste into a bowl, his eyes darted from Arith to Risa, then to couples, servants, dancers, and to The Flutist whose body melted into the dark.

Risa understood his silent methods from their intriguing talk at the prince-priest's hunt.

"Hope and delight are at this banquet," Asba brazenly said. "I'll be in the tomb chamber at dawn to do a rendering."

"Its success thrills me." Risa sank onto a cushion, reviewing her day, still upset with Arith's showy late arrival.

Quizzically, Asba gazed at her.

In her dreamy repose, Risa didn't see lightning flare, bright as day. Thunder exploded through the clouds, shaking goblets and plates.

She knew her mistake. She hadn't sacrificed the goat! The augur-priests' adage had to be true.

Sky whiteness announces Tinia's power, he who produces rain in the heat season at whim by raising his eyebrows or flicking fingertips.

Fearful of Tinia's wrath, servants unrolled sheets of cloth over the courtyard, with not a moment to spare. Chilling rain on the roof congealed into hail, clicking like dancers' cymbals. Godly discharges streaked through the canopy seams.

Candles fizzled and died, sending the banquet into semidarkness. Guests reacted to the elemental powers slowly, non-caring in their own inert states, not put off by poor illumination. Charged by Tinia's lightning, talk grew loud. Gesturing hands and bobbing heads gyrated like orgiastic participants at Flufluns' parties.

Bursts of that eerie whiteness dimmed Risa's eyesight. She pressed a handkerchief against her eyes to ward off the sparks.

I've drunk too many cups and will dream of gorgons and snakes, Risa cautioned herself. Tomorrow's consequence could be a glum headache.

A sudden movement from the shadowy cushions joggled her. Parth was lounging in the corner. Lightning showed Arith next to him. How improbable for Parth to sit cozily with Arith. Around them, others were preoccupied by food and drink, not worrying about Tinia's wind rustling through the house. In the wavering candlelight, Parth's hand was caressing Arith's shoulder.

Risa moved closer.

"...However, you are most beautiful," Parth was saying.

"Beautiful enough for you to bed me?" Arith offered him a goblet of wine. "Touch my nipples. They're tipped with gold in the Hellenic and Aegyptian style."

With a husky gurgle, Parth's hand stroked her breast. Arith's glittering ringed hand was on Parth's knee.

What unbearable sight is this? It must be Mammarce, not Parth. They look alike. I haven't seen anything, Risa denied to herself.

She stared again. Arith's hand was up Parth's thigh and he was laughing like a youth.

Riveted by that image of husband and sister, Risa sidled to another couch before they could discover her watching them. He's laughing in orgasmic delight, she thought grimly. Arith, who he has disliked since they met, charms him.

"More wine, Master's Wife?" A wine server held a pitcher to Risa's goblet and filled it, not waiting for her answer. "Where there's wine, love and song, there's enchantment."

"Enchantment." Risa swilled a mouthful. She knew men strayed, particularly at feasts, but not her husband. How odd that lately he had become more loving. Had Flufluns joked by enchanting Parth to stray? Or had a quirk from the gods transferred his love to another, of all women, her sister? Was Parth's devotion to her out of guilt that he had strayed?

Her lawfully given cresting banquet that she had strived for, lost pleasure. The goblet in her trembling hand splashed wine on the cloth cushions, fell and crashed into tiny shards on the floor. Shattered with her goblet were her earlier fantasies of lovemaking.

Joy of her wonderful banquet withered, the wine vinegary in her throat. The flute player's face floated before her eyes. She wished he would be here now to take her far from her usually beloved dining place. A hot iron seared the core of her being, a stab of pain in her belly, dizziness in her forehead, and blackness behind her eyes. Weighted by that iron, Risa swayed from her cushion and careened down the hall into the storm.

39

The rain-laden winds died. Tinia's freakish storm raged towards the mountains, leaving wet dripping branches, soaked grasses and a rush of humidity, bringing out the chitter of crickets.

What was supposed to be the best night of Risa's life turned out to be the worst.

She staggered back to the house. Her elegant hem dragged in the mud. The once polished, gem-studded leather shoes were caked with dirt. She tore off her delicate garments and dropped onto the bed, knowing Parth wouldn't pursue her.

The night went cold, then hot, then cold. At the first streaks of light, she awoke from demonic dreams. Tears matted her head pillow. Made of her birds' softest feathers, the pillow gave no comfort now. Parth wasn't by her side. A hair from his beard and the indentation on the mattress showed he had lain there.

Tinia's rumblings persisted throughout the dawn.

"Vesta's fire has gone out," Risa heard the servants cry. "The wind blew it. Woe to us!"

Parth stood at the doorway of their marriage room, his face taut. "You were in Flufluns' cups, frenzied like a wild woman. How could you desert your own banquet?"

"Leave me alone," she snapped, plagued by a throb in her belly. "I'm going to the uplands. Asba will be there."

"How could you think of the painter? Yesterday there was banquet. Today, Asba. Has that ill wind overtaken you too?"

"Asba will paint the banquet's entertainment on our tomb chamber walls."

"What about our household? Get the servants to put the dining place and courtyard back in order!" Parth snatched his cloak. "We need foodstuffs after what was provided for your enjoyment."

Risa got out of bed, hearing a horse clomping its hooves. Squeaking cogs of a chariot's wheels ground into the rutted stone road outside their dwelling, a sign that Arith was leaving.

"Good. Farewell to the sister who always tries to ruin me. May Tinia rain pebbles on your house, Arith," she cursed aloud and threw on a soiled tunic and old mantle. Parth was also leaving for his toil. He was probably saying farewell to Arith and arranging for their next bedding. Disgusted, she didn't want to see either of them.

Hurrying from her room, she averted the house disorder and went through the messy cooking room, the sight of food scraps turning her stomach. Each detail of the ghastly banquet remembered, she tore out of the animal gate and passed the cypress hedge that marked their property.

I've displeased the gods, Risa's mind worked feverishly. Asba promised to paint the truth, the most memorable moments of my life—my banquet! What will he paint? Parth and Arith looking like orgiastic gods on a marriage training bowl in the temple, her legs around his body, her flesh melted into his.

Without doubt, she had to get to the tomb.

The path towards the uplands was slippery from rain, but the climb wasn't insufferably hot. Between clouds left from the storm, shafts of early sunlight threw a misshapen shadow of her at the earth.

Shame is my legacy if I don't stop him, she thought. My life in this cosmos and the next will be devastated.

On the uplands, watchmen on extended shifts kept guard against Phoenician and Hellenic pirates.

"What causes you to be here?" a bleary-eyed watchman questioned Risa. "Zilath's new decree is that no one walks here except workers, tomb building slaves, or members of a procession visiting the afterlife home of the deceased."

"I'm a noble visiting my tomb."

"Nobles shouldn't be on the uplands unaccompanied by elders, family and servants."

"I must oversee the work being done. Don't I have cause?"

"Tears in your eyes tell me you do, and your white flax cloak marks you as a noble. Go on," he relented.

Once, the wide upland grasses had been uninhabited. Then the sacred ancestors came and knew its altitude would be an ideal defense against potential enemies from the sea. How original Prince-priest Zilath had been to use these innocuous fields as a burial ground. The arable land was flat to plow and fertile to plant barley. Rival sister city Cisra or barbarians would never think the dead were underneath. Newly deceased Tarchna had begun to populate the uplands, sheltered in underground chambers. They slept safely on feathered pillows, tranquil in afterlife with earthly household furnishings and ornaments.

Deprived of sleep, Risa envied the deceased as she passed by. The earthly Etruscan cosmos was good, but the eternal home was better. She and Parth tended it as regularly as their life dwelling, making certain that the rock-carved walls didn't crumble, that dampness was purged with minted herbs on the beds. Neither cold nor hot, the chamber was right for Asba's wall scenes. With few household possessions for furnishings, the paintings would be most noticeable.

Vesta's cooking fires smothered the city in soot. The uplands were refreshing. Dew lay on the verdant grasses colored with lavender. Gathering flowers for the tomb, Risa walked up a path of earth-covered tombs. The new burial sites couldn't be seen from above, set apart by paths across the landscape. Carefully she skirted around tufa stone boulders that she knew to be chamber covers. When she reached theirs, she saw that it had been moved to open the stairwell. Light shown from below.

"Yesterday my cresting banquet was my accolade. Today I'm as tarnished as a copper pot." She gritted her teeth as another pain hit her belly, a knot of hardness never felt before.

Risa descended, awaiting her foreseeable disgrace, the banquet that would be indelibly painted on the sanded walls of their eternal home.

With vigorous strokes, Asba had sketched The Flutist and dancers among trees, outlined with decorative bands of paint.

"You work fast, Asba."

"The banquet inspired me. I've been here since the rains quit." Asba beamed, wiping his hands on his splattered work tunic.

"You told me you paint the truth. This wall lies. You omitted the images of..." she breathed deeper, "of carnal love."

"I'm the least of your worries. I uphold your honor." He lifted her chin so that his candlelight showed her eyes. "You glory in loving. Your steady love for Parth and his for you is what I paint. If you look at the opposite wall, Noblewoman Laris, you'll see the whole scene."

There they were. A portrayal of Parth and Risa reclined on cushions, sensually exchanging gifts of duck egg and necklace.

"It reminds me of how we once opened our hearts to each other," she sighed.

"I glimpsed your past and made it true." Not waiting for consent, Asba kissed her forehead and her cheek.

Had the mood of the chamber made her lazy? She hadn't stepped away from him. Irritation grew, at herself and then at his impropriety. Where he had kissed her burned like hot coals.

"You're a craftsman. I'm a noblewoman."

"Cannot I claim a kiss? I saw you with The Flutist. He wanted to kiss you."

"He was a banquet flutist. He lulled me with the gods' love songs. He pleased the guests. Nothing else happened."

"My kiss makes you tremble." Asba grinned like a youth eating honeycomb.

She couldn't justify being in the tomb with the painter. If he forced her into his cushions, he could damage the rest of her life by smearing walls with frescoes of disrepute. Bringing her body to its full height, she garnered her pride as Menvra taught and said haughtily, "May the gods thank you."

"They will," he said.

"You aren't that important." Risa placed the lavender in a bed niche and took a last look at the-soon-to-be painted walls. "But your sketches are artful."

"They must be."

She went to the steps. "You don't keep the eighth day work ban. How did you get past the watchman?"

"I'm an artist, outside Zilath's law. Life calls me, not days."

40

After the clayish dampness of below, Aplu's sun rejuvenated. Risa walked briskly towards Tarchna, trying to get Asba out of her mind. The heat had dried the mist to unveil outlying jagged foothills. Taking in the sight, she exalted in the geometrically trimmed vineyards curving with the land's contours, continuous fields of plentiful vegetables, beans and grains midway to harvest. How does rain and sun spring forth this exquisiteness? she wondered.

From hills to upper mountains, roaming flutists continued to lure waking stags, boar and partridge from lairs. "Be our sacred food. Come joyfully to serve Goddess of Hearth and Fire. We hail your sacrifice."

Those hollow pipes echoed in her head like an unplaced memory, leaving her sad and elated within a moment, soothed yet chilled. She hummed a melody that her banquet flutist played. One, she hadn't known. The music enchanted, but how absurd that Asba thought she dallied with a common flutist.

Her banquet guests would howl mirthfully this morning about Parth and Arith, how they had pawed each other like two felines in heat.

"Arith, my wanton sister was so beautiful, captivating men to make me look shabby," Risa wailed to the cosmos. "I am the moon. She is the sun!"

Her mind rotated from Arith's licentiousness to Parth's infidelity, to Asba. Anger turned to fury until she lost the look of a respectable wife and mother.

So stricken, her eyes became colorless. Her exposed neck and arms took on a sickly pallor. The knot in her belly wouldn't go away.

Grimly, Risa raced over wind-blown grasses. Her cloak blew and her tunic whipped at her legs.

Tarchna's third gate was ahead, built into the massive city wall, not used by magistrates but convenient for Risa. Slowing her steps to a woman's leisurely pace, she bowed her head from the onslaught of Tarchna citizens and servants going to market.

Uproarious laughter came from the Tatanu family as a flutist played a high-pitched tune, and the family clapped to the smashing of kernels. A neighbor responded with a cry to be invited. Merchants clamored for their worth of barter from carts reverberating as they moved goods. Mash pulverized by mortar and pestle interacted with birds chirping and goats bleating.

Too much noise, Risa's head thumped wildly. The usually convivial morning sounds of the city brought anger instead of accord.

Almost new day, Risa was overdue for tasks. Carelessly, she charted foods needed from market. Her respite from chores was over. For nine seasons until yesterday, she had prepared for her feast.

Raising children, managing a large household of servants and slaves, and drudgeries of weaving flax to linen cloth, had been the scope of her existence. Today, the household repetition was annoying and meaningless.

Her cresting banquet, the rite of passage she had ached for, had ended. There was nothing to look forward to.

41

"A visitor is in the courtyard to see you, but who would come before the sun's height?" Lethi reproved. "Noble Vella has already gone to lay out a south road with other road builders. He'll be back late."

"A visitor? Do I know her?"

"A man."

"Wait here while I see what he wants," Risa answered brusquely, her lips tasting like hearth soot. Asba? The Flutist? They wouldn't be at her door.

"You speak coldly to the one who raised you."

"Don't scold, Lethi."

At the courtyard, Risa sobbed at the remnants of her banquet. Garlands that she had painstakingly twined had fallen to the floor. The reclining couches sagged. In the far corner, the water supply in the cylindrical tin cistern dripped noisily into a shallow ditch, unheard last night. No one would think of leaking water with loud music and gab.

Until he shifted, she saw a dark sculptured stone. The visitor sat upright in a shapeless robe, uncovering his tunic that reeked of kill. Topped by a cone-shaped hat, tied by ribbons under a goat-like chin, one eye squinted while the other assessed her.

"You were in the market place at my accolade," Risa said, trying to calm her voice.

"That's right. My cloak and hat prove who I am."

"Why are you in my courtyard, wearing soiled garb, sitting on my couch as if you own it?" she asked.

Large hands with knobby fingers darted out with a steaming viscous mass. He brightened. "Noble Parth's Wife," his watchful eyes gleamed through strands of hair oiled with animal fat, "You're a fiery one. Sparks fly off your being. If you were a goddess, you'd be goddess of thunder and lightning, for your eyes scintillate and your face is a storm cloud."

His singsong voice hurt her ears. "Your perceptions startle, but you're not a high priest. If you were, you'd stay in the sacred temple, divining ways of the cosmos and forecast thunder. You're a lesser augur who walks the city, foretelling fortunes."

"Noblewoman, your anger is visible." He examined the gelatinous mass in his left hand.

"What makes you sure of your words?" Curiosity bested her. "Where are those entrails from?"

"These aren't entrails. This spleen is from a sheep in your animal yard sacrificed for your table tonight. No matter sheep or hare, because it associates with you. Your animal yard reflects your house."

Softened by his frankness, she apologized, "You're blunt, Haruspex, not discourteous as I am."

" 'Risa' is a suitable name. She who smiles on life. But your desires are unsatisfied and you frown." He poked his right finger into the organ meat. "The source of humanity's spirit and courage."

"You didn't lie about the spleen. It's not a common hare's organ that augurs use for a cheap ploy," she said.

Caressing its surface, he searched for formations that related to the celestial gods. "A healthy spleen is propitious. Abscesses, pustules and carbuncles are defects. Bad omens. Hmm, contain yourself, for wildness is destructive."

"I'm tame."

"You resist too much!" Haruspex jumped about the courtyard, flapping his arms, kicking his legs. "You know the *Story of Time and Seasons*. Our greatest ancestor, Tages spoke with Tinia and marked four seasons. At the warming season, hills are in flower, animals have newborn, trees awake and sprout greenery, and mountains lose frost. The heat season is when land dries out and scorches. Workers brown and sweat in the fields until Tinia's thunderstorms and lightning alleviate. The cooling season comes when leaves drop with Tinia's winds, and crops must be gathered. Then hunts are declared. In the cold season, we store the harvest, sleep and talk by Vesta's hearth, eat with no hurry and drink wine with no thought of tomorrow. A year divided into four seasons, twelve or thirteen moons, the rhythm of earth's time."

Risa interrupted. "Haruspex, why are you telling me about time, seasons and predictions?"

"Your household has scattered this season and you're uneasy. Your husband—your sister..." He poked another crevice. "Sheesh! If you continue on your purpose with integrity and honesty, results will be worthy."

"The gods people the cosmos and give each something to do, a path, a destiny, a purpose. Which purpose is mine, what path to walk?"

"The chamber in the uplands and the Great Prediction are tied in your purpose. The entire city of Tarchna hastens tomb construction to prepare us for afterlife. Time has become important. Predictions have to be heeded. You must be involved in Tarchna's tomb completions."

"I'm a noblewoman, not a builder."

"Don't you see? Time is the connection with Parth and Arith."

Risa's head ached like a wild bird walloping its cage to get out. "I see none. Parth admires the elders and augurs and knows the prophecies but does what he wants. He makes me the fool with his dirty love secrets."

Haruspex sank onto the couch. "Something will happen in each season, under every moon. Your whole life will be considered every year."

"Will Tinia or Turan judge me every season?"

"Only when changes are needed."

"When you cannot forgive, you must seek new means to dissipate turmoil. You have a kindness that must prevail and talents that go unused."

"So kindness and forgiveness are in my destiny," she said. "You banter ideals but can you name remedies?"

"I read the portents and consult the gods." Haruspex brought his feet down, stood and walked towards the outer door, not looking wrinkled or old. Kindly, he said, "Life has bruised you. You quest for contentment. I shall instruct you."

"You're a strange man, nameless, young and ancient. Why have you come at my home unbidden?"

He shrugged.

"You madden me by knowing what I'm thinking."

"Indeed," he said gravely.

"Haruspex," Risa asked skeptically, "who sent for you?"

With a leap, he cackled, "You did."

"I did not!"

"Your soul sent for me." He twirled his black robes and was gone. A faint odor of entrails and animal fat stayed.

His skills were quite amazing, his posturing ridiculous. She stifled giggling at the transformation from his cloddish arrival to his uncanny departure as she went to her cooking room servants.

Expecting her, they squatted with bowed heads, not hinting they knew her banquet embarrassment. Dutifully, they got up to push the shopping wagon to replenish market food even though there were leftovers for three days.

She was still smiling from the astonishing haruspex.

42

"Speed your steps." Risa hurried her servants, her spirits oddly uplifted by Haruspex. "We go to market for the prince-priest's new barley ration before none is left."

She studied the cloudless sky. A good omen. Geese, not her favorite, were flying toward the steep hills where Culni and Ari were. Her boy-children had gone eagerly, taken by dependable slaves who knew the hunt, but she missed their frisky presence.

They resembled both parents, but one was like a thunderclap and the other a windless rain. Culni had already shown manly braveness by hunting on horseback and holding up his dead fawn for family to see before it was grilled. Ari had warmly hugged Risa upon departing and told her, "I'll miss you, Mother, but it will be quiet without our noise."

While Tarchna girls went to the warmer interior valleys to learn ways of the land, the girl-child Larthia was too young, kept out of sight with other little ones to be nursed by women servants. Curly-haired Larthia, who charmed with perceptive remarks for such a young thing, would make costumes with cloth from the chest and saucily get those in the courtyard to see her dance to the servants' music. "One, two three. Clap your hands!" If no one watched her antics, she would run to the stream, unafraid of its waters.

My winsome daughter grows up to be like her namesake. She's a handful,

Risa thought, dallying in the market stalls, picking out fruits and nutmeats for her servants to bear.

She didn't want to see Parth tonight. They had never had such mean words. Enmeshed in loneliness, she groped for a wall and saw she was close to the sacred temple. Sweat beaded her forehead and she tried to breathe slower to cool. A cramping spasm stabbed like a blade into flesh, exploding through her body. Her legs faltered with first blood of the moon passage trickling down her thigh.

Instantly, Lethi's arms held her up.

"Long life for me," Risa muttered in pain. "I'm not for the netherworld, am I, Lethi?"

"No. Too much wind. Too many clouds. Disharmony," Lethi whined. "That abominable Haruspex upset you."

"He's my ally."

"We've gotten food and can go home," Lethi comforted as Risa's servants lifted her atop the barley and millet sacks in the cart.

Risa's mumblings continued, yet through an excruciating contraction, she wondered about Haruspex. He knew the prediction, encouraging her to concentrate on purpose, to strengthen her will. She had no choice. She must believe him.

43

"Uncertainty causes this bleeding," Risa rambled as house servants bore her to the marriage room and laid her on the bed.

She thrashed about her pillows, punching blankets, sweating, then chilling. Her waters released, streaked with blood. She shrieked like a demented haruspex laying a curse. Needing the gods, she cried out for help, naming any who could save her.

The one who answered, cruel god Vetisl, inflicted darkness on the Laris house, smothering life, strangling Turan's gift of love to Risa and Parth. Risa collapsed in a pool of her own blood, screaming as the deformed unborn mass leaked from her womb. The convulsions of her being slowed, then ceased.

Nearby, Lethi mourned, singing a dirge so that the departed would pass in peace to the afterlife.

Risa slept. In nightmares, blood was on Uni's silver face, contorting into a gorgon, tongue sticking out to mock Risa's anguished blood. The moon goddess crackled, icing the earth, sending Risa towards the netherworld.

Days melded one to another until Risa awoke. Restlessly, she combed her mind for what went wrong with her marriage. Once their lovemaking had been joyous, settling to endearment with Culni, Ari and Larthia's births. With each new complication of a growing household, they had moments of disagreeing on what to favor or not, moments where neither spoke. Sometimes

Parth was distracted by his work and didn't hear her words. Other times the days dulled with toil. Looking back, had her union been better than most? Or fair? Or worse?

Her ambiguity intensified. Perhaps they hadn't enough children. That was it! Like her parents, there had been three, not eight like other families. A newborn hadn't arrived three seasons after their first coupling. One had swelled Risa's body briefly and bled out.

"She hasn't puffed liked Tinia's cheeks or seasoned like a plump pear. Too young she is," the Birthing Woman had told Parth. "Not to fret."

Not to fret! Risa had chafed with indignation. The gods taunted by giving her a boyish form. Her body hadn't become womanly like curvaceous Arith and most Etruscan females. Yet, Parth had told her how he loved her slender limbs and sleek torso.

Many seasons later, the gods gave their blessings and painlessly Culni and Ari were born. Risa's breasts engorged with milk. Larthia came five years after, but none since. Was this enough cause for Parth to seek another?

She rose from her bed, wanting comfort by talking with her skybirds. "This unborn gushed out with vehemence. Is losing the child punishment for not satisfying Parth?"

The skybirds didn't respond, not wanting to be disturbed.

"No more children can be made, the Old Birthing Woman told me. I'd been early with child at my banquet." Risa huddled on her side of the bed.

"The gods willed it so, Risa. Three shall do us." Parth turned on his side, not enthused for love.

Perhaps the thunderbolt from Tinia's rainstorm was a message of dissatisfaction that Parth tires of me. Perhaps he could have gained more favors from Zilath if he had married a more eligible woman, one more beautiful, full-breasted, with round belly and curved hips, Risa thought.

Seeded with distress, she had no answer.

44

In the new seasons after Risa's sullied banquet, when her misery was most felt, Haruspex visited as Uni's moon waxed high. He drew out her secrets about Parth and Arith's treachery and read the folds of freshly killed sheep entrails.

"Dishonor," the wizened creature announced gleefully as if he enjoyed finding crisis. "This crease indicates dishonor. At the Temple of the Gods, I'll offer this steamy liver to the one responsible for love's mysteries, our Heavenly Goddess, Turan."

A day later, he related, "Tinia, ruler of the cosmos, shapes our destiny but Turan rules over love's ways. She knows Parth deceived you. In her wisdom she says 'Keep Parth and Arith separate from each other if harmony is wanted in your life.' Shun your sister until Parth's infatuation weakens."

"You respect Turan's words as I do. Your predictions must be right, Haruspex."

"Of course," Haruspex purred. "Harmony means joy and laughter that gives life strength, the same strength that made Etruria great. Harmony will fulfill your destiny."

Uni's crescent moon beckoned Risa to the uplands one night. In darkness, she sat on a hillock away from the watchmen's oil lamps, envisioning that birds with magical wings ascended to Tinia's highest sky and turned into stars.

"Take me with you," she called up.

A powerful force scooped her from the hillock and she rose. Who was there, but omnipotent Tinia, floating above birds and starlight against the quiet space.

"If it was a dream, it strengthened my will and brings a sense of belonging," she told Haruspex.

"Tinia brings harmony to the cosmos and you are part of Tinia's sky," he answered, in awe of her perception.

The woman of the brilliant smile practiced smiling, while food tasted like bitter herbs. She tried to be joyful, but her gaunt eyes marked her unborn's death and her own loss of dignity.

Even if Parth dishonored her, their family and home would remain noble. She would hold her head high at market. No one would ever laugh at her as they did before her accolade.

Risa knew she would abide by Haruspex's advice until Culni, Ari and Larthia were children no more.

Beyond the Great Sea

Nobleman Venu Laris

45

In the great days of Tarchna and Cisra's rivalry, Venu ascended into manhood. His hearty laugh and long stride were more like Shipmaster Alfnis than his own father Vel. The wayfarer-turned-seafarer rode on the Great Sea into the cosmos of Eastern regions, alienated from Etruria. Whenever Alfnis' vessel docked in Gravisca and provisions were unloaded, Venu would go up the Tarchna road to his family's home.

On one of those late moonless nights, an oil lamp floated on the road like an apparition. A human bulge under a hat and unshorn beard said, "Welcome back, Seafarer Venu."

"Who are you to say my name?"

"I am Haruspex." He untangled his robe, discharging heat from his being. "A half-man, half-beast, born in a mountain hovel, raised on uncooked victuals to master my trade through the gods. I came from the mountains to Tarchna for employment, walking among nobles who need me. They never know they do, until I come upon them and see their worries and fear. I help cure their trials, and they give sustenance that I trade for necessities, clothing, bedding or refuge."

"What do you want from me?"

"First, let me tell you of my powers and then you can give what you think I deserve. I got you to take herbs to your mother when you were a child. You were in Anneia's room. I gave you her amulet and sent you into the swamps towards Gravisca."

"My mother's amulet? You made me take it?"

"I stole it from her to give you," Haruspex cackled, "to set the course of your life."

"I don't believe you. Why would you have done that?" Venu started to walk into the deserted city night.

Haruspex trailed, his robe dipping in dirt. "I look in and out of the cosmos to see what others do."

"How's that possible? Give proof of your power."

"I can't. You Tarchna are raised to believe you surpass other cities in intellect, achievement and ability. The Cisra are raised the same. Competition continues, all jealous of what power the other has. Proof will show in ages to come."

"Zilath tells us we're richer," Venu huffed. "We have wealth and industry brought by our ships."

"Maru says Cisra is unbeatable, that Tarchna lacks culture."

"Culture? We have sculptures from the gods. Frieze paintings on..."

"Cisra wouldn't believe you. They haven't seen your paintings."

"And they won't. They're for my people, not for Cisra's eyes."

Haruspex juggled his oil lamp. "Cisra jokes that Tarchna's nobles eat like animals, devouring meat without chewing."

Venu took the lamp to keep Haruspex from burning himself. "Cisra's people eat until their bellies distend..."

"...And Tarchna drinks pails of swillish wine," Haruspex completed. "Round they go to find fault. Tarchna's deceased are subtly buried. Cisra's are venerated in their City of the Dead. Neither declines in power. Not now."

"You're more knowledgeable about Tarchna and Cisra than most, Haruspex." Venu went into the sleeping Laris-Vella household and put down the lamp to get a better view of his guest.

The shrunken priest took off his bulky robe and shook out more heat that went to the ceiling. "I know more because my ancestors descend from Tarchon, the Farmer, who set perimeters of Tarchna's land. Thirty generations are my clan. Our blood intermingled, each generation losing skin, muscle and bone until we shriveled, deformed and mutated into wizened creatures like Tages of old. As ugly as warts and moles we became! We may have lost bodily functions but gained wisdom that brought us from the mountains to be with those who cannot see their own needs. That's why we're called *haruspices*, but we're each called by our *gens* name, *Haruspex*, one who reads entrails of animals."

"Perhaps you brag."

"The Tarchna believe in my kinsmen and me, or they don't. There is no in-between. It takes seasons or maybe years for the Tarchna to realize my predictions. I don't mind. Truth isn't always revealed in the cosmos. If it were, my kinsmen wouldn't have troubles they do."

Venu digested Haruspex's words. "I haven't seen your kinsmen."

"You have. They're the gods, goddesses, augur-priests and haruspices you see, but the netherworld gods are below our realm. We are all one," Haruspex said. "We give hope, confidence and courage."

"So you bolstered my life. Why did you encourage my family's?"

"The Noble Laris Clan? I stay with them because they are extraordinary. Clever. What stamina! They advance society. They intrigue! I am wherever they are. I hear all. I can read private thoughts. I see all. I make their lives move and change." He looked into Venu's eyes. "You have a dilemma."

"That's why you've come. You're here to see what worries me."

"You question whether land is better than sea or sea is better than land."

"I still don't know which is best."

"The story I cannot tell is yours, those seasons when you go beyond the Great Sea for I only venture to the edge. That water is too vast for haruspices. We can't swim. You didn't drown, Venu. That is your hint."

46

The day that Venu waded into the sea, his father's cloak dragged him under the surface. Swept by the current, he let go of his mother's bundle of herbs, ripped off the cloak's fibula and watched it sink. Gasping for air, he bobbed up and saw the precious herbs from his mother's workshop float towards a ship's hull.

Scanning the water from its deck, the shipmaster growled at Venu. "Child, what do you want?"

Venu reached for the herbs, yelling through the blowing sea wind, "I'm looking for my mother to bring her these."

"This is the ship <u>Plentiful</u>. We haul lentils, metal ore, wine and oil. No mothers here." The man's gruff laugh carried over the water. "Come aboard."

Venu climbed the hemp rope ladder thrown to him. Crates, amphora and riggings were piled on the ship's deck of polished strips of wood. He wanted to see more of this ship, but the man had swiped his bundle of herbs.

"Are they fresh?"

"Less than two moons old, dried to snap when bitten, of good color and potent," Venu instructed, remembering Anneia's tutelage. "The texture shows they're of season."

"So they have to be dried for use. Salt is for seafarers, not herbs."

The man's craggy face was wet with sea spray, his beard shaggy from neglect. His eyes showed humor, crinkled lines upward like a ship's prow.

"You're not like Tarchna men. Where are you from?"

"The Great Sea is my home. Tarchna and Cisra's ports are some landings." The man sprinted across the deck with agility.

Venu rubbed the stinging salt from his eyes. The man brought him a round, flat metal piece and put it in his palm. One side had a badge marked *Athenai,* the other side a stamped square.

"What's this?" Venu asked.

"Oh, you're a smart one. You drive a hard bargain." He gave Venu another.

"I would like the usual exchange. Food." Venu foisted the metal back at the man. "Did you steal them?"

"Steal them? You don't know the Hellenic invention. You're not from port." He took another one from his pouch and flipped it in the air. "Coinage. Some are worth more, some less depending on gold and silver content. They hold no worth to Etruscans who want goods." His voice lowered. "Keep them anyway. Come to the galley. Cook will fix you a meal."

So what if the shipmaster lied. He had to be a pirate with metal pieces as barter. Pirates were exciting! They were robbers on the high seas, talked about in Tarchna, but food was what Venu needed. He crossed the deck after the man. Crewmembers were tying bundles raised up the ladder from the water, and scampering up ropes to complete tasks. The shipmaster took Venu to an open door cut into the deck that wasn't big enough for a man or a boy to crawl into. A dank smell with human odor wafted up.

"Am I your prisoner?" Venu whimpered. Pirates always caged their victims. "Please don't send me there."

"No, child. Oarsmen are below. They steer the boat and make it move when the wind's down."

The shipmaster led Venu to the cabin hatch. Benches and table were at one end of the galley. The cook leaned over a brazier at the other. Seeing his ship's leader and Venu, the cook set two bowls of stew laced with fish.

"Is this good smell sent by the sea gods?" Venu asked on his best behavior, lest he be made an oarsman. "I'm hungry, kind shipmaster."

"When did you eat last?"

"Two days ago."

"Eat!"

"The winds, Master Alfnis," an old seaman rasped from the door. "Heed the winds."

Shipmaster Alfnis passed his bowl to Venu and ducked out.

Famished, Venu gulped the stew and took the second bowl, chewing more slowly. He didn't feel the ship lurch, nor hear the crew shouting to slide it through the waves.

Venu rubbed his rounded belly. "I thank your hospitality, Cook, but I must search for my mother." He went around the ropes, bundles and amphorae to the ship's railing where he had climbed up. The ladder dangled to the murky water, the shore at a distance.

Alfnis pushed Venu and laughed. "Over you go. Jump! It's not far."

"The water's higher than my head," Venu said frantically, paralyzed with fear. "I can't walk to the sand."

"Can you swim?"

Venu shook his head.

"Boy," Alfnis said incredulously, "You're about to walk better on sea than land. You're about to get sea-legs."

Venu knew he had been captured.

47

"We go south from Gravisca Port along Etruscan territory," Shipmaster Alfnis told Venu. "Our warships patrol our trade fleet on these sea lanes and guide passage."

The Plentiful sailed on the Great Sea coast, stopping nightly at known sites to eat and bed on land. Leaving the warships in Etruscan domain, the vessel passed Hellenic colonies on the Italic peninsula's soil. Those established communities of foreigners had encroached from eastern Great Sea city-states. They watched Alfnis' vessel but didn't attack.

"We've had to leave shore out of season, lest more would be infected with The Disease. We risk losing our course on Tinia's cloud-ridden days, for he sends a pursuing wind that stops the oarsmen." Alfnis scribbled notes about the sea's horizon, hill projections and enclosed bays, his navigating method and itinerary.

A lead ball and line was dropped over the ship's side to trail on the sea bottom and keep broad distance from hazardous shallows. Without it, the vessel could break apart.

"Anyone can hold the helm in a calm sea," Alfnis said, "but skill lies in knowing the waterways."

One moon passed, days that felt like a saecula. Venu knew he was a slave.

Kept hard at work, he swabbed decks, polished rails, chopped fish with the cook and made knots for nets with lowly crewmen.

He convinced himself that Nethuns' waves had mesmerized him to those grand, dancing ships in port. His bad luck to be captured! It wasn't his fault that he hadn't searched more for his mother.

Alfnis recognized despondency under Venu's brave appearance. He entertained Venu with sea fables. "Bearded Nethuns rules the waves. He sent a bull from the sea to thwart his enemies, dragons to devour foes and sea serpents to punish."

"Bulls don't come from the sea. How could your story be true?" Venu asked cynically.

"It's because we Etruscans believe Nethuns is king god of the undersea cosmos and holds many secrets."

Alfnis' fables about the ancient ocean gods kindled Venu's imagination, and he waited on the deck for nymphs and creatures to leap from the water.

Two more moons passed. The season cooled, then warmed as they went farther from Etruria, into Magna Graecia. The land changed from timber to rock to flat sand. They sailed east through the straits to a new bay, then a new sea.

"This rougher sea is feared by many seamen. Nethuns is violent here. A lapse in steering can mean instant death," Alfnis warned.

"Caution, caution!" were portentous words on mariners lips, whether young or old. "When the gods shudder, it thunders," they would say even though there were cloudless skies. "If the gods are angry, lightning strikes."

When he should have slept, Venu was worked harder, sent up the mast on watch after a day of chores. Drowsily, he came down to lie on deck. He laughed at the seafarers, thinking what old men they were, how disagreeable they became when the wind blew cold.

Menacing clouds blocked the sun as he napped, surprising him with drops of rain the size of his Hellenic coin. A wave tall as the ship, crashed over the deck, the foam of Nethuns' wrath hurling waters as if the god himself rose from the depths to answer Venu about mariners' fears. Crackling lightning zigzagged across the sky, splitting the main mast.

My fault! I caused the nasty weather, he thought, his chest pulsing. I've niggled the sea deities. They send storm clouds from nowhere.

Another monumental wave washed the deck, dislodging half the mast. The ship heaved. An amphora, the size of half a man, rolled towards Venu. He hung on the railing to keep from slipping. The amphora crushed him against the rail and shattered. Shards scraped through his tunic. Blood spurted from his forehead.

His body slackened with the rocking ship, and he entered a netherworld of dreams where Anneia walked behind a flutist who stared straight ahead, playing discordant pipes. Unaware of the merry banquet around her, she headed to a door, dragging her robe like the ship's lead ball. Vel, Arith, Risa and Venu tried to yank her back, wailing in mournful song.

"Get her by the cloth!" Venu screamed as Risa pulled with her entire strength.

"Come, Mother." Arith tugged at Anneia's sleeve.

"Anneia, my beloved," Vel begged, kneeling with upraised arms, "stay with us."

Their laments served only to drain spirit. Sightlessly, Anneia drifted forward through the door, insensitive to the family's weeping, not touching the ground with her slippers, smiling at The Flutist, loving him more than her kin.

48

The gods stopped battering the merchant ship. Gradually, the current rippled lackadaisically towards land. The crew rejoiced by busily re-stacking amphorae and crates, tying them securely to the deck cleaned by the calmed sea. Dexterous seamen hoisted the extra mast, kept aboard with foresight. Their noise didn't wake Venu.

Alfnis washed dried blood from the limp boy's face. "Get up! You're not ready for afterlife."

Venu didn't respond, his whitened face passive.

"Don't be afraid. You're saved from Nethuns." Alfnis pressed wet cloths on Venu's forehead.

Revived, Venu cried out, bewildered, "Mother, here are your life-giving flowers. Take them for your healing."

"You're with fever."

Venu twitched and sat up. "Are we in Etruria, Alfnis?"

Alfnis shook his head. "The storm's danger ends and we make for Hellas. You called for your mother, father and sisters in your sleep."

"My mother is dead." Venu said, replaying the dream in his mind.

"Yes." Alfnis continued to wash the child's forehead with a damp rag. "The Disease took her."

"How do you know that?" Venu asked.

"You were hungry and tired, racked by the elements. I liked your spunk.

While you ate, I asked Port Master." He looked at the little lost boy who would have slain a leopard to save his mother. "She died the night before you came to my ship. How could I leave you in port town? You would have died of The Disease. I took pity and cared for you. We sailed."

Outraged by Alfnis' explanation, Venu bumped into a crate. "You captured me and make me do slave work."

"Slave work? What would you do all day on a ship? A ship must be conserved. Besides, I'm your friend, Venu."

"No, you're not." With almost a drunken swagger, Venu leaned over the railing and retched his venom to the sea.

Venu kept to himself, refusing to talk with the crew who had befriended him, certain they had conspired with Alfnis. The vessel tacked into the first Hellenic destination, Patras harbor.

The town bustled with seafarers. Venu stayed aboard, hearing them from from the deck where he huddled on his straw mat, liverish at Alfnis' deceit. If he had hated Alfnis before, his scope of hate grew to include ship, barter mission and grubby people on the docks, seaweed and the squared white-mud buildings.

In torment, his mind was shut to the new and different. He dreamed of the hunt, his friends who practiced with him, his room in his far-off home, of the mother he would never see again, the father who cursed him, his sister who coddled and everything he could remember of Tarchna.

The seafarers unloaded iron cauldrons, bronze ware and wine amphorae like the one that had crushed Venu. Amphorae were passed from man to man, and then to local Hellenics who loaded them onto donkey carts. New trade arrived at the dock. The seafarers lifted baskets of olives to the ship's deck.

The exchange of goods took days. Each night, laughing at their wobbley legs and sore muscles, Alfnis and the crew went ashore to drink wine with townsmen.

Days wasted in this port and then home, Venu thought when the anchor was hoisted.

He left his mat to see the vessel's ball dragging bottom towards a rocky inlet where grandly proportioned temples suspended on cliff ledges. They didn't look like Tarchna's sacred halls.

Venu spoke to no one and no one bothered him as the ship sailed on.

49

<u>The Plentiful</u> anchored at Corinthos, a major harbor built on a crescent around a continuous dock where stark white box-shaped houses wedged compactly, fishers dried nets and traders bartered wares.

Their journey long, the seafarers grouped oarsmen on the ship deck to stretch cramped bodies. Used to Venu's silence, the seafarers ignored him and went to the agora.

Corinthos wasn't an Etruscan port. On the confining ship, Venu was bored. He waited until the oarsmen fell asleep before hurrying down the ramp.

Keeping away from seafarers, he browsed through merchant stalls. Freshly picked herbs hung like his mother's, but the main foodstuffs were whipped mounds of creamy cheese, tiny fish layered high, and black elliptical olives.

To Venu's irritation, Alfnis was bartering bronze shields and helmets. He spoke the foreign tongue with boisterous Corinthians, gesturing when words didn't suffice. In a moment when Alfnis looked from his customers, he saw Venu and waved him to come.

"Catch me if you can, you—you pirate!" Venu goaded and hid behind a stall in an alley filled with shopkeepers striking bargains. When they moved on, Venu ran through the alley. Alfnis saw him and chased, but Venu was faster, going further from the dock. He turned a corner and collided with a boy of similar stature. Both knocked down, the Corinthian boy picked himself up first, putting spittle on his bloodied elbow, prattling in his language. He grinned when he saw that Venu couldn't understand a word.

Alfnis yelled. The boy must have realized that Venu was running from the shipmaster. He shoved Venu through a doorway. The large room was coated with a layer of dusty clay powder on every surface from round tables to shelves with vases, jugs, platters and bowls in stages of completion. A black robed woman hunched over a flame, brewing herbs in water. Without asking who Venu was, she gave drinking bowls of the liquid to him and the boy.

The boy patted his chest and said clearly, "Nikothenes," then worded a stream of gibberish.

Venu laughed as he gave his own name, the first laugh since before the horrific sea storm. It felt good to laugh. Like Alfnis, he gestured, realizing that was the way to get the Hellenic boy to understand that he was from the ship at the dock.

Three unsmiling men entered the shop and went to the round tables. Each cupped his hands around a ball of clay, anointed it with water from a nearby bowl and kicked his feet rhythmically on the base. Something in the mysterious clay pulled up a shape—a vase, goblet or amphora.

These were no ordinary men. They sat like priests in sacred offering positions, lifting their bodies, growing mighty.

Are they gods who make magic? Venu wondered, unable to budge from the floor where he sipped tea.

Nikothenes tapped Venu's shoulder. Although he didn't know the words then, Venu later learned that the Hellenic said, "You shouldn't see sacred *keramikos*. It's not for your eyes."

The Hellenic boy took Venu up a maze of streets, the girth of two men. The agora was before them, the dock in sight.

The Plentiful was not there.

50

Venu ran.

At the harbor's mouth far ahead, <u>The Plentiful</u> was being steered from land by oarsmen roped together on the dock. Venu walked abreast of the ship's hull with the oarsmen. Nikothenes tagged along.

Unmanned, except for Alfnis at the prow, the ship loomed above them like a sea creature. It rose from the depths, rolling on logs under the shallows. Grinding starfish and seaweed that clung to the dripping wood body, the ship came onto the beach where a planked roadway started at the shoreline.

Nikothenes saw where Venu was leading and shook his head. He unknotted an object from his cloth belt and offered it to Venu.

Venu turned the black cup with earth-hued lines. It was the story of goddess Athenai's birth, springing from the head of the great Hellenas god Zeus.

"You treasure this cup but gift it to me. How can I thank you, my new friend? Do you want coinage?" Venu asked. From under his tunic, he took the pouch of metal pieces Alfnis had given him and jammed them in Nikothenes' hand. "I must go."

<u>The Plentiful</u> continued its path on a strip of land that divided two seas. Venu caught up to his ship.

The seafarers and oarsmen hauled the ship, laboring three days over the *isthmus* of Corinthos harbor to its city. Alfnis had no time for Venu. He moved between the ship and his men to expedite the road crossing.

"What are we doing? Where are we going?" Venu asked Alfnis' first crewman.

"This is a toll way for Persian, Phoenician or Etruscan merchant ships to get to the eastern sea, faster than going around the Peloponnesus Islands," he said.

"What's a toll way?" Venu asked.

The crewman laughed. "Those Corinthians love gold and silver. That's what made their city rich."

The seafarers rested at intervals for food and sleep until they traversed the gateway to a precipice overlooking the Aegean Sea. Below, the water level dropped to the city of Corinthos, crossroads of east and west. With pulleys, they lowered the vessel into deeper waters.

"Why are there two Corinthos, the port and town?" Venu asked Alfnis who sat on a bale of nets. "They didn't build this city like Tarchna."

"This place has a story older than prince-priests. They have kings in Hellas. The king here was known to be vicious and cruel, but he was smart. Once the necessities of life were provided, he had city dwellers make crafts, ceramics, weave cloth and build ships. Thanks to the oracles at Olympia and Delphi whom the king had gifted, Corinthos became a great trading center."

"That must be why pirates like coinage," Venu said.

"The gods granted coinage as a bonus to the king for a source of wealth. And they did something more. They devised sporting games to be held every four years."

Corinthian officials scrutinized the Etruscan ship and approached Alfnis warily. "We heard a boy call you a pirate, Shipmaster. We don't allow pirates here."

"My trade is sincere," Alfnis answered, speaking the right Hellenic words for commerce and his own safety.

"Our spies report that Etruria arranges an alliance with Carthage."

"I wouldn't know. I'm a seafarer, not a magistrate."

"Have you Phoenician goods on board?" the officials interrogated. "They have crooked ways but we like their goods from the East."

"We have none."

This discourse troubled Alfnis. His last words were half-truth. The Plentiful planned to trade with Phoenician Sea People next season.

Short-winded and tired, Alfnis said to Venu. "We've paid dearly for our passage, in flax, barley, iron and tin, but our purpose remains, to steer ourselves near Attica's peninsula until Athenai's port town."

"You talk to me as if I'm a fellow seafarer," Venu said.

"You are now. There are strangers in this new territory to the east who would enslave you."

"It is you who enslaves me. You're the pirate." A shiver ran through Venu's body.

"We haven't stockpiled javelins of war. I bartered for shields and helmets in case we're attacked."

"You could keep swords under the deck," Venu said.

"Our ancestors were pirates. We're merchants, seeking goods to bring Etruria."

"What of the oarsmen? Didn't you capture them?"

"They're slaves, sons of Carthaginian slaves, disobedient on land. But they're not in chains and neither are you."

Alfnis hasn't made me a slave. I've been cared for, like a father his son, Venu thought and repented meekly, "I have erred. I offended you. I'll stay close to the ship."

Alfnis' hugged Venu. "The truth is you're a good boy with a strong imagination. Be safe, my child."

51

Eager to please Alfnis, Venu worked from dawn to dusk, attending crewmen, maintaining ropes, sails and the hull's wooden planks.

Slight winds pushed <u>The Plentiful</u> in a mild cool climate along the limestone Hellenic coast inhabited by goat-herders, bee keepers, growers and gatherers, fishermen, poets and orators who eked out a living the way they had for eons. Their charismatic gods, revered even by Etruscans, blessed them to work the unusable land to full advantage. What contrast to Etruria's esculent gardens.

The ship docked at Piraeus, a working village on the sea. A resilient alliance between Etruria and Hellas, brought on by two centuries of piracy and warfare before truce, made this stay essential for each empire's growth. However dubious the Athenians were, a trade agreement permitted <u>The Plentiful</u> to moor and be restored for seaworthiness.

Piraeus was dull after Corinthos. Athenai, a half day's walk was where seafarers wanted to go after they took on nautical supplies.

"In Corinthos, the people called me 'Etruscan Boy,' not 'Tarchna Boy.' They named our region, not our city. When we get to Athenai, I'll say I'm Etruscan," Venu said.

"Etruscan would identify you better than Tarchna," Alfnis answered as they walked on the road to the Hellenic main city. "The name poses strength and power. I'll use it too."

Athenai's sacred temple of marbled columns soared above the market place. It belonged to the famed goddess, Athena. In her warrior's helmet, she carried spear and shield, but her chameleon personality could also be dainty and serene.

"Let's climb up, Alfnis," Venu said, wanting to touch the translucent stone platform, walls and statues and be closer to the temple's beauty.

"Never. It's not our birthright. Citizens don't worship there as the Tarchna do in our sacred temples, except once a year to celebrate Athena's birth."

In the market place, an impassioned orator was entertaining with written verses from a scroll. The people listened attentively and conferred about his themes when pleased.

"What are they saying?" Venu asked Alfnis, liking the foreign rhythm. "Why do they get excited?"

"They're dreamers," Alfnis replied. "They dream of a virtuous society where artisans, poets, thinkers and warriors work together for the good of the cosmos."

Alfnis listened with the Athenians, having lived among them during enough cold seasons to know their ideas. Pleasure crossed his face as the poet recited tales of gods and goddesses, half-men, half-beasts who were overthrown by warriors.

"Tell me more about these dreamers," Venu said.

"Learn Hellenic," Alfnis joked. "I've had to. That's how I learn about *politikos*."

"What's that?"

"Acts of dishonest wealthy Hellenics."

Venu surprised Alfnis. Hellenic came easily to him for landsmen near the vessel or on the town road spoke the language. Whenever he went into the city, Venu absorbed words from shopkeepers and vendors at the grand agora. Their hands and faces taught him more words. They didn't barter for goods like Etruscans, but haggled with coin leverage like Corinthians.

Flush with good trade, Alfnis gave Venu metal pieces. "Buy a new tunic. You've outgrown yours."

Strutting back like a seafarer, he said to Alfnis, "I won my price at the cloth merchant when I told him I was a wayfarer. Here are two tunics for the price of one."

A cold blast of northern air kept <u>The Plentiful</u> stationed in Piraeus where Venu heard how the Athenians, full of new ideas, were organizing the city-state.

"They are less light-hearted than we," Venu observed. "They don't walk with Etruscan grace or have mirthful faces."

"How do you have so many friends among them?" Alfnis asked. "It's dumbfounding that you can see these foreigners clearly."

"When I try to speak their language, I tell them how much I like Athens," Venu said. "They're so long-tongued that they invite companionship."

The Athenians were dreamers, like Alfnis had said, but they were creative thinkers, purveyors of artistic beauty, who spoke incessantly about their own significance wherever they went. Poets spread words throughout Attica and the Great Sea, talking like they were at one with the gods, preserving heritage tales at festivals and public markets.

Once Venu became fluent, he went often to hear the traveling reciters. They told tales of mystical heroes whose lives were doomed and of gods who resembled humans, fighting in dust and muck. Passages were told again and again about the wrath of Achilles the warrior, greatest hero of the Trojan War, and Hector, great defender of Troy.

The poets knew about that ancient ten-year war, brought on by a golden apple given by Paris to goddess Aphrodite, and the consequences for those at Troy. They knew of brave King Odysseus whose wild adventures took years of wandering, descending into Hades, meeting the Cyclops, and then the romance of getting home.

"Could we Etruscans be Trojans?" Venu asked Alfnis after hearing the poets. "They call us 'Trus' which sounds like 'Troy.' Perhaps Aeneas of Troy sailed to the Italic Peninsula with thirty ships in past saeculae."

"A fine question. Who knows? We mix with all."

The warming season came fast, one day rain and cold, the next a hot sun that brought flower blooms on hillsides. The Plentiful lived up to its name, stocked with olive oil, vases and urns with specific names of *krater* and *hydria*. Set to continue journey, they slipped away from the pier on a bright dawning to weave through the Cycladic Islands whose limpid water evoked the myths of Hellas.

Heading across proven sea routes using islands as stepping-stones, the ship reached one every night to eat and sleep. These bleached rock islands randomly rose from the sea, non-tillable chunks of land, sparsely populated with fishermen living meagerly, awaiting passing boats for talk and trade. On whatever beach space there was, the crew would pray to the gods not to drown them in these waters that brought frightful storms.

"These islands aren't good for anything, save giving birth to the Hellenic god Apollo at Delos or burying oarsmen. There was a fisherman, stranded

181

from his wrecked ship in a storm, who we took with us," Alfnis said as they sailed on to a small gravel bay.

The well-built <u>Plentiful</u> went further east to a trade station on the western coast of Anatolia. Hotter than ever, the sun dried the seafarers' skins, tanned like the Hellenics who waved from shore.

"This place seems familiar," Venu said to Alfnis when they were on ground. "Is it Troy? It's foreign, yet known."

"This is Lydia. Some think that Lydians are our ancient ancestors. Their tongue sounds much like ours. They're admirable seafarers and bring silken textiles, silver, gold and ivory trinkets from the edge of the East. Prince-priest Zilath and nobles crave their goods, so we stop here."

The Lydians were like his own Tarchna friends. "Will we ever go home?" Venu asked.

"Soon our return journey begins," Alfnis said warm-heartedly.

52

From the ship's railing, Alfnis and Venu viewed the unpredictable sea that went beyond the cosmos. Sometimes it was impossible to tell if they were going east or west.

"Rocks, trees, hills or fields are markers to help people get from one road to another. When I ride my horse to the hunt, I see where to go," Venu told Alfnis. "The prize of land people is boar and stag."

"Nets of sea-catch are what I know, not the hunt. Our prize is fish, not meat," Alfnis said, bonding with the boy as they talked about everything under Aplu's sun. "You think horses are better than ships?"

"A ship depends on winds. If the water is muddy or has seaweed, the oarsmen can't see where rocks or sea monsters are," Venu replied.

"You're right about sea monsters. If a ship loses its way at night, sea monsters crash it against the rocks."

"On land, a horse can find home."

"The Fates chose me to care for a rich city child," Alfnis answered, amused when Venu compared the two. "I'm a seafarer, born in a port village of shanty houses, not a city like Tarchna."

Detached from the mother ship, Alfnis and his crew guided their small boat into Gravisca. Gods of the netherworld had blown hoary breaths on the port, selecting diseased victims, fleeing with Anneia, leaving survivors to rebuild.

The village wasn't lifeless. New immigrants lined up at the harbor's temple, holding votive statues and oil lamps, worshipping their gods. "Aphrodite! Demetra! Hera!"

"They're Hellenic, not Etruscans. Why are these sorry-eyed people in Tarchna's port?" Venu asked, puzzled.

"They're artisans and merchants captured by our warriors. They don't want to be here but they are."

"Seven seasons was this voyage. I'm back on Etruscan soil!" Relief swept over Venu, mixed with an ache for his dead mother. He walked with Alfnis to the town center for a horse cart to take them up the Tarchna road. "The gods give a blessing by bringing me home."

"The Great Sea honored you," Alfnis reminded him.

The cart rumbled alongside the swamps, climbed around Tarchna's walls and through the main gate towards the court temple.

"You missed the street to my father's house."

Alfnis shifted his body on the leather seat. "We're going to Prince-priest Zilath."

"I don't want to," Venu said in a hurt voice. "What does he want from me?"

"The choice isn't yours. When we reached port, a little old man came aboard to say that Zilath gives your destiny."

With no escape, Venu dragged his feet, wondering what method of death awaited him.

"The son of Vel Porenna and Anneia the Healer," Alfnis presented. "Venu Laris."

At a loss, the boy knelt and lowered his head.

"Rise up and let me see your chin," Zilath ordered. "Brown-skinned. Shipmaster Alfnis, are you sure he's the son?"

"His skin burned, blistered and turned color from sitting watch in the mast. He sights vessels. He counts trade. In Athenai, he learned Hellenic. He's valuable."

Venu jumped up. "Of course I'm the son or you wouldn't have forced me here."

"Feisty. It runs in that untamed family," Zilath chortled.

"How will you kill me? Will you strangle, stone or drown me?"

"I don't murder noble children."

"What do you want then?"

"Give me truth. Do you want to be with your father in Cisra?"

"Isn't he in Tarchna?" Venu asked, "Does he visit my sister Arith? Don't send me to Cisra."

"Why not?"

Venu boldly stepped up to the throne. "My sister would beat me. I know what she does," he said and whispered in the prince-priest's ear.

Zilath said in disgust, "The sister is licentious. This boy is an innocent. He is Tarchna born and of quality. He will serve me."

Reassured, Venu smiled. "And I pledge my life to you, Zilath."

Alfnis had returned the boy to his rightful identity.

Like the Hellenics in Gravisca, Venu felt like a stranger in Tarchna. The feeling didn't stop when he arrived at his family's stately dwelling.

The man who opened the door wasn't his father, but he spoke kindly. "We've waited many seasons for you. I'm your brother-in-law, Parth."

Risa's eyes shined as her husband embraced the brother. She ran to hug Venu.

"This is Shipmaster Alfnis," Venu introduced. "He's taken me beyond our waters to the Great Sea."

"Come, Young Noble and bring the seafarer," Lethi said as the family cook laid out platters of meats, jugs of wine and fruit.

The luxury of reclining wasn't lost on Alfnis. His charge was a noble after all, not a swamp boy or lost soul.

Warmed with hospitality, each told a story. Risa described Zilath's marriage blessing over them, Vel's new position in Cisra, and the Great Prediction.

Parth said, "Your sister's laugh was irresistible. I had to marry her."

Alfnis talked of the ship and sea monsters with tentacles immersing seafarers until they suffocated.

"It's better to know they're there and not be able to see them," Venu said as if he personally met one.

"Venu's brave," Alfnis said at meal's end, aware that he would miss the boy. "Back to <u>The Plentiful</u> by dusk for me. I leave you safe in your family's care, my young friend."

Family? Venu thought. The family's not the same anymore. Mother's dead. Father moved to Cisra and lives with Arith and Ramnes. Risa and Parth own our house.

The house wasn't oppressive as when Venu left, nor did it show memories of Anneia and Vel's former household. Painted scenes decorated walls, new couches and low tables replaced old. Blooming anemones garnished every room.

"Because of Father, we've made changes." Risa walked Venu through the house. "We knocked out a wall between two front rooms for a compartment when he visits. I chose our parents' room to birth children. My childhood room will be for them."

"This is your home, Venu," Parth added. "Be glad that it will always be."

"Not all is different. You have your same room," Risa spoke to her brother gently, seeing fright in his eyes after all his boasting of sea monsters. "It will help you find your path."

"Home," Venu said dully, jumbled at being in his birthplace, confusion he didn't understand.

53

The sea in his memory, Venu resumed training with other boys on the woodland hunt. They made fun of him. He was older than they but hadn't mastered the horse, or basic tasks to become a traditional Tarchna.

Confined to Tarchna, his life was filled with Risa and Parth's children, his nephews, Culni and Ari, and niece, Larthia. To Venu, they became brothers and sister.

When Venu's boyhood passed to youth, his father sent for him. Compliantly, Venu went to Cisra, staying in Arith and Ramnes' house. His sister and husband were aloof, ridiculing him for wearing garments unfit for a noble and riding a horse poorly. Their son, Avele was occupied at becoming a young noble, and ignored Venu.

"Your behavior was despicable. You ran away!" Vel charged.

"Father, you roam to find rocks. I roamed on water, taken by the gods," Venu answered humbly. "I came back."

Vel's hostility softened. "Let's say your behavior was one of childhood. You're a young man and must take your place in the cosmos. You'll be a rock finder with me."

Venu tried his father's work. Neither metals nor tufa held appeal.

Parth apprenticed Venu to road builders. To learn the trade, he had to layer roadbeds with pebbles, and then top with stone pavings. His hands blistered. Ineptly, he stubbed his toes on rock piles, unable to judge distances.

"Road work isn't for you," Parth observed. "You speak more of your days at sea with Alfnis than of building our city. Perhaps your strange experience has given you a new vision."

Venu remained unsettled in his future.

Risa watched Venu's bungled attempts at farming. "You don't love the earth. The sea nymphs call you."

"The gods have tricked me," Venu confided in Risa and Parth. "They made me yearn for Tarchna. Now I yearn for the sea. I don't belong here. I belong nowhere."

"Tarchna is too still after the bouncing ship," Risa said. "Better you a seafarer than a landsman."

Venu kissed his sister's cheek. "You've taken me in, nurtured me in years of my turmoil and raised me. You understand the truth of my disquiet."

On a day when Prince-priest Zilath was at market, Venu wormed past a guard and went up to him.

"You again?" Zilath said. "What do you want?"

"Although small in size, I am manly in style. Tarchna needs bounty of the cosmos that I will bring if you send me to sea, Zilath," Venu beseeched.

"I believe you," Zilath said, already counting wealth. "I'll make inquiry at Gravisca. The Port Master will signal when <u>The Plentiful</u> is in harbor."

Vel wasn't gracious when he heard Venu's seafaring plans. "You're a child of Tarchna nobles. You defy me. You're not of us. I deny your birth to our family."

"I can't help what I am," Venu disputed. "Land discomforts me. The sea lured me once. It lures me still."

"You're not my son," Vel said, deadly calm.

With a pang of regret for what he had to do, Venu became a seafarer.

54

Zilath and the gods of fate granted Venu's wish. He went to the Great Sea. Watery god Nethuns tantalized him with hypnotic, lapping waves and crashing surf. Tyrannical and capricious, Nethuns cajoled one moment and then played havoc with choppy waves, injecting the effervescent sea into Venu's blood.

With confidence, Venu rode out storms, surviving because of the blood-hued amulet in his cloth belt. The stone keepsake that Vel had gifted Anneia had become his, and he knew it would withstand any offense he might cause Nethuns.

On each voyage, <u>The Plentiful</u> upheld its title, gathering copious amounts of goods on the north and south coasts, traversing the sea to Carthage, sailing eastward for Hellas and other ancient places. The ship roved uncharted waters, selling raw lead, zinc and copper from Tarchna's side of the Tolfa. Alfnis argued prices for olive oil and metal trinkets.

Venu learned sea lore of mariners and ethics of warrior pirates along with studying the sea and guiding stars. He had been an empty-headed youth who left the land of his father and became a successful seafarer. When Zilath promoted Alfnis to "High Master, Sea Merchant," Venu became second crewman.

"With this new title, Zilath pressures me. He demands treasures at any price," Alfnis told Venu.

"Any price? I'm not a sea warrior. Plundering isn't for me."

"Zilath wants gold, amber and jewels," Alfnis replied with sternness reserved for lowest oarsmen. "I do as commanded and so must you."

"I won't do it."

"You're a seafaring merchant. Sea gods and Oceanids bring you home from precarious storms. But if you fail Zilath, you'll be thrown to the fishes."

"Winds must be in our favor to board the Sea People's vessels after they leave ports. We'll take what they carry," Alfnis told his men. "Piracy without killing. Take care not to shed blood. Each of you takes an oath of secrecy."

Should they refuse, they knew they'd suffer a miserable fate.

Making sure the crew outnumbered their prey, they claimed friendship with delicacies of quail eggs, dried meats, cheeses and wines brought from Etruria's bounty. At a signal, Alfnis' crew threw sacks over their foes' heads and tied hands behind their backs, securing them to the mast.

Out-maneuvering other ships, the High Master and Venu brought considerable wealth to Tarchna. Zilath traded this contraband with Cisra, Veii or Vulci until Etruria's cities had a plethora of household goods and tomb relics.

Zilath prospered. Without knowing the source, Tarchna's citizens, including the Laris-Vella clan received distributions.

"My banquet comes next season," Risa said to Venu when he was on leave from a voyage.

"We're taking a hold of blackware north to Aethelia in exchange for iron. A short mission, but the sea decides our arrival." Venu unraveled a bolt of cloth from Aegypt. "Fashion a banquet tunic with this."

His presence was not to be. The load from the iron smelters unbalanced The Plentiful. The ship floundered. Unable to steer to Gravisca's docks, it smashed into another ship. While the crew praised Nethuns on the beach, Venu stayed on board with Alfnis, calculating the loss, examining and patching damage.

"Eat and drink from our jars," the port townsmen invited, setting up tables and stools to rejoice in survival. Soon, cheered by wine, the townsmen idly gossiped. The seafarers, who knew nothing of Venu's family, got an earful.

"She's a harlot," one said. "Always was."

"Yes, and the wife of a Cisra advisor," another put in.

"They're laughing in Tarchna, best banquet they've ever had, some say."

"And snickering in Cisra."

"In front of the honored banquet giver."

"She fondled him while that one saw."

"Arith of the Laris Clan will do anything. That's how bold she is."

"The Road Builder is a rogue, too."

Jabbering stopped when Alfnis and Venu got to the tables. Venu already heard. The names had to be a coincidence. It couldn't be his family. If it were, Risa and Parth's reputations would be smeared. Here they talked. Word could spread throughout Etruria.

Mortification! Venu's head was on fire. Regard aside for his dilapidated ship, darkened as the night was, he procured a horse and raced with Tinia's wind, straight to Tarchna.

55

Venu pulled reins on the galloping horse.

Haruspex dozed against the wall of the Laris-Vella dwelling, shaded from Aplu's sun by a neighbor's house.

"Horses don't race in these streets, Venu," Haruspex yowled at him. "You've come three days too late for Risa's cresting banquet."

"You seem healthy, my friend and don't mince words." Breathless, Venu slid his leg over the horse's flank, showering road dust from his ride. He tethered the lathered horse in the animal yard and banged at the door.

No one answered. He went around to the front entrance and rapped harder. The door opened three fingers worth.

Wearily, Lethi said, "Shh! She sleeps."

"You greet me more like a stranger than your former charge," Venu steamed. "What's amiss? Why is Risa asleep in the mid-day? Where's Parth?"

"On the far Tarchna road," Lethi replied and shut the door. Aggravated by the servant's rudeness, Venu flogged his horse onward, but the horse couldn't trot fast after the arduous overnight journey from Gravisca.

Scurrying like a squirrel, Haruspex kept to the shrubs, out of sight, tracking Venu by smelling dust from horse hooves.

From the upper hill, Venu watched Parth set the groma, the four-pronged plumb lines dangling precisely on the intersection.

The last days weighed heavily on Venu. Putting aside brotherly affection, he slithered down the hill as quickly as he would the ship's mast. His toe hit a rock. Angered further, he raised it to smash Parth's skull. "How could you be calm in your work when gossip surrounds you? You've dishonored the Laris Clan."

His back to Venu, Parth adjusted the groma. "Your shadow tells your intent. If you value your own life, think what would be cast upon us."

He spun around and threw himself at Venu. Off balance, Venu dropped the rock. They somersaulted into a thistle bush. Venu got up. Parth crawled behind and nabbed his legs.

"You don't see what you do. My wife shies from me. Our Cisra sister has degraded me."

Slammed into earth, unable to move, Venu spit dirt and blood from his split lip. "Slander in port ...honor," he panted. "Forgive me."

Parth released Venu and brushed dust from his own eyes. He stretched his limbs. "My aching bones don't care for fights."

"If Ramnes finds out about you and Arith, his prince-priest might cause trouble." Venu swaggered to his knees and righted his tunic.

"I reclined with her for the time it takes to eat a pear and drink a goblet of wine."

"How long might that be?"

"I can't remember. The wine was syrupy."

"So you dallied with her."

"She made my manhood quicken. What man wouldn't with such provocation?"

56

Venu delayed seeing the ruins of <u>The Plentiful</u>. The ship had broken up and the seafarers would have to wait another season for one to be built. He guarded Risa, weakened by her miscarriage after the cresting banquet ordeal, and watched Parth for signs of infidelity. He saw a vague withdrawal of the sociable man who kept the household on course, working to safeguard and increase his family's wealthy position, showing responsibility in front of the children at table or public games.

"Parth and I talk of children and work, not intimately as we used to," Risa said to Venu, reclining in the dining place. "What has happened to stimulating talk of harmony in the cosmos, of gods' and goddesses' myths, of life's interests? He conceals his thoughts and I do mine from him."

"Roadwork will take Parth from home. He builds new roads north and south, going at new moon," Venu relayed to Risa.

"South to Cisra," Risa said tonelessly. "Parth must be bedding Arith when on this construction, for he never speaks of her."

"Don't anguish."

"How can I help it? He breaks union with me by having her."

"I care for you both. It's hard to take sides."

"Marriage has many sides. My marriage with Parth had gone well until my ill-starred banquet. I shouldn't have had it. We quarreled. Sorrow made me lose the babe."

Venu tried to lighten her self-deprecation. "Maybe the time wasn't auspicious."

"Zilath timed my banquet, otherwise my destiny would have been different."

"Destiny makes us do what we least expect. I should have had the traditional life of a noble, training and livelihood, family and children. I question whether sea is better than land or land is better than sea."

"Is union too complicated for you, Venu? Is that why you haven't married?"

"What would I do with a wife on land when I'm not?"

"You don't have to have a love union."

"I like women, but want none after seeing disease-ridden harlots who blight seafarers to agony in Great Sea ports. Some seafarers die in my care when no herbs can cure."

"The augur-priests say that you must behave in the manner of your birth and procreate," Risa recited.

"Procreate? No. The sea is my life. I love its danger and the fear of being swallowed by Great Sea god Nethuns. It's a challenge to ride Tinia's storms, great waves forming mountains. I work the ropes of the mast on bright days, basking in Aplu's sun as we sail through clear calm waters. Then I want to be nowhere else."

"You make the cosmos sound mysterious," Risa said, envying his daring.

After <u>The Plentiful II</u>, a duplicate of the first ship, was launched at Gravisca dock, Venu waited until his sister recovered from her trauma. Then he packed his travel-worn baggage.

"I must leave again. I need to feel the sea under my feet," he said and went to meet Alfnis and the crew.

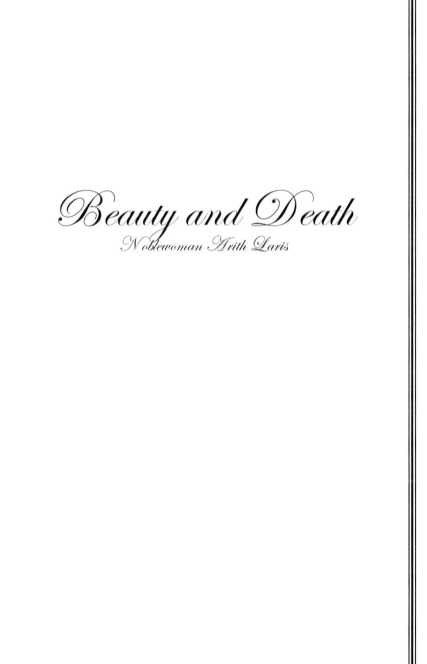

Beauty and Death

Noblewoman Arith Laris

57

"Leave, Arith, before the sun is high." Lethi shuffled around the room picking up layers of tunics, scarves, necklaces and armlets. "It's best you go."

"You wake me too early," Arith yawned from bed, unflustered by her former servant. "Don't you think my banquet was more lavish? Definitely larger."

"Get up." Lethi pulled back the covers. "Your banquets were different, just as you two are."

"Hers was dull," Arith replied and waited for Lethi to comb her hair as she had done since childhood. "Worst of all, that smile of hers. Risa dupes kin and so-called friends with insincerity."

"Her smile is like faces on the gods' statues. A true Etruscan golden smile. Her friendships are true."

"My smile may be less, but my body is more desirable. Risa looks like a youth."

"Arghh," Lethi said. "Tarchna born, but living in Cisra has made your nose stick up. You don't care who you offend. You may be a great beauty, but your mouth is sour. You think you're better than anyone else."

"I am better. Prettier, taller, smarter, richer. Tell Risa that."

"Get ready for your journey. Which tunic do you want?"

"The one of amber color and olive hue cloak," Arith chose. "That will serve for a sunless day."

Not wanting Arith's enmity, Lethi picked up a speckled scarf. "Take this lovely cloth to veil you."

"My gold brooch with clasp goes with this tunic," she said, thinking that her appearances might attract men on the road.

"Don't wear jewels."

"You worry too much. The Osco-Umbrians are dead."

"Those cut-throat bandits who murdered your grandparents had children. Their children might have been taught to hate."

"Father told me they surrendered to Etruscan power," Arith said, "and Hellenics and Latins of the southern Italic Peninsula have retreated."

Opulently dressed, Arith went to the open horse-drawn chariot. Her horse servant, who doubled as her driver, waited in a tunic befitting a noble. If approached, Arith's elegance would show dignity accorded magistrates, and if she planned well, Ramnes would be a magistrate by his late cresting.

Lethi was wrong. Danger had ended. She could travel without threat. Yet she carried a new bronze amulet from Aegypt for precaution, brought by Cisra's sea warriors to ward off the evil eye.

Outside Tarchna's gates, the chariot's creaking wooden wheels labored up the new road that shortened the journey to less than a day in good weather. Consecrated by Tinia, Parth had his men cut those vertical rock walls to lay the dried clay. Overhead, roots hanging like elders' beards, sprouted from the mountain's level top. An ethereal mist hovered, as if shadows of the ancestors permeated it with song. Arith loved to go through this passage, a lush reprieve from both sides of the trachytite mountain that divided Tarchna territory from Cisra.

Few took the coastal route from the port that went through mud flats teeming with vultures, scavenging for fresh kill from The Disease. Travelers feared catching the illness, a horrid death that left corpses sunk in the mire until heat season when they could be retrieved. No one spoke of the illness that snuffed life fast.

Arith counted six transports on the new road. Their occupants waved but she was in no mood to greet. Feigning sleep, she sat back on her cushions, drawing the scarf over her head like a mourning shroud. Her horse, as fine as any Phocaean stallion, forged ahead of the others. Then, her servant slowed the horse.

From the roadside brushwood, a rustling noise startled her. An animal jumped out and ambled alongside. More human than animal, its malformed, blood-soaked hand grazed her cloth. "So, fine lady," it said, never taking its eyes off her, "you've had your amusement. Don't think the gods won't retaliate."

"How dare you debase me," Arith yelped, wondering if the servant could hear. She bunched her tunic to her cleavage, fumbling for the amulet to shine at him. "I do no wrong."

"Vetisl, god of darkness curses your impropriety. Brother to brother, sister to sister, bonds must be unbroken." He spat vehemently on a rock. "May you find ashes in your bed."

"You dare to defame me, you filthy reader of entrails." Arith shivered in the day's muggy heat. Ashes of the ancestors were known to haunt one's life with misery. She shouted to her horse servant, "Drive on. Run over this leech if you must."

As soon as she spoke, he wasn't there to tread upon, gone into the thicket without the howl of one hit by a chariot.

58

Arith held the amulet, willing it to keep her safe. "Driver, did you see that creature? Did it come after us from Tarchna? Did you hear it speak?"

"I'm a lowly servant. I only attend to get you home." He worked the horse slower through the Tolfa side of the pass, having enough sense not to talk to the noble's wife when her mood was dark.

A horse's frolicking would have sickened Arith. The ride steadied her, full from food and drink. Her younger sister's banquet was a mistake, given ten years late. Why Zilath accoladed Risa was a mystery. Vel should have provided it before Risa had children.

Arith had been obligated to go. Few enlivened the wearisome banquet. Childhood friends were too occupied with their lives. Her former lovers bulged from piggish feasting. Good fortune was that they were fat and married.

Disdain for her sister hadn't waned. Risa was such a bore, unexciting and unadventurous. How she wedded Parth was a mystery. She didn't deserve such a good-looking man with intelligent eyes, contoured cheeks and muscular stature.

Arith snickered as it came to mind what she had done when the guests engaged with spouses. What a challenge to prove that Parth could roam.

"Join me a while, Parth," Arith had called pleasantly as he went from couch to couch. "You're a better host than Ramnes. Pity my solitary state with my husband at Maru's errands. I'm so lonely."

Parth pillowed himself at the wall. Arith dangled a ripe honeyed plum from the fruit bowl and he reached for it. She snagged it back, took a bite and offered it again.

Her eyes willed him to look at her. "This moist fruit is as tasty as my tongue."

He ate the plum and spit the pit.

Arith let the juice dribble from her mouth. Flicking her tongue, she laid her fingertips on Parth's lips, down his beard to his neck and chest, onto the fabric covering his manhood.

"You're a temptress, Arith." Parth turned to the guest on his right.

With his snub, she slyly dropped a tincture of liquid in his wine goblet and settled on the cushions, rippling her fingers across his thigh, stopping at his knee.

"You're jealous that I love Risa."

"How can you love her when your manhood grows at my touch?"

"Haven't you love at your home? Or do you want what Risa has?"

"And what do you have? A woman who strays. She looks brazenly at a crafter and he at her with understanding." Arith then pointed at the Flutist. "She lusts for him, too."

"Impossible." Parth spit the plum pit into a bowl.

"He smiles at her like she's his harlot, not a servant to noble."

Parth swigged the wine dregs. "You imagine much."

Arith laughed, waiting for the golden potion to take effect. Bartered to her by a nomadic Phoenician, the syrup was known to light fires within men, to envy, to covet. Provoking jealousy in her victims was the catalyst for unearthing useful secrets or desires. They would succumb to her. She had drizzled the same tincture at Cisra's banquets to learn of magistrates' plotting, and the workings of warriors and merchants. Her method ensured that Ramnes would be the governing eyes of Prince-priest Maru.

"Enough play." Curtly, Parth got up.

"Play? Lust is not play. Play is for childhood. When we were children, I played a game with Risa. I would get her to bring me one of the boiled duck eggs from the cooking room shelf, ones that mother saved for a festive meal. She would refuse until I'd say, 'If you don't bring an egg, then you must take the food basket to Old Grandmother who lives at the dark woods' edge where spirits dwell. It tickled me that she was scared of that old woman who babbled about ancestors, smelled of bat dung and lived in a mucky hut. Risa would shrink into a ball without a word, frightened not to do what I wanted, pathetic with fear."

At Arith's words, Tinia's rain struck, its force as hateful as her story.

"I'll make sure the animals are dry." Parth put on his cloak and headed out of the courtyard, unaware that Risa preceded him.

Arith was delighted. Both host and hostess were gone, leaving her as next of kin to preside over the banquet.

"Wine," Arith directed the cupbearers.

A bronze vat was placed on the low table at Arith's feet. From the second vial, attached to a secret belt within her tunic, she brought out a pomegranate and herbal compound known to cause sexual delirium.

"We need to enliven these festivities. Bring goblets and chestnut meats," Arith commanded the servants and mixed the compound into the wine. "Pour another round. Miss no one."

How long it took to drug the guests depended on how quickly The Flutist's melody lulled them. From his corner, with his muted sounds The Flutist charmed the banquet from lethargy to stimulation.

Lasciviously, an export merchant smiled at Arith, and she went to his side. He put his arm around her shoulder and stroked it.

Arith unclasped her tunic's brooch and held her breast to the merchant's mouth. "Suckle me like a babe at its mother."

59

The merchant wouldn't remember Arith from Risa's banquet, nor would guests in their own enchantments.

She mused about what she had done, small gratification for this tedious day's journey. The chariot approached the Tolfa markings to Cisra. Upward. Higher. Going above the fields and dwellings was as exalting as when she married Noble Ramnes Vibenna of Cisra's hedonistic court, getting out of less indulgent Tarchna.

Flicking dust from her cloak, she thought back to the heated lovemaking that started her marriage. How monotonous it became when she was with child. Her body grew cumbersome until she was frantic. Bearing a child was detestable. After Avele's birth she wanted no more and remedied herself with silphion herb sap. Procured secretly by Old Woman, it was traded from the hills of Cyrene across the Great Sea. The valuable giant fennel came at a price. Arith had to give the hag a gold ingot from her chain.

The sap failed, making her beget for three painful moons. Messy with mucous blood, she lost the second child. Ramnes' interest in her wilted like an un-watered flower. He took to gaming and sports. That was fine with her. She didn't want more children.

The sap had a lasting effect. Arith's beauty ripened with a new urge for sensuality when Ramnes worked long days. Elder nobles began to admire her.

Openly she lusted for these more sexually experienced men, quickly couching at feasts or meeting them in the woods.

Effortlessly she deceived her husband, pleasing him by listening to his politics and hinting answers that gave time for her own exploits. Ramnes was not as slow as she presumed. Her deception served his purpose. It drove him to his true love—ambition.

"How smart I am," he would say. "My solutions bring me higher in Maru's opinion."

Through Arith's cunning, Ramnes became a different man in his cresting. He weaseled into the graces of the elders, boosting their self-images and lessening worries. They repaid him, and consequently Arith, with great wealth and position as Advisor.

"Ramnes the Crafty One," his opponents joked, envious of his status, a step below the magistrates.

"Don't let wealth or station in life guide you," the priests who taught ancient laws said. "The gods give fortune and each person applies it to his cause."

Arith would have loved to announce that she, not the gods, helped the destiny of others and brought her abundance. Those pious priests were self-righteous, yet their coffers were full of bribe gifts. Without her, Ramnes would be an underling. He needed her. She was his backbone. What bliss if the elders knew how she helped Ramnes make decisions.

The chariot pitched into a flat road and skidded. An unshaven shepherd and his flock obstructed the way. The driver yelled and the shepherd prodded the sheep until he saw Arith. His head jerked up and he licked his mouth, wiping spittle on his sleeve. Dried secretions were on his tunic.

The shepherd's dirtiness was appealing. She eyed him until he lowered his head. Lazily he moved the rest of his herd, whistling as he led them by.

Impatient from the delay, Arith's driver beat the horse into a canter. The countryside was a contrast to Tarchna's spelt fields. Cultivated barley, gardens of peas and beans made a patchwork on the Tolfa slopes. Vines and trees grew heartily on mountain ridges of glassy hard rock produced by volcanic fire. She looked for common landmarks from one village to another leading to Cisra.

Risa's banquet kept coming to mind. Arith's aphrodisiacs thrown into the wine hadn't loosened tongues. She hadn't lured Parth to her bed, and the potion hadn't worked secrets from him.

A clean mild breeze from the Great Sea crossed the pastureland that led to Cisra. The horse kicked a stone and bolted forward. A new sense of wildness rushed through her. "Whip him on faster!"

Cisra's walls came into view. The driver reined the stallion and chariot to trot for a noblewoman's entrance. They went through the covered gate to the city, a massive stone arch adorned with sculptures of the hunter god chasing stags, symbols of Cisra's authority over the cosmos. Sophisticated Cisra, intelligent, exhilarating and adored.

More exciting than Tarchna's celebrations was the up-coming prince-priest's banquet to honor his wife, Maruth. Arith imagined the pageantry. She and Ramnes could flaunt two new prancing horses, saddled and harnessed with tooled leather. On their way, people would admire the ornate wooden carriage with cut designs and figures.

At the banquet she could show Ramnes her genius by making up tidbits for the magistrates to worry about. She'd wear a tunic of latest fashion, a brilliant concoction of gossamer cloth set off by armlets and necklaces, but she needed to go to market to see what other trinkets Ramnes might get her.

Arith and driver drove through a market aisle. How delightful to see the array of goods Cisra offered. So much to possess. A tiny glass vial for her perfume. A gauzy cloth of patterned hues to swathe her skin. A gold armlet of animal designs inset with cabochon gemstones.

Nobles choose bone seals to mark documents. Priests took carved ivory figurines and containers. Doddering elders selected fruit bowls.

No need for combs. The tradesman from Norchia sat at his comb table. He had once followed her home, bringing elaborately carved ivory combs from Africa. Their lovemaking had been erotic. Unexpectedly, Ramnes ruined the rest of the dalliance when he came from the court to get a warmer cloak. He might have seen the warm depression on the cushions.

Dancing from one man to the next always roused her. In Cisra, she could do as she wished to excess, without punishment. Encounters like the one with the tradesman made her love Cisra.

60

The maze of paved streets two carts wide, broader than Tarchna's, took them to Arith's grand home. Lined up in front, the household staff gave ready speeches. "Welcome, Mother of the House. The gods have brought you safely."

"Look after these bundles. I'll open them later. Heat water for my bath." Disregarding their salutations, she walked through the tiled portico, more a warrior in charge of the fleet than a noblewoman.

Ramnes reclined in the dining place, eating Phoenician dates without glancing up.

"You were cruel to leave me alone when you knew Risa's banquet was so small," Arith pouted. "What new festival has Maru announced?"

"Honoring those born under the sign of the Moon. Your family's city will be irate that they don't have as many celebrations as we."

"Everything is better in Cisra. Our clothes for banquets and feasts are more stylish."

"How are your nephews and niece?"

"A relief that annoying bunch were sent off. They throw bits of Vel's bucchero clay in the house and mingle with slave children. They pet the yard animals instead of whacking them to move. On the streets they yell and bounce balls. Culni mimics hunters by sneaking into bushes, terrorizing the servants who care for the yard. Ari never walks, but runs in the house, quiet only when he scribbles strange pictures on his slate. Then he embraces his mother for all to see. And that littlest one, Larthia, bangs pots and pans until the animals are skittish."

"They're poorly trained, unlike our Avele. He's a strapping tall youth, intelligent in his questions and replies," Ramnes said. "He does as told. He'll be groomed as a noble's consul."

"A noble's consul is fine for him. We'll dress him in proper tunics."

"I'll teach him the manner of talk. He'll go with a magistrate's son to learn politics."

"His face is too open, too honest."

"We'll improve on that," Ramnes agreed.

Arith smiled as best she could after the ugly ride from Tarchna and took the plate of dates from Ramnes.

She went to her rooms to shed that ghastly journey's dust, wanting to forget Parth's indifference and the bland sister she despised. Into her bath water, Arith swirled bay laurel leaves that blackened like ashes. Once more, words of that whining, monstrous haruspex went through her.

May you find ashes in your bed.
May you find ashes in your bed.
May you find ashes in your bed.

She couldn't get his curse out of her head. Panicky, she scratched her scalp and a tuft of hair pulled loose.

"What enemy is he, that horrid creature on the road? He's far and can't hurt me," she gibbered as she submerged in her tub, caressing her breasts with a bath cloth.

Arith was glad to be in Cisra. She jiggled her bronze amulet in her palm. Unbearably staid Tarchna was her past. Supreme Cisra was her life.

61

From the port of Pyrgi to Cisra, troves of imported merchandise rumbled in oxcarts to the central eighth day market for citizens to see. White cloaked augur-priests, black hooded fulguriators and haruspices weaved among the crowd looking at divine objects, bartering for favored sculptures of Tinia, Uni and Menvra, and household votive statues of Goddess of Hearth and Fire.

"Highest priest of priests, highest magistrate, see what we have," merchants called out.

Maru inspected the goods and went to his platform, trailed by a few magistrates. He announced, "Phoenicia now trades with us, more than Tarchna. Ostrich eggs from Africa, feathers from male peafowl, scarab talismans from Aegypt, bronze cauldrons etched with sphinxes, gold beads and silver pitchers—far places where the sun rises before it does here. Nobles, come get your vases incised with Hellenic myths."

Arith and Ramnes crammed with other nobles to get a vase. All were taken before Ramnes could get one.

The Magistrate of Trade began doling out stone carvings of gods or goddesses to elders for their courtyards. "Those foreign traders from the Great Sea countries leap like Nethuns' Oceanids to wield commerce with Cisra. They give us best wares in exchange for our metals and fabrications. Cisra's products are in demand."

"Keep a steadfast watch on our goods. Our people expect nothing less,"

Maru said, counting each piece as it was taken, knowing the very best wares never made it to market. They went straight to him for his perusal.

"We have to amend our course and give devotion to the gods. That's what Tarchna, that holier-than-holy city does," a magistrate inveighed, "or the Great Prediction might occur sooner."

"How would the magistrate know Tarchna's practices?" Ramnes scratched his forehead.

Because I've told him, Arith wanted to say. Instead she replied, "That magistrate is too outspoken. Maru is right. Get what we can now. Make certain you get what you are owed, Husband."

After each new moon, Maru beckoned his constituents to the massive court and sacred temple near the market place.

Dressed in short tunic of sea-urchin color as a show of opulence and gentility, Maru looked at the frieze over the wooden columns depicting a victorious sea battle, his victory. He waved his scepter and waited for the court's silence. The musician strummed his cithar. The highest augur-priest placed the crown of gold-incrusted laurel on Maru's thick tufts to nest like a bird.

The mood set for this critical assembly, Maru perched on his backless carved ebony chair. His face transformed from roundness to confident.

Somberly, his eleven magistrates, keepers of society's work, sat three steps lower, wearing floor-length tunics with official symbols of authority. In total, the twelve magistrates were a favorable number for Etruscan politics. Each had three personal advisors who stood at the court's periphery.

Ramnes was with them, neither a magistrate nor a personal advisor, but an anomaly. Thirteen magistrates would not be in accordance with law, but Ramnes ranked above the Magistrate of Building, responsible for making the City of the Dead the best one in Etruria. He was below other magistrates at assemblies but their intimate at banquets. At feasts, he sat within the shadow of the prince-priest.

"Name your accounts." Maru reviewed the circle of men with premeditated slowness, neither expecting nor receiving answers.

"Our fertile soil harvested the most barley this season," Magistrate of Goods bravely reported, not afraid of Maru. In charge of distributing the harvest's grains and produce, the task was larger than the small farm he was given for life. His invariable dependability was paid by his appointment of magistrate. "We're stocked for the cold."

"How many can we feed?" Maru said as a servant came with a platter of dried grapes. Maru selected the largest as if it were a gem, offering none.

Averting their eyes to not show craving, the magistrates knew there was no invitation to eat or drink.

"Everyone in our vicinity. There is plenty."

"The forests yield endurable wood from tall trees. Our ships sail to foreign shores and back without sinking," Magistrate of Trade said. "By the full moon we'll have two new ships."

"Capacity, Magistrate Spurinna?" Maru asked, calling this most respected trade magistrate by name. "What will they hold?"

"Fifty tonnages of rock metal to barter, Maru," Spurinna answered precisely. "Perhaps for Hellenic vases?"

"We have greater wealth than at our last meet," Magistrate of Mines said. "Our hills hold more lead, copper and iron in rock crevices. Vel Porenna, the Soil Sampler has discovered a new rich deposit in the Tolfa."

Approval buzzed through the court.

"No one speaks of our slaves." Maru sniffed the goblet of full-bodied red Etruscan wine taken from his servant, wary to set it on a table for an enemy to contaminate.

"They land regularly in Pyrgi, Puni or Palo. These ports are equipped with shackles and buckets. When they come ashore, we cleanse off flies and strip them, wash filth and puss before distribution."

"Are they guarded?"

"Warriors enlist slaves with spears at their backs," Magistrate of War said.

"They're better treated than in Carthage's fly-infested quarters. We'll capture more. Low class or high class doesn't matter. They all submit when we beat them. Use leather, not sticks as our ancestors did. Sooth them with music," Maru said, the sound of leather on skin exciting his manhood.

Magistrate of Cisra's Monuments spoke. "We work them diligently to proliferate our city with buildings for all to enjoy."

"We need more to build superb homes of great comfort," Magistrate of Building added.

"Us too," Magistrate of Water Courses scowled. "We need them to work in irrigation projects, to keep land fertile."

"Some don't mind being here. They know that if they work with fortitude, their children are freed," Magistrate Exchanger of Goods half-lied, not sure if what he said was part of the plan. "Cisra could send ships to the Hot Countries to round up boatloads of those creatures."

The magistrates and augur-priests were quiet. They may have dissented in group, but common interest was loyalty to Cisra, or their lives would be short.

"No one is against getting more slaves? Good. Let's continue. What says the Farm and Vineyard Magistrate?" Maru rinsed grape residue from his fingertips in a hot water bowl.

"He's tasted the harvest and is on his knees." Road Construction Magistrate broke the tension.

"... On his knees," they chortled, knowing his joke meant praying to Flufluns, god of the vineyard, who could reduce the pain of excessive drink.

"Much jammy wine he's had."

"Our organization is efficient." Maru rose and stretched his aching legs, irritated from that old horse accident. "This meeting ends."

Overcome by his own relevance, Maru wielded his scepter upward. "This season we'll show our wealth with grand feasts, festivals and hunts for everyone so Tarchna can see how we shine."

"You are most benevolent, kindest of prince-priests," the magistrates bellowed as the standing advisors applauded, wanting Maru's favors.

No one mentioned the Great Prediction.

62

Of all the rituals and custom instruction Maru was given by his predecessors on how to be prince-priest, his favorite was wisdom of the Lares and Penates household spirits of home and hearth. These spirits made him powerful.

"The gods give me what I want, for I am as wise as they, above mortals. The spectrum of gifts is my due. How else can it be? I am Maru," he said, clunking his scepter on the floor.

"You are revered, Maru, but there is gossip that you lift from the city coffers," his highest augur-priest said, trying to bring him to earthly standards.

"What blasphemy. Who calls me 'looter'?" Maru raved. "I don't care what's said. The gods give me the right to want more."

Relentlessly he craved new objects for his afterlife. He couldn't disprove hoarding an inlaid wood throne, four chariots decorated with war stories, six bronze incense braziers footed with lion paws, Hellenic amphorae, stacked vases, gold rings and armlets.

One morning Maru awoke in panic. He had dreamed of a razor slitting his throat. The night vision wouldn't recede. He sweated. His teeth chattered.

"Who would kill me?" He asked his highest augur-priest. "Our enemies aren't on our soil."

"Drink this tonic, a remedy for enlightenment. It will swell your popularity."

"I'm popular already."

"Ask your magistrates."

Assembled, Maru appraised each magistrate. "A traitor walks among us, one who brands me crook. So I gave bucchero for a Hellenic amphora and a few sacks of corn and beans for the Persian carpet. No cause for any to turn against me. I convey goodness to my people."

"Give up what you thieved," counseled one, knowing how much Maru had taken.

"Don't own up to that," said a second one who took more flour, olive oil and wine than his due.

"Helpful deeds are called for," contributed a third, an honest, but self-righteous soul.

Maru clenched his jaws. "So I must pacify the citizenry."

From the shadow of the court hall, a monotone voice boomed, "I am an elder and a priest. Give up gluttony to save your reign."

Incited by the elusive directive, Maru brawled, "You think I've become greedy. Not so. I keep the standard of highborn."

"So you mean that magistrates, nobles and elders' ashes would be interred in a few dedicated mounds in the City of the Dead, cremated in life-like funerary urns or in miniature house-shaped ossuaries. Common citizens would still pile in mass family graves. Slaves would be dumped into pits, disposed under layers of yonder soil. That won't work anymore. Maru, a floodgate of hostility has opened," the elder priest replied with a clear caveat that any could understand. "It's a new era."

"There must be another way to win back Cisra's favor." Maru flexed his muscles, aching from one of Tinia's approaching storms. "They could get extra food and wine."

"Not good enough."

"What then?"

"Share your burial grounds."

Maru squinted at the audience, looking for the faceless elder priest. "What does the word 'share' mean? You want burial grounds for yourself."

"I'm not a high magistrate. God Tinia must be obeyed."

Taken aback by what he could and couldn't do, Maru fell on his throne. All is not well for me, he thought petulantly. Codes of the Great Prediction may be true.

63

Along with building public monuments, construction continued for the City of the Dead. Maru and Ramnes watched the endless line of slaves going to the funerary valley.

"I need another tomb. The one I built when young goes to Uncle Thefarie's clan," Maru said, thinking how charitable he was. Although Thefarie, the Tyrant was dead, his family would be one to placate. "Should it be a square or round tomb mound?"

"Round hardest rock is easiest to shape for the exterior," Ramnes replied, pleased to be within his leader's circle. "There are many long, narrow ones throughout Etruria."

"Make mine smaller than Ancestor Priestess Larthia's, but place it in the center."

"A sight to see!" Magistrates and elders viewed Maru's dome-structure that rose with a diameter the size of six horses lined up, head to tail. Wide entrances, many straddled by statues of animals brought back from eastern lands, led to steps and sealed main iron doors.

Maru marveled to his magistrates, "Where would we be without slaves? They learn Etruria's beliefs of life's continuation and see results of good labors so that they work and build our tombs with loving dedication, thankful for my kind provisions, fated to spend their whole lives in this cosmos anticipating the next."

Discontent increased among the nobles when they heard about the prince-priest's grand tomb. They gathered at Maru's temple and accused:

"An elder-priest says you stuff your tomb and steal from other tombs."

"You hoard sacred gold goblets…"

"…an Aegytian alabaster canopic jar of a pharaoh…"

"…a thousand votives…"

"…a sarcophagus carved as two humans."

"Like the Tarchna, we Cisra are proud of our ancestors, worshipping gods of sky and netherworld, obeying the infinite order of the cosmos. I don't steal. These objects will shield me in eternal sleep," Maru defended. "Who is that elder-priest? Tell him the contents of the next eastern ship will be yours."

"We want our own mound tombs now!" they yelled.

The magistrates surrounded Maru to protect him. "Give gifts of afterlife land, Maru, and share the creative genius of tomb chambers' designs."

Grumbling that he had no choice, Maru forced himself into an act of piousness and named clans to be interred in the City of the Dead, with remains of preferred servants and slaves in urns.

The Seianti, Spurinna, Urgulania and Velianas Clans took him at his word and met at the necropolis for proof.

Other citizens heard what the nobles had done. They, too, demanded tombs. As a show of hospitality, Maru invited them to the temple. He picked up a small bronze replica of the grand terracotta statue of Tinia. "We prosper. The Great Prediction means we live within rules of the cosmos. Our gods divine our worthiness. Tinia, god of thunder and skies, rewards us. Our City of the Dead will prove Cisra's wealth to future saeculae. We'll be famous."

He often wondered why the statue's piercing eyes and flowing tunic lorded over him.

Small and large tombs were built with precision, slaves working constantly on the sacred land that would become greater in size than Cisra itself. Adding gifts for all, nobles and citizens backed down. Threat of revolt ceased.

Maru sought his prized flask, an ox-headed jug incised with horsemen to put in his tomb and reclined on his cushions, vowing, "When that traitor elder-priest is found, he'll be boiled in olive oil."

64

Cisra bathed in success. Wealth and profit showed in gates, walls and buildings. The magistrates believed that Maru, helped by Vel Porenna's magical ability to find valuable rocks, led to the city's rapid ascendancy.

Vel counted forty-nine years behind him, the third year after Arith's strange return from Risa's cresting. He had settled in Cisra well, living in Arith and Ramnes' home where others took care of his household needs.

No one remembered he was Tarchna after he ingratiated himself with the magistrates, sitting in Maru's gallery at the temple court, learning Cisra's secrets. Vel had friends and their spouses for dark nights, but only his daughter, son-in-law and grandson for family.

A fresh wind rose throughout Etruria. The gods invoked a spell of *amnesia* to make the people forget the Great Prediction, disseminating the forecast into mythology.

"Let bygones be, Porenna," Zilath invited and bragged, "I blamed trade failure on your defection, but a superior soil sampler is mine. I built him a grander dwelling than yours. Come to the city of your early fame."

The gates of Tarchna were open to Vel again. He hardly knew his Tarchna daughter, seafarer son and grandchildren. He went to see them.

"Cisra was a gainful move," Vel confided when he saw servant Lethi loyally doing what she always did in the Laris-Vella household. "Maru kept his word and gives me more power than I had in Tarchna. I come and go without attendants."

"Yet you brood about what's missing in your life," she said.

"There's nothing missing."

"You're lonely for lack of family."

"I see them."

"Hummpf," she replied. "But you don't look at them."

Vel knew it was true. Lethi was more sage than servant, providing the impetus he needed. "What must I do?"

"Honor your children and they will honor you."

"How do I do that?"

"Talk with them. Find out who they are."

Vel took Lethi's advice.

In Cisra, Arith brought libations and fed him latest gossip of Cisra's townsfolk. In Tarchna, Risa tried to win his affection by keeping the house fragrant with flowered garlands, and preparing flavorful morsels as Anneia had. Home from sea sporadically, Venu told Vel his adventures.

"My son muddles me," Vel said to Lethi. "I treated him badly as a child. Is that why Venu doesn't want issue of his own loins?"

"Who knows? You weren't lenient with your children. Too much discipline. They were headstrong like you, but you had to get your way," Lethi replied.

"They were exasperating youths."

"Arith and Risa have grown to be substantial noblewomen. Their spouses are respected citizens. Venu brings trade from the east to build Tarchna's wealth," Lethi said to make Vel see his children clearly.

Living in the Vibenna home was clouded by Ramnes and Arith's awkward marriage. Gradually, Vel extended his stays in Tarchna and realized that Risa wasn't like his dead wife. This daughter had domestic and motherly skills that Anneia lacked. He went to meet Venu at Gravisca dock and was impressed by his son's part in sea trade. To each, Vel told ancestor stories, thinking that's what fathers talked about with children. But they were in cresting, mature Etruscans who spoke of daily routines. He stopped telling about the ancestors and shared what he did. Together, they began to eat and work for the common household.

"They value life," Vel told Lethi, "but their attitudes aren't mine. I'm a finder. They're sowers who put down roots. They're also reapers, benefiting from the rise of our generation's advancements."

The ancestor stories had affect. Risa began to retell legends to Culni, Ari and Larthia that would be passed on. Without issue, Venu could only lay poultices from wild herbs on his father's forehead. Arith was skeptical of her father's stories but told them because her son, Avele, needed background.

"Fondness for my children has grown," Vel said.

"You were grieving for Anneia." Lethi sympathized.

Vel mouthed the newest proverb of the day. "It's better to learn late than never."

His exceptional grandchildren were of good stock and spirit, yet they were like honeycomb, complex and sweet.

Avele, Vel's namesake, the first-born grandchild, had ambitiously entered Cisra's politics. In his youth, he was already practiced at looking for stylish detail among his class. Whenever Vel would ask, "What gift would you want?" Avele answered, "Tunics of spun cloth, leather belts with golden clasps."

In dishonor, Arith's line ended with a child dead at birth, her bearing defective. Vel knew she didn't want more.

"A quirk of the gods," Arith said without qualm.

"Women are meant to bear children. The gods haven't been munificent with my family," Vel confided to Lethi.

Risa's trio was lively and inquisitive. Sedate Culni would make a valiant master of the hunt, his eyes attuned to seeing animals in the bush. Vel witnessed his skill, acknowledging his entrance to manhood by gifting him with horse and spear.

Quick-witted Ari, Risa's second son charmed with words.

"Ari, what do you wish for?" Vel asked.

"To train in letters so I can discuss Etruria's laws and draw diagrams of cosmos and earth to show the priests."

"Remarkable! Your future may be as spokesman for the people, champion of causes," Vel chuckled.

Moments later, Ari hung from a tree, his legs curved around a branch.

"What are you doing?" Vel asked, startled by this strange behavior. "Have the gods made you, a scholarly child, a lunatic?"

"I'm getting a new view of the cosmos," Ari calmly replied, swinging by his legs.

"You're a budding philosopher," Vel said.

Wisdom had taught Vel that love and favoring were two separate qualities. Of his grandchildren, Larthia, the girl child with a goddess's equanimity, was the one he loved most. She was a mix of the entire family, using each personality to her advantage, understanding all at an early age, and finishing last words of everyone's speech. Vel spent more time with her than the others, tolerating her requests.

This old-wise child would beg, "Tell another story."

"Why?" Vel teased.

"I can write them when Ari teaches me the alphabet."

"The alphabet! Of my age, the higher elders and nobles write. Diligently they copy Hellenic letters, changing one here or there to fit the Etruscan tongue. I myself have never learned to read or write, but by repetition I've memorized rock quality as well as ancestor stories."

Vel delighted in these engaging children, removed by a generation, the hope of future Etruria.

They were his legacy. Lethi was right. When he accepted his family, he learned to honor them.

65

Master Soil Sampler Vel Porenna fortified Cisra's wealth more than he had Tarchna's, finding superior metals in the Tolfa. Tired, he began to wake late and shortened expeditions. Feasting excessively, he debauched with vilest harlots for entertainment.

"You're as bloated as a boar stuffed with birds and hare, Father," Arith needled.

"And your hair is as unkempt as a wild sow's mane."

"I can't help it. My hair was shiny and full. That haruspex after Risa's weird banquet put a spell on me to make it brittle and white. There's no mistaking that Risa is spiteful."

"Spiteful," Vel said. "You make remarks that put a curse on family loyalty."

"If anyone's not loyal, it's Risa. She's vindictive because I sat on cushions with her spouse."

"You and Parth?"

"At Risa's banquet, back in the season of the shifting winds. You understand, Father. You seek women."

"I am a distinguished noble and elder," Vel said indignantly.

"And I, a noblewoman of Cisra. But since that banquet Risa and her dumpy haruspex have cursed me. Every day, my hair becomes drier, less manageable. They've played mischief with my scalp!"

"That's impossible. It's many years since you went to Tarchna and saw her," he said. "What remedies have you tried to keep from balding?"

"Boar's lard, chicken renderings, bee's honey, oil of olive, crushed berry waters."

"Your mother used berry water."

"It didn't work," Arith said. "Perhaps Old Woman was right that Mother wasn't a true healer. She couldn't save herself from The Disease with her cures."

With force he had never shown her, Vel slapped Arith's cheek. "You dishonor Anneia! The gods made The Disease to teach humbleness to Etruria. Who could go against them? Not even your mother. That's why she couldn't get rid of it. She helped in vain, healing as she could."

Ramnes barged through Arith's bedroom curtain. "Do you never stop beautifying?"

"I comb at rising, before new day and nightfall."

"Comb later and sit down. Magistrate Spurinna has died. His funeral is the event of the season. Make amends with your father. You, Vel and I must go."

"How can I be seen with these strands?" She massaged a treatment into her scalp, hoping that more wouldn't fall out. "It ages me."

"We all age. Your breasts haven't drooped. Your veins haven't ruptured."

"You don't think I look like an old she-ox?" she asked.

"You haven't fattened like older women after your moon blood ceased," Ramnes said, "but you've got to give up your argument and convince him to come."

"He hit me, his favorite child."

"Vel might lose grace with Prince-priest Maru. It will reflect on us. Our noble position is jeopardized if we don't appear together. You're the daughter. Have new garments sewn to pretty you," Ramnes said to keep peace with his wife and father-in-law. "Apologize, Arith."

66

Hundreds of mourners arrived at the sunrise ceremony for Magistrate Spurinna. Having done this ritual repeatedly, mourners knew the procession must show dignity for earthly life and eternity, a reminder of the gods' work in the cosmos as prescribed by sacred laws.

Vel met Ramnes and Arith at the late noble's house where magistrates, nobles and elders congregated. The room of wood hull remnants paid homage to Spurinna's shipbuilding, skeletal braces, bulkheads and decking. There, the Magistrate of Trade had dealt with bringing prosperity to Cisra. The Soil Sampler and his cronies exchanged practiced small talk, speculating what future trade would be like with the magistrate's death.

"We go past Tinia's sacred temple and the crowds," Vel said.

"The temple will be the best place to be seen," Arith suggested, wanting to parade her fineries to high nobles who would recognize her as the beautiful Arith Laris, wife of Noble Vibenna, mother of Avele, daughter of Maru's illustrious Soil Sampler.

"A prestigious spot," Ramnes agreed.

Arith knew the procedure. Mourning was part of her duty when one of high title died. She wore the correct plain tunic and a veil to mask grief. If seen, her face had to be weepy, whether she felt it or not. She didn't. How ridiculous to mourn for one unknown. She derived pleasure from these funerary proceedings and wanted everyone to appreciate the efforts she made to look doleful.

Assigned with Vel's elite group, the three went to the watching station on the tufa stone curb. Arith hadn't been with her father since their rift, but she had sent a required apology through her servant. That should have sufficed, but father and daughter stood at arm's length. Vel picked up pebbles, clicking them to a childhood tune. Arith smoothed her hair.

Behind them, lowborn spectators clapped and whistled like they were at a horse race.

Abruptly, all hushed.

Street cleaners prepared the route by leveling stony ruts and sweeping animal dung into sacks. Town callers preceded the procession, ebulliently repeating, "The name of the deceased is Nobleman Spurinna, Magistrate of Trade, most esteemed administrator of Cisra. We praise him in his eternal life. Spurinna! Spurinna! Spurinna!"

Augur-priests, fulguriators and haruspices, identifying importance with conical or skull-fitted hats, strutted in slender floor-length capes, palms of hands and fingers pointed up to deflect bad spirits. They chanted prayers to the ruling gods, off-tone verses of their individual cults: "Great gods of Etruria, gods of heaven, earth and netherworld, whose lessons of the cosmos sustain us in wisdom, be pleased with the soul of this deceased, and ease his way into a happy afterlife."

"A good start to this parade. They display strength by not sitting in carts," Vel judged, offering his first words to Arith.

"They could have been carried," Arith contradicted.

Spry musicians weaved in and out among sedate magistrates and high nobles, playing long low notes on curved horns. The elders ambled in measured solemn steps, weighted by heavy tunics and cloaks.

"We'll parade halfway through the procession to the tune of trumpets," Ramnes said.

Arith wasn't listening but admiring Cisra's men who went before them. A parade was a perfect setting to lust when the rest were exuberantly mourning the deceased.

Not one kind of man appealed to Arith, except that the hairier his body, the more she loved to rub against him. If she could get his manhood to erect quickly, she knew he would be wilder on the cushions. Counting those men she had bedded as they filed by, she tried to remember why each was sexually enjoyable, a broad chest or well-curved buttocks and thighs.

Decorously Arith kept her eyes at their shoes. They saw her as one of the crowd. She raised her eyes when the noble from Blera marched by, one of her regular lovers who she had met seasons past at the market place. He spotted her and winked, making her mound itch for his ridged shaft. Later, he would be at festivities and they could slip away.

The street temporarily deserted when the procession idled.

"How inconvenient death is." Arith shifted her feet to find a comfortable pose for the black fitted shoes that came up her ankles. She had craved these new stiff leathers from the shoe-tooler, a harebrained crafter who didn't know how to peddle wares. Ramnes traded three sacks of barley. Ha! The shoe-tooler could have gotten four. The shoes pinched her toes, but she gloried in winning them.

"I didn't cause the delay, Arith. Getting a parade together takes much arrangement."

"Don't whine, Ramnes. My feet hurt. Will this funeral ever go on? I have to get my clothes ready for this feast."

"You're the whining one. You just need to attend the procession. The banquet's not required," Ramnes said sarcastically.

"You're dull since your spy journeys to lands of the dead."

"It's my professional duty to be at all entombments, if it's for a citizen or high official. You wanted to come."

"I participate as a noble should," Arith replied. "At least we don't have to wail like Hellenic women."

"They do that because they protest death. They don't honor death as we Etruscans. Death is a fact of life's ways," Ramnes said in that infuriating, condescending voice he had taken on since he became Maru's confidential advisor. "Wailing isn't for us, not like the childish Hellenics."

Vel stroked his whitened beard. "The gods observed and wrote in the *Book of Tages* that life after this one, under sun and moon, is reckoned as a continuation, a new life in the afterworld. We embrace death as we embrace life."

Ox dung! Arith thought. He talks like Ramnes and Ramnes talks like Father. We only embrace life. There's no life after this one. Worms eat us and we're gone. I'll enjoy this life, lusting for a male's heat, draping myself in gold-spun cloth, wearing garnets and amber, feasting on delectable meats, grapes and melons.

67

"Maru comes." His name zipped through the street, exciting the spectators more than this onerous procession for a deceased noble.

Dressed regally in robes with emblems of lotus leaves, griffins and eagles, the sovereign waved his golden scepter to express majesty and power. Glaring in the sun, his polished gold and silver finery obscured ears, throat and fingers. His face was bathed with red paint to please the afterlife gods. In lofty posture, he reverently bowed to the sky gods at regular intervals.

Drawn by two horses, Maru rode in a chariot that matched his costume, flanked by protective servants spread across the road.

In awe, the Cisra raised both arms in homage as he went by. He hailed them like he was the Hellenic warrior god Ares.

"His colors make nobles look like servants wearing rags. Maru always shows off," Arith criticized. "Had it been a triumphant sea battle parade, he would have donned a tunic to show his bulging muscles. I won't lift my arms like a commoner."

"You talk against Maru? He's central to the funeral. You would have worn something as gaudy if you could," Ramnes derided.

Inwardly Arith felt injustice. She had prided in knowing Maru in the blankets after she spied for him in Tarchna. He had seduced her into compliance that she adored, mounting her like a stallion, his whim for the moment. At the next communal feast, he looked at her with blank eyes. She knew he saw her as an ageing beauty.

Following the prince-priest, Maruth, his wife, rode in a less elaborate chariot, its wheels in her husband's tracks.

"She's an ugly toad. Bags under her eyes. Creases at her mouth. Sagging cheeks," Arith said. "Her boredom with rituals is widely known."

"She's never been popular with the Cisra and suffers for it," Ramnes empathized.

"You take pity on her? She's as pampered as a babe lounging on cushions, served by attendants for each request."

"Her renowned husband leaves little for her enjoyment, except material goods that soon tire her. She's isolated from the Cisra. No one knows if she has friends," Vel confided. "But as husband, Maru is neither companion nor lover. She sleeps alone. Maruth, more shadow than wife, excels in accumulating jewels and riches for afterlife."

"Father, you surprise me with such details."

"I know Maru's mistress is power, not women."

The pompous highborn glided through.

The street momentarily quieted. Then faintly, notes of a lone flute came from the sacred temple.

"A plaintive reed whistling the gods' call," Vel stated poetically.

The tune grew audibly.

"It's The Flutist as messenger to the afterlife, the harbinger of joy and sorrow," Ramnes said.

"Being close to Maru makes you eloquent," Arith replied scornfully.

Behind The Flutist, twelve dark-skinned Carthaginian slaves elevated a cloth-draped bundle on wooden beams. Within his sarcophagus, the magistrate lay in the stiffness of death with bones of his previously deceased wife for their souls to co-mingle.

Three augur-priests ambled alongside the slaves and eulogized to the crowd, "The Spurinna in this temporal life coupled, made children, worked, struggled and laughed together. They are bound in the afterlife to harmony and peace."

"These mourners act solemn as they prance. They're liars, for the moment this funeral is over, they forget tears and go to feast." Arith brushed street dust from her tunic.

"You bite with every word you utter," Ramnes snapped.

"Do you remember that Magistrate Spurinna had his sarcophagus ordered when he was in his cresting? Cisra spoke of it then, for he had it made of clay from the Tolfa. He had the sarcophagus sculpted in his likeness with that of his wife, not as old crones but youthful," Vel tattled to the new generation's soil sampler with whom he spoke.

"An inspiration for us," the younger man said. "Having the image of the departed in their cresting will become custom. Word is that it's a fine piece."

Startled, Arith looked at her father. Vel was babbling like an old satyr, full of himself. He had become as mushy as puls, speaking commonly, gabbing about others like he knew them personally. "Father, how well had you known Spurinna?"

"I am privy to the circle of magistrates," Vel replied.

"And you, Ramnes?" Arith asked.

He hung his head. "Not yet."

68

A solemn moment, one of quiet harmony, flowed from the heavens as the Spurinna sarcophagus passed Arith, Ramnes and Vel.

Three highest augur-priests fluttered by, arms dipping and turning like swallows banking in flight.

A trained horse, decorated in garlands and bronze belts, plodded as if in sorrow. It pulled the open cart in which the dead magistrate's family sat facing inward.

"Our turn." Arith arched her back and upped her head, though her feet hurt from the pebbled road. A blister irritated from her new shoes.

They left the curb and fell into step with their group of nobles, starting the lengthy walk to the necropolis.

"We're fortunate ones," Ramnes said. "These bystanders knew Spurrina—lesser nobles and people of his commerce and his servants who will be entombed with the magistrate at their deaths. They're envious since they can't go to the tomb chambers."

"He had a lot of friends," Vel said. "All favored him."

"I met him once at a banquet. He was charming noblewomen with stories of his faithful wife," Arith said.

The procession passed through Cisra's fourth gate into the hinterland, trudging on the road between the living and the dead, an area of intermittent watch towers among barley fields and olive groves.

"The land slopes. I go no further," Vel said. "I'm weary."

"I had to come. So should you," Arith said.

"The day heats."

"Perhaps you need rest to banquet this night," Arith jeered as he turned around. "I'll honor Spurinna, and go on."

She usually paraded to Cisra's walls and went home, fed up by the repetitive ritual. For this funeral, she'd see the day out to match her father's spitefulness. She had apologized but he had never acted contrite for that face slap.

The procession formed a human ribbon crossing the distance to the valley of massive tombs. Slowing where the road forked and the Avenue of the Oak Trees began, the mourners tramped towards the walls that enclosed the City of the Dead. The sun blazed halfway to high. The walls were like Cisra's bricks, both the height of dry-wood trees. A covered gate hinged open to receive the newly dead.

"How quickly Cisra's slaves build this town, Ramnes. It will be ready for occupation in our life span. We'll have a luxurious tomb here," Arith exclaimed.

"Finally, you've come to see it."

"You've been successful," she said, giving an unexpected compliment. "Spurinna is the highest official to die since you became Maru's privileged advisor."

"His death changes my position," Ramnes smirked like a cat full of fish sauce. "Maru increases the allotment of sacred land for the dead. Some say it might eventually be greater than Tarchna's. I'll be needed to manage all."

The head caller signaled, his hand beckoning like netherworld god Vetisl. The procession advanced on hardened dirt streets bordered by small round tombs. Already, grasses, shrubs and trees brought calmness for the ancestors within. The closer they came to the Spurinna tomb, the larger the tombs were. Moving with joyful cadence, they tread softly to not disturb the dead with only chirping sparrows and robins for sound.

"Our earthly homes are built of wood and tufa, but these afterlife homes are carved in durable stone for a secure future, for eternity," someone touted.

The procession turned right, then left, then straight until they halted at the Spurinna family tumulo.

Knocking aside a mourner, an augur-priest chanted omens from the *Book of Tages* to the stone winged-beasts that guarded the doorway. "The Magistrate will be the second of his clan interred. Fend off evil spirits who try to surround the dead. Make way for slaves to enter and lay Spurinna on his resting place."

Maru dismounted from his chariot, strode to the tomb's entrance and faced the mourners. "By the gods' decree, enter and pay homage to our deceased brother. Under Magistrate Spurinna's supervision, our commerce progressed. He bartered our metal-bearing rocks for Hellenic red and black figure vases and vessels of olive oil. He sent spiked weapons to trade Carthage. The noble's death was neither from disease nor sword, but of twilight, his old age of twelve times four. What fate! He lived in good fitness through the stages of life as decreed by ancestor Etruscan elders who calculated life span."

"With permission, Maru," Spurinna's cousin stood. "He was kind and honest. He will be missed."

Maru ignored the cousin. "Mourners of Cisra, don't the dead have the same needs as the living? Don't they want feasts and games for journey to the afterlife? Spurinna's gala feast will last from dusk to dusk. Funerary games will have combat between wild beasts of prey."

"Sacrificial blood will flow to comfort and energize the deceased magistrate on his journey," a noble said.

Bah, everyone loves blood for its own gore. I, too, Arith thought, not listening to the eulogy. She watched the prince-priest's body sway with strength, sexuality emanating through his skin, no matter what his speech.

69

"Why do those mourners stupidly wait and not call for commencement? Aplu's sun burns. I want this ceremony to end," Arith said irritably and blotted her face with her scarf.

"Clouds start. We may get drenched before the viewing," the funeral planner informed Maru.

"Tinia had confided his plans for a storm," Maru charmed the mourners, grinning. "We go inside."

One by one, the bereaved filed through a passageway to the first antechamber, wanting to keep dry from the impending storm.

Musky body smells mixed with damp tufa. Nauseated, Arith sniffed a cloth of lavender fragrance. "Why haven't they skipped on, keeping the rhythm of procession, Ramnes?"

"Have patience, the space will free to the doorway."

"If I get this viewing done, I can fix my hair for the banquet," Arith fussed.

"All you talk about is your hair."

"The thirteenth clump fell out!"

She was pushed forward to view family possessions displayed on stone biers and niches. Bronze Lares and Penates votive statues, made by the best metal crafters, would comfort Spurinna on his afterlife journey. Animal-shaped *askos* filled with libations were left for underworld god Vetisl.

Gifts from the Hellenics were in the second antechamber. Showing respect, the foreigners paid tribute to Magistrate Spurinna with excellent vases, amphorae and storage vessels created by famed Corinthian and Athenian craftsmen. No better pieces had been seen in the necropolis for less than a prince-priest.

Back and forth, Maru went through the passageways, eyeing the mourners and then the vases. "How did this happen? There was no better collection than mine. His will outdo."

He's jealous that the dead magistrate should receive so many gifts, Arith thought as she entered the main tomb chamber packed with mourners, mewing unintelligible sounds, sighing uncontrollably. Then she said to Ramnes, "Are they dying from lack of air? Get them out if they want to expire."

"Hush, Arith."

Light from oil lamps glowed on the rounded walls and dome ceiling of the huge main vault. Rose petals were strewn on the floor for fragrance. One musician strummed the cithar. His companion played a flute.

Set down from its bier, cloth removed, the terracotta sarcophagus was centered in the chamber. The sculptured noble couple reclined sideways on its tufa stone base. They gazed outward as if sharing an excited moment with someone across the banquet couch, elliptical eyes animated, pupils inset with bloodstones, caught in the light above wrinkleless high cheeks. Contented smiles crossed lips ready to utter profundity. Their stylish fashion was Hellenic, yet hinted of Etruscan flair. From the wife's fitted cap, braids hung to her shoulders and tunic-covered breasts. The husband's contoured hair and tapered beard molded to his face while his half-nude torso propped on one elbow upon cushions. The cozy looking couple, in agreement with the cosmos, no longer seemed of rock.

It became clear why the mourners mewed like cats. Arith emitted a sharp inward cry. "They pulse with life!" Lightness overcame her spirit to feel like she was riding Tinia's clouds above Cisra.

One mourner snuffled, "This doesn't look like Spurinna. What sculptor modeled him in youth with arm around his wife?"

"Don't shout! They're in love's embrace, reclining on banquet couch, looking upon the cosmos."

Another postulated, "Did he know that his mold of a man with sacred egg in hand, symbol of fertility, and woman showing her earthly wealth by fingering her necklace, would draw such response from a viewer?"

The bereavement line looped around the chamber. Mulling over the exquisite scene, Arith backed into a pillar.

When the nobles left, she went to the sarcophagus and touched the golden-brown drapery folds of the stone tunics. She caressed the hands of the heavenly pair, stroked their sculptured cheeks and smoothed their dressed hair. Heat radiated to her fingers. Amazed by warmth from stone, she asked out loud, "Are you listening, gods of the cosmos and beyond? Is the rock living? Or is it the Spurinnas' shining faces, smiling in bliss that enthralls?"

"Move on," called a guard.

"Never have I laid eyes on such a wondrous sarcophagus!"

"That's what all say," he replied caustically.

Overwhelmed by its beauty, tears rolled down Arith's cheeks. She, who had shed no tears for Anneia's death and felt no compassion for those she hurt, kneeled in honor. "The sculptured lid is unsurpassed."

Ramnes came back from the outer passageway and hustled her forward. "What are you doing, Arith? You've embarrassed me by not leaving the tomb."

"Such tender joy. It dazzles. It holds mystery I cannot fathom," she bawled, rooted to the viewing spot, her skin prickled with hair-raising chills.

"Come, Arith. You, emotional about the magistrate? You didn't know him."

She stumbled, her body on fire after the chill. Outside, a drizzling rain had started, and Maru hurried the augur-priests to perform the death rituals. Acting more bereft than a mere acquaintance to the magistrate, Arith went through the chants without collapse.

The procession disbanded. Anxious to resume life-giving activities, the mourners began the trek back to Cisra at their own gait. Ramnes went ahead with them, but Arith maundered alone.

Disoriented, the remaining day was unknown to her. The Spurinna feast and games were a blur. The noble from Blera was forgotten. Her sexual need dissipated. She thought only of the phenomenal pair in the afterlife chamber.

70

In Arith's dreams, the couple from the sarcophagus was alive in journey to the afterlife, greeted by the godliest of the gods, Tinia, who praised their immortality. "Most perfect you are. Turan will reign over you. You shall be known throughout the ages for unblemished love and joy."

One more look at the sarcophagus will satisfy, Arith told herself. The tomb won't be sealed until officials come from other cities.

Telling Ramnes that she was off to Cisra's market place, she turned at the main gate and took the deserted road to the City of the Dead. As she walked, she covered her head in gauze cloth to dress as a bereaved clansman. In case anyone was about, she kept near the trees.

An entrance guard slept next to the tomb chamber door. He sprang up. "Are you a relative of the deceased?"

"Why, yes," Arith blithely lied. "I've come to view my cousin's tomb."

"Cousin? Most have been here. An irregular request."

"My word your lazy conduct will be left unknown if you let me in." Arith held out the basket of death flowers with a silver ingot nestled in the leaves. "Besides, I've brought these."

He blanched at her threat but took the silver and moved aside. She assured him with a smile.

Ringed by yesterday's gifts, oil lamp burners illuminated the sarcophagus. The sculptured beauty compelled her to kneel. From hundreds of mourners' touches, the couple's hair and arms had an oiled patina that made it more exquisite. Overpowered by its magnificence, Arith's limbs quaked with impulses never felt before.

The stone is as alive as me, she thought, slumping to the floor. The sculpture has a message, an eternal understanding of life's ways imbued with godliness.

Jealousy welled up. She wanted a sarcophagus to mark her life, an afterlife monument for all to admire.

A familiar commanding voice came through the passageway. Like her, he wasn't a Spurinna.

"Seize that duck-shaped *askos* and the two-headed cup. No one will miss them. They're local, not Hellenic," Maru ordered the guard.

"But where do I put them?" the witless guard asked.

"I'll take them at the entrance, you imbecile. Not a word. Then seal the tomb to everyone, including clansmen."

Arith couldn't flee. Climbing into a vacant niche, she peered out.

The prince-priest paced in front of the sarcophagus. With his jeweled scepter, he jabbed the stone magistrate's carved shoulder and crowed, "Spurinna, you upstart who wanted my title! It was you who betrayed me! If you were alive, I'd torture you like a slave!"

The painted stone reacted to its punishment by spraying chips of terracotta. From Arith's hiding place, she expected the smiling couple to break into tears.

Maru expected the sarcophagus to react too, but it sat stoically as if saying, "You'll never hurt us."

Startled by his momentary hysteria, he regained composure and apologized to the sarcophagus, "This scepter is the culprit who attacked you, not me!"

Carefully, he tucked the scepter into his belt. From a pouch in his tunic, he withdrew a tiny sharpened blade. Skillfully, more like a craftsman than a noble, he gouged the bloodstone eyes and examined them.

"Flawless." He dropped them into his pouch. "I'll best you yet, Spurinna!"

Blinding the sarcophagus gave him new energy. His laughter echoed through the chamber. With grand strides, he headed for the passageway and waved in last eulogy, more in curse, "May Vetisl swallow you whole."

Arith heard him banging, "Guard, open the door."

A moment of sunlight streaked across the passageway and Maru was gone. Arith waited until there was silence and swung her legs over the niche rim. In the dimness she took an oil light and held it above the heads of the couple. For the damage it sustained, the gashes seemed to have healed, surviving to become part of the sculptural detail.

"He and I want a sarcophagus like you," Arith said, caressing the couples' hair and foreheads until the wick burned low.

She went to the entrance. The guard had left it ajar. Outside, he blocked her way.

"You and the Maru were related to Magistrate Spurinna?" He asked with a pernicious grin as he wrenched a silver bangle from her arm.

Her arm burned. Swiftly, she ran from him down the road to Cisra. By nightfall, the image of the sarcophagus began a craving stronger than her orgasmic lusts. Tossing fitfully in sleep, she chanted, "One for me. For me! I need one. I must have one."

71

After a night meal, Ramnes rolled dice with Avele. Engrossed in their match, they ignored Arith.

"Avele seems older than his years with his instruction in politics. He didn't have to apprentice as advisor. He leaves youth for cresting and his wife births a second child. We don't get younger. My age of twilight begins. I don't feel old, albeit, thirty-six to your forty-one," she said.

"Don't remind us when we're playing," Ramnes said tersely.

"Come, I'll rub your shoulders. The magistrate's funeral reminds me that we must think of our own sarcophagus. We need a sarcophagus!"

"Probably."

"What insult to close your eyes to me, a wife and mother," Arith rebuked, the efforts of her palms wasted on Ramnes.

"This talk is between you and Father," Avele said. "The game's a tie. The dice spin."

As they made their way to a feast a few days later, Arith badgered, "Do you think our sarcophagus should look like us now or when we wed?"

"Interest yourself in the delicacies at table," he said.

"No matter when I ask, you avoid my question, Ramnes."

Arith's craving exaggerated as the sarcophagus of Spurrina and his wife lingered with her like a lover's memory.

When Ramnes went to Sutri, she went to the clay-makers' workshops. None made sarcophagi. "Where are the tomb artists?" she asked, stumped.

"Sculptors labor in unknown quarters. Their society is a meticulous one with work requiring solitude," one clay-maker said.

"They're so secretive that it might take a moon to find one," his partner said. "They're tight-lipped."

Having a Hellenic coin from her brother Venu, she went to the most talkative clay-maker, dangling the piece at him. "Find the tomb sculptor who has done that trade magistrate and his wife. You shall have half a gold ingot."

More convinced than ever of her need, Arith told Ramnes forcefully, "Our sarcophagus must be carved soon! What fame it will bring! Our sarcophagus should look like us as nobles."

"What image is that? You as devoted wife, I, sole recipient of that pleasure?"

"You've become sour, Ramnes," she retorted. "On our sarcophagus I shall recline in my most elegant tunic and you will be draped in official garb beside me."

"We can't start a sarcophagus now. Maru wants my help with the new magistrate who replaced Spurinna."

"You refuse me," Arith smoldered. "Then I'll get it without you."

"No, not possible," Ramnes shouted. "We aren't of Magistrate Spurinna's rank. You've looked up too high. You've gone too far."

"Why shouldn't we have greatness? Spurinna has it with his sarcophagus. You'll be magistrate one day, won't you?"

Enraged with Arith at a banquet, Ramnes fondled the thighs of a fellow noble's wife.

"You try to forget me. You think I'm too ambitious. But what do you know of ambition, you without spine?" Arith harangued.

Unremittingly, Arith begged him with hollowed eyes, sunk from tears. "My heart will burst if I cannot have the sarcophagus I want. You don't care for my wishes."

"I've put up with your wanting costly trinkets and tunics, but yearning for a sarcophagus like the Magistrate's is wrong. The netherworld gods will beat us to death while alive."

"You fancy much," Arith snapped back.

"Your weeping strains me," Ramnes barked at her like he would a mongrel. "You leave my nights cold. Your obsession breaks our marriage."

Ramnes did have spine. Attentively, he plunged into work with the Magistrate of Construction, doing favors and bestowing extra consideration on the elders. Invited to feasts for patrons or nobles where the high workings of Cisra were discussed, he learned sovereign secrets that elevated his power with the officials.

"Your continuous machinations and your flood of tears bore me. My success has taken half a lifetime to achieve and I won't lose it for your whims."

At end of Maru's banquets, women of questionable descent would be brought in to pleasure, sing, dance or copulate. Then, with a vengeance, Ramnes no longer dallied. He showed his manhood.

Seasons of Sorrow - Seasons of Joy

72

"Zilath and the magistrates insist that I accompany my road-builders to explain the use of my inventions," Parth said at the noonday meal.

His reason was hollow to her ears. She could tell by the way he had held her that he was leaving.

"Our territory expands almost to Cisra. I could be leading a hundred men." Parth's eyes were as faraway as the moon.

Risa parted her lips like the waxed smile of the newly dead. Women always knew when a man was unfaithful. She knew since her banquet last season.

Culni came in to eat at his father's last words. "Uncle Venu left for sea. You're going away. I'll be the oldest male. I can hunt quail for the table on my own."

Ari chomped on an oatcake. "How long will you be gone? Will you be here for birthdays?"

Larthia started crying. "Who will tell me a story before I go to sleep?"

"Your mother will, Larthia. I'll come home at the changing seasons with new stories of the cosmos." Parth looked at Risa. "Have you a say?"

"Gods of fate have complicated our lives with tasks that only each could fulfill. If this is yours, you've made your choice."

"It's right. Tarchna's strength depends on ties with other Etruscans. Cisra grows bolder in commerce and we need to compete."

"Keep safe and in good health, Parth," Risa said, a smile pasted on her face.

Vesta's hearth fires in the Laris-Vella home burned low but didn't extinguish. Servants tended the embers, claiming that the gods must be sending an omen, for the driest wood wouldn't kindle. Parth rushed off soon after, with Risa to act as father and mother, master of the house, servants and slaves. While she calmed squabbling children, she was uneasy. How could she do the same for her troubled marriage? Her husband was gone.

In Parth's absence, Haruspex sat beside Risa in the courtyard, doused with two scents, rose water and blood from animal sacrifice. The combined stench was sickening.

"You've become frail. For your instruction, you must contemplate what I say." He tapped his fingers to his head. "What will bring you strength is to speak kindly and show unselfish deeds."

"You think I speak harshly?" she asked.

"Once you adored Parth, but discontent is marked by your flat voice." Haruspex impertinently reclined on her courtyard couch, closing his eyes to rest. "Your husband's amorous interest in the sister you feud with makes you dull. You resent Parth's departure. Animosity breeds harshness."

"Sometimes self-pity tortures my sensations."

Haruspex shook his head. "You understand your condition. Give up pity! Your words must reflect good action. Each moment of life must pile up to form an existence of well-being. Don't change your everyday customs for what smoothes your path."

"My custom is to devote my life to my children, giving them sound teachings of the elders and ancestors."

Haruspex jumped up and put his wrinkled face to hers. "That's not enough. Contentment won't stay. Your childbearing and glorious union had been your sole pleasure. Diversion will add joy to your being. Tend skybirds like the white doves that gave solace in your youth. The wild and tame shall come to your beckoning. They'll guide you."

The day that a dozen speckled birds flew in from the sea, glistening on Aplu's spectral light, she attracted them with barley kernels.

"Wonder of life!" she said when they landed at her feet and she stroked their iridescent feathers. Learning their characteristics, an exchange grew. She became protectress, and they taught preferences of fruit, grain, nuts or insects, yet took what was edible. They were hungry. She was hungry for gratification.

At varying heights, she put food for swallows and storks, honey in mimosa tree water for bee-eaters, puls grain in sacks for vultures. She nurtured hoopoes, swifts and those wounded or starved out of nests. When birds with elongated beaks bored holes to build shelters and shot sawdust from tree bark, or kestrels pecked apples in poor crop seasons, she pondered about complexities of the cosmos.

Much like the mysterious flutist of her calamitous banquet, the plumaged hollow-boned creatures warbled love songs to relay where they were on yard or hill, soothing and revitalizing her spirit. In awe of their sheer numbers, she counted breeds gliding and soaring under sun or cloud.

"Birds see with greater clearness than we," she told her children. "They have seasons of plenty and shortage, and live in balance with the cosmos. In scarce seasons, they store energy for flight."

When Risa spread seeds on the courtyard floor and brought potted tree limbs in clay containers, songbirds came. She sketched them with Vesta's charcoal bits to entertain her youngsters.

"My feathered flocks give musical harmony and bring evenness." Risa fed a skylark from her hand.

Whether the children understood their mother or not, they were old enough to see she had changed and that birds gave her pleasure.

Risa had her family. She kept walking her life path, doing what she could to dissolve the hole in her heart.

She set traditions, making sure the children knew correctness. At table, she showed them how to dine like at a feast, relishing food while talking about their day. As Anneia had, she embellished the table with ornaments, decorating walls with pungent herbs, arranging delicate seasonal bouquets.

For the home's outer walls, Risa had a shallow portico built with columns and roof to ward off rain. She planted vines to entwine squared columns, ends dripping over beams clustered with nascent fruit. The baked brick walls were plastered with paste of tufa sand, filling in cracks of the house built in Vel's youth.

For Venu, she had rooms attached through a hallway at a side of the courtyard. He would need them when home from sea.

It made sense that her life was tied to her family even though she and Parth were estranged. Outwardly she showed that all was light and joyful in their lives, the diligent wife and mother, a loyal Tarchna in thought and deed.

"Your insights encourage continuity," she bowed her head to Haruspex in deference.

"One of life's purpose is to function within a whole society, each member doing his duty," Haruspex replied.

"My birds have to wait for the right time for every action. They've given me wisdom to have patience," she said.

73

Parth came home as he had pledged, his skin rugged from outdoor life. He brought gifts from rural villages and told of hinterland settlements. "Bisenzth makes flexible wooden-soled sandals. Here's an extravagance for the children's growing feet. They're hinged in the middle so that the foot bends without pain."

Culni, Ari and Larthia dipped the new sandals in water so they would conform to their toes. They danced around the house.

"Bizenzth is a town ahead of our time. They also have a toothache cure of false teeth with gold bridges," Parth told the family.

"How funny," the children laughed at the peculiar joke of gold bridges instead of stone ones.

From Cisra crafters, Parth brought votive gifts, small metal acrobats that Culni and Ari pranced across the floor and a straw baby dressed in peasant clothes for Larthia.

"I name her Boobaa." Larthia rocked her doll.

"Boobaa?"

"Papa, she will bed with me."

"Toys. Cisra's new idea. We never played with anything other than pots, pans or stones."

"What are you doing, Parth? You've given the children entertainment,"

Risa said, wondering about what was happening in the city that housed her father and sister.

"I bartered for the votives. I thought the boys would enjoy the acrobats like the ones at your banquet."

"Votives are not toys but sacred statues of worship," she replied, suspicious that he wanted to remember her banquet.

"We replenished supplies at Cisra. Since we haven't seen Arith and Ramnes for many seasons, I went to their home," Parth said on his next visit.

Risa shuddered involuntarily. "How are they?"

"Most odd," Parth frowned. "Vel had left for the Tolfa that dawning. Ramnes was at a magistrate's dinner. I stayed until the moon's height. Arith looked unwell."

"Unwell. Do you think she's with child?" Risa held herself stiffly.

"By holy gods, no! Did you forget that she's past child-bearing, and Avele is a man. Arith's servants served a leg of roasted goat and wine for my unforeseen visit. Avele came briefly."

Risa plucked dead flowers from a garland on the wall, waiting for his confession.

"She seemed dazed, her eyes unclear."

"Arith must drink too much at banquets." Risa shredded the garland's vines.

"She still thinks she's beautiful."

And you do, too, Risa thought when Parth stayed home less than a quarter moon.

Risa paced the courtyard, telling Haruspex, "Arith and Parth ate together. Then, what did they do? Did he bed her with servants at the curtains?"

"Why don't you ask him straightforward? Then your fears will be known." Haruspex sat cross-legged on the floor, wondering if his bones would ache when he rose.

"I can't," Risa said dejectedly. "I'm afraid of the answer."

Haruspex rarely spied on Parth, but the road builder's two faces—a loyal, hard worker with secret lusts for the sister-in-law—made this duty necessary. Waiting for a cloudy day, he followed Parth.

Etruria's road system had grown as Parth connected Tarchna with neighboring towns. His knowledge of landforms authorized him to engineer related hydraulics projects. To bar erosion of his tufa roads, he dug underground tunnels to divert Tinia's rainwater. His solution meant that marsh flooding and field irrigation could allow seepage, causing formerly unusable land to be cultivated.

Impressed by what he saw, Haruspex put a spell on Parth to make him wish to be home, to need family and friends. Under the stars, Parth tossed in his blankets, thinking of Risa's warmth and the fire of their early life. Haggard from sleeplessness, he knew that he was wearied of his lonely life in isolated wilds with other men.

The spell, or a twist of fate, brought a messenger to Parth. "Nobleman Vella, Prince-priest Zilath wants you. Villagers come into Tarchna from the hinterlands. We need more roads for the city."

74

Washing road dust in a river bath, Parth donned fresh clothes to give accounts of his labor, reminding Zilath, "I've been gone for much of my cresting seasons, almost since the Great Prediction started our tomb constructions."

"Your reputation is noted, Noble Road Builder Vella."

"My children grow between visits. I miss their laughter."

"Children are the root of life, but you haven't mentioned your wife. Could it be that it's not only your children you miss but the delights of bed?" Zilath asked, always curious about sexuality, especially of a vivacious, attractive woman like Risa Laris.

"Of course, Zilath. My manliness needs stirring," Parth replied.

"In Tarchna, you must intersect roads where a new temple will be built. You'll be home to bed your wife."

Parth's homecoming brought the hint of a smile to Risa's lips, then a tiny laugh in joy and a cry. "Is it his preference? Will he want to leave again?"

"Ready yourself, Risa," Lethi warned. "I'll lay out your best tunic and plait your hair into a crown."

House servants scrubbed walls and niches, tidied grain storage and shined copper pots. To greet their father, the children's soiled clothes were blanched. Hair was brushed. Nails were trimmed. The cooks concocted a venison stew with rosemary and thyme.

"You don't make such a tasty dish often." Risa dipped a ladle into the pot, inhaling the aroma. "Your stew is fit for Tinia."

"The master doesn't come home every day," the head cook said.

Shouting accosted Parth. Wild with excitement, the children and well-wishers came to toast the reunited couple. Zilath had a sense of humor. He sent a personal trumpeter to play snappy melodies. All that Parth and Risa could do was host this gathering late into the night, glancing at the other like they once had.

When the guests left, the two lounged in the dining place garlanded in asphodel, lit by honeycomb candles.

"These are for you." From his leather road sack, Parth sprinkled berries into a bowl, wetting them with crimson wine.

"They look like gemstones." Risa sampled one. "Hmm. They taste like food the gods must crave."

"Remember when we first met and you tipped wine on me?"

Risa smoothed her tunic over a cushion. "I was bad-mannered. I hated that I was obliged to serve you."

"You charmed me with your obstinacy, but delighted with humor. We became friends." He topped the berries with a stone. "More than friends. We started to love."

"I remember. It was as magical as this berry that glistens in the light." Risa raised it to the candle. The stone sparkled from shafts of light on its facets. "It's the most special gift you've ever given me."

"A garnet for you to cherish." Parth took the stone and kissed it, "as I cherish you, my beautiful one."

"You cherish me? How could you when Arith is more beautiful?" Inebriated by drink and his nearness, inadvertently her words trickled out.

He arched his eyebrows, wrinkling his suntanned face. "As beautiful as Arith?"

"Isn't she your love anymore? Did you tire of her and come home?"

"She means nothing to me."

"The servants gossiped. All Tarchna gossiped after my banquet." Miserably, Risa yanked a cushion to her breast for succor. "My banquet was to be so wonderful. How you and Arith spoiled it. I can't forget the image of you two reclining," she sobbed. "She has everything, even you."

Parth imprisoned Risa's shoulders and shook her. "Did you watch Arith and me all night? Arith wanted to see if I could be overcome. Didn't you see me get up to wash my mouth from distaste? She schemes to get what she can't have."

"And what of you and Arith after my banquet? You met her secretly when your road work took you to Cisra."

"I ate with her once and told you." Parth took her cushion and threw it on the floor. "You don't believe me."

"You ate with her alone."

"Avele and servants were there."

Risa erupted like volcanic lava from the high Etruscan mountains. "Gossip has tortured me for many seasons. Did you bed her?"

"Bed Arith? Why would I do that? A vein of malice runs through that woman."

"You were so harsh after my banquet."

"You made eyes with Asba. You talked with a flutist."

"After the loss of the child, you didn't love me."

"How could I not love you? You've always had my heart." He leaned and kissed her. "I've come home. Don't I always?"

"Yes, you do," she said, breathless from his sudden tenderness.

"Remember that, my dearest."

She saw the desire in his eyes and loosened her hair. "I've loved you since you invaded my father's house. You're more handsome than ever."

"Let me kiss you a thousand times and lie my body with yours."

"And I'll hold you with love to fill your pleasures."

Aroused with foreplay, there in the dining place, site of family meals and her banquet, they renewed their passion, calling out in ecstasy.

75

Praise Haruspex! He divined insightful portents of optimism, cooperation and radiance of spirit to enhance Risa and Parth's love. Their plagued misunderstanding was replaced by heightened harmony, a love that would endure through cresting life, inhibiting gossip and slander from that banquet when winds jolted their lives. Tumultuous seasons at end, goddess Turan gave Risa's smile back.

"The fetid Gravisca Disease is quelled. Enjoy dry winds without fear," prince-priests of Etruria proclaimed.

Life continued, days blending without mishaps. The Etruscans exalted in the cosmos, depicting whimsical portrayals of themselves on sculptures, paintings, vases, pots and pans.

After the first series of secret chambers had been dug on the uplands outside Tarchna's city gates, tomb builders learned that other Etruscan city-states built necropolises.

Prince-priest Maru of Cisra gloated, "Our City of the Dead is largest."

Tarchna moped from Cisra's boast but laughed heartily about the secrecy of their own underground chambers. "We had declared death to citizen or slave who blabbed during construction. How amusing! Now, we can claim our beliefs of eternal households to the cosmos."

And they did. Instead of hiding chambers among grasses, they built a hut over each tomb site with a wooden door and slanted roof. Zilath judged that Risa and Parth's chamber was finished after tool marks and cracked surfaces were smoothed, Asba's paintings were glossed against earth's ravages, and interior walls dried out.

When wood columns and scaffolding were removed, Risa and Parth decided to see it at moon's light.

Minds once again aligned, they walked on the path to the isolated uplands, the tall grasses whistling in the breeze. They passed old Man Pors' grave site.

"Do you remember him, the first Tarchna to go to his afterlife when the tombs were done?" Risa asked.

"Was he the cantankerous old fool who diddled ladies at banquet?"

"You tickle Flufluns' ears! No, Pors was a sage among elders, the one who befriended me at the market and told me how to banquet. Before he died he said to any who would listen, 'You can choose to fear death or enjoy it.'"

"Do you believe those words, Risa?"

"Death doesn't scare me. The dead live in the protection of the tomb. It's another life for us."

"Your Haruspex must be as wise as Menvra. He's taught you more wisdom than Zilath has."

"Not all. Skybirds who fly across sun and moon tell much. They taught me the cosmos is alive, always moving."

"You're like your birds. You soar with exuberance."

They opened the tomb's new wooden door. There was the same rock with bronze loops, sealing the chamber below for temporary closure until interment.

"Rumor is that souls walk night long, sucking the fragile into tombs before they're ready," Parth quoted the augurs, he as superstitious as any Etruscan.

"Then we shouldn't test Vetisl and his netherworld gods by stepping into our eternal home with the moon at fullest." Risa slipped her arms under the folds of Parth's cloak.

"We won't go in," Parth said.

They sat on the grasses next to the tomb chamber and watched Uni's moon go higher, and the stars dot the sky.

"My mid-cresting comes. Our afterlife chamber is done. Calmness has overtaken my being," Risa smiled peacefully.

Warmly, Parth embraced her. "For me too. Our ties are deepened, our love resolved."

"This life has become what it's meant to be, joyous and undisturbed by trauma."

To guard the chamber, they left a bronze votive, the size of a goblet, outside the door. "Tinia, Uni and Menvra have made our future home possible. Our chamber will be sealed until death pries it open."

Hand in hand, they strolled back to the living city to herald the dawn, the uplands forgotten in favor of mortal activity.

76

Sorrowful or joyous, seasons and years whirled past. The family's noble position accelerated with two major accomplishments: Parth's remedies to roads and bounty from afar that brought wealth to Tarchna.

During that time, Risa avoided reunion with Arith, giving excuses until the children had grown up and were on their own paths. She wanted nothing to do with the sister who ruined her banquet.

"The roads are muddy," Risa said in the cold season to justify not visiting Cisra.

"Tarchna's games and ceremonies demand the children's attendance," she lied in the warming season.

To keep the family from being outwardly divided, Risa sent the boys to Cisra when pressed, keeping Larthia from Arith's caustic tongue. Her nephew Avele accompanied Vel to Tarchna on his annual journeys. Deliberately, Risa invited Arith and Ramnes to come when duty required them to attend Cisra's celebrations.

Risa and Parth's boys came into cresting, their age for responsibility. Hunter Culni married into a horse-breeding family from the northern mountains. He had ridden with Iola since they met. She was a tall, willowy, quiet woman who thought more about horses than people. Perhaps that was why they procreated only two.

Road Planner Ari wanted children and selected Caitha without help. They were childhood playmates, having met at a cart stop when they boarded for training. Caitha's hips were ample for childbirth.

"The gods blessed us with seven, a positive number," Ari said, cuddling his adorable wife.

The main attachment between the two estranged sisters was their father, Vel, by day the Soil Sampler, by night a widower.

Vel had become the subject of much talk. Rich widows thought him a handsome catch. His noble good looks had charmed many women since Anneia died, but he was resolute to stay unmatched. The family enjoyed his escapades and bantered as to which woman would unhinge him.

"Aren't there gorgeous women in Tarchna for you?" Risa teased. "Is that why you moved to Cisra?"

"The city wanted my expertise. They think I help increase its coffers," Vel praised himself, not offended by Risa.

"Tarchna's loss and mine," Parth said. "I miss our talks of road building."

"You must be happy there," Risa said with a hug, showing fondness for Vel that he didn't reciprocate.

From the beginning to end of the heat season, Arith pestered with sentimental messages about yearning for closeness. The next flattered Risa's homemaker abilities and tempted with a list of delicacies she could bring on a visit.

"I don't want her here. She's trouble. We have to think of our sons, their wives, and Larthia," Risa said, resisting her sister's hints. The messages became more urgent. Arith's servant pleaded for invitation on her behalf, exhausted from running between cities.

"Arith begs to see me after these many years," Risa told Parth. "What does she want from me?"

"Relent, Risa. You have firm convictions that comes with age. And I'm here for you."

Haruspex witnessed Arith's entrance into Tarchna but made sure she didn't see him, not wanting her slurs. Messengers ran ahead of Arith's chariot calling out her title, like she was a princess-priest. Servants, guarded by other sword-carrying servants, lugged packages as they walked beside the slow-moving vehicle. Flaunting wealth to friends and neighbors as Maru had done at processions, Arith perfected her visage with Aegyptian powders, kohl and rouge. Her hair was styled with combs; bangles were at her wrists. She waved her scarf like a banner as her transparent tunics and mantles showed breasts and hips.

Doors opened at hearing the commotion. Not seeing the golden laurel crown of the highest noble, the Tarchna lost interest.

"She has to make a spectacle," Risa said recognizing her sister, not knowing whether to laugh or cry.

With her bags of tunics, shoes and cold season robes, it became apparent that Arith intended to stay.

"She's settled in. Arith moved our linens off the shelf and put her cosmetics, hair unguents and tunics there," Risa said.

"Not a hard task for us to undo. We'll put them back," Parth grinned.

77

The two sisters spoke of childhood memories, each telling how they were raised in the same family.

"Anneia and Vel doted on me, giving the best gifts they could afford, taking care with my learning, fawning over me like I was an infant. Of course, these are rights of the eldest." Arith brushed oil into her long hair, trying to cure dryness and cover a bald spot.

"Much interest went into your training." Risa watched her sister's grooming as she coiled her own curled strands into a braided knot on top of her head, avoiding Arith's eyes lording over her.

"It's as if we came from different houses, different parents and different families," Risa said, sensing Arith was becoming contrary. "Our lives have been opposite."

"You weren't as spectacular as I, so you deserved scantier learning. Our parents knew you needed less." Arith peered into her mirror, searching her angular cheeks for wrinkles. "When it came time to choose my husband, father and mother wanted one to match my beauty. No one compared favorably, so they hosted a seasonal hunt and I chose Ramnes."

Match her beauty? With a rush, it came back to Risa. Arith lies! Ramnes was a spy for Cisra long ago. This past season, Parth had found out when he met sheep farmers on the Cisra road. They remembered Ramnes as the Cisra man who pretended to buy new stock. Instead, he counted them for Cisra's magistrates and contrived to get an invitation to Vel's dwelling.

Arith was half-lying now. "With his firm muscles, I decided Ramnes would do as a husband. I had to plead with Father, promising to visit home often."

The rest of the story was true. "Father was satisfied after magistrates of Tarchna and Cisra arranged our union." Arith smiled her superiority. "I knew I'd get my way. My wedding was the cause Tarchna and Cisra are civil to each other."

Get her way? She always gets her way, Risa thought, trying to think of what to say so they wouldn't battle. "Ramnes was a good choice for you."

"His sizable wealth gave us a grand life," Arith said haughtily, her face ashen. "But now Ramnes and I aren't of same mind. The magistrate's sarcophagus started our argument."

"A sarcophagus?"

"Avele was still in his youth. Magistrate Spurinna had died." Arith's eyes misted. "I can't forget the sculptured couple carved on Spurinna's sarcophagus. It burned into my being. What beauty!"

"Beauty is wondrous to all. The gods must have blessed the magistrate in death with beauty."

"I loved them so. I was called to them." Arith's chest lifted and fell, heated with her story.

"A piece of stonework can hold magic," Risa rationalized, beginning to wonder at the strangeness of Arith's affliction. "Beauty is magic."

"Another one has been made."

"Like the sarcophagus you speak of?"

"How slow you are. Yes, one like my couple's. The unknown sculptor crafted another for a patron. It's not good. Doesn't have the same beauty."

"You could have one made."

"Ramnes refuses."

Parth's new chariot, given by Zilath, went up the hill to Rasna village. Risa and Parth stood bouncing in its bucket. Risa clamped her arms around his back as he drove. "She craves a sarcophagus. Ramnes didn't. He has other women and stays away from her, so she left him. That's why she's here."

"She ruins her marriage for a sarcophagus?"

"Father will lose respect should Cisra find out about Ramnes and Arith's separation."

"Better to say she's come on an extended visit. We won't be disgraced by her again."

"Must we keep my sister under our roof," Risa chaffed, "after what she has done to me from birth?"

"It's our obligation," Parth answered, feeling his wife's body behind his. "She's aged badly. You're still slim while she's beginning to fatten like a caged pig, plumped for feasting."

78

Arith expected everyone and everything to go her way. The more that was given her, the more she expected. She rose at late dawn and wanted a bath. She only ate food of her liking. She drank wine saved for occasions, not the household ration. She treated Risa and Parth's servants as if they were her own.

"How bland Tarchna is. It dwells on commonness," Arith said.

When Arith spoke of the sarcophagus again, Risa asked, "Why do the Cisra want their souls confined in a box when they're already in afterlife homes?"

"We must be secure," Arith explained condescendingly. "We don't want our souls' spirits to fly, or they may escape through walls."

"We like our souls to rest as they have in life's space with freedom to move about in our chambers, so beds are built," Risa replied.

Arith laughed, primping her locks. "How simple you Tarchna are."

"You deride Tarchna, your birthplace."

"I was born here but I got out. Father smartly left. Venu goes beyond. But you dumbly stay."

A pang of anger pierced Risa. Comparing all of their lives gnawed at her. "You talk about your hair falling out. I'll show you hair fallen out!"

Risa lunged at her sister's head and pulled. She looked at her fingers and saw a clump of Arith's hair that looked like a quill brush to clean birdcages.

Arith clawed at Risa's face. "It's only fair, for one of my hairs, I knock out one of your teeth. How will everyone like your famous smile then?"

Blood trickled down Risa's cheek. She punched out at her sister's hand. Arith missed Risa's face and hit her collarbone. Risa retaliated, ramming her head against Arith's stomach. With a shrill cry, Arith fell backward, thumping on her bottom and sat there, open-mouthed.

The gods have turned me into a raving maenad, Risa thought as she walked away.

Welts rose on Risa's cheek. She felt like a heartbroken slave.

"Arith gets what she wants without struggle," she ranted to Haruspex. "I wasn't the beauty. My face was softer, not striking. My banquet was to be the highlight of life. She ruined it. Is she more blessed?"

"She didn't get the sarcophagus." Haruspex applied a comfrey root poultice on Risa's bruises. "An obscure problem. Too much has spoiled her. You appreciate the moments of your life that have been joyous. Forget the agonized ones."

Risa tried to recall those happiest moments, memorizing helpful words to convince herself she was strong against Arith's torture. To calm her own evil reaction, she found cause to leave the room or house.

There was no accord in Arith's visit.

Like Risa, Haruspex bristled at Arith's prickly conceits. He put potions in Arith's wine as she had done at Risa's banquet. Not effective, he tried spells. His powers were sickly from the miseries of biting mosquitoes. His wisdom cooled.

Risa didn't know Haruspex's malady, but he wasn't who he had been. She consulted a prominent fulguriator, an augur-priest higher than a haruspex, closer to the gods, who divined meanings of the flight of birds and the secret of thunder.

At the top step of Tarchna's wall, Risa met the fulguriator where he sat with a falcon tethered to his wrist. "Arith thinks her way is the true one, belittling me as she did in childhood, Fulguriator. We can't agree."

"I prefer rain and lightning bolts to family adversity," he said airily, his eyes on the view of sky and sea. "You still live in the shadow of your older sister. Envy and greed stand in her path, torment in yours."

"What signs can the heavenly birds give on how to speak with Arith?"

"Voltumna, god of strange and contrasting attributes, sometimes malevolent monster, sometimes earth god spirit, sometimes divine war god, marks your passage."

Shaking from this split warning, Risa asked, "What do I do to please Voltumna?"

"Voltumna cannot help you. There's nothing you can do. It is fated, one of life's flaws. You scorn your sister, yet you love her because you're bonded by kinship," the fulguriator conjectured. "Distortions of life have separated your souls."

"Our fates are circumscribed and even a fulguriator's wisdom can't soften disharmony," Risa told Haruspex.

"Give me another chance to help," Haruspex begged and retreated to his home in the hills to contemplate solutions.

On his way, he saw a flutist on the apex of a cliff, beckoning a fleshy stag from his glen. The Flutist swung his pipes high, then low with a cadenced tune that dissolved the stag's fear. Primed for death, the stag danced after The Flutist.

"How incredible the cosmos is," Haruspex sang to Tinia. "The stag knows his fate. Even as I read the omens, I know that Risa's fate and destiny are wished by the gods."

79

Venu had made the right choice of staying a seafarer in his cresting, and it showed on his ruddy countenance. Sea was better than land, but after eight seasons at sea among the ardent Athenians and bristly Phoenicians, it felt good to be with Etruscans.

Earsplitting horns of Tarchna's city-callers deafened Venu as he marched through brick-paved streets with his fellow seafarers from <u>The Plentiful II</u>.

Shopkeepers, grain-storers, candle makers, elders and young children flooded the main thoroughfare, an amicable crowd enjoying moments away from a day's toil. Granted permission by the prince-priest, they were here to view exotics from the ship. Venu knew what was aboard. They had brought ivories and inlaid carvings from Aegypt, gold-threaded fabrics, dates, figs and pomegranates from Phoenicia, along with Tarchna's mundane trade.

Jubilantly, the rough-bearded seafarers hailed and laughed with those on the curbs, acting as if the sea had charged them with its salt. Moving side to side like he walked on a rocking ship, Venu freed from rank when he saw Risa. She stood out, not in the same disposition as those around her. He grabbed her arm and jested, "Don't you know me, sister? Your glum face makes me think you aren't who I think you are."

"Great Tinia!" Joyous tears of relief filled her saddened eyes. "Venu, you're safe from the sea. You've appeared like a misty spirit from the dead. However, your laugh is very real."

They hugged tightly, but Venu felt her tension. "Your mood is as bleak as Vetisl's sleep."

"I was on my way home when I ran into this crowd. If only I could be as happy as they."

"You didn't mean to come?" Venu asked as more townsfolk came to march with the seafarers.

"I've been consulting a fulguriator who's known to be sagacious."

"What causes you to seek him?"

"Arith. There's no lightness with her. She crushes what is dear to me."

"Join us. We parade our bounty to the court," Venu invited as the horns blew for the oarsmen to usher the vessel's bounty, wheeling crates, bundles, odd parcels on wooden pushcarts.

Gracefully, Risa stepped with him and said, "Arith lets me know of her wealth, banquets, but mostly her beauty. How would I behave if I had Arith's life and could have my pick of jewelry? Would that make me her equal?"

"She has always thought no one equals her."

The man behind Venu coughed.

"Who's he?" Risa pried. "He smells of sea but he's not Phoenician and isn't Etruscan."

"Shh! He's Hellenic from Corinthos. A craftsman of high caliber."

Risa looked back. "How exciting to have new talents from Hellas, but he trails you."

"Zilath frets at losing commercial power to Cisra and commands that we find exceptional barter. Nikothenes is part of that trade."

Risa studied Venu's somber face. "We don't capture humans except slaves for labor. You can't be toting a slave, can you?"

"No, slaves don't parade with shipmasters."

"With so many Tarchna around, you talk low. Does he speak our tongue?"

"He learns quickly."

"It's a despondent man who becomes dangerous. Despair comes from within him," Risa perceived.

"You see that?"

"And your glib speech about trade," Risa said, perplexed as they got to the viewing stands and idled among the displays. "That doesn't seem right."

"Shipmaster Alfnis needed a prize for Tarchna, and Nikothenes can teach our craftsmen to turn blackware decorated with Hellenas gods and great wars. He's of Corinthos and we haven't many of that city," Venu said.

"You took a renowned artist?" Risa's voice rose in disbelief.

"Don't tell anyone. It could mean trouble for Tarchna."

The display and distribution over, brother and sister walked towards the Laris-Vella home with the Hellenic in mute attendance.

"In captivity, Nikothenes sickened almost to death by foul water. Alfnis directed me to make him well. Do you remember the herbs and potions mother taught me? I keep bundles stored on ship and gave him some," Venu said, wanting to make sure the man could hear him.

Nikothenes suffered at their walk. His face, darker toned than most Etruscan people, was dry from hot sun.

"He doesn't look strong."

"I saved his life." Venu said without pride. "Alfnis was relieved that the Hellenic hadn't infected the rest of the ship and increased my wealth as sea merchant by making Nikothenes mine."

"So he is bound to you like a slave," Risa said, beginning to pity the man treated as baggage.

"He's for service to Zilath but is part of my household."

"Household is a land lover's word. When did you become housebound?"

"Since we anchored in port, Nikothenes has been with me. Alfnis enjoys seeing how discomforted I am by my new possession because he can tease that I was born a noble, stolen by the sea."

Risa glanced at the Hellenic. "Alfnis isn't being levelheaded, but you agree."

"I have to."

"Be careful, Venu. New arrivals are first taken to the fields, toiling naked to prove their worth. That's no place for a craftsman. For his own protection, we can't safely shelter him in our home. He must stay among the servants so that no one will know he's a slave."

Venu winced at his own trumped up story, part truth, and part fib. Many nights he had brooded over how Nikothenes could meet his family.

Feeling the undercooked barley in his stomach, he said, "Your solution is good. Nikothenes will have to be treated as a servant."

80

"Tell me what I missed, Haruspex," Venu implored, resettled from his voyage, his thinning hair bleached from sun and wind.

"Much," Haruspex said. "The Zilath of your early cresting died in the last warming season, the same prince-priest who brought Tarchna to greatness and ordered growth to that southern city, Ruma. Popular, much loved Zilath had been in his twilight."

Venu blinked back tears. "How will we survive without our Zilath?"

"The Flutist made Zilath's death known with the strangest song. He droned on for a day, buzzing flat tones until magistrates urged him to desist. That's how Tarchna learned."

"Buzzing?"

"It reflected his death. He was stung by a bee."

"A single bee couldn't kill."

"Actually, a swarm of bees attacked him as he inspected the fields. One gave the final sting. His skin bloated. He became feeble. His body withered."

"He's ruled over my family and that of my father Velthur Porenna. He's given us a good life. Old Zilath's death is a blow."

"I went to his funeral, a festive sight at a mound chamber on the hillock away from the uplands, a rich sepulcher made richer with offerings left by citizens. Hundreds of bronze votives encircled his death couch where his nostrils and orifices were stuffed with linens. Rose and lavender petals adorned his gold-leafed tunic. Opinion was he had been a supreme prince-priest, one of the best since Tages founded Etruria."

"Who will lead?"

"The next Zilath is chosen already. He's a lusty young stallion and lacks restraint. Be aware that the priests teach him to be stricter on nobles."

"Tarchna can't be the same with the new prince-priest."

"This new Zilath has a puny chin, but augur-priests trained him in his first season. He carries on Tarchna's cold-blooded traditions—to hate and compete with Cisra. He has his scribe write decrees to bring downfall to the Tarchna king branch of lineage that remain in both cities," Haruspex said.

"My family must be careful," Venu muttered.

"Can't hear you. I'm getting deaf," Haruspex squeaked.

"Have you cared for my family?"

"They take up my daily life. They have learned how to feast, delight in banquet and live in the gods' good graces. I am always with your clan."

"Since when?"

Haruspex calculated for awhile on his fingers. "Lost count. I'll start with your mother, Anneia. Everyone was affected by her death, a grueling time when the might of angry gods played havoc with the cosmos and the Vella-Laris household."

"That I know," Venu said softly.

"Her death caused events that shaped all of your lives." Haruspex cleaned drool from his hairless chin. "Everyone in the Laris family had their own version of Risa's cresting banquet, even the children who weren't in Tarchna. When Culni and Ari arrived home after hunting, they saw their parents act like strangers when they spoke. Larthia was too young to understand why her parents played less with her. Ramnes' wife returned to Cisra, prone to shrieking. Vel was unmindful of them all, in the cosmos of his own making."

"How did you find out?" Venu asked.

"Without watching those I instruct, it would be impossible to serve. I sneak around, listen at doors and walls, mix with crowds, hide in travelers' bags, behind trees or turn into stone by my black cloak. I can't rest for many important words are said when Tinia's skies darken."

"You're the crafty one," Venu laughed. "I like how you take part."

"If I could blush, I would. Hostile babble destroyed something in this stubborn family."

"We're not stubborn."

"Your clan is full of resistance. At that time when the shifting winds swirled, leaving a taste of ashes in everyone's mouth, they rarely mentioned the scandal, humiliation and grief, preferring memories to stay in the past.

They had dignity." Haruspex shook his head at that tragic episode. "What a cosmos."

"You have skills of a prophet."

Haruspex broke into his first-ever true smile. Eyes twinkled like Tinia's stars. "Each and every Etruscan since Tagus acquired the secret to life: 'Make the most of what you are given. Enjoy this day. Seize each moment as if it's your last breath.'"

81

At new day meal, Risa saw that Venu's bowl of hunter's stew wasn't emptied. "Isn't this better than fish?"

"Food is less salty than at sea."

He couldn't eat more than a mouthful, only barley cakes and meat scraps, nor did he want boar, stag or hare.

"Our entertainment must bore you," Risa said when Venu napped during a performance of dancers at a friend's banquet.

"I miss the rocking ship and sleep poorly," he fibbed, kept awake envisioning Nikothenes on a cushion-less pallet.

Days later, Risa peered at Venu's blotched face. "Has a spider stung you?"

"Spiders don't sting."

"Are you listless from not being at sea?"

"Perhaps." Venu smiled vacantly, lying on the reclining couch in the courtyard, looking at clouds forming with rain.

Risa said to Parth, "Venu's been here a half moon. Discontent is within him. Nothing removes his melancholy—neither rest and air, friends and family at table, nor work in the yard. I fear his mysterious illness, incurable with his own herbs, will take him to the afterlife before his natural time."

"We could show him Tarchna's newest buildings and inventions. He might want to go to athlete's contests."

"Frivolity isn't the solution. That augur-priest I saw at the temple may have a remedy," Risa suggested.

When food held no appeal, Venu's waist began to thin. His shoulders became bony.

Parth drew his brother-in-law from the couch. "Lean on my arm."

"Leave me be."

"No. Your sister won't have your death on her hands and neither will I."

"You have a secret," the augur-priest intuitively divined, piously sitting on a temple platform among his votives.

"Seafarers have no secrets. We shout at the wind," Venu protested. "Who are you to talk of secrets, you who keep many?"

"It distresses you," the augur-priest replied mildly. "You're scrawny from lack of food."

"Your presumption annoys. Haven't you heard me? You're wrong," Venu said rudely.

The augur-priest became less pious, thundering at Venu, "Unburden yourself!"

Shocked by the diviner's astuteness, Venu folded to the floor. "When I was a boy, I got off our ship in Corinthos, not telling my shipmaster Alfnis."

"You ran away," the augur-priest corrected.

"Nikothenes was in an alley and saw my problem."

"Nikothenes? A Hellenic name."

"Yes. The Potter, Nikothenes. He fed and sensibly took me back to ship. We were both youths, but he was levelheaded. On this past sea voyage, at Corinthos dock, Alfnis woke me from sleep. 'I've goods as valuable as gold,' he said and dragged in a man with bound eyes and wrists. Alfnis had abducted my childhood friend."

"The gods of fate were at work," the augur-priest intoned.

"I was embarrassed that Zilath forced us into piracy. Nikothenes didn't utter a word that he knew me. He was quartered under-deck and took ill, wasting of ship-motion disease. His disappearance must cause his family as much misery as I have to keep him."

The augur-priest droned incantations until a bell tingled in the distance. His eyes flashed with lightning as he said, "Remorse has set in you, Noble Seafarer Laris, you who hold blame. Menvra, the Wise One, decrees you must surrender your spirit to the gods' divine will. Pay homage to them by reuniting your own family, since you can't reunite Nikothenes with his."

"You ripped open my guts, pulling words out I didn't know I could say." Venu bowed his head. "I never believed an augur could have such power."

82

With his wretched admission, Venu's appetite grew. Rid of deceit, he came up from his couch with the vigor of a bull. His recovery surprised everyone, even himself.

Venu offered the augur-priest a deerskin.

Fingering its hairs as if it were a talisman, the augur-priest spoke. "In the cold season, we sit at the fire to ward off stinging chills and muse about why we eat voraciously. Remains of crops are buried in the soil and Aplu's cloudy sun hugs the ground. Leafless trees stick out from frost while fallen blooms decay into mulch. Grasses turn to straw, interspersed with weeds. The once verdant hills are stripped naked. Only cypresses that touch Tinia's sky show life. Time shouldn't be wasted in dreariness at nature's cold season. You must feast."

"Feast? Seafarers don't feast. We eat barley cakes and dried fish."

"Food isn't just for nourishment but the source of life's delight."

"Feasting isn't my pleasure."

"Didn't you learn that Tarchna youths feast every fourth season when voices alter or prizes are given for hunting, wrestling or riding? You must have hated your own manhood banquet," the augur-priest surmised.

"I didn't have one. I was at sea. Zilath never granted one when I was in Tarchna."

"You were an awkward child, Venu. Any cause justifies celebrations when changes occur—a child's body blossoms, a young woman starts her blood, or a man's hair whitens. Don't become a dour elder. I'll teach you to feast."

Tarchna was ablaze with cold season festivities. On the shortest day of the year, the prince-priest and the richest nobles, magistrates and elders in the city gave feasts. Land owners, wealthiest trade merchants, metal-smiths, architects and engineers were invited with spouses to the great temple court or dwellings. The augur-priest took Venu on his round of those banquets where Parth and Risa were sometimes among the guests.

"Make raucous noise to wake the hibernating gods. Cajolery in the temple's halls must be loud, loud, loud to beg heat from heavenly gods to warm the cosmos," Zilath insisted jocularly to his subjects. "Look at the cosmos with a merry eye."

Venu learned to consume food for a man twice his size, vomiting it out at the end of night like the others. How different the winter feasts were from Venu's childhood memories. He became less somber, singing and dancing to the flutists' pipes with the other celebrators.

"Surely, no other people throughout the Great Sea live life as we Etruscans do. None have our blessedness."

"Or abundance," Venu said.

Venu announced to his startled family, "A time of rejoicing begins. The Goddess of Wisdom manifested to the augur-priest that we hold a feasting, a family reunion to reconcile our Laris-Vella-Vibenna Clan scattered over time and distance."

Relieved by Venu's rapid recovery, they kidded:

"In days, you left death's sleep for a feast."

"Now you want to eat yourself to death."

"Should a feast for our seafaring noble be small or large?"

"After going to feasts with the priest, one just for our family, Alfnis and Nikothenes," Venu requested.

"You want to invite the Outsider. He's a servant," Culni said.

"He's not a servant in bondage, but an artisan," Venu answered to vouch for his trusted friend.

"Mother fed him and Uncle Venu cared for him until he healed," Larthia replied. "Now he works like Lethi, doing chores in the house. Isn't that servants' work?"

"Nikothenes lives among us and has already made a place for himself in the family," Ari said. "He's more than a servant."

"Do you still call him Nikothenes?" Larthia asked Ari. "I call him 'Nikos.' That name is easier on the lips."

"Either name is fine with him. He's told me a lot about his craft."

"He doesn't seem to threaten Etruria," Culni agreed.

"The augur-priest mouths Menvra's wisdom, and we'll do whatever you want," each member of the affluent family told Venu. "We'll celebrate in style, without budget."

They hadn't guessed Nikothenes was the cause of Venu's deceit. Delighted by this discussion, Venu invited Nikothenes to the feast.

Risa praised Venu's decision and reflected, "It's been many years since we've had a family gathering. Anneia's death sent our family to different corners of life, Tarchna, Cisra, the Great Sea and the Tolfa Mountains. We're tied by threads, unlike most Etruscans whose families are sewn together."

"Even sealife is full of threads. Seafarers sew nets and patch holes in masts," Venu said, connecting land and sea.

"Threads are not as strong as sea rope," Risa answered cryptically.

As chief nobleman of his clan, Parth sought Zilath's approval for Venu's feast. "Seafarer Venu survives the sea's perils. Our family has had few feasts."

"Seafarers need to be placated when back from turbulent seas. Celebrate," Zilath said, not obliged to host and supply food and drink.

Gladly, the family began preparations. The feast would be held at the end of Tages' sacred year when the full moon would ascend in the cold season.

"Your recovery is justified and festivity is yours," Venu's augur-priest pronounced.

"No one declined invitation except Alfnis who sails north without me," Venu said.

83

"I've made a few changes." Risa laid upholstered cushions she had stitched with lotus leaf patterns on the reclining couches. "They make the dining space cheerful. I've put up dried yarrow garlands of late seasonal plantings around our votive statues."

"You're more excited about my feast than I am," Venu laughed.

"That's because it was ordered by Menvra. A good portent. Father journeys from Cisra with Avele and his young wife. They will cart the boar Avele snared himself. Arith was in Vel's former rooms, but we moved her into Anneia's quarters."

"Mother's workshop?"

"It was time to let go of the past. I restored those rooms for Arith."

"Arith must have been in a frenzy."

"She was, but your feast is reunion and we needed to find places for all. Larthia has her own room, and her future husband has been invited. Culni, Ari and spouses live nearby and will sleep at home."

"And Ramnes?"

"He remains stubbornly in Cisra."

"I'm glad you're matriarch of this house, Risa," Venu complimented. "You've kept up tradition."

Risa had altars built in the niches of the courtyard walls to set bronze stick figurines posed in heroic actions. When she put her fingertips on these ancestor spirit votives, she felt the gods' kindness. "I pay homage to you, God Lares of Households, and to all Penates gods who care for the cosmos. You warm my hands and bring good omens."

Arith kissed them mockingly and said to Risa, "That sheep dung in a black bag, Haruspex, told me he visits you. He still tells you what to do."

"I obey the gods and follow Haruspex's words," Risa calmly replied.

Arith brushed by Risa and flounced to her rooms.

Haruspex peeped around the water tank. "Your outlook has improved, Noblewoman Laris. You've become unfettered and proud from my portents, but you're competitive with your sister."

"That's over."

"I think not. She makes you miserable." Haruspex swirled about in a robe twice his size. "For the many lessons I've given you, I insist on more payment. Make animal sacrifices to God Tinia when I visit, perhaps a deer."

"A deer is too big when we'll soon be feasting," Risa objected.

"What about a hare, or a chicken?"

"Too much blood sickens me since the bloody loss of my unborn. If I may, I will gift Tinia with other Lares and Penates votives."

"I won't refuse your theistic proposal. Your wisdom grows," Haruspex said. "I'll go elsewhere for food."

"I was in the hallway and heard you bargain with the savage-looking creature," Venu said to Risa when Haruspex left.

"He's not savage," Risa said with an amused smile. "Do you not want to say you're his friend, too?"

Venu avoided answer. "You believe Haruspex but bravely stand against his demands."

"Where would I be without him?"

Before Venu's celebration, Risa appealed to her family. "Don't forget to touch the Lares when you enter or the gods get angry."

Circled by kin, patriarch Vel, his whitened beard kinked from age, approved of Risa's house votives. "They're on our side if we honor them. The cosmos becomes good with whatever one wants." He went to the dining place and raised the silver goblet that marked his status. "We offer libations to Nethuns, who piloted the course of Venu's ship. Thankfully, my son escaped danger from the Great Sea to have this feast."

"To Nethuns." Reverently, the family drank.

Risa turned toward her brother. "To your continuous health, Venu."

"To feasting!" Avele, the least outgoing of the family said with a display of emotion.

With affinity, cousins, spouses, aunts, uncles, even Vel, laughed at Avele's outburst and clinked goblets.

"Father gives me good will. After these years, he has let rest that my path wouldn't be his, forgiving me for going to sea." Venu toasted Vel. "To your happiness, Father."

Venu's favorite land foods were laid out: suckling pig on spit basted with barley meal, oil and wine, dressed with grilled rabbit and grapes. He walked around the tables and said, "Rancid meat on board ship nauseates and turns seafarers into fishermen. A fact. We eat fish stewed with sea water. Our bread is rock hard, made when there's no wind. The ship's cook tries to make meals palatable for the crew with herbs I pick on shore. But nothing compares with meats of the untamed when we reach ground. The smells at this table awaken me to eat as much as my belly can hold."

"We enjoy your words as much as these victuals." Parth peeled and offered hot chestnuts as a start. "This feast stimulates your hunger."

"Don't wait, Uncle," Larthia recommended with the vivacity of youth. "Steaming meat doesn't last."

"Whatever shall I do with you when we marry?" Arun the Hunter hugged his bride-to-be. "Will you always count on bounty of the hunt?"

"I'm sure you'll provide for me, Arun," she said, returning his embrace.

Plates of lamb shanks, trimmed with portions of boiled chard and wild mallow were served with figs. A rich harvest wine made the rounds.

"Your wine isn't tart from resin, like ours." Nikothenes drained his goblet. In keeping with the feast, he wore a traditional Hellenic chiton, the full-length tunic pinned at both shoulders, gathered above the belt, with a stitched key pattern hem, his form of freedom from Venu's bondage.

"We drink wine when we're happy." To symbolize Menvra's wisdom, Venu refilled Nikothenes' goblet as a servant would for master. "Etruria's vineyards grant us good fortune."

"And we Hellenics drink wine to make us happy," Nikothenes said, inhaling the wine's smell.

After first courses of the meal, Parth joked, "This feast is just starting. We could figure out the cosmos if the gods give us a longer night to eat and drink."

"Hellenics figured out the cosmos long ago," Nikothenes said. Realizing he might be speaking out of turn, he went on. "I don't boast but state the studied viewpoint. Hellenics think Zeus and Athena have smiled on them."

"We think that Tinia and Uni have, too," Ari said, willing to philosophize.

"While we've stolen some of your gods to worship, ours are not winged but of earth rather than sky."

Nikothenes thumped Ari's shoulder. "You remind me of my Corinthian friends."

"You'll see," Ari said kindly, knowing that Nikothenes was destined to live in Tarchna for the rest of his life. "Our gods are more human and you'll come to love them."

"We take what we like from Hellenic legends and make them our own," Risa told Nikothenes. "Most of our gods were once yours, but our augur-priests made them sacred and divine."

"Risa sympathizes with your plight," Venu interjected.

"I don't just sympathize. I admire your fortitude," she answered.

"Please tell more of your people's attitudes, Nikos." Venu chewed on a piece of pig earskin. "My family highly approves of wicked humor."

84

Nikothenes' face crumpled. "I doubt you will like what I say, but Venu encourages honesty. Hellenics frown on Etruscans, saying that you're vulgar to let women enjoy what they want, that women who recline with men at banquets are no better than harlots."

"Nonsense! They make a song and dance about reclining. Tell us more," they all exclaimed, Culni the loudest.

Nikothenes chugged another goblet of wine. "Hellenics think Etruscans are lewd to let women toast with men other than husbands and show love in front of each other."

All of the wives and daughters clapped and acknowledged the males. "Hellenics don't know bliss."

"You don't insult us, Nikos." Parth leaned against his cushion and drew Risa towards him. "We're glad Hellenics don't know our views."

"It's the nature of my kinfolk," Venu said. "Your words don't slander but broaden our understanding of the cosmos and make us laugh."

Arith moved about testily, rejecting imperfect fruit bits, tugging her garment to her curves. She fixed her eyes on the potter. He wasn't a sculptor but a crafter. All artists had the same quest, expressing perfect imaginative love with their hands. He would be a passionate lover.

"Your candor pleases me, Nikothenes," Arith said, captivated by her own smartness.

"She's interested in our Hellenic," Risa whispered, nestled against Parth's chest.

"Hellenics think they know more about the Etruscans than Etruscans, telling of Etruria's origins that baffle other countries of the Great Sea," Nikothenes said. "They vilify you with the name: 'People of the Mysterious Smile.'"

Risa perked up. "A remarkable title. Mystery is exotic. My smile is an Etruscan trait."

"Our heritage is a closeted matter, our secret," Vel said with the loftiness of nobility. "Others can speculate if they wish, but Etruscan history is ours to keep. We're unique in the cosmos."

"We fit our landscape as easily as a horse crosses a meadow or a tree roots into earth," Ari versed poetically.

When the citharist began to play, Nikothenes told the family, "Hellenics ridicule Etruscans for baking bread, doing chores and beating servants to music. It's confusing if I'm slave or servant, but I haven't been beaten. This family hasn't been cruel."

"Rhythm is necessary to knead bread," Risa said. "The cithar makes baking pleasant and shortens time. Don't worry. We Tarchna don't beat servants. They'd be hostile and revolt."

"Culni is vile when it comes to food," Parth joked. "He wants more. The hunt makes him ravenous."

"You banter with levity and flatter with kindness. I admire you for that, Risa," Nikothenes said, made careless by wine. "But my people heard of the grizzly sport of a blinded slave given a club and set upon by a leashed dog. The cruel master then strangles the defenseless slave with the hound's rope."

"That's one of Cisra's entertainments, not Tarchna's. A coarse sport of uncouth masters," Vel denounced.

"Cisra has to beat slaves into obedience or they become lazy," Avele defended. "Maru says so."

"Not servants." Arith came in from combing her hair again. "We correct them by taking away a day's meal."

"I've seen too much of the cosmos to like these customs," Vel ranted like an orator at court. "Never forget we are opposed to the Hellenics and barbarian Ruma tendencies."

"Ease up, Father Vel," Parth appeased. "We're here as brethren."

"Don't talk down to me, son-in-law." Vel retreated to his bed, satiated with food, stomach protruding from too many goblets.

"Set that episode aside," Parth said when all quieted.

Risa's eyes darkened. "Ugliness spoils happy occasions. Let's speak of other amusements. Here's one that Tarchna gabs about, that Venu's ship brought baskets of Corinthian erotica to the Zilath."

"That's talk of meddling elders. Our barter changes every season," Venu frowned.

"Erotica, Mother? This new Zilath doesn't need instruction," Culni said. "He has a reputation for Hellenic harlots."

"Zilath doesn't mind saying he needs pleasure after long days of decisions," Ari confirmed.

"Nikothenes, you don't grace our dining with sensational bowls and plates. Does the Prince-priest hoard them for his delight?" Risa baited, knowing lewd stories were depicted on Zilath's blackware.

He grinned at her while the boys burst out with laughter.

"Ah." Arith's unsmiling face gazed at Nikothenes' sensuous eyes. "Could we view their deliciousness first?"

"My feast loses joy if these talks continue," Venu yawned, overcome by swollen belly. "I'm not used to such food at one setting."

The tenacious family went to the next round of feasting. Chops of Avele's sacrificed boar were garnished with bowls of fruit, goat cheeses and olives.

Venu lay back on his cushions and listened to his family's chatter. He, the visitor, could clearly understand their harmony and tolerance, discomfort and anger. His feast had turned as bleak as Vesta dampening her cooking fires and then resumed when Risa mentioned his ship's newest bounty.

Jugs of the ubiquitous grape wine were placed for libations to Wine God, Fufluns, and Wisdom Goddess, Menvra. The citharist slid against the wall, pinging a string.

"Wake, Uncle. You doze at your own feast." Ari rocked Venu's sluggish form. "You're like a sack of barley meal."

"Get you old, Uncle?" Avele tickled Venu's hand.

"Have too many storms weathered you?" Culni chuckled. "Do you think he needs refreshment? Perhaps water on the neck." From a flask, Larthia dribbled cold drops on the back of Venu's tunic.

"Enough!" Venu humorously played along and shook off the droplets. "I will last the night."

The family drank thimbles of refills, touching goblets in playful silliness that came with the joy of celebration. At the rose-tinted dawn, slothful from food and wine, they bid each other good sleep.

85

"We keep secrets under upturned smiles," Larthia told her uncle Venu, days after his feast was over.

"So do I, but I missed being an Etruscan child. I want to know how you, your brothers and cousin grew up," Venu said.

"There are talkers and listeners. You're a listener. Whatever we tell you won't be spread across the waters."

Venu was honored by their trust. They wanted to confide in this uncle who ventured outside Etruria, made mistakes and paid for them with a lonely life.

Arith's son, Avele, was formal and vague, conduct admired by Cisra's magistrates who took him into their council at an undeveloped age. With political fervor, Avele went to sporting events of athletes where humans raced animals. Athletic and competitive, his Tarchna cousins thought him tiresome when he showed off. They were pleased when he went back to Cisra. Venu was also.

Culni was dourly earnest. Ari was merrily serious. Their inescapable bond of blood was part friendship and part hostility. Venu saw that the brothers protected their younger female sibling, high-spirited Larthia, who defied taming. As she blossomed, she gained passion to learn alphabets and numbers, taking over the chore of household accounts.

"I'm a killer," Culni, Master of the Hunt, said virtuously, stringing sheep gut to bow, chipping arrow tips from flint. "I pierce hearts of sacred beasts with bow and arrow, not just for sacrifice but for satisfaction. Is that wrong, Uncle Venu?"

"The gods gifted you with agility on horseback and a true aim," Venu replied. "The opposite of what the gods blessed on me."

Ari had learned his father's skills, the intricate study of road building. Parth took him on journeys where new construction linked hill towns, creating a network of Etruscan power. Ari's scholarly mind was on road design, debating his practical drawings to convince Tarchna's magistrates that they worked.

"I've tried to persuade the elders to change deplorable conditions of slaves who labor on roads," Ari said. "They need more care and less severity. They're humans and have wants like us. We must treat them better. Elders and magistrates dismiss my pleas."

"They're part of our hierarchy decided by the ancestors. We need the labor. That won't change. If you drum dissatisfaction, Tinia's thunderbolt may strike. Withdraw, Ari, if you want no harm to come to the family," Venu advised sadly, harboring Nikothenes.

"Men pursue me to marry, but my brothers inveigled me to choose Arun, the Hunter, Culni's friend," Larthia told Venu. "He's a fine hunter and is soon to go up in the prince-priest's favor. He gallops in the hills after The Flutist's song, snaring sacred animals during the day but feasts with nobles at night. Is that whom I want as a husband?"

"You care for him. He's ambitious and likeable." Venu listed Arun's obvious aspects.

"I can be devoted to him."

"Can be? There's something you're not saying. You come and go all times of day."

She laughed but didn't answer.

Ancestral custom dictated that Parth would have final say on marriage, but as everything else she did, Larthia chose her own husband.

Venu found Larthia extraordinary. He went to her about Arith's strange obsession for a stone-carved husband and wife sarcophagus.

"I've heard Tarchna craftsmen say, 'We are judged against Hellenic arts and found wanting. Their artists idealize life. They don't imagine the inner forces that drive life.'" Venu pointed to the votives in the wall niches. "Our art works show the core of personality."

286

"Do you think, Uncle, that the personality of the sarcophagus Arith craved shows a life force that taints those who view it?" Larthia asked.

"Perhaps Arith was tainted by something else before," Venu said, knowing Larthia was most astute, understanding life with the clarity of an elder.

"It startles me that my daughter weds. She was an infant a moment ago," Risa said nostalgically, throwing crumbs to her birds. She and Venu sat on her childhood rock in the animal yard under the stars. "Age comes quickly to us, but I've never felt old. Our time is brief in the cosmos, yet stars seem ageless. I sometimes wonder how old they are."

Venu looked at Tinia's sky. "Stars must be older than our most ancient ancestors. We guide our ship by the constant North Star. It steadies our course. Stars will be here after we are shadows."

"We're too young to be shadows." Risa slid off the rock to sprinkle grain for the birds that wouldn't come near. "It astounds me that my children have attained maturity. Tinia and Uni granted them a wholesome life. They've made the most of what is given. Their children make me a grandmother. Me, a grandmother!"

"And I a grand uncle. The boys have married well, and Larthia's union will be fine. My niece and nephews gratify me more than having my own. They fill the gap of no offspring."

"Your words are kind, Venu. Don't you need your own?"

"I don't regret not having children."

"Shy of land women?"

"I have a sea woman. The sea is my wife. She wakes me. She lulls me to sleep. You have more than I, healthy kin who will thrive."

86

"The gods are playing tricks or giving me a phenomenal fate. In Corinthos, artistic rules of proportion for gods' myths must be abided for in each vase," Nikothenes explained to Venu. "You Tarchna accept what I do with delight, allowing me to be creative. If I concentrate, I could stand out as a crafter, not one of many as in Hellas."

"You'll be established in your livelihood," Venu promised and had Nikothenes moved into his rooms. "A new peace is forged between us, a friendship solidified by Menvra."

In the season after Venu's feast, family servants set up a workshop for Nikothenes with a potter's wheel and mound-shaped oven as he prescribed. Vel gave him advice on where the best clay could be found in the hills. The black mud, different than Hellenic chalky base, exceeded Nikothenes' expectations. He planned shelves for clay models and supplies. He mortared bricks for his firing house. Whittling wooden tools out of tree branches, he polished them into precise instruments. He mixed colored pastes from powders, testing consistency.

Conceiving blackware animated him. Re-established in his craft, he shut out the cosmos. Kicking the wheel's base with his heel, he bent over the spinning circular table, determining the clay's usage for an oversized bowl or amphora. Intermittently he sponged water on the clay, his strong arms, wrists and hands curving it into shape.

While Nikothenes mastered the Etruscan tongue, the family questioned his methods and praised, "What finely turned ceramics."

"There's good black soil here," he said as his thumbs lifted pliable clay.

Appreciated, his lot improved. When he lay on his pallet at night, he thanked Tinia, not Athena, for placing him in the seafarer's hands.

Nikothenes' contentment was short-lived.

Arith came to watch him. "You work magic with bucchero to transform earth into art. You have much vitality at your wheel. Your muscles bulge from throwing clay."

Her compliments, full of sensual hints, made him feel awkward.

Venu walked through the shop, seeing unfinished bowls, disfigured goblets and shoddily painted vases heaped on disorganized shelves.

Nikothenes was sitting at his potter's wheel, staring at the wall.

"Your shop doesn't lack work, but you're not producing vases. What ails, Nikos?"

Half-heartedly, Nikothenes answered, "Nightmares. I imagine a snake coiled at my throat, its head like Arith's face. During the day, Arith is like a sea serpent, slithering around me, baring her shoulder, breathing on my neck as I work."

Venu drummed his fingers on his knees. "Dreams or truths? Does my sister have another reason to see you?"

"I'm younger than she. When she comes, my wheel unbalances and my vase distorts. Alarm spreads through me like a chilling wind. Her eyes follow me with fire."

"Arith's days are empty of a man," Venu said, weariness coming over him as if there were more to bear than he was capable of handling. "And you work alone."

"She's a seductress. She talks like a harlot."

"Do you talk to her with lust?" Venu asked, not really wanting to know.

"Lust is for uninitiated youths! Yesterday I collapsed my bowl and threw it in the slush bin, scraped the clay off the table and said I was done."

"You've been decent, Nikos."

"I was curt, but she was unruffled. She asked if Etruscans should go to Corinthos.'

"Corinthos," Venu chuckled despite his worry. "Arith threw you off guard."

"When there's interest in Corinthos, I get chatty. I told her about our king Periander who built the temple of Apollo with seven great columns and hired peasant dwellers for its construction. He's a vengeful master, but he doesn't import slaves like Etruscans."

"What did Arith say to that?"

"I didn't stay to hear."

"That's why the door was left swinging on its hinge."

"You make fun. I don't want to be involved with her, Venu."

"Arith habitually needs lovers. She marked Risa's life and damaged her spirit. Now she campaigns for you," Venu warned.

"If I displease her, she could ruin me."

"A family member is always in the house. Move to the courtyard where you wouldn't be alone if she comes," Venu counseled, not certain he would be able to keep Arith away from Nikothenes.

Nikothenes obeyed Venu, eating family meals quickly, delving into the black clay for solitude and solace.

"My clay will dry out," he learned to lie.

"You haven't escaped from her, have you?" Venu asked as he repaired a stone wall with Nikothenes.

Nikothenes lowered his eyes. "She is unyielding and harps, 'a foreigner lives at the whim of his sponsor.'"

"So that's her ploy. Not only does she threaten you, she goes against me. My sister made you think she's your sponsor." Venu's anger mounted. "You know I am, not her."

"If Arith would only go home." Nikothenes gave Venu a rock of exact shape that a craftsman's eye could see.

"My sister's demands concern us all, you, me, Risa and Parth. She's a plateful of misery for our family. We all want her to go home."

"I want to live until my twilight, not in servitude."

"Dear friend, your craft will protect you as I will," Venu said.

They joined stone to stone without mortar. The stones fit so well that the wall seemed to be made of one piece, as solid as the pact they made.

87

Nikothenes labored over the first of two vases for Risa and Parth. His hands burned with energy from the gods, pulling up the black refined clay for the pedestal, out for body, in for a tall neck, creating a gigantic hydria to bear water in the afterlife. Delicate strokes of his stylus showed ancestor love incised in friezes of tenderness, contours decorated with bands of palmettes and plant tendrils.

Risa and Venu watched the miracle of Nikothenes' craft. He recalled, "In Hellas, poets described the gods to me, and I depicted them on the sacred vases. I conformed to purpose. I didn't make erotic vases for Periander as I must for Prince-priest Zilath."

Fancifully, Risa took scraps of clay waste. "Without a wheel, I'll form a vase and paint the surface with light brushstrokes. I don't have your talents, Nikos, so my vase will be for cooking oil."

The second vase was a pomegranate-shaped amphora for sacred wine to offer netherworld gods of Hellenic myth, Dionysus among Maenades and Satyrs dancing sinuously under vines at banquet. Two handles arched out of the vase's lip, curving downward to attach to the vase body.

As Nikothenes was finishing them, Arith came into his workshop. She stammered when she saw the hydria. "The gods rejoice in the beauty of your work."

"Nikos preserves ideal love like heady perfume that brings joy," Risa smiled.

With her fingertips, Arith traced its beautiful incisions in the hardened clay. "NIKOTHENES EPOISEN is written on a frieze," she said. "What does it read?"

Venu answered for Nikothenes. "It means 'Nikothenes made.' He's famous enough to sign his work."

"I've not seen such beauty." In genuine fascination, Arith caressed the hydria's surface, her body quivering as she examined the ancient love theme, tears in her eyes. "The craftsman put his love in this exquisite vase."

"The hydria is designed to be used with the amphora. A pair. They're for Risa and Parth," Venu said. "A gift of gratitude."

Arith gaped at the Dionysian banquet amphora. "How fortunate you are to have Nikothenes' work."

The vases were stored in Nikothenes' workshop until they could be put in the Laris-Vella tomb. When nobles learned of his mastery, they visited and offered barter.

"These aren't for commerce," Nikothenes said.

Arith began to crave the breathtaking vases, dreaming of them at night. If she couldn't have a sarcophagus, these vases would do. They would bring honor to her and be a shrine for the Vibenna family tomb.

"I'm going home. A messenger brought word that Ramnes loves me and is lonely. He wants me," Arith said, and readied to leave Tarchna, stacking her fineries in her cart stored in the animal yard shed.

At the dark of night, she went to Nikothenes' workshop and covered each vase with a cloak. Under the moon's shadow, she hauled the amphora, then the hydria, to the cart. Packing them in straw and flax bundles, she layered worn tunics on top for protection.

In the glory of possession, she breathed, "These supreme vases are for me, mine to covet."

The family gathered to bid farewell as Venu and Parth secured the overloaded cart, binding it with rope.

Caustically, Arith said to Risa, "Other men are hard to attract as I age. It will be more difficult for you."

"Parth is my only one. Other men don't interest me," Risa replied equably. "Can't you understand that one man is enough?"

"So pure." Arith's voice sprayed antipathy. "You've missed variety in love-making."

"No more," Risa sighed. "Leave this time with good feeling. Our debates wear thin."

With arrogant stride, Arith swept past Risa and went to see her servant attach the cart to horse.

Risa waved at her sister's departure. She wouldn't again have to defend how she lived her life.

"The vases are gone," Nikothenes told Risa and Parth after he went to his workshop. "Arith stole your hydria and amphora!"

"That's why she rushed away," Risa said, incensed by her sister's thievery.

"We'll retrieve them," Parth assured her.

Venu nodded agreement.

Risa thought about the consequences. She would have to go to Cisra and confront. "No. The vases were beautiful, but perhaps their loss is for the best. We got rid of my sister."

"She needs the vases for her afterlife. We don't, "Parth said.

"For this life, I'll make a finer drinking cup with your image, Risa, and a drinking horn for you, Parth, a *rhyton*," Nikothenes consoled.

Risa's anger softened. "You've become a life-giving Etruscan, Nikos."

"Aha! So Arith leaves for Cisra with the best bucchero ever made." Haruspex appeared between Venu and Risa. "She lives in despair. Vetisl will guide her path."

"Who are you?" Parth asked.

"I've never visited you, Noble Vella, but you're a fine man," Haruspex judged. "As for Arith, I think she never liked me."

"She saw you twice," Risa said. Later she would tell Parth about Haruspex.

"Perhaps I steered her course and yours." Haruspex picked dried dirt from his filthy robe and held it in his emaciated palm. "Turan and Menvra sit in their temples. I trod the land doing their labor."

"You are mortal, Haruspex, aren't you?" Venu asked. "You haven't the capacity to plan this fate for Arith to reconcile with her husband."

Haruspex hopped and skipped around Risa, flapping his arms madly.

She smiled gratefully at his antics. "Menvra's wisdom has touched us all. Venu is in good health. Nikothenes is safe. Arith will no longer plague me. My home is again serene."

Haruspex stopped his wild gesticulations. A grimace came over his cunning face. He threw the dirt skyward, dusting the air into fog. When it landed, he was gone, disappearing as quickly as he had come.

Shadows of Dusk

88

"Who took Aplu's sun away?" Vel questioned in his last years as he slept in the day's heat.

Risa ladled soup into his bowl. "See? The sun in your soup is the yolk of our chickens."

As Vel aged, Arith refused to care for him. He went to Tarchna often and in due course stayed, grumbling, "I want Lethi. She'll take care of me."

"She went to her people," Risa replied. "I'm here for you."

In truth, Lethi had peacefully gone to sleep and never awakened. Her remains were covered with Vesta's hearth soot and buried near the cooking place.

"We're her family. We won't have her thrown into a cremation pit," Risa had intervened. "She was with us so long. We can put her in our tomb."

Vel could have built a family tomb in Tarchna, but Anneia's death caused him to lose heart. Her bones hadn't been found in the time of the noxious disease when victims were tossed into massive grave mounds. It was supposed her corpse lay there.

"Were her bones mingled with seafarers and merchants?" Vel raged. That virulent memory lasted until he offered a sacrificial goat to the gods, with castanet, tambourine and flutes playing in a farewell observance.

The new generation's emphasis on tombs disgusted him. Arith's obsession with a sarcophagus appalled him to say, "I want neither. They're made of flesh-eating stone. My ancestors had cinerary urns and so will I. Have a carved alabaster urn fashioned with my image on its lid, sprinkled with herbs that Anneia used. Let it be inscribed that in death I honor the ancestors. Place my urn where you will."

The patriarch went to the afterlife as a cranky old man. On his last day, he put down his soup bowl, slovenly wiped his mouth on the back of his hand and gargled, "The cosmos is chaotic. Defiance grows in Etruria. Curse those demon gods."

"He ate only a few mouthfuls each day and was thin as a razor," Risa defended her father's final ramblings. "His teeth must have ached. Yet his life ended peacefully."

Given that Cisra had been his home until he couldn't climb the Tolfa, the family agreed that he would live his afterlife in Arith and Ramnes' tomb in the City of the Dead.

The esteemed elder was eulogized in death with ceremony larger than Spurinna's but without a sarcophagus. Peer elders and magistrates of Tarchna and Cisra led the funeral parade to Cisra's City of the Dead. Rarely had the two cities combined in ritual and feasts, but they did for the Soil Sampler who brought great geologic discoveries to both cities.

"Vel Porenna never hesitated to oblige Prince-priests Zilath and Maru before his own needs, his own family, honoring societal laws and traditions," an augur-priest, who didn't know Vel, extolled.

"The gods bestowed wondrous magic on Etruria through the Soil Sampler," all said, praising his deeds.

"He would have enjoyed the fuss over his death procession, and the dignity it brought us," his descendants recalled.

89

In Cisra, Ramnes' power was increased by the workings of the elders. He represented them at magistrates' banquets in his secondary role of Maru's hierarchy.

"Stay with me," Arith cooed. "You go to so many banquets that I'm lonely."

Cinching his tunic with the fibula bearing Maru's insignia, Ramnes said, "Cisra talks that some citizens want new laws that will change our fundamental beliefs. This banquet is to squash rumor."

"I haven't heard rumor," Arith contradicted. "I can't imagine anyone against Maru."

"Not only him," Ramnes rebuffed. "There are those opposed to magistrates and elder nobles who rule over our city."

Arith watched her husband smear pomade of rose in his hair and comb his strands. She had known what he did for a long time. Viciously she persisted, "Who are you primping for? What magistrate will come near? Have you a new woman? Will there be harlots at tonight's meal?"

"Because you weren't invited, you don't believe anything I say. Ever since Risa's banquet, you don't trust anyone," Ramnes hollered as he left. The household cringed hearing the master and his spouse having another spat.

In good banquet form, the already fat-bellied guests drank Cisra's best and ate generously at the magistrate's house. As the starless night blackened, they were lulled into festive conviviality, glutted with delicacies decorated with wild parsley and carrot leaves.

One by one, magistrates and nobles, whose lineage stemmed from the ancestors, drooped onto restful cushions with numbing drowsiness while swilling wine and eating chestnuts and grapes. Cisra's chief leader and judge, the greatest, highest Maru toppled over Ramnes whose face was in grapes. Nobleman Cneve of the Seianti Clan laughed as he drooled the remains of boar skin. Magistrate of Farm and Vineyards sighed and dropped his goblet into Magistrate of Road Construction's lap.

Eyes fixed, mouths open, the banqueters' slumber was to be enduring. Cold and stiff, they were poisoned. All dead.

Unfavorable Vetisl gods ruled supreme. Purposefully, the magistrate's servants had chosen that night to annihilate. They stayed to make sure the elite were dead, kicking the corpses into an alley for the vultures' pleasure.

At the owl's desolate nocturnal hoot, Arith's personal attendant brought news of Ramnes. In horror, Arith screeched so loudly that the household heard her. "I'm not part of it. It's not my fault! Will they kill me, too?"

Her cries lengthened until she collapsed into a black sleep. Her attendant sat by, until Arith woke and ordered, "Get out! Get out with your lies."

Clothes and hair in disarray, Arith dashed towards the cypress borders.

A servant at morning chores in the animal yard said, "I couldn't be sure it was Master's Wife. She had lost her refinement."

A shepherd saw Arith running across his field, bound for the high mountains.

Trumpets sounded for Cisra citizens to come to the court at late dawn. On the platform, a phalanx of Maru's servants spread out. 'They' of Arith's rantings, weren't true servants, not of Cisra. The one who had posed as an elder at Maru's court and spread stories of Maru's tomb plundering, marched forward.

"We are the Opposition." He tore off his servant's tunic. On his chest, the bronze armor of a warrior shined. He picked up his shield. The other servants, all warriors, did the same. "Once Maru had total power but gave unsatisfactory performance. He was impious to the gods. He wanted to be a god."

The crowd gasped.

A citizen stood up. "We love Maru. He's been our prince-priest since we were children."

"Not any longer." A servant-warrior jumped from the platform. His sword flashed. The man was decapitated.

A woman screamed. Some fainted.

"In Tinia's name, lay face down in the stones," the leader commanded.

Tumult ensued. In conformity, all bent to knees and flattened to the ground.

The leader walked on their spines, calling out Cisra's new order for the cosmos.

Terrified that the warrior's henchmen would kill them, Avele, with his wife and children, fled to the Laris-Vella house in Tarchna.

"We'll do what's expected. We'll keep them with us," Parth said.

Risa tried to calm Avele, hugging him like a mother, tears welling in her eyes. "We'll make our clan survive."

"I saw my father's corpse. He was foaming chewed leaves at the mouth." Avele shook and held onto his aunt.

"Wild parsley and wild carrot look like hemlock. Your mother may have been poisoned, too." Parth gently touched Avele's arm in sympathy.

"Mother wasn't at that banquet. Her attendant told me that men from Tarchna were with her earlier."

"Arith hasn't been in Tarchna for years," Parth frowned.

"I searched hills and valleys that the shepherd indicated and the forests beyond, but she's not to be found."

"Arith could have fallen in the woods," Risa said to her nephew, thinking that her sister might have been unable to move and starved to death. "It's been known that gushing torrents can bring misfortune while cupping hands for drink."

"No one knows. I despair over my mother's disappearance."

Risa felt her sister's death upon them. She hoped Arith had gone peacefully, but a nagging thought went through her head. She wondered if Arith had the eyes of a hunted wolf before death.

"There must have been a wicked culprit who became disloyal to the ancestors, one who led the opposed to the banquet. Who turned enemy? Could it have been Arith?" Risa said as she and Parth rearranged space for the additional family.

"She loathed Maru for slighting her."

"How ironic that the fulguriator recognized that there would never be harmony between Arith and me. I hated when she acted like the highest noblewoman. I loved my sister. Were we not of the same roots? I was jealous of Arith my entire life."

"Blood ties matter," Parth said.

"It's the final say of the gods that Ramnes and Arith will never enter their tomb," Risa consoled Avele. "No one knows where their remains are. At least, your Grandfather Vel's alabaster urn sits in their tomb, close to Nikothenes' Hellenic vases made for Arith and Ramnes."

90

"Heroes home from Cisra are here to greet you!" The second prince-priest Zilath announced to the special citizens' meeting. "Meet the Democratic Magistrates."

The guests stood. "Why should Tarchna bewail the fate of Cisra's Maru and magistrates? That unholy city defies our holy laws. The Great Prediction began when they turned against us. They murdered our Old Zilath. They're enemies."

Behind him on the platform, an unfamiliar augur-priest said, "Cisra got what it deserved."

Equally curt, another augur-priest said, "Old Zilath's death caused by bee stings was the work of Maru's henchmen. We retaliated. That took many years."

Not missing a moment, prince-priest Zilath advocated to his people, "We have faith in all our leaders. Our city won't unbind. There is no cause to doubt our fidelity."

Risa and Parth were among the audience, sequestering Avele, his wife and children in their home.

"These men scare me. What are they doing in Tarchna?" she nervously asked him.

"They must be the Opposition that Avele told us about. Zilath's mercenaries are against Cisra."

"So mercenaries are killers. They're responsible for the overthrow," Risa said despondently.

In Cisra, the Opposition began to channel the behavior of Cisra citizens by threats and torture. Having seized power, they nullified Maru's royalty with their own beliefs based on the Hellenic model of separating ability from hereditary rank.

"We'll have no more leaders from the family of our Etruscan ancestors!" The new leader, named 'Land and Sea Warrior,' proclaimed to the horrified city.

Magistrates and constituents of deposed noble families were hunted, brutalized and murdered until the roots of old Cisra nobility were annihilated.

Avele's quick escape had saved him and his family from the despotic rulers.

"The wealth of the City of the Dead is ours," the warrior and his men claimed, prying open tomb entrances sealed with the cippus stone, pilfering each one, stockpiling riches for themselves. The Vibenna tomb mound, four hearse carts wide, butted by two smaller mounds, lined a small road off the main necropolis thoroughfare, convenient to plunder. There, one of the warriors came upon the hydria and amphora. He rolled over one and read the crudely-written inscription on its base:

Nikothenes of Corinthos made this amphora for Risa Laris and Parth Vella. Tinia, god of lightning and thunder blesses it.

The warrior blubbered as he turned over the hydria. "The gods' love stories are on these vases. I feel their beauty."

The others laughed at his unmanly behavior.

"What goes on here?" The head warrior strode across the tomb chamber, pushed his man aside and beheld the vases. They emitted a powerful history, one that could be his nemesis and bring his death. "We'll leave the City of the Dead to the ancestors and wield new wealth elsewhere. Seal the tombs again."

Abandoned to eternal rest, Vel's urn and Nikothenes' crafts sat in the airless tomb until Avele's generation would stealthily open the door to install their dead.

91

Tarchna was safer than Cisra, but disagreement between Etruria and neighboring Italic tribes from the southern mountains couldn't be contained.

On a road in the oak and pine hills, Parth and his road crew were attacked by a roving band of barbaric thugs who wanted Etruscan land. Brought to Tarchna by villagers from the hinterland, Parth was scarcely alive, carried on a canvas frame.

When Risa received him, she purified his blood and bandaged his injuries, weeping to the villagers, "Had he been planning the road's path at that time, sighting with his *groma* or talking with his men? His crew must have resisted and fought back."

"Those fiends hacked at them, stabbing and slashing every road builder with swords and hatchets. They were left to die in pools of blood oozing across the unfinished road. We hid behind bushes and waited. When they had gone, we crept to see. We feared for our own lives," the villagers said squeamishly.

Risa's heart screamed at their cowardly retreat, but the voice of Haruspex entered her core, saying, "Don't condemn the innocent villagers. They may have been overpowered as Parth and his men, but they deserved to live."

Parth's bloodied body was too wounded to save. In his last moments, his hands reached for Risa's, and he pledged as fervently as at their union, "We are forever, my love."

With that final lingering touch, Parth went to the afterlife. She was bound to him in death as on earth.

"The Italics stole intricate tools, but they'll never steal the sacred knowledge and skills of men who studied drainage systems, erosion, silting and flooding. Those savages won't gain Tarchna's secrets of road engineering, our network of complicated highways that cross the landscape," Zilath said in eulogy. "I'll see to that."

"My grieving is less since our destiny is assured," Risa told her bereaved family as they prepared for Parth's interment, walking his chariot to the tomb chamber. "It hasn't been open since completion. Your father will be protected in our tomb."

Culni and Ari dismantled the chariot, angling pieces through the threshold to descend the stairs. Wiping off mud, they reassembled and polished the bronze ornaments and horse bits to shining perfection.

Finished, they looked at the vivid wall friezes. The most prominent showed the best scenes of Risa's cresting banquet. Asba had captured the spirit of the moment. Parth's handsome face looked devotedly at Risa as he held up the golden ingot necklace, and she smiled delightedly while they reclined on patterned cushions.

"Your smile is immortalized like that of the gods, Mother." Ari soothingly held Risa's hand as he saw the tomb chamber, hoping his praise would lighten grief of his father's death.

On another wall, Asba had painted the Laris-Vella sons throwing darts. Daughter Larthia danced to music of a youthful flutist who mingled with banquet guests. In the background, Risa's larks flitted among them.

Risa draped Parth's prize ribbon on his chariot, placed where he had wanted. Running her fingers over the hammered bronze, she saw him standing proudly, tall and smiling, whip in hand. He urged his stallion over cobble roads built with his men. Not pausing, he passed her on his afterlife journey.

"*A phantasma!* It was a phantasma I just had of my dear husband," she murmured as the image dissolved, leaving her at the chariot's frame. Happiness rushed through her for the first time since Parth's death. As she scattered lavender for his funeral parade, she saw the entrance wall. Painted leopards reared up on muscled hindquarters, guarding the doorway.

"I've never seen them before," she said to her children. "They're so alive, joyous!"

"Mother," Larthia hugged her, "why didn't you tell us of all these paintings?"

"Why wasn't it known?" Culni inspected each segment of the colorful walls. "They're splendid."

"I knew." Ari grinned at besting his older brother. "Mother came to the uplands into this chamber often. She walked fast, so unlike her that I wanted to know what she was doing. Once, when she left, I went down."

"You spied on me?"

"I was nosy. You were mysterious. Asba and I became friends. He cautioned not to tell of our meetings. That was the time when Tarchna didn't want other Etruscans to discover our tombs."

"What kind of meetings could you have with a crafter, Ari?" Risa asked.

"He taught me how to draw," Ari revealed, letting his mother know part of his secret cosmos.

92

Wearing his finest tunic, Parth's body was carried to the uplands tomb chamber where his sons laid him on a bed of bird feathers.

Sprinkling lavender petals, Risa greeted mourners, elders, nobles, friends and clansmen holding candlelight. They paraded through the chamber, circling twice. Before exiting, some complimented, "Asba, the crafter, honors the Vella family. These are the best paintings of Tarchna."

As candles burned out, the Laris family surrounded Parth's bed.

"Everyone goes to our father's feast," Culni told Risa. "It's time for us to leave him."

"Give me more moments." Risa knelt by Parth's bed, caressing the fabric of his robe.

"Don't delay. I'll host the meal until you attend."

In spite of her depleted spirits, Risa smiled at how mature her eldest son had become since Parth's demise, the strength of the next generation surging. She gazed numbly at her husband's resting body. "I miss you, my beloved. You're in my thoughts, alive with me. We shared a bed, arms locked in falling asleep, warm comfort after the day. Turning in dreams, we clasped our hands together."

"The cores of your beings are entwined." Haruspex materialized from a tomb niche like a vapor from the heavens. Older than ever, he stood by Risa and intoned kindly, "Invisible cords bind you. It has always been so."

"We had a romantic love, my soul mate and I, not knowing what would be our fate. Then the celestial gods struck Etruria. The cosmos became strange with the Great Prediction."

"It's not strange when one considers that the powerful Etruscans are envied by other peoples," Haruspex reminded Risa with lucidity of one able to see and argue all sides of an issue, whether good or bad. He raised Risa to her feet. "Go to your guests. Partake of cheese and fruit, toast Parth with wine and honor his goodness."

Hand in hand, they went up the chamber steps, not disturbing Parth's sleep. "You have much life ahead and the gift of energy. Use it well."

93

Noble-turned-seafarer Venu loved <u>The Plentiful II.</u> The prince-priest had awarded the ship to his care after old Alfnis resigned from his post. Sailing across the Great Sea and to the Greater Sea, Venu became a better merchant than his predecessor, riding out Tinia's storms to victoriously bring new goods to Tarchna.

Rotted from barnacles, the ship's hull gave out in sight of Gravisca port. Abandoning the goods, the crew swam to shore, salvaging their pride.

"Nethuns sent the Oceanids to alter my life. He gifted the sea with our barter as offerings to him," Venu said. "Now, I'm at a disadvantage. I haven't the strength of youth anymore to take on another ship."

He came to his rooms within the Laris home in a new role, the surviving eldest nobleman, and patron of the family, Risa's sole protector who nurtured her grown children, nephew and their spouses.

"Landsman Venu, you enjoy your new status," Risa cheered.

"I miss the sea salt, but I'm content that Nikothenes' tomb vases are in great demand."

"He's created the ceramic works with your help," Risa said, aware that his penitent smile may have expressed misdeeds of being a seafarer.

"Nikothenes trades bucchero and terracotta for home and tomb adornment to Etruria's other cities. He barters with Phoenicia and Carthage. More Hellenic crafters have arrived from Corinthos and are in the shop, spinning red and black ware on their wheels. Exekias migrated. He incises Dionysus and the Tyrrhenian pirates on vases that Tarchna craves. Lydos decorates hydrias with the fight between Hercules and Geryon. Nikothenes doesn't want to be outdone. He makes more pots with Hellenic myths in red-figured scenes on black," Venu listed.

"You're a land merchant now, too."

"And you, Risa, showed me how to treat Hellenic crafters as brethren."

"With cause. The truth is, Venu, that Hellenic crafters didn't migrate. Like Nikothenes, they were abducted, a fact the magistrates and seafarers never admit. Those crafters will marry into our clans in the next generation, more loyal to Etruria than Hellas," Risa forecasted.

Risa had fewer household chores. Her days were lengthy and empty since Parth's death. She watched Nikothenes throw mud at his wheel, turning *kylix*, *olpe* and *oinochoe*.

"There's something lacking in my life, a void that leaves bleakness," Risa confided in him.

"Your hands are firm and graceful. Try the wheel," Nikothenes suggested.

She kicked it until her leg and arm muscles ached, yet her clumsy pots ended in the slush bin.

"You've a sensitive touch, but not the roughness for clay grit. You could make delicate strokes with a paintbrush. Go to that crafter, Asba. He'll instruct you," Nikothenes advised.

"You've met Asba?"

"All crafters know another. Whether Hellenic or Etruscan, concepts of ideal beauty bond us," he answered.

94

"I've seen Asba in the market place since my cresting banquet, but I don't know where he lives. I can't go looking for him," Risa blushed at the idea.

"I can," Nikothenes said. He found the quaint tufa house within the walls of the third city gate.

"Learn the rhythm of the brush, Noblewoman Laris." Asba was mixing pigments from crushed iron with powders, sandstone into ochre, purple inks from squid and murex. "Color is part of the cosmic mystery. Tages wasn't a fool to give Tarchon white oxen to contrast the hues of Etruscan life. From the land he made it possible for me to reap pigments to texture walls."

Buckets of paint sat on a bench. She dipped her fingertips into watery aqua sediment. "What god or goddess made me do that?"

Asba watched Risa's pleasure and dunked his finger into paint, printing a mark on the back of her hand.

"I've waited for you." His eyes were on hers. "I've felt your longing."

If she hadn't remembered when they first met at Zilath's hunting feast, his forwardness would have shocked. She didn't want him to know how much he impressed her, yet she couldn't help smiling. "Your gray beard has more paint than the walls."

"Paint with me."

She looked at the mark he painted on her hand. A bird's wing. Allured, she went to see his wall friezes.

Risa cleared out a woodpile in an unused storeroom at the rear of the house where meddlesome neighbors couldn't view her new venture.

"I'm a widow. I honor my husband's memory," she reminded herself when her nights remained secluded, but thoughts of Asba's eyes left her sleepless.

At sunrise, Asba and Risa would go into the cool, damp tomb chamber and leave with the setting sun. Intent on their work, sunlight went unrecognized during the day. Asba would apply a paste of lime, sand and water to the walls and deftly paint scenes of rich tomb owners. Risa filled in his lines with color.

"You paint with such liveliness. The colors from earth and rock dance on the walls. Human and animal forms are caught in the moment," Risa admired. "Did you always draw as rapidly as you do now?"

"Time grows less, so strokes must be sure," Asba sketched swirling lines, stippling with color.

Without his spontaneity, Risa studied Asba's wall paintings and mimicked his methods on bare unfinished walls. She learned to hold brushes, applying the right glob on tips, whorled lines light or bold, to portray the figures' *dynamis*.

Asba painted with brilliant flair. The gods smiled on his artwork, he, the master who showed Tarchna's enthrallment for life and guided the deceased to the afterworld. Jocular banquet givers reclined as if speaking of important life interests. The spectral portrait of a flutist could nearly be heard playing. An eminent magistrate strode with robust determination, trailed by servants from the Hot Countries who labored in slow rhythm. Wild beasts underfoot and birds overhead filled the walls.

When Risa re-examined the animals and birds, Asba paced the tomb and asked flatly, "What is my failing?"

"I can't voice my opinion to the master."

"I've never been criticized for my art but tell if you find error."

"Asba," she said, "This animal needs a touch of iron tint for his flanks."

He stippled it with a brush and admitted sheepishly, "Better."

Absorbed in their work, they stopped only to partake of bread and wine. Food and friendship blossomed with talk of her clan and his wives.

"I married young. My bride died in childbirth. In sorrow, I immersed myself in art." Asba tore a loaf of bread in half to offer Risa. "It became my life's work. I married again. My obsession to paint was more interesting than home. To spite me, my wife went to her village and bedded with the town's grain merchant."

"How humiliating for you."

"Then, yes, but now I don't care. I seek friends, not a spouse, for pleasure."

In unspoken accord, they worked underground, the tomb quarters not offensive to either. He respected her perseverance to learn his craft. She became as devoted to painting as he. Their companionship solidified like the rock walls they painted.

After working with Asba for a season's cycle, Risa became aware of her own ripening skills and saw that Asba's thrushes and swallows detracted from his icons.

"Asba, your birds are like straw, stiff and dried from sun's heat."

"Have you a remedy?" he teased.

Confidently, Risa told him, "You haven't the feeling for skybirds, but I do."

He dabbled his paintbrush and handed it to her. "Let your birds fly through the background."

With a stroke, she conveyed the flittering of a bird's wing.

"Your skill has developed and your style defined," Asba commended, "You've learned the secret of making pictures live on the walls with charm and originality."

"I feel the delight that comes from our people's souls."

"Your passion is evident. Creatures of the wild will be your talent. Paint a cat and dove on that band. Choose if they're friends or enemies."

"The gods must be at work, giving me ideas that I didn't know I had," Risa laughed when her painted cat pawed at a hovering dove.

Asba stared at her depiction as he stroked his bearded chin. "You do well. Goddess Menvra fills my head and hands with sacred thoughts. I paint the signs she tells me, of laws of our cosmos, lion against deer or bull against ram. She fills yours with pleasure. We're the chosen ones who release those thoughts with joy through our hands."

He pointed to the wall at the entrance door where ferocious animals stood guard for the deceased in afterlife. "Practice painting those creatures," he said with a wry smile, "for we're partners in our work."

Asba inspired her. His techniques, patience and compassion fed her spirit. They went from one tomb chamber to the next, painting the essence of Tarchna.

95

"I won't deny what I do," Risa announced to her family at an eighth day meal.

"Mother, being the eldest, I have the first say. We know that you've been going into the tombs with Asba," Culni said.

"Be comforted, Mother. I accept Asba's place in your life," Ari seconded. "I'm happy for you."

"Tarchna women melt over him," Larthia said enviously.

"You think we are bedding?" Risa seethed.

"It's right that we turn our heads," Ari said.

"Holy gods of the cosmos! Turn your heads if you must, but you haven't understood," Risa boiled.

"But..." Culni protested. "But..."

"Like you, Ari," Risa continued, "Asba has taught me his craft."

Chewed food stayed in their mouths. Goblets were half raised.

Larthia broke the spell. "His craft?"

"I've chosen to be an artist." Risa aligned herself to fullest height like a prince-priest delivering law. "A painter."

Abashed, Culni asked, "Have you lost your wits? May I remind you, you have an obligation as a Tarchna Noblewoman, an Etruscan, a mother, to know your place. You'll lose your good reputation."

Risa laughed. "How self-righteous your speeches are."

"Mothers don't become artists. Artists are born into craft trade. They're lower than we," Culni sputtered.

"Lower? Dismay of my disclosure sours you." Risa glowered at her haughty son. "Beauty is what we strive for in life. Beauty is in Etruscan blood. We delight in our surroundings that we mark with beautiful touches."

Her family stared at Risa as if they had never seen her before.

"I always wanted to be more than I was, and now I am an artist." She emphasized her next words. "Don't hamper me, for it has been willed by the gods."

"I don't doubt you. Your speech is convincing," Ari buzzed in her ear. "Your eyes sparkle, Mother."

At the beginning of Risa's twilight age, she became widely known for her art, independent of Asba's popularity. Risa Laris, Woman Crafter. With a whip of a brush she could preserve the very soul of her people. Her works were sought for comfort and homage in the afterlife. What magic she expressed when her creatures warded off unknown fears.

She didn't expect to paint animals, but their prowess and movement of colorful limbs, part of sea, land and sky wrapped in one being, fused in her memory. Her ducks swam on the water's surface, lifting wings to dive into the sea. Her birds sang blissfully through Asba's landscape friezes that depicted Etruria's philosophies.

To Risa's surprise, the Tarchna adored the horse-like animal that came to her in a dream, a galloping horse with a fish-like swishing tail, a fantasy that folks started to call a *hippocampus.*

"The gods say that all nature works as one," Risa said to Asba.

"You're truly a marvel. No other noblewoman thinks like you. The death journey of a newly deceased ancestor is blessed by your tomb chamber paintings," Asba agreed.

"Our tomb chamber paintings," she reminded him.

Risa outlived Asba, her beloved friend and mentor, whose health had deteriorated from dampness, having spent the greater part of his life underground. Neither healer, haruspex, fulguriator nor augur-priest's prayers could stop the rumbling cough that lay in his chest.

"Why did you forget to paint your own chamber walls?" Risa asked him as he lay dying.

"It's harder to tell the truth than maintain a lie. I waited for you all my life." His voice was almost inaudible. "I wanted us to paint together, you who have become master crafter with me."

"I'll show my devotion to you, Asba," she wept, "by painting your tomb walls with creatures at sacred dances to bring joy to your afterlife."

Risa kept her pledge and went alone to paint the tiny chamber that was given him, he without family or descendants. There was no dampness in that small space.

"Asba must have breathed so much air in this cosmos that none was left for the next," Risa told the chamber walls as she set about to do his requests. He had wanted leopards and griffins to ward off evils. She painted them with curled tails belying their snarling jaws.

Taken by an odd mood as she painted leopards crouching low and griffins leaping high, Asba's voice echoed: "He who fears death is unworthy of life."

96

The seasons quickened with events that stimulated, or dragged. God Vulcan's cone mountain smoked. Ash spewed and lava clouded Tinia's air. Crops fell to the ground. People of Tarchna, Cisra and the rest of Etruria aged and tired.

"We are replaced by youth who spring forth like my newly hatched birds, ready to meet life's challenges," Risa told her children and grandchildren. "Your own lives are full of purpose and joy."

Only Larthia seemed to lose glee, childless with Arun, away from home with irregular frequency. Arun made excuses for her until Risa demanded answers. Larthia was doing work for Zilath, but what and where was unknown. Risky work, Risa feared. Then Larthia disappeared and scandal tore at the family once again. Larthia, dear Larthia, was labeled liar, traitor and thief. She vanished. Word came that she was dead.

"She is alive! I know it in my being," Risa protested to the family. "She is beyond Tarchna, lost in a fog. I can hear her cries and feel her speak to me from a hinterland outpost. I never thought that so many tears within me could flow like the river I see her on."

"She is dead," Arun said abrasively. "Don't think about Larthia. Block her from your mind. Work in your tomb chambers to stop your grief."

Rumors circulated of war against Hellas. There was cause. Insatiable to colonize land that was more productive than their treeless, rock-bound country, the Hellenics wanted Etruria. To fight the invasion, the twelve prince-priests recruited warriors of land and sea.

"Etruria is the garden of the gods. The dead Etruscans are already protected in happy afterlife. We must protect the living," each prince-priest decreed to his citizens to deflect the pain of upcoming war.

After learning that battles would be fought to regulate trade, Risa and Venu gathered the surviving clan to assuage fears. "We've lived within a good time, before these warmonger magistrates. War was in other lands so we lived unafraid, in peace. Tarchna and Cisra were splendid cities of my family. We knew no poverty. Menvra will brighten the future."

Augurs preached life's changes, citing the Great Prediction. "Tarchon, the Ancient One, the Field Plower, prescribed time for Etruria. That's why we need more tombs."

"How many saeculae are left?" Risa asked Venu as they ate barley soup at the cooking room hearth. "I can't remember anymore. Time is marked with each elder's death, governing the length of a saecula. The gods must laugh at that foolishness."

"Four, five or six."

"Haruspex must have joined the elders in ideological discourses to learn wisdom. He must be decrepit for he wasn't young when he first came to our house."

"He was old then," Venu said.

"His irritating voice and grimacing face became a comfort," Risa said wistfully.

"He could have disintegrated of entrail smells."

"Hold your tongue, Venu. He guided my life's path and lessened my problems. He taught patience and enlightened me with the meaning of sweetness. In truth, I came to care for him. To me, he was just 'Haruspex.'"

"Whatever happened to that grumpy old prune?" Venu asked.

"I went to those who might have used his services. Odd that he wasn't there when I began to paint," Risa answered.

When her fingers couldn't bend to hold paint brushes, and the wet walls resisted her trowel, Risa put down paints and went home, still walking with a young woman's energy, arms swinging loosely at her sides.

Risa's voice became tingly, but she hummed bits of melodies that her banquet flutist seared into her head. More often in her twilight, she sang while bathing in the river pool of underground bubbling hot water.

Not to forget. Not to become muddled like Vel and the elders. She had become afraid when old Vel couldn't understand the little things in life that were important. So sad that such a great man acted like a newborn.

Yet, she too began to push her mind to remember.

"My darling daughter, Larthia, must be at Zilath's court, paying loyalty like Anneia and Vel did," Risa told her sons. "She's blessed by the gods."

97

In Risa's twilight, sorrow from the deaths in her family mended with time. When Aplu's sun fell into the Great Sea and Uni's moon grew at night, Risa covered herself with robes, chilled often by aged thinning skin.

Wanting the serenity of sleep, her breaths became shallower. Spots and wrinkles blemished her skin, each line defined in ravages of the heat season sun. Her skin coarsened and sagged. With eyes sensitive to bright light, her shrunken skin bruised if she bumped into a table or door. Favorite foods tasted bland, and her appetite dwindled to nil.

"Where did the days go, the seasons and years? Did they wane into the misty sky gods' homes? Did they blend into the earth, the seas or outer cosmos?" she'd ask attendants as she lay on her couch. "I'm the last of my generation, respected as an elder. The augur-priests say that marking the next saecula will be based on my death."

Even Venu died long ago in his twilight years, the younger brother not outliving his sister. A seafarer until the end, he walked to Gravisca's shores into a stormy Great Sea. Fishers dragged the water with nets to find his body, but it had washed to the depths. Where he disappeared, only the gods saw a rare sea-land bird flying to the sun's rays.

To honor Venu, a bucchero *situla* of Great Sea water was brought to the Vella-Laris tomb chamber in a cart, the sides painted with Nethuns' face smiling up from waves as dolphins leapt above. The water was left to evaporate for the *situla* to be interred. Dried shells, anemones, starfish and seahorses remained on the residue of sand.

"A fitting afterlife begins for our uncle," Risa's sons had said. Now in their twilight, they came to see their mother with their children. All except daughter Larthia.

"Something bad has happened to my daughter—and I can't remember what it is. Where has she gone?" Risa asked each one, shivering with cold. Her rickety bones grated with indignation. Pain shot through her, enraging her spirits.

And then her old mind cleared to the truth. Larthia had been banished from Tarchna, never to return.

"We believe in Anneia the Healer's herbal potions, but music is a good remedy for elders," the next generation's cult of healers recommended and sent lyre masters and itinerant musicians to treat Noblewoman Laris.

After the sunset meal, they played for her. The quivering lyre strings spiraled songs throughout her being. Risa listened and sipped wine as the melodies dislodged aches from her bones.

Most meaningful were the flutists who revived her memories. They had always been in her life—flutists who went to banquets or sat in house corners or on landscape, their pipes whistling rhythmically to the pounding of mash. They walked the hills, beckoning woodland animals from caves for sacrifice, dazing them with pleasurable notes about the glory of land and sky. Music soothed her monotonous days, bringing echoes of the seasonal hunt, abundant food, prelude to celebration and joy, the ingredients of Etruria's cosmos that gave her longevity.

"The flute pleasures me for it makes a mellow sound through the air like the wide-winged hunting birds crossing a windless sky," Risa told her great-grandchildren. "The tones of the flute's pipes are like honey. They resonate in my soul."

Missing Parth as she walked to their tomb chamber, one particular flutist came to mind. He was the one who had been at her banquet, whose melodies intoxicated her dreams, repeating through her head like old chants.

Dusk was when she welcomed him most. A soft spot in her being grew for him over the years. He guided her day, playing gentle notes that faded as the sun's residue streaked the sky and the stars came up from the black unknown.

"Flutist," she once had said, "you bring peace to make me whole, so that I am part of the cosmos, part of the stars, wind, earth and water. To you, my mysterious god, I give fathomless love."

Never did he speak to her. Had Risa told Parth, family or friends of her feelings for a common flutist, they would think her crazed.

At the end of her twilight, his music flowed into her being most intensely as the loud voices of her past dimmed. She shut her eyes and heard his notes singing:

> *I caress you*
> *stroking your skin with feather's touch*
> *I kiss your lips*
> *removing the crust of weariness.*
>
> *Life's lightness remains, life's lightness remains.*

98

A noise in Risa's room startled her. "Is it the wind stripping branches of leaves?"

No one answered.

"Parth, are you getting ready for the night?" she murmured through her haze of sleep. "Did you secure the animal gate and blow out the candles? Are the children in bed?"

A shadowed figure advanced towards her.

"Who comes? Aah, it's you, Flutist, not Parth." Risa relaxed on her cushions. "You're late for your visit."

Silently he approached, the air quiet of song.

"You look like my flutist, but my eyes trick. You must be a new household servant." She stared at the illusion. "For a moment I saw the window through you." A chill, then heat pounded her chest. She said hoarsely, "I know who you are. You are Ancestor."

He loomed over the farthest end of her bed, smiling placidly.

"What do you want?" Risa stilled her body, not moving a blanket. "I've heard that an ancestor could appear to some, a hallucination that could disintegrate if an Etruscan uttered a blasphemous oath."

His smile broadened at her perception, a resplendent grin that left her light-headed and her body prickling with sensation.

"Here I am for you, Noblewoman." His serene voice floated like a breeze carrying a hatchling songbird. "Banish fear."

Sobered by his words, her own smile stopped. His voice was her flutist's. His image was of an ancestor, regal and dignified by afterlife. "I have no fear. Are you taking me to Parth?"

Without reply, he glided to her bedside.

In awe, Risa said, "You're as luminous as Uni's harvest moon. Light shines through you each step you take. You're transparent! How can that be?"

"Who knows? The cosmos doesn't give up every secret."

He kept coming toward her until she bathed in his glow.

Flashes of childhood flickered through her mind. She could feel her body move as sprightly as a deer.

The image oscillated in his moonbeam clothing. Risa was in her cresting, walking hand in hand with Parth on the windy cliff.

The image became The Flutist. He spun around. Her banquet's ugliness surfaced, and she writhed in discomfort seeing Arith's face mocking her.

He kept spinning and became Ancestor. Soon Risa's birds flitted overhead as she played with her children, hugging Ari, throwing a ball for Culni, splashing in the river with Larthia.

The scenes fused. Anneia waved her on to gather herbs in a sunless canyon. Vel stood on a mountain ridge, calling her to see his newest stones that glistened with morning dew. The pictures revolved around until she wilted from exhaustion.

"Ancestor," Risa whispered, overcome by these memories, "am I in the beyond?"

His image disappeared with her question.

"A dream," she mumbled. "The ancestor wasn't there nor was my flute player. The best dreams uplift into oneness."

Her blankets were tugged and she blinked in disbelief.

"Our cherished ones are happy," Parth said, healthy in his prime. He got into bed, warming her body. "The gods care for them."

"Chills end with you here, my love." The cold damp that penetrated the walls evaporated, and Risa smiled in relief as sunlight miraculously bathed the room. "And the heat season is upon us."

She turned to Parth and knew him to be another dream.

On a wisp of air where the Ancestor had been, The Flutist rose from the shadows and gracefully took up his pipes. The familiar song filled her with gladness. Risa closed her tired eyes and let the smell of lavender disperse in her nostrils. A far-off bird signaled her mate, and he chirped back in harmony.

Between his notes, The Flutist puffed his cheeks like Tinia's wind and blew, "Your time ceases. The journey to afterlife begins."

Comfortable in her cushions, Noblewoman Risa Laris listened tranquilly. Calmness seeped into her breasts and through her body. At the moment before death, or at death, his joyful melody muted to sadness, and then impassioned, as flowers bursting open in bloom. The song came not from afar but from her being.

Cast me not to the God Fates
without
garlands on my head
Anoint me with oils, fragrant of flowers
so I may bask in the glory
of my journey.

Attendants: dress me in fine linen tunic,
breastplate embroidered.

Gold earrings
looped under plaited strands of hair,
ringed-fingers entwined for my journey.

Best leather, pointed skyward,
lying on my bed of lavender.
Berries in my mouth to feed me
on my journey.

Here comes my family, here enter friends
the dance of death in their feet
paying homage to Vetisl and to me
in my journey.

Rejoice! Rejoice in journey
from light to dark to light again.
Flutist, play your pipes tenderly
notes poignant with love, seduction of death
for my journey.

Cast my shadows
on the walls of eternity.
Cast my shadows as one of the
People of the Shadows
into eternity.

Her breathing turned into nothingness, the moment for eternal slumber. Her journey began.

99

More than twenty years had gone by since Parth's journey to the afterlife before Risa joined him. I was there. I know, for I am he who composes the spirit, words, deeds of my dear people. They do not fear me, for I comfort them in time of distress. I pleasure them in time of need.

I am the Ancestor. I pose as Flutist.

As the air above met the dank below, the Laris-Vella tomb chamber was cleaved open, intact as if no time had lapsed. With that gust of freshness, Parth's noble garments crinkled and disintegrated. Rapidly, his chariot's metal corroded and wooden axles splintered into musty decay.

First came the city mourners carrying a hundred honey-wax candles. Bearing their mother on a pallet, Culni and Ari set her on the stone carved bed, where the candlelight threw off a floral smell and sent warmth to Risa's sleeping face and rose petal crown.

"She is still beautiful." Larthia stepped quietly down the stairs and removed her veil. She stood next to her brothers, her hands on their shoulders in greeting.

"Larthia, the gods praise your presence. We hoped you'd come. Mother would have been pleased."

"The gods willed that I honor Mother. No one else must know of my exile from Tarchna."

The brothers nodded disconsolately.

Larthia picked up a wad of flax cloth on Risa's stone head pillow. "What is this?"

"It wasn't here before," Culni said.

Larthia unraveled the cloth. Inside, a shimmering stone was set on an inscription:

I adored you in life, my beauty, and I shall in death. I beseech you to lay this gemstone between your breasts and feel the heat of my love on our afterlife journey.

"Father wrote this. The stone is from northern mountains." Larthia handed it to Ari.

"Fire of Turan! Who could have put it there?" Ari laid the gem on Risa's breastplate and sprinkled lavender petals on her body, letting a tear fall on her smiling lips.

I, Flutist, placed it. It was part of my music to bring harmony.

The chamber brightened with mourners' candles.

Gathered in the chamber, mourners brought food gifts for Risa's journey and cried in delight, "The walls are still alive with banquet. The paint vibrates with love and joy. This tomb is blessed by the gods!"

Out they danced, leaving the siblings alone.

"The mourners are right. Our parents depicted on these walls breathe with life," Culni said. "After the Prince-priest designated her cresting banquet, Mother's preparations for her day became magical. Whatever she wanted, she got."

"We were at training for the hunt. We came back a half moon later. Mother had changed. Her face held a painful expression that was upon her for seasons," Ari reminisced.

"I was too young to remember. Her banquet must have been the highlight of her life, her dearest moment," Larthia wept.

Just then, a colorless mist undulated from the stairs, and the wailing of an ancient dirge began. Unseen, The Flutist descended and passed through the tomb chamber with his slow lament. Abruptly, he began a whimsical tune, signaling entrance to the afterlife.

They looked around the tomb.

"Where does that sound come from?" Culni asked baffled.

"Our souls." Larthia touched Risa's reposeful face. "The brightest miracle of the gods."

Epilogue

I prowl the cosmos savoring what evolves from generation to generation. Tages gave philosophy to the Etruscans. The augurs developed new attitudes of civilization. Seeing my people reap wisdom brings me contentment.

"Leave the workings of the cosmos to the gods for your fortune," the *Book of Tages* instructed and predicted. "You will live in an era when Etruria luxuriates in rich industry, in abundant food, in elaborate dwellings—when neighboring semi-barbaric societies live on gruel and water in mud and wattle huts."

I danced with the Etruscans at their celebrations, and sang, "Good fortune triumphs."

The noble Porenna-Laris-Vella family, products of sagacious ancestors, three generations strong, concurred. "We are cared for and blessed by the supreme gods. When we journey to our most sacred cosmos, watched by our saving god, Tinia, we will sleep peacefully, laugh with families and friends in perpetual life."

How contented I was that Risa induced her family to accept death as part of life's ways.

"Welcome your fate," the gods had decreed.

"We do," the Etruscans chorused. "That's why we banquet and wear fineries now."

And I will play my pipes to cheer you on until no more music is in you.

Less than a saecula after Risa's death, more ugliness entered the burgeoning Tarchna and Cisra populations, corrupted from life's purpose.

"Has too much banqueting debauched you? Are you too arrogant in your powers?" Tinia thundered, aggravated by his once favored people. "You debase our knowledge and admire Hellenic gods. You mix their images with ours, sculpting their images more. Clouds of the cosmos! Another fate awaits!"

Their hideousness frustrated me but I could do nothing for it struck the majority, and I am but a small force who soothes individually.

Then, Tages, creator of Etruria appeared. From the shadows, bones poking through his skin, he reamed his way up from the earth's bowels again. "Tinia, Uni, Menvra, celestial gods, gods of nature and earth, and gods of the afterlife, you have abandoned the Etruscans and escaped to a distant cosmos. Their magnificence crashes, brought on by decadent and irreverent excesses that cause a prolonged demise."

Undetected by his people in their coarseness, Tages walked through Etruria's lands inspecting his creations over the next three saeculae, three hundred years of sea battles with Hellas, bickering among city-states, and disenchanted slaves who turned on masters.

Invincible, almighty Etruria fell to pieces. The Great Prediction came to pass.

Knowing they could take advantage, the ascendant Ruma, latinized to Romans, swept through Etruria's territory. Hateful of the Etruscans whose gods were alien, whose women were treated as equal, whose language was foreign, they brought a whirlwind of death and gore. What joy they took in defiling men and women, murdering magistrates and citizens, eliminating city after city, mutilating temples, bashing sculptured gods.

Mighty in unified forces, those Romans burglarized Etruria's tombs north and south, desecrated cities of the dead, vandalized necropolises, plundered the cliff niches, and dug through the shattered skeletons for gold. The conquerors buried the rubble of their desecration, obliterating the Etruscans' existence, hiding evidence and history of Rome's crime against humanity. Seasons and years sped. Mounds of dirt smothered generations. Drainage systems filled back into swamps. Roadways were overrun with weeds. Sly Romans claimed that Etruscan architecture and land use was of Roman and Hellenic derivation. When the Romans fell in decay and squalor, uncouth grave robbers thoroughly filched Cisra's City of the Dead, sacred monument to wealth and industry.

At the end of his foot journey through Etruria, ragged and emaciated with age, Tages climbed the steep cliffs to Tarchna's uplands. "The gods flew across the mists in golden chariots, renouncing their very own people to be overtaken by enemies," he conceded. "No one cries for the Etruscans. There is no one left to mourn."

That said, The Flutist appeared at the one place kept sacrosanct by the gods, lighted by the sun's glow.

Tages hummed, "Perhaps there is one left who mourns the Etruscans."

In greeting, The Flutist raised the pipes to his mouth to trill the sacred music.

"Who are you, creature, more human than beast?" Tages asked. "You aren't a phantom."

"Don't you recognize me?" The Flutist caressed with a mouthful of air. "My kinsmen are myths, legends, the gods, and you, Tages. Some hear my songs when I embrace them. Others don't listen or call out for me. I never stop moving. Unrelentingly, I seek all."

"And I protect the Tarchna from invaders who trample the uplands listening for susurrations of the dead, not finding them," Tages retorted. "Seasonal grasses and eroded stone slabs disguise these sepulchers so that the Tarchna sleep in their underground tombs, undisturbed by plunder, plough or war. They were smart in secrets."

"Etruria was a success, Tages."

A hot Great Sea Wind howled across the uplands as Tages scrutinized a farmer's crop. "Here it is. The Romans missed these beloved Etruscans, Risa Laris and Parth Vella. They were worthy folk who helped shape Etruria's brilliance with inspired purpose, revering the gods, delighting modestly in life's joys. I shielded them during the Roman bloodbath, concealing the tomb entrance by mixing earth and seed to become field."

"They believed their souls would be with family for eternity," The Flutist replied, "but no one joined them. Venu's watery death left remains to the fishes. Their sons, prevailing nobles Culni and Ari, built chambers to house offspring. Daughter Larthia went to her tomb in a northern land. Yet, they all rest in tranquility."

"You, Ancestor, work well with me." The wind swirled ferociously around Tages' robes, gusting him about. "Changes proliferate! A year of new shifting winds begins. My predictions are complete, my work done."

With his residual power, Tages flicked his fingers as Tinia had, and vanished into a lustrous radiance not seen before, fleeing the cosmos.

Photograph by Steve Barrett

Rosalind Burgundy's enchantment for the Etruscans' amazing culture began when she worked with a renowned archeologist in Rome as Technical Illustrator and Curator of Etruscan artifacts. After more than 40 years as educator/lecturer, wife, mother and world traveler, Ms. Burgundy returns to her life-long interest to create a trio of novels about that ancient civilization.

Song of The Flutist, a multi-generation family epic, and *Odyssey of an Etruscan Noblewoman* are set in Etruscan Italy, two thousand six hundred years ago. *Tuscan Intrigue,* a contemporary archeological escapade, takes place in modern Tuscany and Umbria.

Ms. Burgundy divides her time between the Central Sierra in California and Palm Beach Coast in Florida, feasting with family and friends in Etruscan tradition.

Praise for *Odyssey of an Etruscan Noblewoman*

"...Selected by the Sons of Italy for its National Book Club. Members in 700 chapters around the country choose one or more books each quarter and discuss it during the monthly meetings."

Dona De Sanctis, Deputy Executive Director
Native Sons of Italy
Italian America Magazine

"...A wonderful narrative with realistic characters, filled with excitement and surprises to satisfy any reader. It is indeed a well-written book."

Dr. Ralph Ferraro, Director
The Italian American Press

"...Draws the reader in immediately and takes him/her deeper and deeper into the life of early Italy, the people and their rituals. Through Burgundy's creation of Larthia, we are treated to a unique experience of a noblewoman's trials and triumphs despite much adversity. This book would go well with a feast fit for a king (or princess!), goblets of wine and an occasional cold wind blowing."

Lane Wiley, Book Reviewer
Sierra Mountain Times, Twain Harte, CA

"An extraordinary read. So little is known of the Etruscans. Ms. Burgundy has pulled off a nearly impossible feat. The story of Larth/Larthia is unpredictable and heart wrenching. As Mary Renault is to the Greeks, as Steven Saylor is to the Romans, Pauline Gedge to the Egyptians, Ursula K. LeGuin to the Early Latins/Trojans, and Mika Walteri to all of the above...So I believe Rosalind Burgundy is a "scribe" for the mysterious Etruscans. This is historical fiction at its finest. A pearl of a story that I hope more people will discover and enjoy."

Review for amazon.com books by Ms. K
Los Angeles, CA

Praise for *Tuscan Intrigue*

"…Engaging…compelling…unique…suspenseful. The entire novel is lived exquisitely through Amanda's perspective…the story unfolds in a seemingly self-propelling manner…[explored with]…questions about her relationship with Wes, her father, her brother and ultimately with Trent. The descriptive phrasing is so vivid that the scene in which Amanda discovers Joanna comes alive with the dank smells of the putrid cave, the darkness, and finally the whiff of fresh air leading them out of the tunnel. Excellent!"

Editorial Board, an iUniverse Editor's Choice Award

What Readers are saying:

"…Is like a many-layered elegant dessert. The first layer is a mystery: Who nearly killed Amanda's father? The second is a detective story as Amanda tries to uncover the bombers. The third is suspense, as Amanda becomes the target of the villains. There is also a layer of romance with an additional dollop of magic, perfectly blended. Throughout, like icing, is information. The reader learns about international art dealing, Tuscany and Umbria, fine restaurants (the real name of some of the best in Italy) and the fascinating Etruscans of pre-Roman Italy. Taken together, with excellent writing and careful construction, this dessert is truly a special read!"

Jack Karshaw,
Manhattan, New York

"…Makes me want to take off for Italy, like Amanda Oliver, the main character. I didn't realize the back-story of archeologists and collectors was so intertwined. Greed, betrayal and love with lots of surprises, makes this a fun read."

T. Promessi,
Reader, CA